I0682573

HEART OF ASHES

Namesake Chronicles: BOOK 3

By Rachel Marie Lang

ISBN-978-0992077358

<u>Dedication</u>

To the dreamers.

To my family for their support,
my brother for the map,
and to my readers.

Signed Rachel Lang
July 8, 2019
Orillia, Ontario

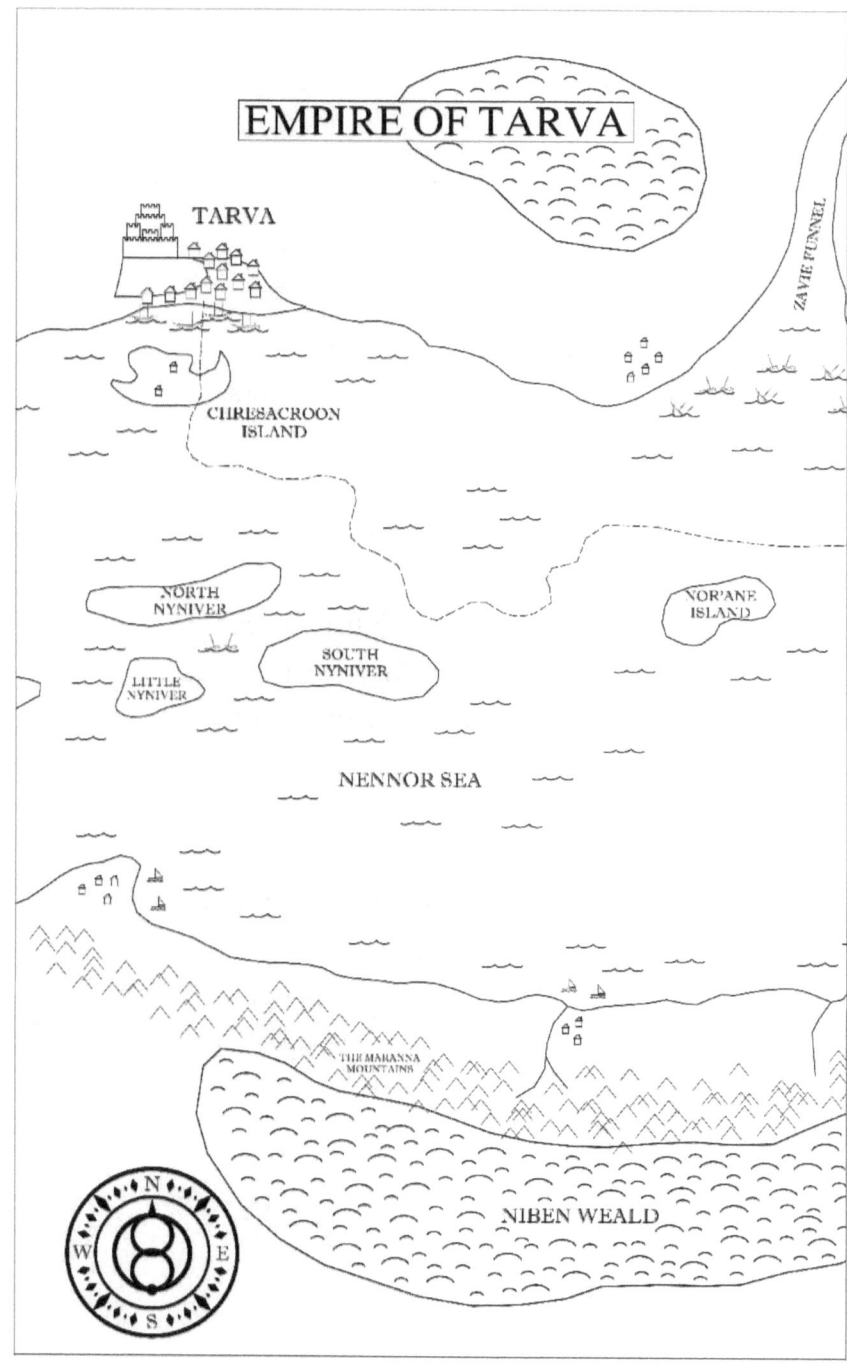

Table of Contents

Part one - Westland's

Chapter 1   The Death of Eamer

The roof beam collapsed sending sparks raining down on the girl's copper coloured hair, still she did not move- she couldn't! Her feet were like weights holding her in place, her fear was so tangible it was like strong, heavy hands on her shoulders, holding her in place, making her uncomfortably aware of something deep inside her; moving. Something that was not a part of her. Coughing black smoke out of her lungs, the girl looked about herself at the great banqueting hall- only the fire feasted now. On her left, beautiful tapestries hanging on the stone wall flared-up as the hungry flames found and devoured them. The copper haired girl could feel the heat on her fair skin as the noxious smoke crawled down into her lungs again, and her eyes smarted and blurred as she caught sight of someone else at the far end of the hall. She knew it was a king from the jeweled crown on his dark head, but even as she watched, he doubled over coughing and the crown slipped from his head. Looking up he pointed a finger at her.

"Why have you done this!? WHY!?" Just then his cape caught fire, and a curtain of ash fell between them, obstructing her view.

"FATE!"

Eighteen-year-old Fate awoke with a start from her violent dream when she heard her father call her namesake. But her dream of fire had come true. Fa gasped for breath and found herself sucking in smoke, coughing she sat up and looked about her attic room in shock; had she woken up at all!? Smoke seeped in around her closed door, and the thatch roof above her dripped flaming straw as if it was a leaky roof and it was raining fire outside- and why not!? She must still be dreaming! This couldn't really be happening.

"Fa!" this time it was the voice of her younger brother franticly calling her.

A piece of burning thatch fell onto her blanket and set it to flame, Fate threw it off herself and jumped to her bare feet. "RAVE!" she screamed her brother's name as she reached for her door latch. Her door swung open and gray smoke billowed in as if it had been leaning on her door waiting to get inside, along with the smoke her brother stumbled in, coughing violently.

Like her, he had been awoken from his sleep and still wore his night clothes. Grabbing his arm, Fa tried to run to the stairs; they had to get out!

'This CAN'T be happening!' her mind rebelled again at the horror of the situation. Before they could even run from her room the smoke overwhelmed them and Fa and her brother fell to their knees as the very air betrayed them. Forcing her stinging eyes open, Fa saw her father come bounding up the steep narrow stairs. He held a cloth to his mouth and a wet blanket in his other hand, with it he whipped at any fire that got in his way.

Fa and Rave crawled out of his way as their father slammed the bedroom door; shutting out the fire for a few moments more.

"How do we get out!?" Rave's voice was unnaturally high with panic.

In reply, their father hacked a cough and pointed to the only wall with a window. But the window was too small, Fa thought in distress, even she would struggle to fit her slender body through- let alone her father's broad frame!

But her father didn't go to the window, he first draped the wet blanket over her and Rave, and then bent over double as he neared the sloped roof that he had hit his head on so often. Stepping onto Fa's trunk that sat against the wall, her father slammed his strong shoulder into the four-inch-wide roof beam that he had once cut and put in place. Again, he slammed his shoulder into the beam- this time it cracked- next he braced his whole back against the slanted roof and pushed out. The beam broke in half and the whole section that it had been supporting caved in with a shower of dry mud, thatch and fire.

"COME!" their father beckoned them with another cough. Throwing the wet blanket on the flaming roof debris, brother and sister leapt up beside their father on the trunk.

Through the gap in the roof, the whole Byla wilderness opened before them, the eastern horizon was crimson with the approaching dawn. Fa blinked in surprise when she saw her grandfather's cottage ablaze along with their little stable. Their horses had escaped and were running a safe distance away. Below, their grandfather and mother were calling their namesakes; a twelve-foot drop separated the family.

"Quick now!" Fa's father placed a hand to her back. Fa didn't hesitate further: stepping out, Fa stretched her arms out as if hoping to grow wings and leave this waking nightmare far behind her, she jumped.

      *   *   *

"You should get dressed."

Sixteen-year-old Brave looked up as his sister approached him, the late morning light highlighting her ash smudged face. Before jumping to safety, their father had had enough foresight to rescue both Rave's and Fa's clothing trunks. Rave had always thought his father was brave- far braver than Rave himself, despite his namesake. Fate had already traded in her ash-smeared nightdress for a tunic and pants; it's what she wore when there was work to be done.

"HO THERE!" a voice called out.

Rave looked over his shoulder; it was the old man who lived two miles west of them (as a child, Rave had called him a crazy old man, and he secretly still did).

"I saw the smoke- and said to myself 'the end of time's come!'" the old man pulled his horse up to a stop and surveyed the charred ruins: the cottages and stables had been reduced to haphazard piles of smoldering thatch and still burning wood.

Rave remained sitting in the hard-packed dirt of their homestead, while Fate stood beside him, but their mother, father and grandfather came over to their old-time neighbor- what was his namesake? Rave could never remember.

"Thank you for coming so swiftly", Rave's Grandfather said stepping closer.

"Looks like I'm too late", the old man commented grimly as he dismounted.

"This is my fault..." Rave's father said as he placed his hands on his hips.

"Treas..." Rave's mother murmured and touched his shoulder tenderly.

"I saw a pile of kindling too close to the fire last night- I should have moved it!"

"Perhaps the kindling helped," Rave's Grandfathers voice always had a calming affect, "But my cottage was where the fire started. But placing blame won't serve a purpose, son."

Brave's father was an orphan and had never know his own father, but sometimes his father-in-law would call him 'son'. Rave had often wondered who his father's parents were- and *where* they were. Did Rave have aunts and uncles somewhere out there?

Turning to his sister, Rave stopped listening to the adults and asked, "How long do you think it will take to rebuild Eamer?" Eamer was what they had always called their homestead.

Fate looked around sadly, "I don't think we will... the only thing left of her is the cold room- there is nothing to rebuild; I think Eamer is dead." Fa stood for a moment as if to honor their dead home, then moved off to join their mother.

Brave shivered in his white night shirt and thin pants. As if to back up Fa's statement, one of the still standing walls of their burning cottage moaned and fell over.

Rising from the cold ground, Rave's eye caught something in the remains of his grandfather's cottage. Rave picked his way in his bare feet through the charred rubble. The fire had run out of fuel on one side of the cottage, allowing Rave to get close to the still standing stone fireplace. He had sat in front of it as a child countless times, but never had he considered that there was something hidden among the stonework. Its hiding place laid bare by the fire and crumbling stone. A little weather-worn and fire-scorched trunk had caught Rave's eye.

Picking it up, Rave frowned at how unfamiliar it was- he had lived in Eamer his whole life- how could there be anything unfamiliar to him!? Unclasping the lid, Rave's eyes widened in awe and surprise at the contents.

*   *   *

"Did you find something?" Wilderness asked as he carefully maneuvered the debris and noticed ruefully that his grandson hadn't put on his boots.

Grandson... When his own daughter, Destination, had been sixteen, Wilder hadn't given much thought to having grandchildren one day- and now he had two! How time had flown.

Wilder stopped short and sucked in his breath when he saw what Brave had found. Both his grandchildren knew about his past- but NOT in any detail. There was no need to tell those dark stories- he had been a different man then- not even Desti knew the full extent of his past life. Wilder had forgotten about the trunk that he had hid in his fireplace so long ago- would he never be free of his past!?

Reaching out, he shut the trunk and smoothly took it from Rave's hands.

"You should put your boots on- and some proper clothes", he said lightly, as he tucked the cursed trunk under his arm. "There's a lot of work to be done; don't want the fire spreading", Wilder added, turning away.

"What is that?" Rave asked.

Wilder sighed; of course, Rave had to know! But Wilder had stolen the innocence from so many lives, he wouldn't let his grandson be one of them. "Just some old rubbish I should have disposed of long ago", he answered elusively, before walking away.

      *   *   *

Fate had been right about Eamer, by noon that same day there had been nothing left but rubble and ash. They had spent the rest of that day and night trying to contain the fire and stop it from spreading into the grass lands around them. They were helped by a rainstorm that came early the morning after- but the rain came too late to save their beloved home.

The list of things they'd been able to save was small: the horses (6 of them) were high strung but safe, as well as their saddles and gear, they had also saved two hunting bows and three small trunks of clothes. Destination and Treasure were able to find clothes that fit amongst their children's clothing, and everyone had boots to wear- but everything else of their home was destroyed.

After two more days of staying with their neighbor, it was agreed upon that Eamer was truly dead, and that rebuilding would be a hopeless affair since there wasn't enough trees in the area to do so. It was decided that they would travel to the Westlands, and perhaps find Courage and his family; the Tarven friend who had left nearly 16 years ago. Courage had returned to visit them a year later, Fa had been just three and had no memory of the man- or his family, but Courage had told an unbelievable story of how he and his wife, Loyal, had won the favour of a powerful Duke who had made Courage a lord over a manor in the north of Garatin. Courage had invited them all to go live with him- but Wilder couldn't be persuaded to leave Eamer... but now that the home he had lived in for forty years was gone, there was only one thing that made Wilder hesitate to leave; the grave of his wife.

Now, five days since the burning of their home, the little family of five stood about the grave of Dream; the namesake of Eamer.

"Leaving this place will be like leaving her", Destination's soft voice was almost lost in the sound of the brook that ran nearby.

"Your mother is in you, Desti", Wilder said in a deep rumbling voice.

Fa had never seen her grandfather without sad eyes, but now it was as if he wore a mask to distance himself from the pain.

"She is in your smile. In your laughter. In your eyes…" Here, Wilder shifted his gray eyes to Fate.

Dream had died when Destination had been little, already Desti was older than her mother had been when she had succumbed to fever. So, for Desti, the pain was from letting go of a perfect memory made from her father's stories. And as for Treasure, Brave and Fate- they had never met the woman to whom Wilder had given his heart. To Fa and her brother, the pain of leaving Eamer didn't come from leaving a grandmother they had never met; it came from leaving the only home they had ever known. However, leave it they did.

After standing around the pile of stones that was Dream's grave for what seemed like forever, they turned their backs on Eamer and set out north-west. Their plan was to travel through the northern tip of the Corfin forest and from there travel around or through the western end of the Quy marsh to get to the manor and village of Fray. But their plans went amok when they reached the far side of the Byla river.

"What is it?" Destination called out anxiously as her husband came riding up to their almost packed up camp.

They had arrived at the river in the evening and decided to cross right away. By the time they had reached the west side, darkness had claimed the land. That morning they had been alarmed to spot smoke columns from dozens of campfires, rising from the forest directly in their path. Treasure had ridden ahead to scout. Now he returned swiftly with a frown.

"I'm not sure, but the forest is full of people- men, and they didn't look friendly!" Treasure said sliding off his horse.

Fate looked again at the columns of smoke, "I thought it was the southern end of the forest that was filled with bandits", she said, remembering her parent's stories.

Wilder tightened his horse's saddle, "Times change", he said grimly.

"The men I saw were Quy marsh folk- and they certainly looked like outlaws- something must have happened in the Quy to drive them into the forest", Treasure surmised.

"What will we do now?" Brave asked as he got their pack horse ready.

"I think it best if we try crossing the Corfin a day south from here", Treas suggested.

"Do you think that will be safer?" Desti voiced her concern.

Wilder squinted at the forest, "It can't be worse than trying to cross here- no point in taking a risk like falling into the hands of bandits or slave dealers", Wilder reasoned.

Slavery was outlawed in the country of Garason and had been for decades. But although the law was enforced in the cities to some degree, there was a large black market for slaves. And it was not uncommon for those traveling along the outer reaches of the country to be captured as slaves and then be taken out of the country to be sold where there were no laws against human trade. Treasure had firsthand knowledge of the dangers of traveling in the Corfin forest, so understandably the adults of the family were wary.

So, they started south, parallel to the forest edge. It took them further from their destination, or so Fate worried, but even then, she was unknowingly being drawn to her destiny.

Fa was not the only one who thought they were being 'blown off course'. Rave thought it was completely unnecessary and silly to travel a whole day south- surely, they could handle a few bandits! But he was sure that no one would listen to him if he shared his opinion.

'Instead we'll travel a whole day south and add four more days onto our journey!' Rave thought grumpily as they rode along, 'we'll probably go so far south that when we come out on the west side of the Corfin we'll.... be within sight of Garason!' The sudden realization made Rave pause in his silent grumblings, and his horse, Breeze, actually stopped. The city of Garason... the thought sent waves of excitement through Rave. For as long as he had been listening to his parent's stories- he had wanted to see that city! And not just see it- but walk its streets. The city his grandfather had haunted as an assassin. The city where his father had grown up as an orphan, and where his mother had gotten lost and met his father! But most of all, the city where Eternity did the impossible.

Rave nudged his horse on again and let his mind spin with the possibilities of being so close to Garason. His mind continued to spin all that day and into the evening when they made camp. It was deep into the night and still he lay awake, his head too full to rest, when he saw his grandfather rise from his bedroll. Rave was about to sit up- then he saw what his grandfather was holding: the trunk Rave had found in the fireplace!

Brave lay still as Wilderness walked past him and waited till his footsteps receded into the damp night air. Rave shot up and strained his eyes till he saw his grandfather's figure disappear behind the slope that led down to the marshy riverbank.

'What is he doing with the trunk!?' the possibility of never getting an answer was too much for Rave to bear! Carefully, so as not to wake anyone, Rave rose and not bothering to pull his boots on, followed his grandfather. Keeping low, Rave ran up the slope and crouched in the long grass at the top. Below, on the edge of the thick reed and bulrushes bank, stood Wilder, with his back to Rave.

What was he doing? Was he looking at the contents of the time scarred trunk? Just as Rave was wondering what he should do next, Wilder bent down and placed the trunk on the ground in the reeds. Standing up, his grandfather pushed the trunk into the soggy earth with his booted foot. Over head, a cloud passed over the half moon, and Rave darted down the slope and hid behind a clump of marsh grass, he peeked through and saw his grandfather look around before giving the trunk one last shove, then he returned the way he had come.

Brave kept his eyes on the spot where the trunk had been buried, and as soon as Wilder was out of sight, Rave darted to the riverbank. Without a moment's hesitation, he stepped into the bulrushes and felt the spongy cold ground embrace his bare feet, while he searched for the trunk. Just before he gave up hope, the moon reappeared and revealed where the mud had oozed over the trunk, only one corner still visible. Digging it out with cold fingers, Rave opened the trunk and caught his breath… then a smile spread across his boyish face. Wiping one hand free of mud on his pants, he carefully lifted a wicked looking dagger by its smooth handle and held it up to the moonlight.

Now what? He couldn't take the trunk; it was too bulky, but he could hide the knife easily enough in his bedroll. What would his grandfather do if he found him with it though? 'Oh well', Rave thought recklessly, he just couldn't let such a beautiful thing be forgotten in the mud! He just couldn't! Nearly losing his balance, Rave returned the now empty trunk to the mud, and pushed it down till it disappeared with a sickening gurgle.

Brave pried his feet from the cold mud, and remembered that his grandfather would still be awake, and he would be caught if he returned now, so he sat on the hillside and shivered in the dark as he gripped the dagger and fantasized about it for long minutes in the dark. A half hour passed before he dared to creep back to his bedroll.

Morning came, and much to Rave's relief, no one went down to the riverbank. 'Grandfather must really want to forget about it...' Rave thought with a sudden pang of guilt. He harboured his guilt for the entire day as they entered and crossed the Corfin without incident, and then made camp on the far side in the thickening dusk. They had come out north of the town of Hirfly and were a mere two-hour ride from the great city of Garason. It was then, in the quickly fading light, that Rave got his first glimpse of the city- and all his guilt melted away. He slept barely at all that night, and minutes after the first songbird announced the coming of morning into the darkness, and before anyone else had even stirred, Rave knew what he would do.

*   *   *

Fate stilled her ragged breath as she realized that the 'thing' was behind her, coming closer. Fa dare not turn and face it- whatever it was; she could tell that she was not strong enough to stand against it, her only hope was to run! And so, she did. Fa practically flew down the wide hallway but skidded to a stop when a large heavy door loomed up in front of her. Knowing that the 'thing' was coming ever closer, Fa reached out and pushed the door open- but quickly snatched her hand back with a gasp; the wood of the door was as hot as a smith's oven! The door swung open and Fa threw up her arms to shield her face as a blast of heat hit her. Forcing her eyes open, Fa peeked at the room beyond; it was burning.

Fate rolled over and gasped for breath, cold dusk air filled her burning lungs, and she was certain that her face was hot from the dream fire! Had she been too close to the campfire?! Fa looked over her shoulder at the campfire that she and her family had slept around; it was only embers now. Sitting up Fa realized that the sun must not have risen quite yet, and she noted that her family were still fast asleep- they had agreed that they would rest for a few extra hours that morning after leaving the Byla behind them.

Slowing her still startled breath, Fa put a hand to her forehead- but gasped in pain! There was a burn on the palm of her hand! The skin was red and blistered. That settled it, Fa decided, she must have flung her hand into the fire while she slept and given herself the bizarre dream.

Fa stood up, and subconsciously stepped away from the fire, pulling her cloak closer about her slim shoulders. Fa pulled two hankies from her pants pocket, returning one, she used the other to wrap around her burnt

16

hand. Deciding to check on the horses, Fa made her way to where they had hobbled the horses the night before. She looked like her mother as she walked lightly through the shin high grass. Fate had her mother's- and her grandmother's copper coloured hair, it had a gentle wave in it, and she wore her hair in a loose braid down her back. Fa also shared the gray-green eyes that came from her grandmother. Her face was kind, pretty and delicately featured. At eighteen, she was still slender- 'a slip of a girl' as her old neighbor use to say. But unlike her mother at her age, Fa was shrewd and sure of herself- it came from growing up with a mischievous little brother who was always getting into trouble of some kind.

Yes, Fate knew her brother quite well- and could always see through his tricks. Brave had inherited their grandfather's straight nose and Garatin blond hair, but unlike Wilder, Rave's hair had a wave in it, and he liked to wear it long, so it was almost always hanging over his blue eyes. He had a quick smile and a devious mind. At sixteen he stood an inch shorter than Fa, and his own shoulders were still slender- but he was growing every day to look more like their father. But no matter how old Rave got, it seemed his appetite for trouble never lessened.

Trouble. That's what Fa thought when she saw her brother at the horses with a saddle in his hands. Silently stepping up behind him Fa spoke, "What are you doing?"

Rave jumped and spun around- his face reminded her of the time when he was seven and she had caught him sneaking a box of baby rabbits into their cottage.

Rave pressed a finger to his lips, "Don't wake anyone!" He hissed pleadingly.

"What are you doing Rave?" she asked again, only slightly quieter.

"Nothing! Just... going for a little ride!" He said innocently, throwing the saddle over his horse's back.

Fa gave him a hard look until he gave in.

"I'm going... into the city alright!? You wouldn't understand!" He turned his back on her and fastened his horse's saddle, "You can live your whole life in the middle of no where and do nothing your whole life, if you want - but I HAVE to see that city!"

Fa could hear the excitement and determination in his voice, and she gave him an exasperated look, "Ask Father and Mother- ask Grandfather; they would take you if you just asked!"

"No, they wouldn't," he replied grudgingly, as he unhobbled his horse. "All their grand stories of all they saw and did there, it all comes down to one thing; they hate that city- they won't go back there for anything!"

Fa recalled everything her parents had said and had to agree with her brother, that they really didn't have too many good memories of the place.

"Father would take you- if you asked him," she insisted tightly.

Rave didn't reply but continued to ready his horse.

Fa took a deep breath, "I'm going with you," she decided suddenly. "You need more looking after than a nest of fledglings!" Taking her extra hanky from her pocket, Fa fished out a piece of chalk from her nearby saddle bag and began to scratch out a note.

"What are you writing?" Rave asked anxiously as he peered over her shoulder- he seemed to have accepted her company.

"If you would let father teach you to read- you wouldn't have to ask!" she said sassily, "I'm telling Mother and Father that we'll be back by nightfall."

"No! Don't say that-" Rave said, eagerly stepping closer "Say tomorrow instead!" he stepped away again when Fa glared at him.

Telling Rave to get her own horse ready, Fa tip toed back into their camp and placed her note on her bedroll. Glancing briefly at her mothers sleeping face, Fa stole back to the horses.

Her note read, *'I and Rave have gone to see the city. I will look after him. We will return by nightfall.'*

If Fate had known what her future was, she would have written something more, but alas, that is the trouble with the future; it hasn't happened yet. And so, not knowing what would befall them, the two siblings took little with them, just their cloaks, some food in their saddle bags, and seven copper coins. Fa and Rave mounted up and with one last fleeting glance of uncertainty on Fate's part- they were soon hidden from view in the grasslands leading up to Garason.

*   *   *

Wilderness slept longer than he had intended to, the journey west had been more taxing on him than he had realized: two weeks was a long time for a man his age to be in the saddle! When he did wake, it was an hour after sunrise. Wilder took his hunting bow, and as he did, he glanced at his grandchildren's bedrolls; he smiled, the two lumpy forms of his grandchildren were still fast asleep- just like their parents!

He returned to the camp an hour later with two forest pheasants slung over his shoulder, his daughter and son-in-law had woken at last, and looked up as Wilder approached.

"Where are Fa and Rave?" Destination asked.

Treasure, who had come back from the horses looked up and waited for Wilder to answer.

"Aren't they here?" Wilder asked as he paused and looked at his grandchildren's bedrolls; all eyes went to the lumps under Fa and Rave's blankets. With a mounting feeling of unease Wilder went quickly to the bedrolls, Desti was right behind him. Wilder stooped and pulled his grandson's blanket away- only to find nothing there. Desti turned to Fa's bed- it had been a trick of the light; Fa and Rave were gone.

"Their horses are gone- could they have gone hunting?" Treasure suggested, as Desti spotted her daughter's hanky.

"Fate doesn't like hunting with Rave- she says he's too noisy…" Wilder said as Desti picked up the hanky.

"They didn't go hunting," Desti said and looked west with a defeated sigh, "They went into the city."

Treas huffed and put his hands on his hips, "Of course our children would run there," he said with a touch of irony.

"Fa wrote they'll be back by nightfall," Desti said, handing the hanky to her husband, who read it and shook his head.

Wilder smiled, "There's no denying that they're your kin!" he said ruefully.

A similar smile touched Desti's lips, and Treas half grinned, "You're the one who ran to Garason," he said looked at his wife, "I'm the one who ran away from it." His grin faded as he looked at his daughters writing, "I'll go find them." He said with resignation.

Wilder's own smile faded, "That city could have changed much since last your eyes saw it," he warned.

Treas nodded and smiled grimly at his wife; she understood what going back there meant to him.

"It won't be the first time I've searched for a needle in that haystack." In those words, he communicated to his wife that he would be all right, and that her understanding- was deeply appreciated. He planted a kiss on her lips, "You two should stay here in case they come back early- otherwise I'll be back with them by nightfall."

Treasure remembered how bothersome a horse was in the crowded streets of Garason and preceded on foot, as he went, he was also reminded of the last time he had been this close to Garason; the morning Nity defied death and showed him that a new future was possible. That day he had runway from Garason, and towards Destination- and he had never looked back... until now.

Oh Garason! It had once been home to him; a sad, lonely and cold home. Years of emptiness and yet full of longing for more. The place where an orphan boy had learned how to steal and lie without a trace of guilt. Such was how Treasure remembered the city, there were only two memories that made that place bearable to him; the first was a copper haired girl who looked at him without judgment, the second was Eternity.

Treasure would have to cling to those memories if he was to get through this day. Closer and closer he came to Garason, until it seemed to swallow up all the happiness, he had found over the past twenty years, reducing him to that lonely orphan boy longing for a place to belong.

He forced himself to think of his children, they would be just like their mother when he first met her; wide-eyed and vulnerable. He had to find them quickly- before something happened.

Chapter 2   Wrong Place

"I can take your horses for you," the stable boy said, as Brave and Fate stood out front of the 'Cobbler's Inn', wondering what they should do.

"Ah, perfect!" Rave said happily handing over the reins of his horse, Breeze, and giving him a pat. Fa did likewise with her horse, Gale.

The stable boy held out his hand; Rave frowned, "I just saw that man pay when he came out." He pointed out.

The stable boy- who was around Rave's age smiled sardonically, "That's because I knew he'd have enough to pay me."

Rave's frown deepened; he had never dealt with someone like this before. "What do you mean by that!?" he said, feeling his temper rise.

Fate rolled her eyes, "Just give him a copper- better yet, give me the money to look after." She said, snatching the coin pouch from his belt.

"That'll be two coppers- actually," the stable boy said, as he refocused his attention on Fa.

After pressing two of there precious coppers into the stable boy's hand, Fa led the way inside as Rave muttered about how rude the exchange had been.

They both stopped and stood frozen; they had never been inside any kind of establishment before, and their impressions of the place ranged between disgust and enchantment. The alehouse had low ceiling beams and only two small windows; the rest of the light came from greasy lanterns that didn't give off nearly enough light. Large, poorly crafted tables cluttered the room, with chairs littered about; it was impossible to walk through the room without bashing your hip against something. The place was mostly empty, with only a small scattering of people eating quietly.

Fa looked about herself and recoiled slightly, "Why are we here?"

"To eat! I'm starving!" Rave said with forced cheerfulness, he was clearly overwhelmed; they had stopped at the first inn they had found, yet even still, the short walk in the city streets had stunned them. Brave sat down at a table in a corner with a view of the window and the street beyond.

"We packed some food- remember?" Fa said as she sat down with her back to the wall.

Rave gave her a look that said, 'stop being a miser', and she stopped trying to point out his idiocies.

"What do you want?" a sharp faced woman asked, as she stepped from the kitchen and pointed at the siblings. Fa and Rave jumped a little and thought they were about to be thrown out. They stared at the woman with wide eyes.

"What do you want to *eat*?" the woman clarified, seeing their confusion.

"Ah..." Rave faltered still.

Fa spoke up, "*A* simple meal," she said. She wondered if five coppers would cover the cost. The woman looked unimpressed but nodded and disappeared back into the kitchen.

When she was gone Rave grinned foolishly, "I thought she would run us out for sure!"

Fa glared at him- she didn't think it was funny in the least!

"Come on!" Rave coaxed, "Your glad we came- admit it!"

A smile tugged at Fa's lips, and she looked out the window hoping to hide the fact that, yes, she was glad.

"Do you think Mother or Father ever came to this alehouse?" Rave asked with bright eyes.

Fa shook her head, "This city is huge!" she said doubtfully.

"There you are then," the woman said, as she made her way to their table and placed a plate of bread and cheese down. "That'll be five copper."

Fa held in a sigh of relief till after the woman left with their remaining coins- that was the end of their savings! The two siblings began eating, but their wide eyes kept wandering about the room and out the window, at the street, as if they ate with their eyes instead of their mouths. They had no idea how fortunate they were that they had wandered into a Garatin establishment and not a Tarven one. Sheltered as they were, they had yet to discover how cruel the world could be because of something so trivial as skin colour.

Suddenly the door burst open and a group of a dozen men and one woman came in. The other customers jumped up and shuffled out without comment, while Fate and Rave sat frozen in the corner- forgotten. The woman from the kitchen poked her head out to see her alehouse suddenly filled with tense looking Garatin men.

One of them pointed at her and said sternly, "Go back and keep quiet and no harm will come to you!"

The woman did as she was told without hesitation- 'did this sort of thing happen often?!' Fa wondered as she shrank back.

"Sit down quick- the guards will be here soon." The man who spoke seemed to be in charge, for the whole group sat down in pairs and the alehouse hummed with their forced, fake conversation.

The leader had blond hair and a short full beard, he looked to be in his early thirties. The lone woman looked similar in age and she was as petite as Fate. The leader held her firmly by her upper arm and pushed her down into a chair. The corner where Fa and Rave sat had been overlooked and remained empty aside from the siblings- who sat as still as they possibly could!

Fa leaned close to Rave and whispered, "We shouldn't be here! - These men must be part of the Garatin rebellion!"

"Or Eternity rebels!" Rave whispered back excitedly; even two weeks into the wilderness, their little family had heard rumors and tales from tradesmen about the ever-changing rebels of Garason. There were three main types: those who were part of the Garatin rebellion and spent their time organizing riots and uprisings, they consisted of board young men, outlaws and anyone else who didn't have a high moral standard. The second type were Eternity rebels; they were guilty of looking at the world with only vengeance and twisted justice in mind. They chose not to remember that Nity stood for forgiveness and love, and only wanted a figure to rally behind, to lead them into war. The third kind were Nity followers; they were less like rebels and more like idealists. They followed Nity's teachings undauntedly. They, unlike the Eternity rebels, clung to Eloi and when they fought- it was for the poor and the oppressed.

Fate gave her brother a look that said she didn't care what 'type' of rebels these men were- she just wanted to escape without being noticed- but that was impossible! To get to the door they would have to walk right past several tables full of rough looking men- and the windows were too small to climb out of even if they could stand up without being noticed!

"Just don't move- maybe they'll leave soon," Fa advised, with a feeling of helplessness. She was exasperated to see that Rave's face was glowing with excitement. Both their attentions were drawn to the conversation that the woman and rebel leader were having a few tables away.

"Turn me lose at once!" the woman hissed, her long blond hair was pinned up and her nice face was strained.

"Don't you recognize me?" The rebel leader sat down close beside her and shifted his grip on her arm to a kinder one on her wrist, "Graci of Hawthorn?"

The woman paused and her face hardened, "You know the village of my childhood- who are you!?"

"We grew up together..." he said tenderly, "it is I; Vanished, son of Obedience."

She searched his face, "Van?" she breathed.

He smiled as recognition lit her face, "When they took you away that night, I was sure I would never see you again!"

The woman was silent for a moment, outside, a group of soldiers ran by. Van gripped the woman's wrist harder and everyone tensed- but the soldiers passed by.

"What gives you the idea that you can just kidnap me like this?" Graci asked coldly.

Van leaned back and all tenderness fled from his face, "I rescued you from servitude to that fat Tarven lord!" he said contemptuously.

"No! You have *no* idea how long and hard I have worked to get to where I am! I had a bed to sleep in and decent food to eat- But now that you and your band of street thieves have snatched me right from within the manor walls; they'll never take me back! They'll think I invited you in- they distrusted me as it was!"

Van looked at her in disbelief, "You have been too long among your enemies Graci! Or have you forgotten that it was the likes of them that allowed you to be torn from your home and carted off like cattle!"

Graci's kind face twisted in anger, "Do not speak to me of what hardship I have endured- you know *nothing* of it!"

"I did not travel across the country and risk capture to be reprimanded for saving your life! You clearly are not well and have forgotten who you are! Well let me remind you; we have come to kill the man responsible for your suffering- yes Graci! The traitor is -even as we speak- on his way out of the city to the coast where they'll take him to Tarva and deny us our right of justice! But on my life; he will never leave the country he soaked in blood!"

In the forgotten corner, Brave made a faint sound of shock at overhearing the deadly plot. All eye's darted to the two hiding in the corner.

"Grab them!" Van ordered sharply. Brave sprung to his feet and pulled Fate up with him as three men lunged towards them. Rave tried pulling Fa to the door, but she went suddenly limp and collapsed to the floor; she had been subconsciously holding her breath and had now fainted! Rave panicked and went rigid as he was seized roughly by one of the rebels.

"Where did they come from!?" Van demanded, but no one had an answer.

"They heard everything- they could be sympathizers of the traitor! We can't let them go!" the rebel said, as he tightened his grip on Brave.

Rave looked down at the unconscious form of Fa, 'wake up!' he silently pleaded.

"The soldiers are coming back- they're searching for us- we have to leave!" A rebel at the window warned.

"We should silence them now!" another rebel said as he viciously yanked Fa's limp body up.

"We *do not* kill children!" Van insisted forcefully, "Take them both and get out through the back door! We meet a mile south of the city- go!" The room emptied and Rave was shoved to the kitchen door as Fa was thrown over a rebel's shoulder. Across the room Van jerked Graci to her feet, "I'm taking you away from this cursed city- maybe then your head will clear up and you'll see reason again!"

*   *   *

'I'm dreaming again…' Fate told herself; she was standing in a dark stone hallway lit only periodically by a torch on the wall. She felt the 'thing' swell deep within, 'trust me', it seemed to say. 'Alright', she found herself answer, and she began walking down the hall carefully, as if she walked a thin ridge between trusting the presence within and being betrayed by it.

Turning a corner, Fa paused; there was a prison cell with rusty iron bars, inside huddled a man. He was Garatin and had a timid face and small stature- he looked frightened beyond comfort. Fa watched him till she realized that she was not alone, beside her was a Tarven prison guard, he was escorting a young Garatin woman, much younger than she was now- but Fa still recognized her; it was Graci!

"D-do n-not weep for m-me daught-daughter!" the prisoner had got up and was reaching through the bars to hold Graci's hands. "All w-will b-be we-well," he stuttered painfully.

The guard then took the young Graci away, passing right by Fa as if she were invisible.

The 'thing' inside Fa impressed upon her that what she was seeing was real- it had actually happened; did that mean her other dreams were real too?

"FA! Your awake- are you alright?" Brave asked anxiously as he bent over her.

"I think... did I faint?" Fa mumbled and looked around- she sat up quickly; they were inside a wagon! The windows had been nailed shut and the floor was littered with blankets, bags, barrels and crates. A single lantern hung from the roof and it swayed as the wagon jumped and jolted along; they were moving!

"Where are we?" Fa asked in alarm.

Rave sniffled and wiped his nose with the back of his hand- he had a red mark across his face; someone had hit him!

"I think they're taking us out of the city..." the excitement from earlier had melted away on his face and he was only frightened now. "But now that your awake we can try to escape!"

"I wouldn't try that."

Sister and brother looked up to see that Graci sat in the front corner of the wagon.

"Van doesn't want to hurt you- but I think he would." Her anger from earlier had given way to reveal that she was really a soft-spoken woman, and her kind face encouraged the siblings.

"You know him," Rave's voice trembled, "can't you help us?"

Fa had never heard him sound so scared- not even in the fire of Eamer!

"No," Graci said quietly, "I don't know him; sixteen years is a long time. That man is as much a stranger to me as he is to you."

They were silent for a moment as the lantern swung, casting its light first on Graci then on the siblings then back again. They could hear muffled voices outside the wagon, and they all shifted as they hit a large bump. Fate thought about her dream and felt the presence swell again inside her, 'trust me'.

"Graci..." Fa began hesitantly, still unsure.

"It's Gracious," she said softly.

Fa swallowed and remembered her manners, "I'm Fate, and this is Brave."

"Those are good namesakes," Graci said politely.

It encouraged Fa- but she was still nervous to say anything about her dream, "Will they let us go?" she asked instead, trying to gage the soft-spoken woman, who, as Fa already had seen, had a scorching temper.

"After they kill the traitor, I expect so," Graci said shortly, as if holding her emotions so tightly that she found it hard to concentrate on speaking.

"Who is the traitor?" Rave asked, some of his fear being taken over by curiosity.

Graci's face hardened again and her lip curled up as if the namesake was distasteful in her mouth, "Horizon."

"Who is he?" Rave asked blankly, the namesake meant nothing to him or Fa.

"Where do you two hail from, that that namesake doesn't fill you with hate!?" Graci watched them, and Fa noticed a change coming over her. "He was the one who brought pain and suffering to thousands! And then 'repented' and said he had changed," Graci's quiet nature shifted and hatred and contempt filled her voice. Her grip on her emotions was carelessly loosened as she told them who the 'traitor' was. "He's traveled the world preaching his lies, claiming that he is now a follower of Nity and that he only wishes to continue Eternity's work! He has all Garatin under his spell- they've forgotten that it was he who tore men from their wives, and children from their parents and had them murdered for following Nity! People who extend acceptance to that monster invite death into their homes- they think because he's 'changed' that he deserves forgiveness! Even his old friends in the Garatin high council are against him- they had him arrested for treason against Garatin- but he's evaded justice by appealing to the king of Tarva." Graci stopped abruptly as if ashamed, she regained control of her rapid breath and swiped bitter tears from her eyes.

Fa was taken aback by the woman's burning hatred that apparently lay just beneath her quiet exterior.

"The rebels are going to kill him…" Rave said, his sheltered disposition on display, "Your going to let them murder him?"

His innocent face and shocked voice seemed to shame Graci even more, for her face softened, "I hate the traitor, but I've never known bloodlust to make anything right. But as you can see from my present situation; I have no control over Van and his men."

'Trust me', the presence again whispered inside Fa, she was enheartened by Graci's subsided anger, and decided to take a chance, "Your father…" Fa felt her confidence waver when Graci looked at her sharply.

"Was, your father one of the people taken by the traitor?"

"You know my father?" Graci asked softly.

Fa glanced at Rave; would he think she was crazy? "I dreamed I saw him in a dungeon…"

Both Graci and Rave frowned, and Fa felt slightly foolish, "I think we could rescue him-" Fa cut herself off when she saw Graci's face harden with subdued anger.

"Rescue him?" she asked- and Fa knew better than to answer. "My father's namesake was Trust; he and my whole family were arrested for giving shelter to Nity followers. We were taken to Garason to stand trial. Before even reaching the city, my mother was sold to a Tarven lord. My little brother died of starvation while we waited in the dungeons for the Ambassador to have time to pass judgment on us. Then two of my sisters fell sick and the guards killed them for fear of their sickness spreading. It was nearly a year before the *Tarven* ambassador held our trial. My last two sisters and father were beheaded- the only reason I lived was because one of the guards took a fancy to me and brought me to his manor to be a servant for his wife." The longer Graci talked the less control she had over her voice, and tears had begun to drip from her face.

Fa shrunk back and cursed herself for trusting the 'thing' inside her.

"That was sixteen years past; my father is long since dead. Remember that the next time you have a 'dream'. You've changed my mind; the traitor must die." Graci's voice was heavy with raw bitterness.

*   *   *

Treasure had searched for two hours before spotting his children's horses in an alehouse stable. Treas had run his hand along Breeze's flank before a stable boy appeared. "Are the masters of these horses inside?" Treas asked, after he had confirmed that no harm had come to the horses.

"That's right- they've been inside for hours; they owe me more than the two copper they gave me!" the boy complained.

Treasure handed the boy several coins. "Saddle the horses," he instructed before entering the alehouse. But upon scanning the room he saw that Fate and Brave were not among the half dozen people there. Treas went up to a woman who was holding a tray of dirty dishes.

"I'm looking for two Garatins- a boy and girl, they would have been in here recently."

The woman refused to look him in the eye and tried to inch past him, "Aye, they were here but they left over an hour ago."

"They left their horses here- they wouldn't have done that; what happened?" Treas stepped in her way and commanded her attention; he knew that something was not right.

"There was a group of men- and I think the two left with them," the woman said offhandedly.

"Who were these men?" Treasure heard warning bells sounding in the back of his mind.

The woman shrugged.

Treas lowered his head and waited till she met his intense gaze. "Please... help me find my children," he implored.

The woman looked about the room and lowered her voice, "They were Eternity rebels, and they took the boy and girl with them," she confessed.

"Where did they go?" Treas felt his heart thudding inside him as his calmness betrayed him and fled.

"I don't know-"

"You wouldn't know anything if you hadn't overheard- so tell me; where have they taken my children!?"

"South!" the woman hissed clearly disturbed at Treasure's rising voice, "They said south of the city, they left in a wagon with a blue roof. Now *please*; leave!"

Treas turned and made for the stables- the stable boy hadn't finished saddling the horses. He hastily lent a hand, and it gave Treas time to think. There were two villages directly south of Garason (or there had been twenty years ago) one was Hirfly, and the other was a smaller village called Marsuthe, those would be the first two places to search. It was still mid morning, and the city streets were beginning to grow crowded; he would have to ride Rave's horse and lead Fa's horse behind him. Then, as fast as he could, he would ride to their camp; then he, Desti and Wilder could begin searching.

Treasures heart quickened as he thought of the village of Hirfly; he had once been betrayed there and sold into slavery. He would die before he let his children fall prey to the same fate!

           *   *   *

"If they've been taken by slavers there won't be any need to use force," Wilder tightened the girth on his horse's saddle while he spoke. "Families of slaves don't often come looking for them; if you claim to be their parents, they'll simply release them to you."

"Would slavers be so bold to take people from within the city?" Destination asked as she swung up onto her horse.

"As long as they are careful with who they take I'm sure no one cares," Treas said casting the city a condemning look, "But the Inn keeper called them rebels- not slavers." He pointed out as his horse snorted impatiently

"Rebels don't have any use for children- they would probably sell them first chance they get." Wilder steadied his horse before fitting his boot into the stirrup.

"Whatever's happened, we will find them- probably by nightfall. Now remember the woman said a blue roofed wagon," Treas reminded, as his horse pranced about nervously; he could sense the urgency.

"Be careful," Desti cautioned her father, before she and Treas rode off to Hirfly.

Wilder would ride slightly more south and search in Marsuthe, which was further from Garason but closer to the Dinco river. They had no choice but to leave their children's horses behind at their camp along with everything else; it would be better to lose their possessions to thieves than to lose Fate and Brave to slavers.

As Wilderness rode out across country, thunder rolled in the distance, drawing attention to the western horizon where dark clouds were gathering. As he went, Wilder kept a sharp eye out for a wagon with a blue roof. He inspected every farmer's cottage and barn, he checked the roads for signs of wagon wheel ruts- but every road was riddled with them. With each hour that passed in his search, the storm grew closer, the wind picked up and rain could be tasted in the air.

Always on his right, the city of Garason stood like an everlasting reminder of his gruesome past, like a bad omen; the city that had turned him into a killer, and now, the city that had stolen his grandchildren.

'Forget those memories!' he told himself; how many times had he done so? 'Think only of finding Fa and Rave; let the ghosts sleep.'

Chapter 3   Too Late

"Fate? Did you fall asleep!?" Brave asked softly in astonishment as he crawled over to his sister's slumped form. After Graci's heated outburst, they had ridden in silence for a long time. The sounds of the city were long since gone, and Rave figured they had been traveling all day and it was now nearing evening. At one point outside the city, the wagon had stopped, and Van had invited Graci to join him and the others outside to walk, the invitation had not been extended to Rave and his sister. So, the two of them had been alone with the sounds of a coming storm. But the wagon had rumbled to a stop a few minutes before Rave looked up to see his sister sleeping.

"Fa," Rave touched her shoulder and she sat up with a start, her eyes filled with panic.

"I don't see how you can sleep!" Rave said with wonder as she evened out her face. Rave then lowered his voice and leaned closer to her, "I've loosened two of the floorboards over there; I think we can squeeze through and get away!" Fa looked at him in disbelief and he grinned slightly, his fear of the dangerous rebels had grown weak after riding in their uncomfortable wagon for a day.

"We'll have to make a run for it- just don't pass out again!" He grabbed her hand to pull her up, but she snatched her hand back and gasped sharply, Rave looked at her hand in bewilderment.

"When did that happen!?" in the palm of her hand was an ugly, raw burn blister, and he took notice for the first time that her other hand was wrapped up in a hanky.

Fa moved her hands as if to hide them from him. "I must have burned myself this morning," she explained lamely.

Before Rave could say anything, the wagon door opened; outside Rave could see the sky was dark with storm clouds and the evening air was damp. Vanished stepped in and shut the door behind him firmly. He scowled at them and adjusted a glowing pipe with his teeth.

"The traitor's armed escort will soon be crossing this way. During the ambush, you two will remain absolutely silent! Two children can easily be killed by mistake on a night like this."

"We're *not* children!" Rave said scornfully.

Van looked at them both without comment, then as if Rave's words meant nothing, Van walked with stooped shoulders to the front of the wagon, Rave watched nervously as he walked over the floorboards that Rave had loosened. Van removed his pipe and knocked it out and grabbed an oil skin cloak from a trunk.

"Please leave!" Rave turned in surprise at Fa's strained voice, she sat against the wagon wall and looked up at Van like she was a frightened child. "Take your men and leave this place!" she continued, "Something terrible is about to happen here- I know it! Eloi is with Horizon and will not let any harm come to him! So please; leave!"

Van didn't seem to react to her warning and only shook out the cloak and dropped it over his head, he didn't speak until he had adjusted it around his neck, "Graci said you were an odd one. Take my advice, and don't try to speak for Eloi; people who do, end up dead." He walked up to them and looked down at them, the lantern light was behind him and his face was shadowed ominously, "I'll decide what to do with you two once the traitor is dead." He stepped back outside into the night, and Rave heard him slide a bolt across the door, locking them in.

Rave swallowed hard as he stifled his fear of the man, "What is going on with you?!" he said turning to Fate, "First, what you said to Graci and then *that*?"

In response Fa only shrunk back as if ashamed.

What was happening to his sister!? Rave thrust the thought aside for later and crept up to the door and put his ear to it; Van was giving orders to his men in preparation for the ambush. If he and Fa were going to make a run for it; now was the time.

"Rave!" Fa's voice was loud with alarm, Rave turned and to his horror saw that a fire had leapt up in the front of the wagon where Van had nocked out his pipe! The fire spread quickly along several more flammable oil skins; soon the wagon would fill with black smoke!

"Quick the boards!" Rave didn't even think of calling for help, instead he jumped to where he had been loosening the floorboards from their nails. He pulled his grandfathers wicked looking dagger from his boot, he saw Fa give it a bewildered look, but he ignored her, and he set to work to pry up one of the boards. The nails held fast for a moment then the board came lose; YES! Rave could see the ground four feet below them! But the hole wasn't large enough to fit through yet. Rave set to work to loosen the nails that held the second board down. Meanwhile Fate had tried to smother the growing fire with a blanket- but she was too timid to get close enough to do any good.

"Is this water!?" she asked stifling a cough as black oil smoke began to fill the air, she opened a barrel and peered at the contents in the dim lighting.

"I think so," Rave grunted- what else could it be?

Fate dipped a nearby pan into the barrel and splashed it on the burning oilskins. The whole thing roared and leapt higher, Fa jumped back and dropped the pan with a clatter, "That's not water!" she said as the fire stretched higher, it was now blackening the ceiling! It was like Eamer all over again!

Rave franticly stuck his fingers under the board and pulled.

"Hurry up!" Fa hissed as she crouched behind him.

The nail bent as Rave heaved the board up, "Go!" Rave coughed and his eyes smarted as Fa slid through the hole and crawled out of the way. Rave jumped down after her- but he got stuck halfway with his knees on the ground and his head still in the wagon! Afterward, Rave could never remember if he had screamed in terror or not, as he looked up at the seemingly towering fire. He shifted his shoulders to one side and squirmed out.

Once on the ground, they crawled to the front of the wagon, and Rave was reminded of Fa's burnt hands when she carefully crawled on her elbows and forearms. Reaching the front of the wagon, they saw that the horses had been unhitched, and they could also see the dark shapes of cottages to their right but everything else was hidden in the dark. Glancing behind them, they realized that the road that Horizon would be coming down, was that way, and so too, must be Van and his men.

"I think that's a river there!" Fa whispered as she strained to see ahead of them through the thickening dusk.

Rave ignored the faint sounds of the fire above them, and followed her gaze, "Is that a boat on the bank?" he whispered excitedly, "That's it! We can push it into the water and let the river take us back to our camp!"

Fa looked behind them again, "Alright- But we should wait for a distraction of some kind; Van could still catch us."

Rave frowned, "What kind of 'distraction' do you expect!?" as if to make him sound foolish, Horizon's company of armed escorts approached the village; horses screamed in fright as men with swords jumped out in ambush.

"Now! Go now!" Fa shoved him as a din of screams and orders filled the night. Rave wiggled out from beneath the wagon and peeked around it; there was a real proper ambush happening right in front of him!

"Rave- help me!" Fa was having a hard time getting out with her burnt and bandaged hands, turning away from the ambush, Rave grasped Fa by her forearm and pulled her free of the wagon. Running to the riverbank, Rave threw his weight into pushing the boat down the grassy incline into the water. Fa jumped in as it splashed into the river, and the boat caught the strong current at once. Rave slipped on the wet grass and had just enough time to jump in, sending the boat rocking wildly.

Looking back, the village road was lit up with torches and they could see the rebels fighting, but even as they watched Van was struck down and his men overcome by the soldiers. Black smoke began to rise from the wagon and the first drops of rain from the mighty storm fell. Soon the village disappeared into the night as the river carried them away.

"It's just like you said!" Rave breathed in astonishment, "Van and his men lost- how did you know!?

Fa looked frightened and bewildered as she sat back against the prow of the boat with a thump, she shook her head.

*   *   *

Wilderness blinked rain out of his eyelashes and dropped his horse's reins, his horse was trained not to wander off. The heavy rain streamed off Wilder's raised hood as he stood in the shadows and watched the soldiers in the street of the tiny village of Marsuthe; they were Tarven soldiers. There was a time when the sight of them would have filled Wilder with pride and longing, but now all he felt was dread, for behind them was the blue roofed wagon, and worse still, they were dragging dead bodies off the road. One soldier was overseeing the work and held a torch, by its light Wilder scanned the bodies for his grandchildren; with a tight sigh he determined that they were not among the dead. Had the soldiers come across the rebels and killed them, and were they now holding Fate and Brave in the wagon?

Wilder watched the soldiers with trepidation, he could see that some of them had removed their hard leather breastplates, and the two working to clear the dead had even left their swords leaning against the wagon, as if they were tired after winning the fight and didn't expect any more danger.

Wilder himself had no weapons- but unlike the soldiers; he didn't need them.

"Good sir," Wilder said, approaching the nearest soldier, he stooped his shoulders to hide his height and shuffled his feet through the mud, he kept his voice quiet so that the other two soldiers who had their backs turned wouldn't hear him, "Please, I'm looking for my grandchildren." Wilder kept his voice soft and looked at the soldier with a slightly pleading expression; perhaps things could still be resolved peacefully.

"Go home old man, I haven't time for you," the soldier said rudely.

Wilder would give him one more chance, "Please, my grandchildren; a young woman and man-"

The soldier stepped forward and gave Wilder a shove, "I said go home!"

Wilder faked a stumble and reached out his hand for support- quick as lightening he delivered a smart chop to the soldier's throat. The man clutched his temporarily silenced throat and tried to call for help- but only a sickly gasp came out. Wilder grabbed hold of the soldier's breast plate to keep him from stumbling away, then Wilder half turned to the second soldier who had just turned about and was peering at Wilder in the flickering light.

"Where are my Grandchildren?" Wilder asked, he felt his dormant temper rising to combat his growing fear, "They're Garatin and my granddaughter has copper hair."

The second soldier disregarded his words and pointed to his gagging comrade, "What've you done?" before he could get the last syllable out, Wilder released the first soldier- who stumbled and fell. Wilder seized the second soldier's outstretched arm and pulled it behind his back- spinning the soldier around and dislocating his shoulder. Wilder kicked the back of the soldier's knees and allowed the soldier to fall face first into the mud, crying out in pain.

Wilder straightened to his full height as he stepped over the downed soldier and walked towards the third and final soldier, "My grandchildren were taken in that wagon- release them to me!" he let his voice rise- his hooded face adding to his intimidation.

The soldier stared in shock at his fallen men, then he threw aside his torch -it fell into a puddle and hissed out- and valiantly drew his sword.

In the darkness, Wilder confidently stood still as the soldier lunged at him with sword in hand. Wilder reached out and expertly deflected the clumsy thrust with his forearm. Taking one step more, Wilder was behind the soldier looping his arm around the man's neck.

The Tarven soldier gasped in surprise then dropped his useless sword, as he no doubt realized his peril and clawed at Wilders arm around his neck.

Wilder held him for a moment fighting his old instincts to snap the man's neck. With an effort of will, Wilderness squeezed the soldier's neck, the mans struggles becoming weaker by the second. At last the soldiers struggling grew still and his body went limp, Wilder held him for a moment longer, taking note that the first and second soldiers were trying to pick themselves up. Wilder released the unconscious soldier, he collapsed into the mud.

Turning swiftly, Wilder went to the wagon and threw open the door- he sucked in his breath; the entire insides of the wagon were burnt black and stunk of smoke. Fate and Brave were gone.

Wilder clutched his heart as his disappointment and surprise turned to pain; he was getting too old for this.

*   *   *

"Where did you get that dagger?" Fate asked just loud enough to be heard over the pelting rain.

Brave flashed her an impetuous grin, "I found it in grandfather's cottage after the fire!"

Fa gasped in disapproval.

"I gave it back to him!" Rave said defensively, "But he didn't want it- he buried it in the marsh."

"So, you dug it up!?" Fa accused in disbelief; she couldn't believe the things he did sometimes! "Rave! Don't you know what that is!? It must be from when Grandfather was..." she fell short of saying the word, even though she knew that no one could possibly overhear them as they floated down the river.

Rave's smile returned, "An assassin," he finished for Fa.

"Rave", Fa said impatiently, wiping her wet hair from her eyes. "It is *not* something to be proud of! Grandfather has always been ashamed to tell us anything from his past- and you should be ashamed for taking that thing!"

Rave blinked rain out of his eyes and refused to meet her stern gaze.

"It doesn't matter now. I have it and it saved our lives back there."

Fa gave in grudgingly, "Fine- but you're getting rid of it as soon as we get back- and your telling grandfather!" she said in her best big sister voice.

Rave glared at her but didn't say anything, and for long minutes they sat in silence as the boat drifted, at a steady slow pace down the center of the river. They were cold and wet; their cloaks long since saturated and offering no protection against the rain that had soaked through to their clothes. After a time, Rave started to doze off.

Fa told him to lay down in the bottom of the boat and sleep while she kept watch, "We don't want to float past our camp while we sleep."

Rave did as she suggested without comment- obviously still mad at her.

Fa sat shivering in the dark and watched the right and north shore for any sign of distant campfires that betrayed the location of their camp. In the dark, Fa found it hard to tell how fast the boat was going, and she knew she should pay close attention so that they didn't pass by the camp. But Fa's mind was full, and she became lost in thought trying to bring order to her scattered thoughts.

Why was she having strange dreams!? Fa began to retrace the past two and a half weeks and realized that the dreams had started in Eamer. Her first dream had been of fire; and she had woken up to Eamer burning. And then early that morning, before she caught Rave running away, she had been awoken by another dream of a burning room- and then again that day when she had fainted she had a dream of Graci- a woman she had only just met- and she had completely misunderstood that dream! Fa swallowed hard when she thought of her third dream that day; she had dreamed of the traitor, Horizon. In the dream, Horizon (she didn't know how she knew who he was, she just knew it was him) was riding a horse surrounded by Tarven guards, but suddenly the Tarvens transformed into knights in brilliant white armor! The knights held spears and white strips of cloth fluttered from them in the wind.

Fa had tried to warn Vanished- she really had tried! But he didn't listen, and from what she saw, Van and his men were all killed- or taken prisoner. And to top it all, the wagon had gone up in flames!

Fa moved uneasily as she thought of the 'thing'. The presence inside her, the 'thing' that was not part of her, moving and growing, compelling her to trust it; a mistake, as was clear from her experience with Graci. Whatever the thing was, Fa decided that it was connected to the dreams, and most certainly meant her harm!

Removing the now soiled hanky from her one hand, Fa turned her hands, palm up in her lap and let the rain, which had now lessened to a drizzle, splash and cool the burns. She winced at the pain and examined them closely; it was as she had feared. The burn on her first hand had grown from that morning, and there was a new burn on her other hand- and she had gotten it *before* the wagon fire...

What was happening to her!?

The boat suddenly bumped against the shore, bringing Fa out of her troubling thoughts. She realized then, that they could float right pass their camp and never know it, she decided it was best to secure the boat to the shore with a length of rope and wait till morning.

*   *   *

Brave woke up with a start as thunder cracked through the air leaving a trace of electricity behind it. Rave was laying in the bottom of the little boat in a puddle of rainwater, looking up at the sky; it was overcast with gray storm clouds, but the rain had stopped, and the dawn had come.

'It's morning!' Rave realized with another start, 'Why didn't Fa wake me when we reached camp!?' Rave sat up and looked behind him, Fa was curled up asleep in the boat stern. 'Why are we still in the boat?' Rave's sleepy mind struggled to make sense of the situation. He looked up and saw that the wind had pushed them against the bank, and long grass with spider webs were hanging over the sides into the boat. The grass was dry, the rainstorm must not have come this way; but that didn't make sense.

The boat rocked side to side as Rave stood up and looked over the grassy bank at the landscape around them; it was hilly! That wasn't right either! The land should be flat, and where was the dark smudge of the Corfin forest!? He wobbled to the front of the boat and pulled up the rope that hung over the side; a broken bush branch was tied to the end of it. Rave looked up as he began to realize what had happened while he and Fa slept.

"Fa wake up!" he said sharply and made the boat rock, mirroring his uncertainty, as lightning flashed across the sky. Fate's arms twitched before her eyes opened.

"Fa- I think we're lost!" he said, as panic once again filled him, and he held up the unsecured rope.

In disbelief Fa sat up quickly and looked around at the unfamiliar and empty landscape. "No…" she whispered as she franticly stood and looked at the horizons, "Oh Rave…" her voice quivered and made Rave's heart sink.

"We went the wrong way!" Thunder cracked again as they both looked up and down the river.

"We haven't just gone too far east?" Rave asked with one last shard of hope.

"No; that's east!" she pointed upriver the way they had come to where the rising sun shone through the clouds, "Home is that way! We thought the river was taking us back- but I forgot; this is the Dinco river west!" Fa touched a bandaged hand to her forehead as their situation overwhelmed her.

"It flows west towards the sea- not east…" Rave finished her thoughts and sat down heavily, 'how could we let ourselves forget!?' He cursed himself for not knowing the Westlands better, and irritably became aware of his soaked back from sleeping in the puddle.

Fa bit her lip as she gazed upriver, "I tied us to the shore- but it must have broken while I slept… We must have traveled miles west last night! it could take us days to get back to mother and father- and I said we'd be back by nightfall…"

Rave let another defeated sigh escape him- then he noticed his sister's hand; she had torn her hanky in half and wrapped up both her hands, but one half came undone and fell to the boat floor.

"Fa- are your burns worse!?" he asked in bafflement; he could have sworn that her burns hadn't been that big- or as bad, the night before!

Fate held up her hand and sucked in her breath. "I don't know what's happening to me," she whispered, as she sank back down into the boat and studied both her hands before wrapping them up again.

Rave was disturbed by Fa's burns, but his attention was drawn to behind Fa on the far bank- the south shore; there was something there that flickered- but he couldn't quite see it…

"We could try and row back…" Fa suggested half heartedly, "But it would be hard- and I couldn't help with my hands like this… so I guess we should start walking."

Rave hardly heard her as he stared intently out at the grasslands, a flash of lightning momentarily lit up the dark clouds and Rave at last understood what he was seeing.

"This can't be happening," he murmured. The lightning had started a grass fire! As he watched it tore through the grassy rolling hills towards the river, as if fleeing from the wind, a wall of smoke rose behind it like a smothering cape- in another few minutes it would be close enough to hear the crackling of the grass burn.

"What...?" Fa looked over her shoulder and froze.

"We need to get out of here!" Rave brushed the long grass aside as if to jump out into the shore.

"NO!" Fa warned, "It's too late! The fire's jumped the river!" her voice was full of fear. Brave looked and sure enough, as if trying to block their way back east, the blowing northwest wind had picked up a spark and planted it on the north bank.

"We can't go back that way now," Fa spoke tightly.

Rave glanced back east; already the north shore was high with red flames and smoke masked the river east.

"We have to outrun the fire on the river; keep ahead of the smoke before it chokes us," Fa instructed as she pushed off the bank with her boot, sending their boat back into the strong current of the Dinco.

Brave fumbled with the heavy oars, then sat down with his back to the fire and slid the oars into place. He had never rowed a boat before, and it took him a moment to get any momentum. The wind overtook them and engulfed them in billowing gray smoke, for a moment Rave couldn't see anything- but he kept rowing. Then with the rivers help, they emerged from the smoke cloud, coughing and scared.

"Faster Rave!" Fa shouted, her voice high in fright, "We need to go faster!" her eyes reflected the deep red flames behind them.

'Backwards!' Rave thought suddenly, 'I'm sitting backwards! Aren't you supposed to sit facing the way you came!?' Rave nearly lost both oars over the side as he swung his legs around, grabbing them he looked up and froze; the river behind them looked like a fiery tunnel of death! Feeling the heat on his face, Rave threw himself into the effort of rowing faster than the flames, and... further from home.

When Brave had been little, he had gotten a rope tangled around his foot, he had mistaken it for a snake. He ran and ran, but the 'snake' was always right behind him. Rave was reminded of that time now; no matter how hard he rowed, he could only seem to get them just ahead of the smoke and flames. And the wind that blew the fire after them, was also blowing them constantly into the north shore, so that Fa had to keep pushing them back into the center. The river that had carried them so far from their parents now seemed to flow painfully slow, seemingly unaffected by last nights rainstorm further east. Rave's muscles ached from the unfamiliar work- but he couldn't stop to rest, otherwise they would choke on the smoke.

Fate had lowered herself off the seat to the bottom of the boat, her rebandaged hands held against her chest and her knees pulled up like a protective shield. Sometimes she would watch over Rave's shoulder at the fire, and then rest her forehead on her knees; blocking out the sight. This went on for three long hours. They realized that the fire around them was from new lightning bolts, as if they could never escape the fire!

Rave blinked in surprise when a large drop of water splashed under his eye; it was beginning to rain!

"Fate!" he said excitedly, "The clouds are full of rain!"

Fa looked up and laughed in relief as the rain began to fall in earnest. The fire around them hissed and the smoke thickened.

"The fire is dying!" Rave slumped over in exhaustion and didn't bother to adjust his cloak to keep him dry, but let the rain run down his face and flatten his blond hair against his head and neck.

The rain worsened suddenly and the puddle in the boat began to grow.

"Help me scoop it out!" Fa directed, as she plunged her cupped hands into the puddle and splashed it overboard. As they worked, Rave noticed that Fa would hold her burnt and bandaged hands under the water for a moment longer than was necessary, how much pain was she in!? Rave wondered. After scooping the water out, on and off, for an hour, Rave realized that the river had curved south, and the current had grown stronger; the wind no longer pushed them against the north bank. Soon they had been carried out of sight of the dowsed grassfire, but the rain continued to drench them, threating to fill their boat, keeping Fa and Rave busy for another hour. Neither of them was keen on getting out of the boat and walking back through the scorched and now drenched grassland behind them, and they had little hope of steering their boat to shore- the river was hurtling them along at a terrific pace. When at last the rain turned to a drizzle, Fa and Rave sat back and rested, and soon began to shiver in their soaked clothes.

"Do you think…" Brave's voice was quiet, but he knew Fa could hear him, "Do you think father will be angry with me?" he looked up at Fa anxiously, 'I'm sorry Fa!' he wanted to say, but the words stuck in his mouth.

"He would have been if we got back last night. Now he'll just be relieved." Fa said gloomily.

Rave pushed his guilt away with a laugh, "After this- nothing will be exciting!"

Fa smiled ruefully, "I've had enough excitement to last me my whole life- so count me out of your next stupid idea." Rave grinned mischievously, but their smiles faded.

Chapter 4   Ree

Fate and her brother drifted down the Dinco river another hour, too tired and defeated to realize that the longer they sat, the further the walk home would be. The swollen current of the river carried them along faster than they realized, and it was early afternoon when they noticed that the landscape was changing. Through the gray curtain of the soft, steady rain, they could see slabs of rough gray rock strewn across the hilly grass lands like old scabs. Purple lichen grew on the rock in flower like patterns, giving the rugged terrain a lavender haze. They sat up with interest when they passed a huge white pine that stood near the bank. The siblings had never seen coniferous trees before and were struck with awe at the towering pine. Looking north east they saw a dark smudge filling the horizon.

"That's the Cokhawk…" Fa said in astonishment of the giant forest, "I didn't realize we'd gone that far! We need to get to shore."

Struggling a bit with the oars, they made it to the north bank, and climbed out onto a platform of rock shaded by another pine. Looking up they realized that not far from the shore was a road; they didn't know it, but they had gotten out at a common place to cross the river. The road dipped closer to the river there, and there was a road sign clumsily nailed to a wooden post, it pointed east, and the carved letters read, 'Cinders Grove'.

Reaching the road, they shook their wet cloaks and wished that it would stop drizzling, then they looked up and down the road; it was empty in the late afternoon gray sunlight.

Fa turned west on the road- but Brave hesitated, Fa looked back at him with a question. He huffed and put his hands on his hips, Fa had an idea of what he would say.

"Somethings happening to you Fa- I mean to your hands; and I don't understand it!" He failed to meet her gaze, "They're not normal burns- and they're spreading, so either I've missed something, and you tell me what that is or…" he faltered looking at her; hoping she would explain it to him.

Fa subconsciously brought her hands inside her cloak; she couldn't explain something that she didn't understand herself!

Rave huffed again, "Or…" He continued, "We go into that village- there might be a healer there who can help."

Fa stubbornly remained where she was; this role Rave was taking on as concerned brother was quite new, and Fa didn't often do as Rave asked.

'A healer...' she thought, with apprehension, as she looked down the road; she could see the outcropping of buildings among a grove of tall pines. What would a healer tell her about the burns? Would they tell her something terrible was happening to her? If she didn't go; she wouldn't hear it, and somehow that made it better.

"Come *on* Fa!" Rave took a step towards her; was he begging!?

"I know our family doesn't trust healers- but they can't all be bad! And we'll need to ask what road to take to get back anyway!" he reasoned.

"We don't have any money to pay a healer," Fa said a slight triumphantly.

"Never mind that! I'll... work something out."

Fa stiffened against the idea even more.

"Please Fa..."

Suddenly Fa's resolve vanished- since when did her brother EVER plead with her!? If he was that worried... then she couldn't dismiss her own concerns.

"Alright," she relented, "But we leave as soon as we can!" She refused to move until he agreed.

"We find a healer, hear what he has to say, then we leave; I promise!"

Fate had never seen her brother be so somber! It made her nervous.

Soon they passed by the village sign, 'Cinders Grove' it read, the carved letters looked old and the wood of the sign was whether worn. Fire was the only thing Fa could think of in relation to 'Cinder'. She did not comment on this and pushed the memory of the grass fire behind her.

Cinders Grove was a quaint collection of Garatin style cottages with thatch roofs, and Cokhawken cottages, tall and narrow. The Cokhawken cottages looked very strange to Fa and her brother, and they stared as the came upon the first of the cottages. Elegant fur trees and tall white pines stood like sentinels among the village, shedding their needles to make a soft carpet on the yards and roads. Even in their wet clothes and dripping hair, the siblings couldn't stop staring at the village in childlike awe; they had never seen anything like it.

At the crossroads of the village was a large inn and alehouse, as this was a common stop for merchants and travelers. The murmur of pleasant conversation from inside met Fa's ears, and a painted hanging sign over the door read 'The Cokhawks Feather'; it all seemed cheerful and welcoming-

very different from the alehouse in Garatin where this whole misadventure began!

"Well… come on," Rave encouraged as she hung back from entering, "If there's a healer here, this is as good a place as any to ask."

Reluctantly, Fa entered the alehouse by Rave's side; there was a large spacious room, and unlike most alehouses, it was well lit, clean and free of clutter. The walls were decorated with giant iridescent blue and green feathers, and a large fire crackled in a well-made fireplace (the fire made Fa slightly nervous). Thick yellow candles were on every surface, and a stair to the second level could be seen in the back. Nearly half the village of Cinders Grove seemed to be inside, seeking shelter from the rain. A family of four caught Fa's eyes and although they weren't doing anything special, she couldn't look away as she and Rave walked up to the counter.

A man stood behind the counter and was scraping off scraps from plates onto the floor where a dog hungrily ate them up. The man was tall and thick, with large hairy arms and a mane of black hair, his eyes were startling brown against his pale skin, and he wore a sparse beard around a wide mouth. His classic Cokhawken features unnerved Fa, but he smiled in a friendly way as Rave approached him.

"What can I do for you two, then?" the man asked, in a pleasant manner, happy from a day of good business.

"Is there a healer in the village?" Rave asked, and Fa watched the innkeepers' response closely; he made a face and shrugged, "Of sorts, but Ree doesn't like to treat strangers. How badly do you need a healer?" he asked ruefully.

Fa bowed her head and Rave didn't answer.

"Well… you can ask her…." the innkeeper spoke after an awkward silence. "The Cokhawken maiden sitting there- by herself." He pointed across the room. "Freedom's her namesake, she's a seamstress and she dabbles with healing herbs now and then… you never know- she might decide to help you," he said doubtfully.

Rave nodded his thanks, then he and Fa turned to the woman the innkeeper had indicated; the woman did indeed sit alone, and no one seemed to want to sit near her table either. A tin plate with a few scraps for the dogs had been pushed away, and she sat with her feet propped up with a little book in her hand. She looked younger than their grandfather- but older than their parents, and she seemed to be of average height and slim build. Like the innkeeper, her skin was pale, and she had black short hair streaked with silver, the front of it had been loosely pulled back from her face with a string.

Fa noted that the woman, like herself, was wearing pants; it made Fa feel slightly more comfortable, knowing that she didn't stand out too much in her own masculine attire. Fa couldn't help but wonder why no one sat near her.

"Come on," Fa whispered as Rave hesitated, seemingly taken aback that the 'healer' wasn't a man. Rave took a deep breath, and together they walked up to the woman.

"Are you Freedom?" Fa heard a tremble in her brother's voice; was he frightened of the woman?!

The woman didn't look up from her book, "That's right." There wasn't even a spark of interest in her voice.

"You're a... healer?" Fa felt embarrassed for Rave when his voice squeaked.

This time the woman lowered her book to her lap with a short sigh, and looked up at them, clearly annoyed; Fa would never have guessed that brown eyes could look so brittle!

"No, I am not," she shot a glare at the innkeeper then picked up her book again.

"It's... just that I have these burns," Fa tried once more and undid one of her bandaged hands. "They seem to come from nowhere." She lifted her hand up to show the frosty woman.

The Cokhawken woman glanced at her hand- and paused... then she looked up at Fa sharply; her gaze was intense, and Fa couldn't hold it.

"My house is just down the street." She stood up and snapped her book shut, Fa and Rave glanced at each other before wordlessly following her to the door.

"Your treating strangers now Ree?" the Innkeeper called out with a mischievous grin, "That's a first!"

Ree opened the Inn door and looked at him as if realizing there would be no end to his comments on 'treating strangers'. "I'll see you later," she said before stepping out into the street and the light drizzle.

"We can't pay you- we don't have any money," Rave said, as he turned up his cloak against the rain.

Freedom didn't seem to care, "Who are you than?" she asked, looking Rave up and down as she set a quick walking pace.

"I'm Brave," Rave said, trying to keep up with her.

"No; who are you to her?" Ree clarified and hitched a thumb at Fa.

"Um- she's my sister." Fa could tell that Rave disliked the woman more every second, and he dropped back to walk behind Freedom.

"And what's your namesake?" Ree asked looking over her shoulder at Fa, who skipped a step to try and catch up to her.

"Fate," she answered breathlessly.

Freedom stopped abruptly and gave Fa a curious look, Rave nearly bumped into her. After a moment Ree smiled ironically, "Ha…" she breathed. "I should have been able to guess that namesake. Come on, my cottage is this way," she added and started walking again.

'These burns will be the death of me' Fa thought as they reached Freedom's cottage, 'why else would she react this way to me?'

Freedom's cottage was of the Cokhawken style; tall and narrow, the cottage had three stories, the top was used mostly for storage and drying herbs and flowers; Ree used it to hang up her fabrics after dyeing them, and one wall of the top floor was only half height, allowing the wind to blow in. The bottom floor was often used as a barn to keep a horse or goats in, but Ree didn't have any animals and instead had her firepit and kitchen on her bottom floor. Just like how she had sat alone at the Inn, her cottage was set back and seemed separate from the others.

Once inside Ree shed her dripping cloak and eyeing her drenched guests, invited them to do the same. Draping their cloaks by the fire to dry, their host moved a worn kettle into the fire, the unspoken promise of hot tea made Fa shiver.

With a touch of sadness Fa was reminded of her home in Eamer, but it was gone now.

Ree pointed to a narrow, steep stair to the next floor, it was so steep it could have been a ladder, "I'll take a look at your hands upstairs," She said leading the way.

On the second level, Fa and Rave looked around with mild curiosity; there was a small bed in one corner, and a table and two chairs by one wall. A large chest dominated one corner, while various little chests lay about, their contents spilling out as if Ree didn't often have guests over. A ladder to the top floor was in the corner opposite the stairs, and a strange smell, which had been noticeable at ground level, increased in pungency and tickled the sibling's noses.

"Sit down," Ree waved to the table.

Since it was clear that Ree wasn't speaking to Brave, Fa did as she was told.

Displeased with being passed over, Rave sat down on the second ladder rung, and fixed his best glare at the Cokhawken woman.

As Freedom moved about the room collecting several things (a book, a jar, some herbs), Fate sniffed the air and realized that the strange smell was from a dyeing vat outside in the yard. And Fa also noticed a pile of fabric on the chest. If Freedom was a seamstress- how did she become interested in healing herbs?

Lighting a hanging lamp in the middle of the room, Ree also lighted a candle and set it down on the table before sitting down next to Fa. Again, Fa felt overpowered as Ree stared intently into Fate's eyes, but this time Fa determined to return the gaze. Ree looked down at Fa's hands, she had placed them palm up on the table and had removed both bandages.

"Tell me about them," Ree instructed, suddenly gentle, "When did they first appear?"

"Two days ago. I thought I had burned them on our campfire while I slept, but since then they've spread and gotten worse…"

"Campfire?" Ree asked with interest, "You were traveling? Interesting…" she whispered, "Were you traveling alone?" Ree sounded very keen to hear Fa's answer.

"No, with my family."

Ree glanced over at Rave, as if just remembering he existed. "What else can you tell me about the burns?" she said, looking back to Fa.

It seemed to Fa that she was fishing for a specific answer. Fa hesitated and looked at Rave before saying anything more.

"Just that they grow after I sleep… and I have strange dreams- mostly of fire." It must have been the answer that Ree was looking for, because one corner of her lips turned upwards.

"Before the burns appeared- did you meet any strangers?" Fa shook her head, and Ree looked downright disappointed!

"On the road while traveling?" Ree pressed.

"No, we live… we lived deep in the wilderness, we didn't meet anyone until after the burns appeared. Why? What do strangers have to do with the burns?" Fa was growing frustrated and on edge over the whole thing.

"How old are you?" Ree disregarded Fa's question like it wasn't worth answering.

'She's doing it again!' Fa thought angrily as Ree again stared intensely into Fa's eyes; despite herself, Fa squirmed under her gaze.

"I'm eighteen," Fa replied tightly.

"What could a child like you have done?" Freedom whispered to herself and sat back.

"Can you help my sister or not?" Brave asked, Fa could hear the agitation in his voice.

"The people in this village are afraid of me," Ree wasn't responding to Rave but instead focused her full attention on Fa.

Feeling more frustrated by the woman's behaviour, Fa was tempted not to say anything. "Why do you say that?" even as she said it, Fa remembered how Ree sat alone at the Inn, and how she appeared to live alone too.

"They're not sure themselves why they're afraid, but they are. I've lived here longer than some of them- but they still don't trust me. They think I have a dark past; why else would a Cokhawken live on the forest edge but refuse to enter it." Fate thought she heard sarcasm in her voice.

"So… they're wrong about you?" even as she said it, Fa realized that she had misunderstood the woman.

Ree let a smile spread across her face, "If they knew the truth; they would run me out with torches and pitch forks this very day." She let the shocked silence hang in the air for a long moment.

'Is she playing with us?!' Fa wondered in anger.

"I killed a man in my youth," Ree said evenly.

Fa didn't allow herself to react, but she saw out of the corner of her eye that Rave sat up straighter.

"I ran from the forest and hid, but Eloi knew what I had done; I became plagued by a black mark on my hand. It grew till it covered me completely. It was called a heart stain." Ree paused for effect, but Fa had never heard of such a thing, she glanced at Rave to see what he thought and saw that he hadn't a clue either.

"Eventually, I was caught and tried for my… accumulated crimes. They were going to kill me," Ree paused and waited for Fa to respond.

"What happened?" Fa didn't like being controlled in this way- but she did want to hear the rest of the story. Ree tilted her head to one side.

"What do you know of Eternity?" she asked calmly.

Fa blinked in surprise and Rave leaned forward, "*He* helped you!?" he blurted out.

"Nity took my place; the stone he was buried under was meant to be my tomb." Ree still didn't look at Rave, it was as if everything she said was for Fa's benefit alone.

Fate couldn't believe her ears! Her mother and father had told her many stories of Eternity, including the impossible story of his death; could Freedom somehow fit into those same stories?!

"As Eloi as my witness, I speak the truth," Freedom said plainly, when she saw the disbelief on Fa's face. "And when the Eloi-man died, my stain went with him. Pardoned for my crimes, I returned home, a new woman, but my village didn't exactly welcome me back with open arms, so I made my way here."

Fa couldn't detect any falsehood in the woman's story- and yet she was having a hard time believing it.

"Since then, I have searched to find out all I can about heart stains; I haven't learned much if your wondering." Ree leaned back in her chair, lifting the two front chair legs off the floor, and shifted her slim shoulders, "Heart stains are of old magic from before the foundations of Garason were laid. Old magic, that has been mostly forgotten and misused through the years, sometimes gaining the name of 'black magic'."

"What does this have to do with me?" Fa asked feeling less angry and more afraid.

Ree brought all four of her chair legs back to the floor with a thump, "I have learned that heart stains can come in many forms; a black mark on the skin, a dark mist over the eyes causing blindness, or it can come in the form of burns."

Chapter 5   Heart Stain

Rave jumped to his feet in outrage, "What are you saying!?" he demanded angrily.

"Do you have another explanation for your sisters burns?" Ree said, addressing him for the first time since entering her cottage. Rave frowned and tightened his lips in frustration. Turning her back on Rave once again, Ree fixed her eyes on Fa. "Your dreams; describe them to me," she instructed.

Fate frowned and her breathing became quick and uneven, Rave stepped closer to her.

"Um... what do you want to know about them?" Fa asked with an effort to calm herself.

Ree shifted impatiently, "Is it the same dream each time- or do they change; how many dreams have you had? Are there other people in your dreams? Are you yourself- or are you something else like an animal?"

Rave watched his sister with growing concern; how many of these strange dreams had she had? He had only heard of two of them- but had she had more?

Fa glanced at him as if ashamed to admit the truth, "I've had five... And they're all different- most involve fire, and yes- there are people- sometimes people I've only just met. But why would I be an animal!?" she seemed overwhelmed and frightened, and it made Rave angry.

"What does this have to do with the burns?" Rave demanded; this whole thing was nonsense!

"Intense, life-like dreams often go hand and hand with heart stains," Ree explained to Fa.

"But- but you said your heart stain was because you killed someone; I'm not a murderer!" Fa said leaning back from Ree slightly.

Rave glared at Ree, he almost wanted her to accuse his sister of killing someone, then he could give her a piece of his mind!

Ree was still, seemingly unaffected by the tension, and her gaze on Fa had never been more searching, "No," she said at last, "You're not a murderer, you don't have the eyes of someone who has killed.

"Then what is happening to me?" Fa asked with a tremble.

Ree relaxed into her chair, "In times of old, Eloi used heart stains for his own purposes; sometimes as a mark of guilt, and other times for more subtle reasons."

"Like what?" Rave asked bluntly.

"Some accounts describe it as a guiding hand, some go as far as to say that the stain is a life force unto itself," at this part Fa paled and stiffened, "a handprint Eloi left in our hearts, only to make itself known in a whisper, a dream... a mark. A spell woven into our souls with the intent of one day bringing us back to Eloi. Some think it's asleep in all of us." Ree paused and pointedly looked at Rave, it made him retreat a step, "Waiting for a time we are at our lowest, to reveal that even then, Eloi will still welcome us into his own. But you, Fa... I believe there is something more to your heart stain."

"What?" Fa sounded as small as Rave felt.

"Only your dreams can answer that."

"But... my dreams are vague and- nonsense! They raise questions, not answer them."

In answer Ree held up a glass bottle of crushed leaves.

"What is that?" Rave asked suspiciously and stepped even closer.

"It will make a tea that will make you sleep and give you vivid dreams."

Fa sat back in her chair.

"If you want to learn the truth- I must know more about your dreams."

Fa shook her head, "I don't know..." Rave relaxed a little.

Ree sighed and was silent for a moment, "I'll let you think on it." She stood up, looked at Rave, then descended the stairs. The siblings were quiet for a moment.

"You didn't tell me that you'd had so many dreams," Rave said at last, he felt a little betrayed that Fa had told a total stranger before telling him.

Fa looked up at him, "I was too scared... I still don't understand what's happening to me."

Rave put his hands on his hips, "Coming here was a mistake- I'm sorry I made you, I think we should just leave now, and... figure this out when we get home."

"Home is gone," she whispered sadly.

"You know what I mean," he said with agitation, "So lets just leave." He had a misgiving when Fa didn't stand up or agree with him, "You don't believe everything she said do you?"

Fa took a deep breath, "I don't know."

Rave turned away and ruffled his hair in frustration; dreams, heart stains, invisible handprints and life forces asleep inside him- Rave much preferred things he could touch, see and control! Believing his parent's stories about the impossible things that Nity did was one thing but believing that a part of Eloi was asleep inside him, was too much of a leap for Rave.

Freedom returned with a tray, on it was loaf of bread, some carrots from her garden and a wedge of cheese. She also had a steaming tin kettle and cups.

As soon as Brave saw the food his stomach growled audibly, Ree raised a dark brow at him and placed the tray on the table, "I thought you might be hungry after your travels.

The siblings hesitated, but it was as if they both remembered at the same time, that they hadn't eaten at all that morning or the whole of the day before! Rave stepped up to the table gingerly, and shyly took a helping, then returned to his seat on the ladder. Ree poured herself a cup of steaming tea and sat silently as the siblings ate hungrily.

"*If* I drink that," Fate said suddenly and looked at the bottle of leaves, "I'll be alright? It isn't dangerous?"

Rave looked up with a full mouth and saw that Ree wasn't even mildly surprised by Fa's reconsideration.

"Of course not; many people drink these leaves to make them sleep- it's quite common in the Cokhawk."

"And if you know more about my dreams," Fa paused and Rave swallowed his food with a gulp, "you can tell me what they mean?"

Ree nodded confidently.

"Alright... I'll do it," Fa said at last and nibbled on her bread.

"Fa- NO!" Rave stood up again.

Ree gave him a knowing look and sipped her tea, as if confident she knew what the outcome would be.

"Fate you can't do this!" Rave found himself forbidding his sister for the first time in his life.

Fa must have noticed too, because she swivelled in her chair and fixed him with a hard look, "Its my decision to make."

Rave wanted to say something more, but the look Fa gave him silenced him, instead he huffed and glared at Ree.

"How quickly will I fall asleep?" Fa asked, turning her attention back on Ree.

"That depends on how tired you are. It's best to do it at night, you may both stay here the night, if you wish."

Rave remained silent as Fa thought about it. "Yes, thank you," she said, and Rave knew that her mind was completely made up.

They spent the next two hours sitting and drying themselves by Ree's fire, giving Rave the chance to observe how timid his sister was around the flames. They didn't see Freedom much in this time; she kept herself busy on the top floor working. Rave took this opportunity to look around the ground floor of the strange dwelling, he hoped to find something that would make Fa see how ridiculous it was to trust Ree. But all Brave could find out of the ordinary was a little doll sitting high in the rafters, it looked like it had been made by a child.

But when he pointed it out and commented about how there were no children about, Fa simply dismissed it as having been made by Ree herself when she was young. The tension between the siblings was tangible, and not many words were spoken. When Rave noticed that it had stopped raining, he suggested that they go out for a walk, and ask directions to get back home. He was relieved when Fa agreed. He had a hope that once he got her away from Ree, that Fa would change her mind.

They wandered about the village for two hours, still only speaking to each other in short clipped words. The clouds parted slightly to let the light of the evening sunshine through the tall pines of the village. The villagers took advantage of the afternoon after the wet morning. They didn't take much notice of the siblings, Rave supposed that a lot of strangers came through the village.

Going into the Inn again, they found a hand-drawn map nailed to a wall. "I don't get it..." Rave said as he tried to make sense of the different red and black lines that were drawn across the map, "Where are we?"

Impatiently Fa pointed to their location. "These are trade routes," she explained, "You'd know that if-"

Rave cut her off with annoyance, "Yeah, I know, if I'd learn how to read." With this new information Rave studied the map again, "It doesn't go far enough east to have Garason on it…" the map mostly had paths and trade routes through the forest marked in red.

"It says that this one goes to Garason," Fa said, pointing to a black line that went off the right side of the map. "Seven days," she read with a sigh.

Rave was taken aback by how far they had traveled, "Oh… Father just might be mad at me after all." Rave was glad when he saw a smile twitch on Fate's face.

"I didn't realize we were so close to the sea…" Fa pointed to the far left of the map, her new bandages looking very white against the yellow parchment. "Just three days away… that's the seaport of Larsanne across the mouth of the Dinco River there," Fa said, brushing her finger on the spot.

Brave let his eyes wander up and down the coast; he had never seen a map of the eastlands- and had most certainly never thought he would ever be a three day walk from the Neenor sea! What a story to tell! "I think father might have been in this village when he was young!" Rave realized with excitement, "Remember his story of traveling with Est and… and- that other guy?"

"Fin," Fa answered as she looked again at the map, "Maybe they did come through here," she said with a small smile.

"Did Freedom fix you up, or did she chase you away?"

The siblings looked up as the bear-like innkeeper spoke behind them; he was clearing away a table. He wore a large grin on his wide face as if he thought it was funny.

"We're staying with her for the night," Fa answered. Rave's mood darkened as he was reminded but took interest in the innkeepers' response.

"No! She invited you to stay the night!?" he asked in disbelief, "You're not kin of hers, are ya then?"

Rave shook his head, and the man smiled widely, "What's next!? Inviting the village to have tea?" He seemed to think it was funny.

Just then Ree walked in and spotted them, she gave the Innkeeper a glare before he could even speak.

"We'll have dinner here," she said, kicking out a chair and sitting down.

"Ah! You and your, 'houseguests'?" the innkeeper asked with a smug smile. She continued to glare at him, it didn't seem to bother him though. "I'll put it on your tab," he said, walking away.

Ree actually smiled, "Or I could consider it as payment for that cloak I made you last week."

The innkeeper shrugged his shoulders, "Fair enough." Rave thought he saw him give Ree a sly wink before disappearing to the kitchen. Their interaction didn't fit Rave's impression of Ree, and it made him all the more uncomfortable.

Fate sat down at Ree's table, giving Rave little choice but to do likewise, he was slightly cheered by the promise of another free meal, but having to share it with Ree sapped his enthusiasm.

Ree leaned back in her chair and looked about the room easily, Rave noticed the change in her demeanor, although she still seemed frosty, she was less aloof, as if she had accepted that he and Fa were part of her 'company'. The thought didn't comfort Rave- instead it made him nervous.

After a moment Ree looked at Fa and raised an eyebrow "Reconsidering your decision?". Rave listened hopefully for Fa's answer.

"No, I want to get to the bottom of this," Fa said, without looking at Rave. Ree nodded.

Brave slouched in his chair, and the three sat in silence waiting for their food; when it came, they ate in more silence. Ree seemed to like it that way.

It was after sundown when they walked back to Freedom's cottage, and Brave noticed for the first time that there were lanterns throughout the village, that were now being lit.

Ree saw Fa taking note of this too, "It's expensive to keep lanterns lit every night, but we do it to keep away the Cokhawks; they hunt at night, and have been known to snatch goats and dogs, and children now and then too. It's not wise to travel these parts at night." she concluded airily.

Rave wasn't sure if he should believe her or not, it sounded like she was trying to scare them from leaving. He made sure not to stray too far behind though, just in case.

Once back in Ree's cottage, they took up their earlier positions; Rave on the ladder, Ree and Fa at the table. Rave watched Ree like a hawk as she prepared a cup of special tea for Fa, using a pinch of the leaves she had shown before.

"How long will I sleep for?" Fa asked as Ree stirred her cup and tested it by sniffing it.

"Hopefully through till morning- I prefer not to examine your dreams in the middle of the night," she said with a slight smile. "You may sleep in that bed there, there's an extra blanket for your brother to sleep on the floor. I'll be downstairs." Ree handed the steaming cup to Fa, and with a moment's hesitation, she drank it down. Rave winced when she screwed up her face at the taste.

"Alright then," Ree said standing up and going to the stairs, "I'll see you in the morning."

Getting up, Fa went and sat on the bed. Rave walked over and sat beside her as she removed her boots.

"You alright?" he asked cautiously.

She nodded but didn't say anything, then she lay back, legs curled up. Brave sat on the foot of her bed, wondering if he should try saying something more, but she refused to meet his gaze, and soon her eyes grew heavier, until at last she closed them. Rave waited till her breathing slowed down, and he knew she was asleep. His eyes went down to her hands, Ree had told her to unbandage them for the night, so that they could air out.

Poor Fa… what was happening to her?

With a determined face, Rave descended the stairs and found Freedom sitting in the semi dark by the fire, a steaming wooden cup in her hands.

"You weren't surprised when Fate agreed to do this; how did you know she would?" Rave asked as the firelight flickered on Ree's pale face and dark hair.

"Because I was her," she said softly.

Rave felt uncomfortable with comparing his sister to this woman. He twitched his mouth, then awkwardly started up the stairs again, but stopped on the second step, "Did you really kill someone in your youth?" he asked impulsively.

A humoured smile crept across Ree's cold face, "That's right."

"Who?" he hated how small his voice sounded in the dark.

Ree's voice was softer still, "A young man." She was gazing into the flames as if lost in thought and was clearly done speaking.

Rave swallowed; he wasn't sure he believed her, but all the same, *he* didn't intend to sleep much that night!

$*$ $*$ $*$

It was one of those dreams where you know your dreaming, Fate was even aware that Brave and Freedom were waiting for her to wake up.

'What if these dreams are just rubbish?' Fa wondered with misgiving, 'like normal dreams are?' but there was nothing to be done about it now, so Fa took in her surroundings. She was standing in a stone courtyard, to her right was the outer wall and rampart. Looking to her left, Fa marvelled at the grand castle that filled her view. Her eyes fell to a door across the courtyard, without thinking, Fa started towards it. As she went, Fa glanced up at the ramparts; there was a Tarven guard keeping watch over the castle. Fa didn't know why, but the scene seemed to impress deeply on her, and she knew she would not soon forget it.

"When will the morning come?" Fa found herself asking. The guard looked down at her and opened his mouth as if to speak, but suddenly her dream changed!

Fate found herself standing on a cliff top overlooking a foaming sea, across a bay from her, was a grand sprawling city. It was all castles, towers and ramparts. A great fleet of beautiful ships waited in the harbour with white sails and blowing flags. Fa could see a large garden in the center of the city, it was full of cherry trees in bloom, Fa was certain that she could smell them.

"You must hurry."

Startled, Fa looked beside her; there was a child standing with her on the cliff edge, looking up at her, "You must hurry; they don't have long."

Fa frowned, "Who?"

The child pointed to the city; it was then that Fa noticed a terrifying black cloud mass rolling in off the sea towards the city.

"You must warn them," the child said, and then Fa felt the 'thing' shift inside her, searching for more room to grow.

Fa gasped and with a strength of will stifled the movement within her; it had already taken more than she wanted to give. "Will they die?" she asked with concern as the storm grew closer.

The child beside her grabbed her hand, "You must hurry Fate."

"Where?" Fa said pulling her hand away from the child; it felt too similar to the 'thing' inside, "Where do I go?" she cried out suddenly growing frantic, she spun round to face the child, but the action made her dizzy, and her body grew heavy.

Quicker than thinking, the dream was gone, and Fa was awake. She had turned in her sleep and woke in time to put her hands out in front of her as she fell off the bed. Her hands and knees made contact with the floorboards and Fa yelped in surprise.

Curled up on the floor at the foot of her bed was Rave, he snorted and jumped awake, "Fate!" he exclaimed and fumbled through his blanket till he knelt beside her, "Are you alright!?" he asked anxiously.

Fa galped and nodded.

"REMEMBER YOUR DREAM!" Freedom yelled as she ran up the stairs, "Remember it- don't let it slip away!" Putting down a candle on the table, Ree caught her breath, then the Cokhawken knelt next to the siblings and searched Fa's eyes intently, "Quickly; tell me what you dreamed- don't leave anything out!" she instructed.

"Give her a moment!" Brave said defensively.

"No! Tell me now- while it's still fresh in your mind!" Fa took three deep breaths as she braced herself on the floor with both hands, 'is it morning!?' she wondered as silver twilight crept in through the windows.

"I was in a courtyard…" Fa recounted all she had dreamed, she left nothing out- except for the part where she had resisted the growing presence. When she was done, the early morning twilight had grown enough to see clearly. Ree stood up with a groan, and went to a window, her face deep in thought.

Fate leaned back-and gasped in pain as she peeled her unprotected hands off the floor, she whimpered and turned her hands about to see the new damage; the burns now covered her whole palms and the skin was peeling away as new blisters formed underneath the old ones. Beside her Brave caught his breath in alarm, Fa tried to hide her hands from him a little- but he had already seen.

Ree grabbed new bandages and crouched by her to carefully wrap up her hands.

"Well?" Rave asked with impatience, "What do her dreams mean?"

Ree stood back up with a moan and went to sit at the table, before speaking she pinched her eyebrows together as if wondering how she should start. "You said you lived far from here- didn't you?" she asked slowly as though still thinking.

"That's right," Fa answered uncertainly, 'we did' she added mentally, "Why? What does that matter?"

"And why are you here?" Ree disregarded her question.

Rave huffed, obviously growing impatient.

"We… were washed downriver by the storm," Fa said trying to keep the peace between the two.

"So, you came here by accident…" Ree said to herself

"What of it?" Rave demanded, still Ree spoke only to Fa.

"I don't believe finding the only person who knows about heart stains in all of Garatin- was an accident." Her gaze had grown intense again, "Your path has been chosen, Fa, the heart stain is leading you somewhere."

"To that city?" Fa felt the mystery unfold itself a little and she knew that she was right.

Ree leaned back and her face became thoughtful again, "I admit, I don't understand the first part of your dream in the courtyard."

Rave tightened his lips in annoyance, but Fa laid a bandaged hand on his arm to keep him from speaking.

"But I believe I know what the second half means," Ree finished.

Fa sighed, for she understood the second part as well, "I must warn the city of the storm."

"You are to warn them of something, yes," Ree said cautiously.

"But where?" Fa felt a sense of relief when she realized that the city's name hadn't been revealed to her, did that mean she was off the hook!?

Ree looked surprised and Fa's heart sank.

"A great city by the sea. A cherry tree garden in the center of it. A Tarven guard on the ramparts?" Ree repeated what Fa had said as if she thought it was clear, Fa looked to Rave but he was as clueless as she.

"Fate, Eloi is calling you to the capital, and city of Tarva!"

"TARVA!?" Rave burst and stood up in disbelief.

"That's right," Ree said, calmly shifting her gaze to him, "Tarva is on the sea and is known for its beautiful cherry tree garden."

"But… why Tarva?" Fa asked from where she still sat on the floor, she felt very small.

"What you mean is, why send you, a Garatin girl to Tarva," Ree said shrewdly, she shrugged her shoulders "I don't pretend to understand the ways of Eloi. But your dream is clear; 'you must hurry' the child said, and you must! For cherry trees bloom in the spring, and winter will soon come to the Neenor."

Rave turned to Fa, 'what will you do?!' he seemed to ask, but Fa avoided his gaze, for she had no answer.

Chapter 6   Far From Home

"Where are you going?" Brave asked his sister as she continued to stumble and march ahead of him. Cinders Grove was now lost to sight behind them and the road west wound and curved through the tall white pines. They had left Freedom's cottage after she had served them breakfast. Ree had also given them a pack with blankets and some food for their journey, which Rave had to thank her for, since Fate had been stubbornly mute all morning. Rave also had to carry the pack and was left asking questions of the air since stepping foot out Ree's door.

Without discussion, Fa had turned west in the morning dusk, and refused to respond to anything Rave said, not even with a look, as he doggedly followed seven steps behind her. They had been walking at a good clip for a half hour now, and Rave had had enough of being ignored- AND of walking west!

"FA!" he shouted at her.

"I'm going to the coast! Where do you think!?" Fate hollered back over her shoulder, Rave thought he could hear a sob in her voice.

"And what do you think you'll do when you get there!? Hop a ship and sail to Tarva? FA!" he stopped and shouted at her. Fa stopped and hesitated a moment before facing him; her eyes were red rimmed, and tears streamed down her face.

"I don't have many options- do I Rave!? You heard what Freedom said!"

Rave took a breath to calm himself, since when was he the one making her see reason!? "You can't believe all she said, Fa," he said, trying to sound reasonable, "You just can't take her word for it!"

"I don't HAVE to take her word for it!" Fa refused to calm down and thrust her bandaged hands out towards him, "Rave- I am living IT! Every time I close my eyes, I have another dream. She only put to words what I've been experiencing! And I can't go on like this- you heard what she said; she had her Heart Stain for THREE years! I have something inside me that's woken up- and it won't rest till I do this!" Fa was near hysterics; she hadn't bothered to re-braid her copper hair and it blew about her pale distraught face.

Rave took a step toward her and lowered his voice, "But *Tarva?* Fa, just calm down, we'll go back home- and fix this together."

Fa took a deep shuddering breath, she seemed to regain control of herself, and she shook her head, "Mother and Father can't help me. I must go to Tarva. I don't know how I'll get there…" here she faltered and lost confidence, "But I know that I must go." She sniffed and wiped her face with her sleeves, "I go to Tarva. I do what Eloi wants. I warn the city of the storm- or whatever is coming; then I go home."

They were silent, and Rave knew that this was the part where he should say that he would stick by her side no matter what… yet the words stuck in his throat, "But *Tarva?*" he was startled to realize that he was terrified of the idea! Why wasn't Fate?

As always Fa saw right through him, she sighed and turned away; she was disappointed in him! He had let her down… Rave swallowed hard; what was he to do? 'She's not herself' he thought in defence to his own short comings, 'She's not thinking clearly, Ree got her all riled up and scared. I'll let her stew about this for the day- soon she'll see reason and we can go home'. He hitched up his pack and followed her again.

But he was fooling himself; the truth, was that he was afraid. Far from home, alone for the first time, and Fa, the solid one- his anchor, couldn't be relied on!

They walked on like this, Fa ahead, and Rave trailing behind, for another hour, until the morning light was strong, and the birds were singing. As they walked, the quiet was broken by the sounds of a lonely cry somewhere up the path, it sent shivers down Rave's spine and he thought about what Ree had said about Cokhawks hunting; but it was well past dusk- surely, they were safe!

Turning a corner Rave paused at what he saw; on the side of the road was a small group of men and women, in the center of them, cramped in a large wooden cage, was a creature the size of a horse, and it seemed as strong too. It was all feathers and sharp claws. Its dazzling plumage consisted of royal blue, emerald and gold, it had a curved beak and glittering eyes of violet. Its regal head feathers had been ripped off, and its strong legs quivered due to the violent struggle it had undergone before capture. It was a female Cokhawk! She opened her sharp beak and released her lonely cry again as her captors stood about.

Fate saw them and quickened her pace to walk past, and without realizing it, the distance between Rave and his sister grew. Rave slowed his pace as he approached the scene and stared with open curiosity. There appeared to be two groups of people around the bird.

"And you can assure me that someone will buy her?" the leader of one group asked as he looked over the creature with a critical eye, he was Garatin and had a scar from his collar bone up to his cheek bone.

"Believe me; rich folk from all around want one of these! And they'll pay good money for um- that's why my price is so high- Watch it!" he warned as the bird fit her head through the bars and shot a jab with her beak at someone's head.

"I still say it's too high a price!" a woman, who was standing far back from the cage, said grudgingly.

"I didn't ask you- did I?" the scarred man snapped- but stopped short when he looked back and saw Rave who was just passing by, he also glanced at Fa who had walked past. The group went silent.

"You aren't from these parts- are ya?" the man asked with a friendly grin, it made his scar pucker.

"Rave!" Fa called impatiently as she turned about to see what was happening.

"We're just traveling through," Rave said, as he glanced at the caged bird again.

The scarred man's smile widened and two of his men stepped closer, "See that's what I thought when I saw ya. But I own this road see?" he pointed up and down the road, "and I tax travelers."

Rave had never heard of someone 'owning' a road, and whatever sense of caution he possessed evaporated. He looked at the man sceptically, "You own this road?"

The man frowned, "That's right; and you owe me."

"Rave!" Fa hissed, but he ignored her, "Well that's too bad, because we don't have any money!" Rave retorted, feeling clever.

The man stroked his chin thoughtfully, "No money? And traveling alone? What an opportunity!"

Rave realized what was happening too late; the two Garatins came at him, and one of them carried a large staff, they moved slowly, as if lazy and not interested in fighting hard.

"NO!" Rave shouted and struck one in the face, the man reeled back in surprise and Rave wrenched the staff from his hands and swung it around, striking the second man. Jumping clear Rave held the staff out- ready to strike anyone who came close, just then he heard Fa's strangled cry! He looked up and saw that the woman of the group had snuck up beside Fa, and the two were now in a struggle- but Fa was quickly subdued and was thrown to the road. The woman had a fist full of Fate's hair and had placed a booted foot between her shoulder blades pinning her to the ground.

"Go ahead boy- run away!" the scarred man jeered, "Leave behind your pretty friend- OH she does look scared!" he laughed as Fa struggled, pressing her tender hands into the dirt.

Rave felt a heat rise inside him; NO ONE treated his sister like that! With a roar Rave charged towards her but was caught from behind by his pack and thrown to the ground himself. He grunted in pain as a foot stomped down on his back, pushing his face into the dirt. The owner of the staff angrily ripped the weapon from his hand.

"HA!" the scarred man laughed, "Not too shabby! A Cokhawk and two young slaves to sell at the coast!"

The angry staff owner struck Rave on the back of his head, and Rave's panic gave way to blackness.

*   *   *

"HEY! LEAVE THAT!" Brave warned angrily and tried to kick as the woman removed the assassin's dagger from his boot. Fate and her brother had been tied up with their hands behind their backs and feet together. Their captors had thrown them aside on the road while the scarred man completed business with the hunters. The woman of the group searched their pack, and then had spotted the dagger in Rave's boot.

"Who'd you steal this from?" the woman asked, as she inspected it with interest.

"It's MINE! Give it back!" Rave said twisting around on the ground, the woman laughed at his efforts. Just then another of the slavers came over, he was also Garatin and had gray in his long hair and beard, he was tall and slim, and he seemed to out rank the woman.

"Give that to me," he said tightly, when he saw the dagger. The woman obeyed without comment and left; the man caught his breath as he ran his hand over the unique sheath. 'He's frightened!' Fa realized and watched him closely.

"How did you come by this!?" he leaned down over Rave and hissed.

"It's mine- and you better give it back!" Rave said boldly.

"No boy your age could be the rightful owner of this blade; where did you get it!?" Rave frowned as beads of sweat popped out on the man's forehead.

"It's our grandfathers..." Rave was confused- but Fa understood.

"It's an assassin's blade," she confirmed calmly.

The man laughed nervously and shifted his attention to her, "I'm no fool; I know what this is!" Fa noticed a slight tremble in the hand that held the blade. "The owner of this blade belonged to the Assassin army! They say they could walk through walls and kill a man with only a word... this blade must surely be cursed with the blood of a thousand," he whispered and looked at the dagger with growing fright.

"That's ridiculous!" Rave mumbled, but Fa cut in before he ruined their chance.

"'Cursed' is exactly the word I'd use!" she had the superstitious mans' attention at once.

"Ever since we got that dagger, we've been kidnapped, chased and narrowly escaped *two* fires!" The nervous man gobbled up every word, Rave on the other hand twisted around to look at her in disbelief,

"That's all rubbish!" he complained.

"Says the boy who's now a slave!" the man pointed out, pointing the dagger tip under Rave's nose. Rave went silent and swallowed hard.

"Exactly! For all we know- the curse has been laid on us now!" Fa whimpered dramatically.

The man raised his eyebrows as if just realizing his horrible misfortune, he stood up and stumbled over to the leader with the scarred face, who had just finished bargaining for the Cokhawk with the hunters.

"We can't keep those two!" the frightened man hissed to his leader.

Fa watched eagerly, "It's working!" she breathed.

"What do you mean?" the scarred man asked with a frown.

"They've been cursed!" he explained, and the leader rolled his eyes.

"I'm serious! They had this dagger (their grandfathers)- don't you know what this blade is!?"

"I most certainly do!" the scarred man said snatching the dagger away, "Go dunk your head in some cold water!" he said dismissing the man, and then he fixed his eyes on Fa and Rave.

"Fa?" Rave whispered nervously.

"This is your grandfathers?" he said holding out the dagger, neither sibling answered.

The scarred man stepped forward grabbing Rave by the front of his shirt, "Answer me!" he ordered.

"Yes, it's our grandfathers," Fa said boldly., "And yes; he will come for us," she challenged, with a false sense of confidence.

The scarred man looked up the road towards Cinders Grove, then back at his men. "Get the bird on your shoulders; we leave now! And make sure these two don't run off!" he said pulling Rave to his feet and tucking the dagger into his own belt.

Fate's heart sank; her plan had failed! Their captor's lust for money outweighed his fear.

Fate and Brave were made to walk and were pushed and shoved along by the man with the staff- who obviously held a grudge against Rave for hitting him. Rave's eyes kept wandering to the forest edge- but Fa quickly banished the thought from him; there was no chance they would escape!

'Is grandfather coming for us?' Fa wondered sadly, she tried to imagine their Grandfather galloping across the scorched grasslands at break-neck speed and crashing into the Inn at Cinders Grove, demanding the whereabouts of his grandchildren. But the hope died inside Fa, when she thought of her bandaged hands and her ill-fated mission. 'Maybe I'm the one who's cursed.'

Part Two - Sea Voyage

Chapter 7   The Neenor

Rustling wiped his brow with his wrinkled hanky and let the sea wind cool his face as he surveyed the group of men and women before him. Nine; nine prisoners intrusted to his care. Nine souls that he must either deliver safely to Tarva to await justice, or if that proved impossible- deliver justice himself.

There was a lord and his lady, who's crime was withholding taxes for forty years; the next was an earl who had also neglected to pay his dues. The fourth was a young woman who had tried to steal her brother's inheritance; the fifth was a man who had fled justice in Tarva six years ago and had just recently been caught. The seventh was a servant who had told one too many lies to his master, and the eighth was a young man who had loved the wrong woman.

But the last prisoner, the ninth soul in Rustling's care was different from the others; he was the only Garatin, his namesake was Horizon, and Rust didn't know what crime he had done. But they were all there for the same reason; each one had appealed to the king, demanding that their trial be held in Tarva. Appealing to the king was a way of buying time, it would take two months to reach Tarva, it was also a way of escaping the local judges, who may be harsher, depending on the crime. But a sea voyage was costly, so it was only the rich who could afford to appeal to the king, and that fact, among others, made Rust curious about the Garatin man- since he did not strike Rust as wealthy.

As for Rustling, he was a Tarven soldier, a knight, on his way home after serving in Garason for three years. But upon arriving in the seaport of Larsanne, Rust was surprised with a new order to escort nine prisoners across the sea to Tarva. He had also been assigned five soldiers, each one anxious to return home to beautiful Tarva.

The afternoon sun had turned west and was casting long shadows behind the city of Larsanne, the tide went out at sundown and that's when Rust and the others would start out on their charted ship; 'The Liberty'. They had only to wait for the captain's word to board.

Once again surveying the group standing about the base of the docks, Rust sighed; this would not be an enjoyable journey! The prisoners were all (aside from the Garatin) rich, entitled nobility, who honestly believed that they were better (despite their circumstances) than everyone else. Rust could tell just by looking at them that they would be rude, demanding and offended when he wouldn't accept their bribes- for if nothing else, Rust was an honest man.

"Sir? The captain sends word that the ship is ready to receive the prisoners," one of Rust's men reported, after saluting.

Rustling nodded, then examined the soldier, "You're the one who's been with the Garatin prisoner since Garason- aren't you?" Rust inquired.

The young soldier looked weary, "Aye sir, and you've heard correct; we had nothing but trouble trying to keep that man alive!"

Rust looked at the Garatin; thinning blond hair, ice blue eyes and a firm jaw. How much trouble could one man cause? "What is his crime?"

"Ahh, something to do with the Garatin high council- I don't know the details," the soldier shrugged, "But I do know this; everyone wants that man dead! We were ambushed *twice* on our way here- and we took the quick route along the river. We were ambushed once by Garatin rebels (Eternity rebels no doubt) and the second time, our hind guard was attacked by some kind of highly trained soldier. The ones who were attacked called him a phantom. He simply attacked and then disappeared- with no attempt on Horizon's life!"

"Were the soldiers killed?" Rust asked, anticipating the answer to be yes.

"That was the strangest thing- he didn't try to kill them, they said he kept asking for his grandchildren!"

"Strange…" Rust commented with a frown, he wondered if it was some sort of code.

"The Garatin's the reason we were given orders to sail right away; we were going to stay here till next year, but it's too risky to keep that man around, and so we leave now. I just hope that the further we get from these shores the easier it will be to keep that man alive!"

Rust managed a laugh, "And I hoped this journey would be peaceful!"

"You are wrong about that," a voice behind them made both men spin round. It was Captain Provide of 'The Liberty'. "It's almost too late in the season to be starting a voyage; storms will soon break out there. And I don't like to take 'passengers', but… orders are orders," Captain Vide said grudgingly.

'I'm sure money helped make up his mind too,' Rust thought ruefully.

"Be that as it may," the captain said without realizing the irony, "I will only take you as far as Nirin on the north of the Neenor, I will introduce you to my partner, who will take you the rest of the way in the spring. We know better than to venture further west in the off season. Now, you may board the prisoners," the captain said stiffly and walked away.

"Is he right? Will we have rough seas?" the young soldier asked, concern showing in his face.

Rust shook his head, "He's just the sort who worries about everything. I can't delay this voyage a half year just to ease his mind; orders are orders." Rust wished he could send the prisoners back into the city and continue on his own… but instead he started to move the prisoners down the dock. He stood aside as the prisoners passed by in single file and was taken off guard when the Garatin smiled pleasantly as he passed. Just then something else demanded Rust's attention.

"Alright, alright, one hundred and eighty silver for the Cokhawk."

"And one hundred and thirty for them." The captain of 'The Liberty' was haggling a price with a group of land merchants who stood about cluttering the seaside square. In a cage on the paving stones was a Cokhawk who looked worse for wear. But the bird wasn't the only thing Captain Vide was buying; there were two young Garatins, with bound hands, a young woman and man. The young man looked defiant and touchy.

'This is new to them' Rust thought as he watched and mopped his brow again.

But the young woman, with copper hair, looked calm as if she was right where she wanted to be. Rust watched as the captain handed over the agreed upon silver then directed that the bird and two Garatins were to be sent aboard. Rust knew the laws on slavery, but the sight made Rust uncomfortable, he was familiar with lords and serfs, but this kind of slavery was different somehow; uglier.

But Rust knew how to pick his fights, and this was one that he knew he could not win.

*   *   *

Fate had gained a calm in her spirit over the past four days that it had taken to get to Larsanne; she was going west, it didn't matter how she got to Tarva, all that mattered was that she got there. She regretted that Brave had been pulled into her mess- but she was glad that he was there with her, and she was confident that they would escape their slavers when they needed to. But for now, they were headed the right way- yes, she had a calm spirit, that is, she *did*, until she stood on the deck of 'The Liberty'. Then it was as if the towering white sails and creaking deck stole her peace and replaced it with fear.

'The Liberty' was a merchant ship built for size, it was an 'out rigger'; it had a second hull off the starboard side connected to the main ship with six sturdy beams wide enough to walk across. This style of ship was only made in the famous ship building city of Jiggitwo. The main ship had four masts with seemingly endless sail and rope, the second hull didn't have any masts, and was used only for cargo.

Aloft and all around the ship's crew were busy making the ship ready to sail, and they hardly took any notice of Fa and her brother as they stood in awe. It was all too much to take in at once, and Fa felt incredibly small. Behind them, the sailor who was given charge of them for the time being, pointed to a large hatch in front of the second and largest mast.

"Get moving then!" he ordered impatiently.

Fate grabbed Rave's hand, and they started forward, her bandages had become dirty and ragged over the past four days, but her burns didn't smart anymore and seemed to be healing. Fa supposed this was because she hadn't slept since Freedom's cottage, 'if I don't sleep, then I won't dream. And if I don't dream, I won't have new burns' she had reasoned, 'and... maybe that 'thing' can't grow anymore.'

Beside her, Rave looked around with wide eyes and a set jaw, a few times in the past few days he had challenged their captors and had paid for it, as the bruises on his face testified, but it didn't seem to have damaged his spirit at all.

On their way across the deck, they were nearly run over by the busy crew three times, and when they reached the open hatch and looked down the steep ladder-like stairs to the second deck, Fa felt fear grip her tighter and she balked.

"Rave, I- I can't go down there- I can't!" she took a step back and felt panic rising inside her.

"Get a move on!" the sailor complained intolerantly and gave Fa a shove.

Rave put his arm around Fa and shot a glare at the sailor, "Come on Fa," he said in a low tone, "We'll be alright, look I'll go first."

Fa watched as he descended the ladder giving her an encouraging smile before disappearing into the darkness. Hesitantly following him, Fa tried to calm her breathing, but found she couldn't- and her heart throbbed in her ears. Never before had she encountered this feeling- this fear, for she had never been in such a closed-in space before, she hadn't even been in a cave! She knew her fear was irrational, but she couldn't control it- she felt like she was being swallowed!

Brave was waiting at the bottom of the ladder for her, and Fa grabbed onto his hand as soon as she could and took in the second deck at a glance; the ceiling was low, making most men stoop in places to avoid supporting beams. Dim light came from small circle windows, that had thick panes of glass and were impossible to see out of. Brighter sunlight came from the hatch and an iron grate that also allowed the air to circulate. Down the center of the ship were four thick pillars- Fa realized that they were the bottom ends of the masts, on either side were hung hammocks for the crew. In the stern of the ship was the galley; where the kitchen was located and where the crew and passengers would eat. While in the bow, two doors led to the cabins for the first mate and the quartermaster, the captains' cabin was on the top deck on the bow.

Above, below and all around them, the ship creaked and groaned like something breathing.

Coming down behind them, the sailor pointed to another hatch, Fa didn't see how she could possibly make herself go further into the wooden beast. Her breathing became erratic and nothing she did would calm it, sweat was beginning to form on her neck and back, and her head felt light as if there wasn't enough air to keep her thoughts from cluttering up. Rave watched her with concern… and something else, was it despair?

'Steady' Fa told herself sternly, 'I *must* be steady- and brave for him.'

Somehow, Fa did make herself descend to the third and lowest deck; because it was below the water line, there were no windows, the only light coming from another grate and the stair they had just come from. As her eyes adjusted to the near darkness, Fa saw that even more hammocks hung from the ceiling, and there were two more smaller cabins in the stern. Standing about the hammocks were a group of Tarvens, they struck Fa as wealthy; she learned later that they were prisoners.

"And just where are we expected to live during this voyage?!" a Tarven man asked with disdain.

A Tarven soldier who oversaw them mopped his forehead and replied wearily, "With the rest of the crew, my lord."

The man glanced at the cabins pointedly, "I would pay you if you arranged for me and my lady to have one of those cabins."

The soldier looked as though he had expected such, "That is a matter that you will have to address with the captain at a later time, my lord." The weary man turned to some other soldiers, "Keep them from going top deck for now", he ordered in a low tone. He gave Rave and Fa a side glance before going topside.

After the soldier had gone by, Fa and Rave's escort sat down on the ladder, "Sit tight you two, the captain will assign jobs for you when he has the time."

Rave sank into a hammock and with the cover of the dark room, glared openly at the sailor. Fa sat down on the edge of a hammock next to his and concentrated on controlling her claustrophobia. She noticed that one of the prisoners had laid down in a hammock across the passageway. He stretched out and closed his eyes as if he hadn't a care in the world, and soon he fell asleep! Yet more surprising still; he was Garatin.

*   *   *

Brave turned his head to watch Fate being led away to the galley where she was to help the cook. A strong hand clamped down over the back of his neck, and Rave hunched his shoulders and winced.

"Pay attention to what I'm saying to you boy!" the sailor beside him warned sharply.

The captain had sent Fate to work in the galley, and Rave had been made into the 'if anything needs doing, he'll do it' boy. His first task was to move two dozen crates, from the bottom of the ladder to the galley storeroom.

After cuffing Rave on the side of his head, the sailor went top side, leaving Rave to glare at him as he went, then grudgingly Rave began the exhausting task. He was grateful that at least he could be on the same deck as Fa.

'Grateful?' he pondered the word, 'Grateful to who? Eloi?'. Had Eloi been responsible for their circumstances? Perhaps being taken captive was the only way to get himself to accompany Fa on her 'task'. For here they were, going West, just like Fa had wanted to.

Rave was not accustomed to wondering about such things- but considering recent events, the hope giver, life changer that his Grandfather and parents had raised him to honor, suddenly sprung to mind. Eloi, the unseen leader, protector, and sovereign of Garatin, had always been a part of Rave's life. But Rave had never stopped to give it much thought; Eloi simply *was*. And Rave had never cared to wonder why that was. But he gave it thought now!

His grandfather had said that no matter how dark his life as an assassin had been- it was never so dark that the light Eloi shone couldn't brighten it. And Rave knew that his father thought much the same- from firsthand experience.

Too much of that kind of wondering would give Rave a headache, besides he had better things to think about- like his grandfather's dagger. He had seen one of 'The Liberty's' crewmen buying the dagger from that scar-faced man; that dagger belonged to Rave- and he *would* retrieve it somehow!

*   *   *

Fate leaned back to see out the galley door to where Brave was working, he had been at it for an hour now, and he was beginning to slow down in exhaustion. Fa frowned; she could only imagine what kind of punishment he would receive if the captain thought he was being lazy. But Fa wasn't any better off herself.

The ship's cook was an old Cokhawken man with heavy eye lids and a pot belly. The sleeves to his stained shirt were always rolled up, revealing scarred and hairy forearms. He was a man of few words and his dour face seemed to be in a perpetual frown. He was not pleased at all to have Fa's help, but grudgingly kept her busy, which Fa was grateful for; it kept her fear and claustrophobia at bay. Fa had peeled more potatoes and cut more carrots than she could eat in her whole life, and by dinner hour she and the sullen cook had made a thick stew.

Slowly the crew came trickling in when their shifts were done, each one passing by Fa so she could ladle out stew into their bowls. Fa supposed that at first glance the sailors mistook her for a boy, since she was still wearing pants and had braided her copper hair back from her face. But soon she noticed that some of the sailors were laughing and pointing rudely at her, some even dared to flash a wink at her when they passed by, but Fa felt more annoyed than scared. In an effort to look unattractive and uninviting, Fa screwed up her face in a scowl that she hoped matched the cooks.

Fa kept her eyes trained on the door waiting for Brave- but he didn't come, instead the Tarven prisoners came one by one to get their dinner. Fa's scowl almost turned honest when some of the prisoners turned up their noses at her stew.

"Thank you," a kind voice said, as she filled up another bowl.

Fa looked up in surprise at the first person to thank her; it was the Garatin prisoner. His eyes were frosty looking, and he had a long angular face that looked a bit gaunt from hardship. His smile held a question.

Fate realized with embarrassment that she was still maintaining her scowl, her face broke to its natural, pleasant, look, "Your welcome sir…"

His smile widened, and he sat down on a bench against the wall near to her, "I didn't expect to see so many Garatin faces on this voyage!" he commented good naturedly. For the first time Fa looked about the eating area and realized that a quarter of the crew were her own countrymen, the rest being a mix of Tarvens and Cokhawkens.

"Have you worked on this ship long?" the Garatin asked her politely.

Fa smiled despite herself, "No! this will be my first voyage. I don't see how anyone could spend their life in a ship!" she swallowed hard as she was reminded of her new-found fear.

The Garatin seemed to understand and he studied her as he ate his stew, "I take it then that you did not choose to voyage."

"I and my brother had about as much choice in the matter as you," she glanced at him and was surprised by his reaction.

"Ah, I'm afraid to say that I *did* choose to voyage."

Fa looked at him curiously.

"Tarva is exactly where I want to go," he said, a touch of steel entering his gaze.

Fa wondered at him, then a thought struck her. "Who are you?"

He smiled as though he had expected the question, "My namesake is Horizon."

Fa's ladle hung in mid air, dripping into the pot as she searched his face, her mind running to all four points of the compass at once. Horizon, the so-called traitor. The man that Van had so desperately wanted to kill. The man who Graci had hated so much. Could this kind, and smiling man be one and the same Horizon!?

"Yes," he said staring down into his stew as if ashamed by his reputation, "I am the same Horizon that you have no doubt heard of."

Fa looked away, embarrassed, and wondered what Rave would do when he found out, "Oh, I- I can't say as I've heard very much about you." She filled another bowl.

"Just enough though," he assumed sadly, "Well let me speak for myself." Reluctantly, Fa found the image of the man being changed in her mind as he spoke. "Nearly fifteen years ago, the man I was died, and who I was, was reimagined. I did many things that I regret- a great many things- and I did them all for what I thought was a just cause. What I thought Eloi meant me to do. I lived with eyes closed, denying the truth. But Eternity, the Eloi-man, opened my eyes, and redefined who I was. Since then I have striven to be who Eloi truly meant me to be."

Fa searched his face again; could she believe him? '*He's traveled the world preaching his lies*', Fa remembered Graci's words about Horizon, '*He has all Garatin under his spell*'. Fa wanted to believe the man sitting there, but what if Graci and Van were right? '*People who extend acceptance to that monster invite death into their homes- they think because he's 'changed' that he deserves forgiveness*'. Who was Fa to believe!?

'He can't do any more harm now' she reasoned in a way of not making a definite decision either way, 'he's going to Tarva to stand trial for treason'. Just then Fa's stomach dropped inside her, and she stumbled, her feet seeking even ground. The stew in the pot tipped wildly to one side, and she felt the whole ship lean with it. Her claustrophobia came crushing down on her. 'What's happening!?' her disorientated mind demanded, and Fa quickly guessed; while she had been serving stew, and talking to Rizon, the sailors top deck had weighed anchored and moved "The Liberty" out of the protected harbour and had now encountered her first sea swells of the voyage.

Fa wanted nothing more than to get out into the open air and found it near torture to help the cook clean up after all the sailors had eaten. But when she stumbled into a nailed down table for the fourth time, the cook waved a hand with dismissal, "Ah! Your no good to me until you get your sea legs. Get below!"

Greatly relieved, Fa stumbled to the ladder, she lost her footing on the ladder twice as the ship rocked, and nearly fell down to the third deck. When she reached the bottom her knees felt weak, and she clutched the railing to support her as she peered through the gloom of the third deck. After a moment she made out Raves outline sitting with his back to the ship wall.

"Where have you been?" Fa asked once she made it to his side, dropping down beside him she noticed that he was clutching his stomach

"They wanted me to work on deck," Rave moaned, "But I don't know how to do anything- and I kept falling over... so they sent me below."

Fa pressed her lips together in sympathy, "Do you want something to eat?"

Fa tried to hide a smile when Rave gave her a very green look.

Chapter 8   Sincere

A week? Three weeks? She had lost track of how long 'The Liberty' had been at sea for. One day just blended into the next without the distinction of sleep to separate them, for Fa had refused to sleep, afraid of what the next dream would bring. She had dozed off many times, sleeping only for a few minutes before waking up with a start, afraid that she had started dreaming. A few times she had become so tired that she started to hallucinate! After the second hallucination she had reluctantly allowed herself to sleep, carefully timing it so that she would be awoken in a few minutes by the cook calling for her to prepare a meal. But a few stolen minutes here and there, hardly made up for the hours of rest that she had denied herself.

Fa closed her eyes, oh how she longed to sleep; to lay down and let the world carry on without her. Let the cook scowl away as the dishes piled up, let Rave be tossed overboard, let the ship crash and sink! She wouldn't have to worry about any of it, if only she could sleep...

Fa jerked herself awake and took a deep breath- it turned into a yawn. In an effort to wake herself up, she rubbed the heels of her hands into her closed eyes.

"Can't sleep- don't dream! Mustn't sleep..." she muttered to herself. Holding her hands out before her, Fa studied them in the near darkness; they were criss-crossed with pink raised scars, and the skin was still red- but they didn't hurt anymore, and she had stopped wearing the bandages a few days ago. She reminded herself that one dream was all it would take to bring the burns back with a vengeance. Wearily she hugged her hands to herself, one dream was all it would take for the 'thing' to reawaken. She had blissfully been free of it for some time now- but she knew it was still there.

Fate pushed herself off the hard deck, careful not to wake the other women. That first night, the two Tarven women prisoners had hung up blankets to create a little square of privacy, and had out of decorum's sake, invited Fa to join them. Fa had almost preferred not to join them- but had gotten use to the feeling of being inferior to the dark-haired, rich women. They were both snobbish to her and hardly ever talked to her, but Fa didn't mind; their company wasn't pleasant enough to make her lonely for it.

Feeling the ship's ever constant movement beneath her bare feet, Fa slipped past the blanket wall and paused, it was late at night, and nearly all the hammocks were filled with snoring sailors. But sitting on the ladder, in the pale moonlight from above sat two men; it was Horizon, and the Tarven soldier, Rustling. Fa stood in the shadows, and was too tired to question whether or not she should be listening in.

"- The Fort is *the* center of Garatin- where every Garatin heart beats," Rust said in a soft voice, the two men appeared to be having a friendly argument, Rustling went on, "Surely to stray from the boarders of Garatin is to leave Eloi behind."

Fa listened with interest; she knew about the Fort and the Vase within, but she had never considered what Rust had just said. If Eloi had sent her on a mission beyond Garatin- had Eloi sent her away!?

Horizon looked like he enjoyed such debates, "Ah, but as we have previously established; Nity's life and death changed all we know of Eloi."

"So, you say, but if the 'Eloi-man' was the 'bridge' to Eloi, or the… ambassador, then surely all connection with Eloi was severed with Nity's death."

Fa looked to Rizon and waited to hear what he would say.

Rizon nodded good naturedly, "Perhaps that would be the case- *if* that were so. But Eternity lived again after his execution."

Rust sighed as if annoyed by an old argument, "So the story goes," he conceded, "but what proof is there of this phenomenon?"

As if to quell Fa's fears that Rust was right, Rizon actually laughed, "Is two hundred eyewitnesses not enough 'proof' for a logical man like yourself?"

Rustling chuckled himself, "I give up! You could convince a fish that water doesn't exist!"

"Have I convinced you though?" Rizon asked seriously. Rust only chuckled again and shook his head.

Fate realized that she had been holding her breath again- she scolded herself for the bad habit and chose that moment to let her presence be known, she stepped forward until they noticed her.

"Good morrow Fate." Over the past several weeks, Rizon had talked with her often, and Fa had grown to appreciate his light-hearted view of circumstances. Fa had been relieved that Rave had taken the news so well when she told him who the Garatin prisoner was, Rave had been more curious than anything.

"Actually", Rustling said looking up to the top decks open hatch, "I believe it already is the morrow."

"I hope we didn't wake you Fate?" Rizon asked when he realized the hour.

Fa smiled thinly, she hadn't told Rizon of her dreams and burns- but she had considered it, "No, I just couldn't sleep."

"A bit of fresh air would help," Rust suggested.

Rizon bowed his head and pressed his lips together; he knew as Fa did, that Captain Vide had forbid her and Rave from going topside.

After a moment of awkward silence, Rust realized what he had overlooked. "Ah…" as if ashamed to look at Fa, he stood to his feet, "Well, good night Horizon," he nodded his head politely at Fa, then ascended to the second deck to his hammock.

"What you were saying…" Fa said shyly, and steadied herself against the ladder, "About Eloi not being bound to the Vase- you believe that?"

Rizon hesitated as if unsure how serious she was, "I do. Eternity began a new age- for everyone; for Garatins- and Tarvens, for the free and the slaves. He opened a door that once entered, will allow you to be close to Eloi- regardless of who you may be, or where you may be. Distance is a non-issue."

Fa frowned; how could this be the same man who tore Graci and her family from their home along with countless others?

Rizon smiled, "You have another question for me," he guessed.

Fa sighed in defeat, sometimes she was just like her mother; wearing every thought on her face!

"I can't reconcile the man I have gotten to know, with the man whom I have heard described as a monster! I look at you, and you are either a liar- in your past and now- or you are sincere. As sincere about telling Eternity's story, as you were about stamping out his followers. How can anyone so drastically shift their passions?"

Horizon might have been taken aback had he not already discovered that Fate was a discerning young woman, "One could say that my passions haven't shifted at all, I have always been passionate about the truth! However, I was misled on who Eloi was. All that changed was Nity revealing the true nature of Eloi, as he does for everyone," he added softly.

Before Fa could really consider this, Brave who had woken from his nearby hammock, called out softly "Fa?" He asked sleepily and struggled to rise from his swaying hammock. He had been seasick on and off much of the time and even now looked greenish, "What are you doing awake?" he whispered and came closer.

"I woke up thirsty," she lied; she hadn't told Rave of her solution for her burns- she knew he would worry over her lack of rest, and she also knew that he couldn't help. She glanced at Rizon; did he catch her fib?

Whether he did or not, Rizon did not indicate. "Well, I better get what sleep I can before sunrise," he smiled at Fa and Rave and went off into the darkness, to his own hammock.

"He's nice for a traitor," Rave whispered flippantly.

"Hush!" Fa scolded, glancing to where Rizon had disappeared. "Don't call him that!" she could just make out his impish grin in the darkness.

"Have you had any more dreams about him- knights and white flags and all that?" he whispered suddenly serious.

"No... I haven't dreamed since Cinders Grove," she said holding out her healed hands.

"That's good- right?" Rave sounded as uncertain as Fa felt. She nodded, not trusting her voice to lie to him again.

"What about you?" she asked instead in a hushed tone, "Are you feeling any better?"

Rave clutched his stomach and raised his eyebrows, "Yeah- I think so. I'll be useless if we ever go through a storm though!"

Fa smiled her sympathy, for some reason the rolling waves didn't bother her as much as Rave- instead she was just constantly biting back claustrophobia. She moved to go back to her hammock.

"What would Mother and Father say if they knew where we were?" Rave asked suddenly, his tone had gone back to serious.

Fa sighed with pain, "I can only hope they think we're lost in Garason somewhere." She had imagined her parents' faces, worry stricken as they searched for them, many times.

"Lost? Fa we've been gone for weeks!" Rave pointed out.

Fa turned to him, glad that the darkness hid her glittering tears, "It won't do us any good to think about it. It won't do us any good to wish that we had never left our camp that morning. It won't do us any good to wish that you had turned back at Cinders Grove so that at least they would know what had happened to me!"

Rave was silent for a moment, as though struggling against words that didn't want to be spoken aloud, "I'm not going to leave you to do this alone." He promised, "Wherever, or what ever you have to do; I'll be there."

His promise touched her more than Fate could ever say, she nodded with new fortitude, "I'm going where Eloi wants me to go; where the heart stain demands... We're just getting there in a way I didn't expect, that's all."

Rave nodded his head in encouragement, "I heard one of the sailors say that we'll be making port in Nirin next week... do you think we'll be sold there?"

Fa sighed, "I don't know, we'll worry about that then." She turned away and went back to her hammock behind the blanket, but what she said had been a lie; she *was* worrying about it! If the captain sold them in Nirin- how were they to get to Tarva!?... but, if he didn't sell them in Nirin, and instead took them back to Garatin... if that happened, did it mean that Eloi was letting her go home?

As Brave had heard, 'The Liberty' made port the next week in the coastal city of Nirin, the city was positioned at the southern tip of the valley of Zavie. It was home to a people who generally had slightly lighter skin than Tarvens, and had brown eyes and to Garatin ears, thick accents. The valley of Zavie had been a part of the Tarven Empire for nearly 80 years, so there was an even mix of Tarvens and true locals. This was as far as Captain Vide had promised to take Rustling and his prisoners, there was still another month of sea voyage before reaching Tarva.

Chapter 9   Confess

"WHERE IS THE CAPTAIN OF 'THE PRESTIGE'?!"

Rustling wiped his forehead with the back of his sleeve (he had lost his hanky) and swallowed his disliking for Captain Vide of 'The Liberty' once more.

"*Well!?* Where is he?" Captain Vide shouted impatiently at the crew members on deck of 'The Prestige'.

'The Liberty' had made port in Nirin the night before, and Captain Vide had waited for his partner, Captain Devotion of 'The Prestige' to meet him- but the man had never shown. So, Captain Vide had gone over to 'The Prestige' in a fit of impatience the next morning. Rust had accompanied him in the hopes of negotiating his passage on 'The Prestige'- but no one seemed to know where the missing partner was.

"Can any of you sea mongrels tell me where your captain is!? I would like to go back to Garatin before winter comes if you don't mind!" he shouted angrily.

"My husband is dead."

Rust turned in surprise at the hard woman's voice; slipping over the bulwark and stepping firmly onto the deck, stood a fierce looking woman. Her Tarven dark brown hair was pulled back from a high forehead in tiny braids, which were then arranged in a messy knot at the back of her neck. She wore men's pants and tunic with rolled up sleeves. She was average height, but her presence was so intimidating that people always remembered her as being taller. Everything about her was masculine, from her strong arms and broad shoulders to her wide chin and high forehead, in fact, Rust might have mistaken her for a man had she not suggested otherwise by her comment.

"Devotion died a few days ago from sea fever." The woman said coming towards them with confident strides.

"Ah…." Captain Vide was momentarily silenced, whether by shock at his partner's demise, or because of the unorthodox woman before him. "I apologise for my conduct, my lady?" he said reaching for her hand to bow over it- but his courtly manners were wasted.

She stood before him and held her hands behind her back like a superior would do when dealing with their underlings. "I am Confess, widow of Devotion," she said, her face betraying no emotion, "And you are Captain

Vide of 'The Liberty'; my husband's partner." She turned her dark eyes on Rust but seemed to dismiss him easily.

"Had I known of Devotion's- demise, I would have left you to your grief, my lady." Rust noticed how Captain Vide seemed to be having trouble looking the woman in the eye. "Alas I have goods to trade before going back to Garatin, and Sir Rustling is seeking passage," he said indicating Rust, "so if you will direct me to the new captain of 'The Prestige', I will gladly do business with him in Devotion's honor."

Rust noticed another man who had come on deck after Confess and recognized him as a first mate. Confess also seemed to take notice of him, for she half turned, and the first mate took a step forward. Rust thought that they would do business with the first mate- but to everyone's surprise, Confess turned her back on the first mate, and fixed her eyes on Captain Vide, "*I* am the new captain of 'The Prestige'."

There was a moments silence, Rust noticed the first mate flinch, and he feared that Captain Vide would be less than delicate with his next choice of words- so Rust spoke up, "Surely, it would be more appropriate for you to appoint someone else, you must rest after the ordeal of losing your husband." Rust thought his words showed tact- but the look Confess gave him said that she did not appreciate it.

"This ship is now my property, and I have chosen to become its captain- I do not have time to spend the customary year in mourning. Now," she gave Captain Vide a challenging look, "I have goods waiting to be taken to Garatin- will you trade with me or not?"

Rust knew from that moment on, that Confess was a force to be reckoned with. Captain Vide still seemed hesitant to do his business dealings with a woman, but reluctantly agreed, and they went into the captain's cabin along with the first mate, to discuss the terms of their trading.

The first mate seemed sullen, as if he too, were displeased with how things had turned out. But Confess knew what she was doing and didn't let Captain Vide short-hand her in any way. However, she seemed a bit hurried as if she wanted to get things underway.

"You… you don't intend to sail right away… do you?" Captain Vide asked suddenly.

"I do, yes," Confess stated without flinching, her first mate looked like he would burst if he kept silent much longer.

Captain Vide smiled in an extremely patronizing way, "But it's late in the season- I may have trouble getting back to Garatin, to sail west now would be…" he fell short of saying 'foolish' when Confess glared at him.

"I believe that concludes our business," she said, standing to her feet and leading the way back out on deck. Once back outside, Rust saw Horizon climbing the side of the ship and marvelled at his timing. He had allowed Rizon to stay with friends in the city overnight and had sent a guard with him- but Rust wasn't worried that Rizon would run away, he knew that Rizon wanted to go to Tarva. Rust was pleased to see the Garatin- since, apparently, they wouldn't be staying in Nirin over the winter but were instead leaving soon!

"One more thing, 'captain'," Vides' tone betrayed what he really thought of Confess, "I also have some livestock, a Cokhawk- in good condition- to name only one."

Rust raised his eyebrows at the man's description of the bird, Rust had seen the poor Cokhawk earlier and it most certainly was *not* in good condition.

"Very well, I will trade you another two dozen barrels of the Kryp wine for the bird," Confess conceded without looking at her new partner, "What other livestock do you have?"

"Two slaves; young man and woman, Garatin."

Confess turned cold, and gave her new partner a look of distaste, "I don't care what was the norm with my husband- *I* will not be dealing in slaves."

Captain Vide raised his eyebrows at Confess' venom over the topic, "Very well, I'll sell them here-"

"I think not captain," Horizon's voice interrupted and all three looked up at the Garatin.

"I was just in the city, and I doubt anyone will want Garatin slaves now; a man was killed by his Garatin slave last night. I was very nearly mobbed in the streets- had it not been for my escort, they would have killed me."

Rust looked to his soldier who stood close by Rizon, he nodded to confirm the story.

Captain Vide cursed, "Someone will always buy slaves!" he argued.

Rizon shook his head and came closer. Rust knew from his own experiences that Rizon would win this argument, and he watched with a hidden smirk.

"Were you not listening!?" Rizon asked boldly, "if you bring those two Garatins into Nirin- they'll be killed, and you most certainly won't get paid for them! You could bring them back to Garatin- but the longer you transport slaves the more likely it is that they'll become sick and weak."

Rustling hid his growing smile behind his hand; he had never liked Rizon more than he did now.

"I do have a solution for you though captain," Rizon continued smoothly, "Sell them to me."

"You!?" Captain Vide exclaimed doubtfully.

"I'll pay you one hundred bronze and ten silver for them", Rizon offered, holding up a pouch.

Captain Vide sputtered, "I paid one hundred and thirty *silver* for them!"

Rizon shrugged, "I guarantee mine is the best offer you'll get for them."

Rustling had to turn away to hide his amusement.

*   *   *

"If the captain was going to sell us, he would have taken us with him," Fate said confidently as she and Brave sat waiting alone below deck on 'The Liberty'.

"But if he doesn't sell us here- then he'll take us back to Garatin," Rave pointed out, as he leaned his head back to rest against the bulkhead.

"That's not so bad."

"In case you forgot, Tarva is in the other direction," Rave said sarcastically.

Fa turned to him, "This is happening because Eloi is *allowing* it to happen, Rave- Eloi is letting us go home!"

"But you haven't warned Tarva of the storm in your dream. Besides your being a little quick to guess what's going to happen- aren't you?"

Fa turned away, "Eloi is letting me go home..." she said quietly and looked at her healed hands, she didn't say anything more for fear that Rave would further question her hopes and rattle her fears.

'Of course, Eloi was letting her go home; a mistake had been made- she should never have gotten the heart stain! Eloi wouldn't ask so much of a simple Garatin maiden. She and Rave would somehow escape their captor and return home no worse for this accidental adventure!'

As if to shatter her hopes, a sailor came halfway down the ladder and pointed at them, "You two; above deck, now!"

With a thudding heart, Fa led the way above deck, and together the siblings blinked in the sunlight, their eyes smarting in the morning sun.

They were instructed to climb the ladder down to a longboat, and for the first time in weeks, they left the deck of 'The Liberty'. Attached to the longboat by a rope was a large flat barge and secured to it was the caged Cokhawk.

Seeing the poor beast again made Fa remember the day she had first seen her. The bird's lonely cry seemed to lament the unjustness of her circumstances and seemed to vocalize what Fa herself felt. As the Cokhawks raft was towed, the waves washed over the sides and drenched the already ragged looking creature, and she ruffled her feathers and tried to spread her wings in her small cage to keep balanced. Fa felt like it was her own soul in the cage; torn from home and helpless.

"Where are we going!?" Rave whispered in alarm; Fa looked around; the sailors rowing the boat were *not* taking them to shore- they were heading towards another ship!

The ship they approached was of the twin-hull type and painted in bold yellow paint across both prows read 'The Prestige'. With apprehension Fa looked up at the ships railing, there was a young Tarven man leaning over watching them.

"Up you get!" one of the sailors instructed when they pulled along side a rope ladder. Brave set his jaw and went first, before Fa followed, she looked back up at the railing- but the young sailor was gone.

Fa had a hard time climbing the ladder (she would never like clinging to the edge of a ship) but once she was over the railing, she grabbed hold of Rave's hand tightly; she wouldn't let anyone separate them!

"Good, you're here," they looked up in surprise as Horizon greeted them.

"Rizon! Your continuing your voyage on this ship!?" Fa asked in bewilderment.

"Is this ship going to Tarva?" Rave asked before Rizon could respond.

Rizon gave a nervous laugh, "I hope so."

Fa felt like the air had been sucked out of her lungs. A false hope of going home, then the brutal truth; how could Eloi be so cruel!?

"What are *we* doing here?" Rave asked as he looked around at the sailors making the ship ready.

"Well," Rizon began delicately, "with the help of some local friends I paid Captain Vide for the both of you."

"You bought us?" Fa blinked in surprise.

Rizon winced a bit, "Only to free you from Captain Vide, you are free to do as you wish, you are not bound to me in anyway."

Rave laughed in relief.

"Just..." Rizon interjected, "Don't go ashore here. As Garatins you are not safe in Nirin."

"What about you- what will you do?" Fa asked, she felt quite lost- was Eloi letting her go home? Or was she still meant to go to Tarva.

"I will go to Tarva, and no matter how long it takes; I will stand before the king and tell him the story of Eternity. It will no doubt be the end of me though!" he said lightly.

Fa frowned, "You don't think you'll ever go home?"

Rizon looked very serious, "No; my time is running out. There is but one last task before me."

Rave seemed to miss the seriousness of the conversation, "What will we do? We can't stay here, and we can't pay for passage back to Garatin," he pointed out. It made Fa pause when she realized how stuck they were.

"I have a bit of money left over..." Rizon offered and Rave's face brightened, "But, I would advise you not to buy passage back to Garatin on 'The Liberty'- I would not trust them to honor your freedom. I know it's not a perfect solution, but you could come with me to Tarva- you would have to work on the ship to help pay for your keep, but in the guise of my slaves, I would be able to protect you... I realize Tarva is not where you want to go."

Fa let her gaze drift overboard at the frothing sea... Tarva; it was like a whirlpool pulling her in. What was she to do?

It was then- in a fraction of a second, but also it seemed to be old, like it had been there for a long time- Fa felt something inside her, it was different from the 'thing', it felt more comforting more... haunting. Like a familiar, yet forgotten voice calling her namesake. Since Fa had kept herself from sleeping deeply, the presence inside her had faded away, but she knew now more than ever, that it was still there; it would always be there, waiting for her to finish her task.

"Fa?" Rave asked uncertainly.

She looked at him and was grateful for his presence, and she knew that he had meant what he had said the week before; he would go with her whatever she decided.

"We will go with you," she decided, and Rave gave her a reassuring nod, "It seems, I too, have a task in Tarva." Rizon raised a brow, and Fa knew that she would have to tell him what her 'task' was before too much longer, but for now he let it slip by.

"To Tarva we shall go then," Rizon said grimly.

*   *   *

Confess picked up the tiny portrait of herself that had sat on her husband's sea desk; despite everything, she supposed that he had loved her, and now that it was over and too late to tell him, she supposed that she had loved him too.

Fess opened the desk drawer and placed the portrait facedown inside; she could only hope that the sharp prick of loss would one day subside and give way to dull pain. But she couldn't afford to show weakness now, not even to shed a tear for Devotion.

A knock sounded at her cabin door, and she called for the knocker to enter. As her first mate stepped inside and closed the door behind him, Fess firmly closed the drawer and turned to face him.

"My lady," he greeted awkwardly. By the way he wouldn't meet her eyes she knew that he had little respect for her.

"'Captain' will do while aboard," she pronounced the word crisply and raised her chin.

Still he refused to meet her gaze as he gave a curt nod. Fess took a deep breath; the respect of her husband's first mate would be hard won, and she would have to wait a long time before he truly thought of her as 'captain'. "What is it you wish to say?" she asked directly.

He answered in kind with untampered boldness. "I think it unwise to set sail west this late in the season. I advise you to delay the voyage till spring and fairer weather." He still failed to meet her gaze while speaking- and it irked her.

"To delay this voyage a day is out of the question- let alone till spring," she said, wondering how far he would push her.

Her first mate grew impatient enough to look at her directly, "Foul weather awaits anyone who voyages west in winter. 'The Prestige' will take damage if we set sail now."

Fess took a deep breath and considered her options; she didn't have many. She had sailed many times before, but she knew that her first mate had much more experience than she, and his wisdom should not be brushed aside. But she *couldn't* stay in Nirin- and she needed this man on her side! She would have to tell him, "You sailed with my husband for many years. He had a lot of confidence in you."

He shifted, as if wary of her.

"I'm sure you would not want his ship to fall into the hands of his enemies- but that is what will happen if we do not sail at once. Tomorrow Devotion will have been dead five days, it will be legal for his last affairs and business to be seen to. He left a great deal of debt for me to repay- debt that I can't pay; his creditors know this, and they will come for this ship tomorrow and whatever other property they can get their hands on." This was the first time she had told anyone outside of her household about her problem, and her first mate looked uncomfortable- but now that she had his gaze, she would hold it.

"The Tarven soldier's passage fee along with the money we will make when we sell our goods in Tarva will satisfy my husbands creditors. But the rest of the Tarven soldiers fee will only be paid upon arrival in Tarva. Now, I have faith in your expertise and believe that we can make it to Tarva; what say you?" she challenged with a raised brow.

His reaction to her challenge was ever so small; what would he do? Fess secretly held her breath.

"When shall I give the order to weigh anchor?" he asked stonily.

"As soon as we can. See to it that our passengers are accommodated."

He broke eye contact at last and left stiffly. Fess let her breath out and steadied herself against the desk; she had spent much of her younger years around ships, and she knew how the pecking order on a ship worked. But she had never been at the top before, everything was new to her!

When Confess had heard that her husband's trading partner had come into the harbour the night before she had jumped at her one and only chance. She knew that if her plan to save herself from ruin was to work, then she needed to look the part- she couldn't board her husband's ship in her best dress and curled hair, no she needed the respect of the crew, not their good manners! She had her handmaiden braid her hair and she had given instructions for her household servants to abandon the small manor when the creditors came. In time, she hoped she would return and reclaim her property. Forcing her way into a man's position was not new to Fess, but never had she tried to take over such an important position before. A lot would depend on the first mate; if he didn't back her, then all would be lost.

*   *   *

Desert was the namesake of the young Tarven sailor that Fate had seen at the ships railing. He had very dark hair that was as unruly as a mane, brown eyes full of excitement and a quick smile. Desert was hanging up hammocks on the third deck, the morning sunlight shining down through the grate, beside him a fellow sailor was sneaking a moment of shut eye in his own hammock.

"Did you see the Garatins?" Dese asked as he secured one side of a hammock to an overhead beam.

The older sailor opened one eye, "I heard they were pale but sink me if they didn't look like ghosts!"

Dese laughed good naturedly, "When I was a kid, we told stories of a witch with fire hair; that Garatin maiden is exactly how I imagined the witch to look!"

"Are you afraid she'll put a spell on ya?" the older sailor asked, "Here's your chance to find out."

A group of people came down the ladder, including the two young Garatins, there was also an older Garatin man with them. Desert watched with interest as the Garatin boy came down and realized that he was probably only a little younger than Dese himself. The boy had startling blue eyes that looked around the third deck wearily. The Garatin girl was right behind him, she wore men's clothing just like the new lady captain, and Dese guessed that she was the boy's sister, but not from her looks for, to Desert, all her features were eclipsed by her wild fire hair.

"You're not a witch, are you?" Desert asked boldly, a playful smile hovering on his face.

The maiden looked at him as if uncertain who he had spoken to. Dese nodded to her, and to his surprise, she hid her hands behind her back; what was she hiding? The maiden's brother glared at Dese, and he smiled back widely, they seemed rather touchy!

There were now about a dozen people standing about at the bottom of the ladder, including a tired looking Tarven soldier. He pointed down the passageway to one of the cabins, "I've arranged for a private cabin for the women on this voyage, since it will be longer," he informed the group. There were too other women besides the Garatin maiden.

"One cabin will hardly be sufficient!" one of the women snobbishly said under her breath.

The soldier's eyes flicked to her- obviously he had heard her, but his only response was a short sigh of weariness.

"And what of the rest of us?" one of the men asked.

The soldier looked annoyed, "Paying for the ladies to have a private cabin was out of curtesy. If you wish for a cabin yourself- take it up with the captain, but I warn you she is in a foul mood." He said the last part under his breath- but Dese heard it and he tried to hide a smile.

With tightened lips and tilted heads, the two ladies moved to their assigned cabin. Dese kept watching the three Garatins with interest; among themselves they seemed to decide that the maiden should go with the other women. Before the fire maiden left, she shared an intense look with the boy- the kind that spoke volumes.

"This is your hammock," Dese said to the boy when the maiden had left and the older Garatin was speaking to the soldier. He tugged on the hammock he had just hung to test it.

The Garatin sullenly looked at him. 'Slaves'. The thought suddenly occurred to him, the two Garatins were the slaves of the older Garatin, while the Tarvens struck him more as prisoners of the soldier.

"I'm Desert," Dese offered, making no attempt to hide his curiosity as the Garatin came cautiously closer.

"Rave," he mumbled.

"Rustling, see that your prisoners don't hang about and get in the way!" The sharp voice made everyone freeze in place; standing at the bottom of the ladder was the new captain. The prisoners all stepped out of her way at once. She came forward and glared at them. "If they won't work like the other sailors- then keep them out of the way," she instructed, pausing beside the soldier. Her first mate came up along side her.

"I will not tolerate laziness sailor!" she said, turning her eyes on the sailor beside Dese who was pretending to nap in his hammock, "Get to work." He jumped up to follow her orders.

Then the captain turned her hard gaze on Desert- but he didn't flinch or look away; he was already following orders. But he knew that she had other reasons for staring him down.

"You're Desert?" she asked suddenly.

"Aye captain," Dese responded quickly. It felt a little strange to not call her 'my lady' but somehow Dese knew he shouldn't address her in such a way.

She narrowed her eyes slightly and Dese turned the corner of his lip up ever so slightly, 'now we both know who I am' he thought sardonically.

"Have you worked on a ship before?" she asked turning to the Garatin boy, he shook his head faintly.

"The captain asked you a question- speak up!" the first mate boomed.

Rave flinched, "No I haven't worked on a ship before, c-captain."

Desert winced in embarrassment for the Garatin; his voice had squeaked.

The captain looked back at Dese, "Teach him to work the sails- and see that he doesn't get washed overboard." With that she and the first mate swept the deck for anymore layabouts, then went back up the ladder; everyone breathed again when she was gone.

"Don't worry about what the captain said," Dese said easily, and tossed Rave a blanket, "People only get washed overboard in foul weather."

Rave didn't look comforted, Desert laughed.

Chapter 10   Dream Again

Fate braced herself in the bottom of the longboat as giant swells tossed it about the wild sea, the night sky was a dark sickening purple colour as storm clouds blotted out the stars. Inside, like a throbbing headache, Fa felt a heavy dread cover her; she was dreaming. For the first time since Freedom's cottage, she had let her guard down and fell asleep- and now she was dreaming. She knew it wasn't a normal dream- she could tell the difference now; one kind of dream was just stray thoughts and old ideas (she hadn't had a dream like that in what seemed like forever) and the other kind of dream was real. She was certain that if the longboat tipped, she would drown in her dream, and her body would be found soaking wet in her bed; dead.

Lightning flashed, and Fa lifted her head; far off, across the perilous sea on a hill with blooming cherry trees, stood the city of Tarva. To Fa's eyes it looked awfully delicate and defenceless against the raging storm coming its way.

"They're running out of time," a child's voice said from behind Fa. She turned about and in the prow of the boat sat the Dream Child. Lightning flashed again and the two of them were drenched in a sudden downpour. The child moved to get closer to Fa in the bottom of the boat.

"Stay where you are!" Fa warned in a strained voice and an outstretched hand; the child looked at her with large hurt eyes.

"I can't help if you won't let me in," the child's voice was almost lost in the fierce wind.

"The city," Fa ignored the child's words, "They're in danger from the storm- won't you help them?"

"Yes; I'm sending you."

Fa felt her heart miss a beat at the child's words, but then forgot them when her eyes fixed on the fifty-foot wave building behind the child, and cresting the wave, came 'The Prestige'- but her sails and second hull were aflame!

Fa recoiled at the sight and fell back in the boat. The ship tipped over the wave and was suddenly bearing down on the little boat.

"Don't be afraid Fa," the child said, without turning around to look at the flaming ship that filled Fate's gaze.

'I don't know what to do' Fa thought numbly.

The burning sensation on her hands actually woke Fa, she sat up in her bunk and brought her knees up to her chest and whimpered. Inspecting her hands in the dim light from under the door, Fa could see that her hands were once again covered in burns. She held back tears and glanced at the other two sleeping women- they didn't know what it was like to be trapped in a destiny that would be the death of them! If she was doing what Eloi wanted- than why was she still plagued by the burns!? By the heart stain? The ships gentle swaying lulled Fa from remembering the most important part of her dream...

Tarva- the storm! But more urgently; 'The Prestige'! Fa could think of only one meaning to what she saw; 'The Prestige' and everyone on it was in great peril.

Fate jumped out of her bunk to the floor, she didn't know what time it was- sometime after midnight- but she didn't care; the captain needed to be warned! Warning Vanished hadn't done him much good- but Fa would try harder this time!

Fate slipped from her shared cabin and walked bare foot down the passageway between the sleeping sailors. As she went, she snagged a strip of cloth that was laying about. Grimacing through the pain she ripped the cloth in half with her teeth and, wrapped up her blistered hands. She paused and glanced to Brave's hammock; it was empty.

Fa remembered with frustration that he had been given night-duty on the top deck with that other sailor, Desert. She desperately needed to speak with Rave- but she couldn't go out on deck now; she would get them both in trouble! Fa reached the bottom of the ladder and paused in despair; she couldn't talk to Rave, nor could she get to the captain, her cabin was out on the top deck. And even if she did reach the captain- she wouldn't be likely to listen if Fa woke her up in the middle of the night!

'The galley' the thought occurred to Fa, she would sit in the galley and wait for Rave there.

Using her elbows and wrists to steady herself, Fa climbed the ladder to the first deck. It took her some time, but when she got up, she stepped inside the mess doorway and froze. Lit up by a single lantern and sitting alone, was the captain.

Fa had only seen the captain once since setting sail- Rave had described her as 'scary' when he had first interacted with her. Although Confess was exactly the person she wanted to speak with, Fa had a nearly overwhelming desire to go back to her bunk and stay there- but the image of 'The Prestige' burning drove her forward.

*   *   *

Confess looked up from her maps and notes to see the Garatin maiden coming towards her timidly; she looked quite pale.

"Don't tell me you're sick too," Fess said leaning back, "Your brother has been sick every day this past week since we left Nirin."

The girl smiled slightly and shook her head but said nothing. Fess narrowed her eyes and studied the girl and noticed that she had bandaged hands.

"What did you do?" she asked, nodding to her hands. The girl drew her hands back.

"Nothing- I just burnt myself in the galley," she explained hastily.

Fess pushed a plate of rather stale biscuits across the table. "Have a seat," she invited after a moment of silence.

"I'm Fate," the girl said, sitting down across from Fess and picked up a biscuit.

"That namesake is almost as hard to live with as mine," Fess allowed the corner of her mouth to turn up- she didn't need to pretend to be made of stone with only the girl sitting there. "My mother had a cruel sense of humour." Fess stopped herself when she realized that the girl was hanging on her every word, perhaps it wasn't wise to let even this girl know that she was human.

Fa glanced at the maps and nibbled at her biscuit, "Are you worried about the voyage?"

"No," Fess replied flatly, "Do you think I should be?" she raised a brow and dared the girl to question her the way everyone else was.

Fate shrugged nervously, "I've heard people saying that it's a bad time of year to be sailing."

Fess felt a prick to her pride hearing it said out loud. She knew hers was the only ship in the western waters, she also knew that her first mate and everyone else thought she was a fool.

"You don't think there is merit to their concern?" Fa asked humbly.

"Of course, there is; the sea is a dangerous place- it's not meant for cowards," Fess said coldly.

"I'm sure you know best."

95

Fess was mollified by Fa's quick surrender, and she relaxed a bit, "The crew don't think so; they think the first mate should be captain, and that I should be back in Nirin where I belong." Just thinking about it made Fess want to punch something. "They won't be the first men I've proved wrong," she added quietly. She studied the maiden again; this soft-hearted girl had probably never questioned her lot in life- had never thought to fight for more, for better. "Let me worry about the sea," she told her confidently, but still the girl didn't look anymore at ease.

"I'll just go clean up the galley now," Fa said quietly and got up.

Fess continued to stare at where she had sat for a long time after she was gone.

*   *   *

Desert and Brave slipped down to the first deck a little before sunrise. Rave had gotten seasick again and Dese couldn't believe that no one had told the inexperienced Garatin that there was a remedy for seasickness! So, he had sat him down in the mess (far away from where the captain was sitting) and told him to sit tight. Dese knew that the sleeping sailors would be waking up soon and coming for breakfast- but he hoped the cook wasn't in the galley at that moment (the cook didn't like him much).

Poking his head inside the galley door, Desert paused and smiled; the cook wasn't about, but Rave's sister was. The fire hair maiden stood with her back to him, making a stack of lovely smelling frybread. She stood in front of the ship's giant square cauldron, as always there was a hot fire under the cauldron, contained in a bed of sand, and the cauldron had a metal lid covering the boiling water, on which kettles' and pans could be placed. Dese cleared his throat so as not to sneak up on her, but she didn't turn around.

To his dismay, in the past week since setting sail, the maiden had shunned him with the coldest shoulder he had ever known, to the point where he very much wished that his first words to her hadn't been to teasingly call her a witch. Brave had, after a day of sullen behavior, begun to warm up to Dese, and Dese had been teaching the kid the ropes, and how to keep his head down- but the fire hair maiden still wouldn't speak to him!

Desert glanced to where a large bundle of mint leaves was hung to dry, slowing his pace in the hopes that she would at least acknowledge his presence, he went and collected a pinch of mint leaves and a tin cup, then walked up beside her at the cauldron.

She glanced at him out of the corner of her gray green eye, he offered a smile as he crushed the leaves into the cup. He held up the cup before reaching for a kettle with a rag, "Mint tea, its good for seasickness." He explained casually and tried to get a better look at her face.

She refused to meet his gaze and only raised one unimpressed brow, "*You* get seasick?".

Dese straightened, and nearly spilled the hot water as he poured it into the cup, "It's for your brother- not me!" he was annoyed with how flustered he sounded, but soon grinned; he had seen her lips twitch in a smile.

Swirling the tin cup around to mix it, Dese was about to leave when Fate seemed to realize something, "Is Brave down from top deck?" she asked suddenly and looked at him full in the face for the first time.

He nodded and she held out the large fork she had been using to flip the frybread, "Here- please."

Wordlessly he took the fork and watched as she hurried out into the mess. Desert very much wanted to follow her and see what she wanted to say to Rave so badly, but the galley fire couldn't go unattended even for a moment, so he grudgingly poked the sizzling frybread. He looked up when the cook came in the back door, he held a wheel of cheese; only the officers got that special treat. "What are you doing in my galley!?" he demanded, "Get out!" he waved his arm in dismissal.

Before he could get really angry, Desert ducked back out of the galley with the mint tea in hand. But he paused and leaned against the galley wall and watched Fate and Brave with interest. The two Garatins seemed quite agitated and were speaking in low tones as some other sailors began to file into the mess. Dese watched thoughtfully and noticed for the first time that the fire hair girl had bandaged hands; had she cut herself? Rave was inspecting Fate's hands and Dese was trying to read her lips as she spoke- but she noticed him watching and stopped.

Instead of looking away and pretending that he hadn't been trying to eavesdrop, Dese flashed her a great big smile.

Fate frowned and turned her back so he couldn't see, Desert laughed at their strange behavior; what was the fire hair maiden hiding? Maybe Rave would tell him what was going on.

But Brave did not share with Desert the secret he and Fate were keeping. Even so, Dese counted the whole thing as a victory, for after his exchange with her in the galley, her cold shoulder towards him began to thaw. And the mint tea did help Rave overcome his near constant seasickness.

And Fate? Even after telling Rave about her disturbing dream, she still wasn't sure what she should do. And she agonized over it for another sleepless night, but the next morning she knew what she would do.

*   *   *

"You said the ship was aflame?" Horizon asked in a quiet tone so as not to be overheard by anyone in the crowded mess.

Fate nodded, she had watched his reaction carefully as she told him about her dreams, she had left out the part about Freedom, her heart stain and burns; that was something that she couldn't share with him just yet.

"And you say the events of your other dreams... have come to pass?" Rizon asked- did Fa detect a hint of skepticism?

"If you think this is foolish, please say so," she said stiffly, fearing that he thought she was a silly girl who was overreacting.

Rizon leaned forward and looked her in the eye, "I am wise enough to see when Eloi is breaking through to our world; and that is exactly what your dreams sound like to me. Your dreams are the echoes of Eloi's voice, and not many get to hear it for themselves, so count yourself as among the fortunate few."

Fa swallowed hard; she didn't feel fortunate. Her dreams were more like a curse than a privilege.

"You have given me much to think on Fate..." Rizon said rubbing his bearded chin, "I'm not sure what the best course of action is at this point, telling the captain may not do a thing (we can't exactly turn the ship around), but, that being said, I am sure there is nothing to worry about."

Fa raised her eyebrows in unbelief, "I saw the ship in flames!"

"Yes, I believe you, but I also know that I am destined to go to Tarva- and so apparently are you. And I know that we will get there, regardless of storms and fires." He sounded so confident!

"You really do want to go to Tarva..." Fa said in wonderment, how could anyone want to go to the place where they would be imprisoned and then probably executed for treason?!

A look of fierce determination came over his face, "I have never been so content with my destination before."

Fa paused and felt a touch of sadness at the unbeknown use of her mothers' namesake, "Won't you be tried for treason?" she asked, pushing the thought of her mother aside.

Rizon sighed, "Yes, and no doubt found guilty- there are a lot of people who want my head, but I have appealed to the king, and he must grant me an audience before condemning me. And then, Fate, I will have the opportunity to do what no other Nity follower can do; tell the story of the Eloi-man to the most powerful man alive... that is what Eloi expects *me* to do in Tarva," his unspoken question hung in the air - what did Eloi expect Fate to do in Tarva?

Images of the city burning and a crown falling passed through Fa's head like a terrible prediction.

"At any rate," Rizon said with a gentle voice, "Don't worry about this latest dream-" his words ended short when a ruckus voice called out.

"Hey Brave!" a Tarven with a broken front tooth called after Rave, as the sailors who had worked top deck filed into the mess.

Fa watched with growing anxiety from where she and Rizon sat across the room, as the scene unfolded.

Rave's back tensed as he turned to face the offending sailor.

"Were you given that Namesake before or after Tarva conquered your country?" he asked with a laugh.

Soft chuckles of amusement rolled through the room, and silent tension began to build as everyone waited to see how the young Garatin would react to the poorly humoured joke.

Rave balled his fists and went slightly red in the face, but Fa knew that he was not gifted in the art of fighting with words- he preferred other methods.

Several sailors thought Rave's reaction was funny and laughed as the broken tooth sailor mocked him. Fa moved to stand up- but Rizon grabbed her arm.

"Come on Chall, everyone remembers what happened last time you thought you were funny."

The faces of everyone shifted to the smooth speaker and the crowd parted to reveal Desert. Dese stood shorter than most of the other sailors, but he didn't seem bothered by the disadvantage, instead he smiled and innocently touched his own front tooth.

Chall, the insulting sailor, lost his smile quite suddenly, his lips hiding his broken tooth. There was a low chuckle throughout the room.

"Why you-" Chall swung his fist at Dese in a rage, Dese expertly ducked to one side and the sailors fist planted firmly in the sailor behind Dese.

Desert himself slipped out of the way of the confused brawl that broke out, and propelled Brave to a safe distance on the other side of the room to Fa.

"BREAK IT UP!" The captain's angry voice yelled from the mess entrance. The room quieted, except for the knot of men still throwing ill-aimed punches.

"OBEY YOUR CAPTAIN YOU RATS!" the first mate snarled, as he came at the men menacingly. The brawl ended abruptly, and the sailors stood in guilty silence as the first mate and Confess glared at them.

"I will *not* tolerate such behaviour on 'The Prestige'!" she warned. Fa flinched at how murderous she sounded. "The next sailor who starts a fight will be put in the brig- is that understood!?" she directed the question at the broken tooth sailor; Chall nodded dumbly.

"Get back to your tables," Confess ordered, glancing about the room. Afraid she would find a reason to punish them, the sailors found their tables at once, and it only took a moment before the typical low murmur was heard throughout the room.

Desert let out a sigh and sat down across from Rizon, "I knew that the captain was coming but I didn't think it would work out so nicely!"

Horizon raised a brow, and Fa sat down between Dese and Rave.

"You planned that!?" Rave asked in near disbelief.

Desert grinned.

"Very clever, lad," Horizon said shrewdly then he leaned forward and made Rave look at him. "Rave, I didn't give you your freedom so that you could get yourself killed. So, I implore you; *don't* get involved in anymore fights!"

Rave nodded sullenly; Fa could tell that he did not appreciate the reprimand.

"Now, if you'll excuse me; I have some things to think about," Rizon said and nodded at Fa before leaving.

Dese gave a low whistle and grinned again, "That was exciting." He patted Rave on the back. It was then that Fa realized how contagious his smile was.

*   *   *

Brave sat in silence as he ate and looked more than a bit sulky; Fa had left him and Dese and went to help in the kitchen. After he was done, Rave left to go to his hammock and sleep after his long night of work. But Dese- who kept a wary eye out for the broken tooth sailor- continued to sit as the mess emptied, he too had worked all night and was tired but still he stayed. His eyes following Fate as she cleaned up; he would have offered to help, but he was afraid her cold shoulder would return.

'What is she hiding?' Desert wondered as she adjusted her bandages again, 'Whatever it is, it makes Rave very nervous!'

At last her work was done, and Fate sat down with a heavy sigh- why did she carry herself as if she carried the weight of a thousand worlds?

"Need some fresh air?" he asked, his voice loud in the empty room.

Fate looked up and frowned, "I'm not allowed on top deck... am I?"

Dese grinned impishly, "If you have the right escort! Can I take you up?"

Dese held his breath as she thought about it, then she smiled ruefully and stood up, "Sure, then I can blame you if the captain yells at us."

Fate breathed deep as she neared the top of the ladder, filling her lungs with tangy sea air, she had missed the open air! Desert reached a hand down to help her up, but her hands were still tender, and Fa managed to climb up to the top deck leaving his hand waiting.

A few sailors glanced their way but said nothing, for that Fa was grateful. She had been so long below deck that her claustrophobia had almost faded into a mundane feeling, but now at last she felt like she could breathe again. Off the starboard side was the second hull- Fa often forgot that 'The Prestige' was a twin hulled ship- and behind the main mast, to Fa's surprise, was the caged Cokhawk.

"Oh! Poor thing, I forgot she was on board!" Fa said in dismay as she saw that the bird didn't look any better than last, she saw her.

"Yeah... she's here," Dese said, with a slight scowl in the birds' direction, "She screams at us all night long."

Fa frowned in sympathy for the bird- not for the sailors.

'The Prestige' rolled to one side and Fa stumbled, although she could usually keep her feet, she would still stumble now and again. Fa noticed how Desert easily kept his footing, it annoyed her.

"Why did you call me a witch before?" she was pleased to see that her question threw him off and he looked uncomfortable.

"Oh uh, it's just a story," he stammered, "There's this story about a witch with fire hair- I didn't mean any harm by it, honest!" his eyes turned pleading.

But Fa's eyes had drifted off sadly, "My father calls it 'copper coloured'..." a stab of loneliness made her suck in her breath; father...

Just then, the midmorning sunlight disappeared, and both Fa and Dese looked up to see the edge of a great gray cloud that was drifting over the ship, and far to the south were even more clouds; darker clouds.

"Is that a bad storm?" Fa feared the answer.

Dese followed her gaze and shrugged, "It might turn into one." He looked at her and flashed another grin, "Are you afraid?"

Fa was terrified! "How long until it reaches us?" she asked with an effort to make her voice sound calm.

Dese looked up at the sails, then out to the clouds, "Two days, maybe. It might blow off before it reaches us though."

"Are you sure?" Fa asked anxiously, to her surprise he flashed a huge smile, "Of course I'm sure! I'm a sailor- I have to be able to read the sky!"

His boast seemed overconfident to Fa, "How long have you been a sailor?"

"Years; been all over the Neenor!"

Fate narrowed her eyes; she didn't think he was old enough to have been a sailor *that* long.

"It's easier than starving back in Tarva," he added, as if he heard her thoughts.

"You lived in the city?" she asked quickly with a sinking feeling.

Dese nodded, "That's right, another four weeks- give or take- and we'll be there."

Fa looked back to the storm clouds without comment; a flaming ship and a city made of ash was all she could think about. But she noticed after a moment, with a touch of unease, that instead of watching the storm- Dese was watching her!

"That storm could sink us- and you're watching me?" she asked turning on him. He noticeably jumped and looked away. Fa stared at him for a moment with a frown; didn't he know that the end was coming?

Chapter 11   Swallowed by the Sea

Fate spent two more days afraid, confused and denying what she knew to be true. In the quiet moments when she was alone, trying not to fall asleep, she could feel the stirring inside her- once she felt sure she heard her namesake being called. The tension from the storm clouds kept building, until the sailors grew quiet in their tasks, they knew that the storm would break soon. The sea had turned temperamental, like a child throwing a tantrum, but still Fa didn't speak to the captain, and neither did Rizon. He was still convinced that everything would be all right. But Fa knew better; she could feel an *ending* approaching.

At last, when she felt run ragged by the tension, Fa stood in her cabin. Night had come and the sailors on top deck, including Desert and Brave, were working hard to control the ship against the strengthening winds.

Fate needed to know what would happen; the Dream Child was pulling her back, trying to communicate, but Fa feared that child- Fa was afraid of everything! But she needed to know what would happen to 'The Prestige'! She knew there would be fire, there would always be fire, but what else? Was there something *she* could do? Would the ship sink? Would they reach Tarva like Rizon said? Was this the same storm that would destroy Tarva?

Fa knew there was only one way to get those answers. "I'm going to fall asleep," she said aloud.

The older Tarven woman looked up from her bunk with a frown, "Well thank you for letting me know." She said saucily- but Fa didn't pay her any heed. She pulled off her boots and untucked her shirt, then lay down…

For long hours, she stared at the wooden beams above her, feeling the ship pitch from side to side and listening to the strange muffled sounds of the wind and waves. The other woman had long since fallen asleep- but Fa couldn't! After long weeks of fighting her tired eyelids and teaching herself how to doze without drifting off completely, she could no longer fall asleep, even now that she wanted to dream.

She spent the whole night, squeezing her eyes shut, tossing and counting as high as her tired brain could, until at long last, an hour before dawn, Fate fell asleep; the dream started almost at once.

This time Fa was standing alone on the top deck of 'The Prestige' and there was no sign of land to be seen on the dark horizon. The wind and rain pelted her making her hair stick to her face, and the waves tossed the ship about like driftwood. Fa clung to the main mast; over the railing she glimpsed the longboat from her other dream!

Fa let go of the mast and was very nearly flung to the ships side, her hip making crushing contact with the bulwark- she was sure that she'd have a bruise when she awoke. Catching her breath, Fa scanned the waves below; the longboat floated haphazardly beside 'The Prestige' and inside was the child looking up at her.

"Don't be afraid Fate!" the child called through the wind and rain, "No harm will come to you; I won't allow it."

No harm would come to her? What of the others!? "What am I to do!?" Fa tried to make her voice heard- if only she weren't so far away!

Thunder tore at the night around them.

"Horizon; he will need your help. Warn Tarva; warn my people!" Fa could hardly hear the child and she leaned out over the railing.

Time is running out…

Fa's attention was captured by a huge wave building behind the longboat.

"Do not fear the storm," the child said without turning around to look, "for Tarva, it is but a breath of what is coming. But even the storm listens to me when I speak; will you?"

Fa gasped in fear, for she could hear a familiar sound crackle, and she could feel the heat on her back.

Fate sat up in her bunk and forced her eyes to see into the dark cabin; the other two women were still asleep. 'It must be just after dawn' Fa concluded in her groggy mind, above she could hear the storm, and feel the ships restless movement.

Fa pressed her lips together; she didn't have a moment to waste. She sprang to her feet and didn't bother with her boots. She wasn't surprised to find that her hip was bruised, and her hair had come lose from its braid, but when she lifted her hands to push it from her face, she caught her breath; the burns had grown.

Outside her cabin was dark, with only a dim gray light filtering down from the first deck to reveal that all the hammocks were empty- everyone was needed top deck. Her feet felt cold against the wooden deck as she went to the ladder, as before she struggled to climb it.

The first deck was also empty- but Fa gasped in horror; someone had left a lantern lit! It swung erratically from side to side on its chain, hot wax escaping from the smeared glass, splattering on the floor, and the flame danced, as if it too wanted out.

Fa ran to it, nearly slipping in the drying wax, she reached up for the lantern- but she couldn't reach it! It kept swinging out of her grasp. Jumping franticly, Fa snatched for the lantern, her fingers made contact, and it bounced on its chain. Trying again, a scream slipped from her lips as the lantern fell from its chain and landed squarely in her tender bandaged hands. Just then the ship pitched to one side and sent her tumbling through the hammocks to bash against the ships side. Fa gasped in pain and held the lantern in front of her face; wax had spilled out onto her bandages, but the flame was still contained safe inside. Her panicked mind rejoiced, and she blew it out with a puff.

Almost directly above her, one of the top deck hatches opened, it was like a window looking into the heart of fury and rage; the wind howled through, and rain and sea water splashed down the ladder, spraying Fa with brine.

"You're not experienced- you'll only be washed overboard, get below!" Desert fought to be heard above the wind.

"But the captain-" Brave argued as Desert shoved him down the hatch.

"Let me worry about that- get below!" Desert said before the wind tore the hatch out of his hands and slammed it shut just above Rave's head. Rave stumbled down the ladder, he was soaked through and looked pale as salt. "Fa!" he exclaimed and collapsed against the ladder as his knees gave way.

Fa sat where she was and let him catch his breath as they braced themselves against the ships swaying.

"Are we in trouble?" Fa asked, fearing the answer.

Rave looked up at her, and she saw his face change. "We'll be alright," he bluffed.

Fa wanted to let her face crumble and sob- but she had to be strong, "I don't think so." Her voice sounded so much more final than she had intended.

Rave searched her face, then his eyes fell to her bandaged hands and he guessed the truth, "You had another dream..."

Fa nodded, the sea spray and darkness masking a tear, "I don't think so." Her repeated words came out crackled and weak; so much for being strong.

*   *   *

"If we double back and go south-east, we might make it to Nor`ane island and find shelter in a bay there." The first mate raised his voice to be heard over the storm and waved his hand over the map where the island was drawn.

Confess eased herself into her nailed down chair at the captain's desk, she was conscious of how shaky her legs were and how exhausted she was. And she was cold; wet through to the bone cold. Fess had been at the helm from sunrise when the storm had started, to midnight when she had called the first mate to her cabin; they were in trouble, and she knew it.

"What of the mainland?" she inquired as the ship tipped to one side and her glowing lantern swung to the left.

The first mate shook his head. "We could try and fight our way back to the mainland, but we would only lose control and be pulled into the Zavie funnel." He pointed to the map where a hook of the sea curled up into the valley of Zavie, "That place can be navigated by very few in the good sailing season, right now it will be a ship graveyard; these winds would drive us in and shipwreck us."

Fess knew all that, but she also knew that they didn't have many options, "What about the Nyniver Isles- how far are they?"

"Nine, eleven days- I can't be certain, but it would be near impossible with winds blowing from the south-west. Even if we did make any head way, we could easily miss the Isles and be tossed about the sea till we run out of provisions," the first mate said grimly.

"How many days of provisions do we have right now?" Fess asked.

"Three weeks, enough to get us to Tarva... in fair weather."

Fess ignored his jab at her decision to sail at all. "And we've been making no headway going directly west... lost a whole day," she added to herself; she closed her eyes and tried to block out the sounds of the storm.

"Change course to South-East; we make for Nor'ane Island."

*   *   *

The crew of 'The Prestige' fought to make headway for two more days, with little success. Several times it seemed the storm was breaking, but then it would worsen, and another fierce wind would catch them and drive

107

them further into the storm. The sails began to rip, and they lost one of three anchors being used to slow their speed, to the depths. Almost like a mimic of Fates own soul, the entire ship began to creak and groan louder with each passing day.

Every time the sailors were ordered on deck, Brave went, but after a few hours, Desert would catch hold of Brave, sometimes keeping him from being pulled overboard, and he would force him to go below. Rave didn't fully appreciate Deserts actions, but every time Rave came below, shaking and dripping, Fa thought a little higher of Dese.

On the third night of the storm, Confess decided that the winds were too strong to make any headway, so she ordered the sails to be lowered and the anchors to be dropped. Then she sent the crew below, leaving only a few topside, to maintain what little control they had in the storm. But when the sun rose the next morning, it was hard to tell day from night in the dark clouds. The crew gathered for breakfast, and the captain entered the mess to address the crew.

Confess looked exhausted (same as everyone) as she surveyed her crew with a weary resignation. "The hull of 'The Prestige' has been weakened," she said without ceremony. The whole room went silent, and as if to confirm her statement, the ship groaned loudly. "If the storm doesn't break soon, we could all be clinging to driftwood," she announced flatly.

Fate, who had just sat down with Brave and Desert listened silently, she felt like a strong, giant hand was holding her- squeezing her.

"I know it's dangerous, but I believe we must frap the main hull of 'The Prestige'."

A murmur went through the crew and they stirred restlessly.

"Frap- what does that mean?" Brave whispered to Dese, Fa watched Desert's suddenly serious face.

"We have to bind the ship with ropes to reinforce the timber- until it's like a net under the hull," Dese explained in a low tone.

"How's that done?" Fa asked trying to conceive the strange concept; it sounded insane to her!

Dese pressed his lips together, "We have to feed ropes out over the prow of the ship, then secure them tightly in place. It's harder to do on twin hulled ships because of the connecting beams, it will be near impossible to do in this storm though.

"The prow disappears in almost every wave!" Brave pointed out in disbelief.

Dese nodded grimly, "There'll be men lost overboard."

"You heard the captain; all hands-on deck- bring all the rope from the brig- MOVE!" the first mate bellowed, and everyone jumped to their feet, their half-eaten meals forgotten.

"Not you Rave," Desert grabbed Rave's arm, "Trust me- you've got no experience with frapping."

"What about the captain?" Rave asked glancing her way, "You'll get caught one of these times keeping me below," he pointed out.

Dese flashed an old smile, "I can handle the captain! You just stand by and get the cargo ready to be tossed- start with the brig."

Fa watched as Desert lost his forced smile and left to go top deck- would she see him again? Fa looked for Horizon- oh why hadn't he believed her when she said this would happen!? They should have warned the captain when there was a chance! But it was too late now… the dream hadn't come soon enough- maybe it would have if she had tried sleeping sooner, but now just like all the other dreams, the dream of 'The Prestige' sinking, would come true.

'I'm going to die…' the thought rang out like a bell in Fate's mind.

*   *   *

Out on deck the wind and rain whipped about and stung the sailors faces and numbed their ear tips and noses. Nearly every wave was large enough to crash over the bulwarks and wash across the deck like ever present hands seeking to pull 'The Prestige' to the depths below. Any words had to be shouted, but even then, the speaker could hardly make themselves be heard over the sea's angry voice. For that reason, it was important that everyone knew exactly what needed to be done. Confess oversaw the work from the helm where she and another sailor held the ships wheel steady, she was ready to shout orders when needed, but the crew knew what they were doing.

Desert, along with nine others, clung to a long length of rope that was as thick as a man's wrist, another ten men hung onto the end of the rope. On the starboard side, the rope had to be carefully fed under the second hull's connecting beams, and once that was done, the twenty men advanced as one to the prow of the ship. Desert, who was sixth from the front, struggled to keep his footing as a wave crashed onto the deck, blinding them before leaving them soaked in its wake, as if they weren't already wet enough.

When they were as close to the prow as they could get, the front sailors threw the rope over the prow of the ship, as one, the twenty men fed more rope over the edge until the think rope was all the way under the prow. They could feel the waves pulling at the rope and it slipped slightly in their hands, but the water's pulling now aided the sailors as they let the rope slip back wards towards the stern of the ship. It took the strength all of twenty sailors to maintain control of the rope and keep it from slipping too far. When it was in place, they pulled it tight and secured it.

Desert and the other nineteen sailors stepped aside for another twenty men to repeat the process- it had to be done five of six more times- each rope holding the ship together a little more. Many times, men were nearly washed overboard but were saved by their shipmates- Dese himself lost his footing and would have been lost if it hadn't been for the sailor behind him.

Bracing himself against the second mast, Dese felt his skin prickle, he looked up to see the broken tooth sailor watching him in a menacing way. 'Great!' Dese thought sarcastically, 'as if the storm isn't enough.'

When six ropes had been successfully frapped about the main hull of the ship, and amazingly not one sailor had been lost, the first mate signaled for everyone to go below. Dese darted for the hatch- but it was ill-timed, a wave came crashing over him, and he just barely grabbed hold of the hatch ring. When the wave passed, Dese gasped for breath then threw open the hatch before the next wave could catch him.

*   *   *

Fate jumped as another piece of cargo bumped against the outside of the ship before sinking. They had spent another eight days fighting the storm- with no headway, they had been blown about for so long that no one knew for certain exactly where in the Neenor they were. They had a little under two weeks of previsions left- not enough to make it to Tarva, and everyone began to consider the possibility of dying of hunger and thirst. Then with a defeated air, the captain had selected ten men to go across to the second hull to throw cargo overboard, in the hopes that they would be able to make head way with a lighter ship. The men tied ropes around themselves and braved the wind and waves as they crossed the connecting beams. Again, everyone was silently astonished that not a single man was lost overboard in the endeavor. The selected sailors tossed the second hull's cargo overboard as quickly as they could, whether it be crates of horse saddles or barrels of fish oil, they tossed it, until over half the cargo had been dumped. Meanwhile on the main hull, the rest of the sailors were doing the same with whatever could be found there; extra sail cloth, old rope, they even threw over four barrels of ale. They had even released the Cokhawk and thrown the cage over. The bird didn't try to take flight in the storm though, and sat huddled at the stern, screaming and struggling to keep herself steady amidst the ship's wild swaying.

Fate knew what sacrificing the cargo meant to the captain; if they survived this storm, she wouldn't make a profit when they came into port. But Fa doubted that 'The Prestige' would ever make port again, the storm had blown them so far off course that if they did escape the gale, they would surely be lost at sea and die of thirst. That, believe it or not, was the best scenario that Fa could foresee; she thought it far more likely that they would be dragged to the depths in one gigantic wave; sail, anchor and timber. Her dreams had never been wrong before- only unclear, but Fa was certain she knew the future of 'The Prestige'. She had doubted Eloi... she had fought her own destiny, she had tried to work against the heart stain, and now... Eloi would punish her for it; she was going to die.

Fa sat down in the mess and tried to ignore the cargo that bashed the side of the ship. She smoothed out a crumpled bit of parchment that she had found in the first mate's cabin and gripped the quill she had also found. Under normal circumstances Fa would never have ventured to take the parchment and quill- but these were not 'normal' circumstances. Fa also gripped an empty bottle between her knees, that she had found in the galley. Nervously she glanced up at the swaying lantern that the first mate had lit, although she needed its light- she would have much preferred it if she could blow it out, but there were sailors all about busy lightening the ship and they needed the light too.

Bending over the wrinkled parchment, Fa sat rigid and curled her legs under the bench to keep herself from tumbling off every time the ship pitched to one side. Hastily she scratched out her note with the limited ink on the quill, but she paused halfway; what could she possible say?

She had many regrets, her biggest one being, that her parents would never know how she and Brave died... how could she explain it all to her parents on one small bit of parchment? Perhaps it was just best to say that she loved them- but how would her bottled letter ever find its way to her parents?!

"You won't need that bottle."

Fa looked up as Horizon came towards her on unstable feet. "None of us are going to die on this sea," he said reassuringly.

"My dreams always come true- it's just a matter of time," she said sadly- she didn't really have the energy to argue with him.

Rizon shook his head, "You didn't dream of our deaths- what you saw was 'The Prestige' in flames."

"Yes- with *us* on board!" Fa said in frustration- didn't he get it!?

Rizon reached her and touched her hand from across the table, "I am destined to speak before the king of Tarva- I cannot die until that is done. You too have a task in Tarva, and more than this; I *know* that we will all survive this storm."

"How can you be certain?" Fa could hardly dare to hope that he knew what he was talking about.

"You're not the only one who has dreams Fate."

They both looked up suddenly as the captain stood in the mess doorway, water dripped from her braid tips, and her jaw was clamped tight to keep it from chattering from the cold- or was it from fear?

Chapter 12   A Promise

"Captain?" Horizon spoke like it was any other day- only his voice was raised to be heard over the storm, "May I have a word?"

Fess flexed her jaw- she was in no mood to *talk*. She had just overseen her crew dispose of nearly all the ship's cargo, the storm had gotten worse, and her cabin was taking on water. She had come below hoping to be alone with her despair.

"A brief one," she consented grudgingly and walked to her favourite table at the back of the room. Rizon followed.

"Captain- you and your crew have been fighting this storm for nearly two weeks, and no one has sat down for a proper meal in five days. The morale of the crew couldn't be worse; so, cease work, and call them for a meal."

Fess smirked as she sat down heavily and eyed the strange Garatin as he shifted to keep his balance, "Feast, for tomorrow we die- is that the idea?"

Rizon suddenly became much more intense; it unnerved Fess.

"Eloi has promised me that we will all survive this storm."

"Eloi is the protector of Garatin; what does a Tarven merchant ship mean to him?" she asked flippantly.

"Garatin is much too small to satisfy Eloi- and when Eloi promises something; it will happen."

Fess didn't put much stock in Eloi, but she could see no harm in the Garatin's suggestion.

'For tomorrow, we die' she thought sarcastically, "Very well." She looked to Fate who sat watching. "Find the cook and prepare a hearty meal, afterwards, we'll toss what's left of the provisions overboard," she sighed and looked up at Rizon with heavy eyelids, "Then we'll hope for the impossible."

After an hour, the crew came in through the doorway, each one dripping and pale faced after their harrowing experiences top side, and they let their weak knees give way as they sat. Dryer, but also pale faced, the nine Tarven prisoners also came, and sat in the oppressive din of the storm. All in all, there were nearly fifty people on 'The Prestige'... '50 people who will all be dead soon' Fess thought bitterly, 'no matter what Rizon thinks'.

The mood was very somber, and everyone ate in silence, the storm the only sound. Fess sat and watched the room with a dismal face. She shifted as her first mate sat down beside her, he had just been top side and was dripping onto the floorboards. He pushed away her untouched plate and placed a map out before them.

"The clouds broke, and I was able to see the stars for a moment," he said in a low voice, but it still seemed to carry through out the room, "I believe we are much further west than we thought."

Fess searched his face and her heart skipped a beat, "How far west?"

"I believe we are within a few days of the Nyniver Isles."

"That's impossible..." Fess whispered, the Tarven Isles were in the opposite direction that they had been trying to sail, "We *can't* have traveled west this past week- the wind wouldn't have allowed it."

"I know the stars, and we are but a few days from the Isles," his tone was quiet- but sharp, as if to say, 'if you were a *good* captain you would know this too'.

"We'll have to take a sounding- at the speed we're going, those islands could come up fast," Fess said looking at the map.

"We could ram into the reefs, or run aground on the shallows," the first mate finished her thoughts.

"Or be smashed to pieces against the island," Fess marvelled at how their situation could have possibly gotten worse.

Across the room, Horizon stood as if to address the crew, "I know you are all afraid; this storm is fierce, and it was foolish to venture this far west."

"What's the fool doing!?" the first mate hissed in anger, while Fess sat stunned.

"'The Prestige' will never make port again- but don't despair, for Eloi has promised to protect us all. I'm saying this so that you will be prepared; for we will be shipwrecked soon." Rizon's voice was calm, even though every face that watched him was tight in fear.

"*Shut your mouth!*" the first mate ordered harshly as he took a step towards the Garatin. Rustling grabbed Horizon's arm as if to persuade him to sit back down. While Fess sat and swallowed hard; this voyage was her bane from the start.

Horizon looked at the first mate with a defiant air, and the first mate's neck corded in rage.

Just then a heart-stopping crack halted all activity. Everyone froze and looked up, there was only one thing that could have made such a noise; the main mast had snapped.

"ALL HANDS-ON DECK!" Fess bellowed and everyone jumped to obey.

*   *   *

Rustling was more terrified than he would admit to even himself; he wasn't ready to die- not like this! Where was the honour in dying at sea? Where was the reason!? Order, his panicked mind demanded order, something he could control! He had a job to do.

As the crew rushed out of the mess, Rust blocked out the fear of what was happening top side and focused on his job; his mission. He grabbed Rizons' arm and hissed in his ear, "Shipwrecked?" he searched the Garatins' face for something to trust.

"Eloi promised we will all survive. I *will* go to Tarva, and you will be the one to take me."

The man's confidence baffled him and enheartened Rust at the same time; how could he be so sure? The impossible situation washed over Rust like one of the waves top deck, surely Rizon was wrong.

"I cannot risk the chance of my prisoners escaping. Do you understand that?" he asked with a heavy heart.

Rizon seemed to measure him for a moment. "I believe I do," he said soberly, and it twisted Rust up inside- how could this man be so calm!? They were discussing his own execution!

The ship pitched to one side and there was another crack above them, like a reminder of their time running out.

"Your crime," Rust said hurriedly, "you told me it was political- against the Garatin high council- is that true?" for a moment he dearly wished that Rizon would tell him that he had lied and was actually a murderer- and then Rust wouldn't feel so bad giving him a death sentence.

"I would not lie to you," Rizon said firmly.

Rust didn't even consider misbelieving him, and he cursed under his breath. The other prisoners he could live with executing- they were all cruel and selfish people- but Rizon?

Rustling stumbled from the room, with a tortured conscience, leaving Rizon once again alone with Fate. Rizon looked over and saw that Fate had lowered herself to the floor and was holding onto the leg of a heavy table as the ship swayed back and forth. Her face was crumpled in defeat and tears glistened in her eyes.

"Your dreams Fate!" he reminded her, "Eloi promised you would go to Tarva; we will survive this!"

Fa didn't seem to listen to him, "My parents, they'll never know what happened to me!"

*   *   *

The main mast had broken- snapped in two and fallen to the starboard side. The crows nest crashed into the second hull horizontally, and the sails filled with the wild wind, pulling the ship at an angle it was not meant to. The whole ship groaned under the pressure as the connecting ropes pulled at the second, smaller mast, and the captain and first mate fought to keep the ship at a direct angle to the ever on coming waves- but the controls were all tangled up in the fallen mast! If the mast could be cut lose then they might still be able to control 'The Prestige'.

Every sailor had a knife held between their teeth or gripped in their hands, as they battled the wind and sea spray to find a connecting rope and sever it. The urgency to cut the main mast and sail loose mounted as the second mast creaked and bent under the strain.

Desert shook water from his eyes as he grabbed hold of a slacking rope at chest level and began sawing it through. He looked up and saw that Brave was close by trying his best to cut through a taunt rope- but in an effort to hold the rope firmly he had swung his leg over it! When the rope snapped- he could be pulled overboard with it!

"RAVE- LET GO!" he shouted, Rave looked up, but it was too late; the rope was about to snap!

Dese leapt at Rave and pushed him to the deck, his momentum sending Dese tumbling perilously close to the open drain in the bulwarks, where the water gushed back into the sea. The rope broke and flew over his head- two more snapped under the pressure. The mast groaned and sagged enough for the sail to catch a wave – it pulled the whole mast backwards; snapping ropes and splintering planks along the second hull. Five strong ropes still held the mast to the ship, two sailors were already hacking away, but the strain was so great that a cross beam on the smaller mast was breaking.

"CUT IT LOSE!" Dese heard the captain holler. Just then a mighty wave crashed over the deck sweeping Rave and Dese, who was only then climbing to his feet, over to the railing where they clung and tried to catch their breath. Dese pulled himself up on weak legs and looked up as the ragged Cokhawk suddenly decided to brave the winds and took to the air on her large wings. Dese followed her with his eyes, she flew over the port side railing, and off into the gray gloom- but wait; she was flying towards land! Still a long way off and shrouded in darkness, but it was land just the same!

"LAND HO!" the wind picked up Deserts call and through it back in his face. Suddenly there was a shuddering crunch- a crack and 'The Prestige' halted. Rave fell forward, while Dese held onto the railing and looked about until his shocked mind grasped what had happened; the second hull had struck something- a sand bar or rocks and was stuck fast.

The thick beams connecting the two hulls cracked and buckled, then snapped with a sound like thunder. Free from her second hull, 'The Prestige' rushed forward and rammed into more rocks with great force. There was another loud crack, and Dese knew without seeing, that they were taking on water.

*   *   *

"THE HULL HAS BEEN BREACHED!" the young Tarven soldier announced with fear to the mess where the prisoners, Rust and Fate had gathered. The soldier slammed the door shut as if hoping to keep the water at bay.

"We're going to die!" the older Tarven woman wailed, and the rest looked about in fright. Fate's thoughts went to Brave; where was he!? Was he safe?

"I tell you- Eloi will keep his promise; we will be safe!" Horizon's stalwart faith astounded Fa yet again.

The door burst open and they heard the captain bark orders to patch up the breach in the hull as best they could. Brave slipped into the mess and went to Fa, he wrapped her in a wet trembling hug. He was pale and cold to the touch; all Fa could do was hold tight to him- there was nothing to say. She looked over his shoulder to where the captain had come to stand in the door.

Confess' face was taunt and her lips blue, her clothes plastered to her rigid form, "The ship is lost," she informed everyone grimly, "But there is land a mile west."

"Have the longboats been lowered?" one of the prisoners asked, his frantic eyes darting past her to the door.

"No, the boats have been lost overboard," Fess replied in a strangely calm voice.

"What land is it? Will help come soon?" a soldier asked hopefully.

Rave pulled away to see how Fess would respond- but Fa guessed the answer before Fess even opened her mouth.

"It's early dawn, I doubt anyone will even see us before the storm moves on. If you wish to stay aboard, I will not stop you, but if the waves continue as they have, I estimate the ship will fall apart within three hours. I will give the order to abandon ship soon, my advice is to find something that floats better than yourself." She looked at Horizon, "If the Garatin is right we will all meet again on the beach." Fa held her breath as Fess returned her gaze for a moment before walking away with a determined stride. Her voice could be heard giving more orders.

117

They heard the awful sound of timber giving way, and the two Tarven women began weeping, while three of the men went into hysterics.

"Let me pass! Didn't you hear the captain?! The ship will soon sink!" one of the prisoners shouted at a soldier who had blocked the door. The young soldier placed a hand on his newly donned sword, he looked at Rustling, "If they escape and we survive- we'll face punishment for losing them." His tone implying fatal punishment.

Fa's eyes darted to Rust and realized that he too had donned his sword but had left his armor off. He looked deeply conflicted as he looked first at the soldier then to the prisoners, who hadn't fully realized what was happening.

"We need to deal justice to them now!" another soldier pressed grimly, the prisoners gasped and recoiled from the soldiers- all but Rizon. He stood, seemingly unmoved by events and perfectly calm, further demonstrating his confidence in their survival. Rust locked eyes with him, and for a moment, amidst the storm and sinking ship he hesitated- Fa could feel the tension between the two men.

"No," Rust said at last, "There will be no justice dealt by us." He looked hard at the other prisoners, "I expect my act of good faith will be honoured; I will see you all on the beach." With an air of foreboding the soldiers allowed the prisoners to leave. Rizon gave Rustling a nod of respect- and Fa thought, of approval.

Next thing Fa knew, Desert came running up to her and Rave, "I hope you two can swim."

"We can't," Brave said flatly, Fa could hear his panic.

Dese nodded slowly, "Alright, that will make it harder."

Fa looked down when she realized that her feet were ice cold; they were now standing in an inch of water! "What do we do!?" she asked trying not to let her voice fill with fear.

Dese calmly looked her in the eye, "The ship will soon sink, the bottom deck is already half under water." He explained evenly and held her gaze, "The bow of the ship will be the first to fall apart," he broke their gaze to glance at the back wall of the mess where the ship was already giving way to the incessant pounding of the waves; water was gushing through the beams with each serge, "Believe it or not, but top deck is the safest place to be right now, we'll each need to find a board or something to float with. Don't fight the waves- they'll carry you ashore." He looked at them both, "Come on, I'll try and stay close to you two in the water- I swim like a fish; we'll be fine!" he encouraged.

Before following him out onto the top deck Fa hesitated- she wanted to say something to Rave, to say goodbye- or something! But the words wouldn't come, instead she ignored the pain of her burns and gripped his hand. Together, they climbed out of the sinking ship and into the full fury of the storm.

Chapter 13   Die Another Day

Out on deck, the wind and sea spray both stole from and filled Fate's lungs. She, Rave and Dese glanced once more over the port bow at the black lump that was their only hope; land.

CRACK!

Fa felt the lighting bolt in every fiber of her being. It struck the main mast and a blinding purple light flashed. The mast exploded, chunks of wood flying past, and red sparks rained down on the deck. Fa screamed and Rave stumbled to the wet deck. Dese hunched his shoulders and reached for Fa as a delayed shield. Climbing to his feet Rave pointed up and shouted- his voice got lost in Fa's ringing ears though. But she didn't need to look to know what Rave was pointing at. She could sense the fire as it hungrily ate up the ragged sails; 'The Prestige' was aflame.

Suddenly Desert was holding a makeshift raft of broken planks and rope, he held it out and Fa and Rave grabbed hold. With out looking back at the burning sails, all three jumped over the ship railing together. The water chilled to the bone instantly and the towering waves disorientated Fa completely, there was little distinction between the dark sky and the frothing sea. The mile to land seemed to stretch till it felt impossible to reach, and soon they had been carried away from even the slim protection of the wrecked ship. The struggle of getting to land soon changed to simply keeping above water.

Despite what he had said, Fa and Rave were separated from Desert soon after they entered the water, and the siblings were left clinging to their raft, their legs vainly kicking at the dark water, and their numbing hands slipping. Although the rest of the crew had abandoned the ship at the same time as them, the siblings seemed to be alone in the churning water.

"Look out!" Rave warned as a wave crashed over them and pulled them under. Fa felt herself tumble backwards in the water and she struggled and kicked, bubbles flew past her eyes and water filled her ears. Reluctantly the sea released the little raft to the surface and Fa gasped for breath and tried to heave herself up onto the raft, but it flipped and sent her back under. When she resurfaced, she realized with horror, that the reason the raft had tipped was because Rave wasn't holding on to the other side.

"RAVE!" she screamed and tried to pull herself higher up to search the water; Brave was gone.

           *   *   *

Confess collapsed to her knees in the wet sand and turned to watch, as what was left of the still burning 'Prestige' broke free of the sand bar and drifted for a moment before sinking completely. Her only chance of paying her husbands debts was gone. Fess fell back on the beach and let a wave crash over her cold legs; she was finished now- she had nothing. Her manor in Nirin was lost forever, and she would never be able to repay her debts. She had no one to turn to- no family, no friends- not a soul.

Setting her face, Fess rolled over and turned away from her sinking ship; she wouldn't allow herself to mourn- not now, maybe not ever.

Now that they were no longer being driven along with the gale, the storm was beginning to pass. The rain had moved on and to the east, the sky was clearing to reveal morning light- the sea, however, was still vicious. Beside her, spread out on the beach, was her first mate and one other crew member.

Fess scanned the serf for more of her crew- 'are they still my crew?' she wondered, then pushed the thought aside for a later time.

"You two search the beach for survivors that way for a mile," she pointed north along the shore, "then come back here, I'll do the same to the south."

Her first mate hesitated for a moment before picking himself up; he and the other sailor obeyed her without comment- but she could see their already strained loyalty beginning to fade. Fess refused to worry about that, or her future; instead she focused on the task at hand. As she picked her way north, she saw bits of her ship being washed up by the pounding waves- that was probably the best representation of her life.

The shore was rough and stony, and to her right the ground eroded in a little cliff, atop were great twisted oaks that dripped from the recent rain. Fess had no clue what island they had landed on, she still had a hard time believing that they could have traveled very far west in the storm- they couldn't possible have landed on the Nyniver Isles. She decided that they must have found some uncharted small island somewhere between the Nyniver Isles and Nor'ane Island. 'No inhabitants then' Fess thought gloomily, 'that would be too easy. Survive the storm, and then starve on a spit of land- how typical!'

Climbing over some rocks that jutted out into the water, Fess paused in surprise; laying high up on the beach, with one wing outstretched over the sand, her plumage ragged and wet, was the Cokhawk.

Fess took a step towards it, she couldn't tell if it was dead or not. Suddenly the mighty beast raised its head and returned Fess's gaze. Then she folded her wings and struggled to her feet, and there, under the wing, was a body!

Fess hesitated, uncertain of the large bird- was it protecting her next meal? But the Cokhawk looked away and limped further inland, hopping onto the eroded cliff, she disappeared into the trees. Waiting till the intimidating bird was gone, Fess jumped off the rocks and ran up to the body and saw copper hair.

"Fate!" Fess called as she approached her- fearing the worse. The girl stirred and looked up, she was wet through but otherwise appeared to be unharmed. Fess knelt and touched the girl's arm; she was warm! Fess marvelled at the idea that the Cokhawk had been keeping the maiden from freezing- why had it done that? Fess then quickly cast her eyes about, but there was no one else on the ragged shore.

"Desert- he jumped ship with you," she said, her fears mounting.

"We were separated," Fa breathed then she struggled to her feet- Fess had to support her for a moment, "My brother! Have you seen him?" she asked her eyes becoming wide.

Fess found that she couldn't tell her the blunt truth - that most don't survive a shipwreck. Instead she shook her head, "We'll look further down the shore. Can you walk?"

Fa nodded, but Fess didn't have time to doubt her, for a voice called out from the waves. Fess spun about and scanned the surf till her eyes spied a head as it came up- then disappeared, she thought it looked like Rustling! He was having trouble getting past the breaking waves.

Leaving Fate, Fess ran into the waves, catching a mouthful of saltwater, she fought her way to where Rustling was floundering and grabbed his arm. He was weak and Fess had to forcefully pull him to shore before he could stand on his own.

"The prisoners?!" he gasped as they waded through the pounding serf.

"Unaccounted for- we have only begun to search," Fess saw the defeat in the soldier's eyes at her news and felt a twinge of empathy; he had lost everything too.

The three of them stumbled down the beach and found three more sailors who had recently pulled themselves from the sea. Fess waded into the water twice more to help two of Rust's soldiers, who were weighted down by their swords and armour.

The sun was now bright enough to see clearly by, and the dark storm clouds were breaking apart overhead. Fess noticed how the further they went the more distraught Fate grew and the more hopeless Rustling became- for still there was no sign of the prisoners, Brave or Desert. Fess didn't speak, for she found no reason to give them hope.

After walking for an hour, they turned around and went back to where Fess had washed up, along the way they found two more sailors. Although the sun was now shining for the first time in two weeks, Fess foresaw the next problem was keeping warm, for everyone, including herself, was shivering like mad.

'We'll die from cold before we starve' Fess thought wearily as the wind off the sea chafed and chilled the shipwreck survivors.

As they neared the rock outcropping that Fess had climbed over before finding Fate, Rust pulled Fess aside and spoke in a low tone, "If the prisoners have all escaped, or their fates are unknown..." here his gaze drifted out to the sea, "Then say I was lost in the storm." Fess noted how he gripped his sword hilt. "Understand?" he asked.

"Completely." In her younger years, Fess might have thought less of him for taking a coward's way out, but now she envied him a little.

Cresting the rock outcropping, the rag tag group all paused- stunned at the sight before them in the morning light; they were all there! Thirty some people were all flaked out in little groupings, recovering their breath from their swim. The whole crew of 'The Prestige'- to a man- even the soldiers and the prisoners. Horizon, his clothes dripping, stood to his feet and waved at Fess and the others.

Beside her, Rustling was so stunned that he couldn't speak. The small group slowly climbed down from the rocks and stared in silence as they were greeted by the others.

"Report," Fess ordered quietly as her first mate walked up, his weathered face looking astonished.

"With the nine you found- everyone is accounted for! No one was lost," the first mate sounded as stunned as Fess felt.

"The boy Desert?" she asked- was that too much to ask for? The first mate nodded

"And the island?" she asked looking about at all the faces she had felt certain would have been lost to the storm.

"I don't know- but we saw smoke further south, I believe it's a village."

Fess sighed and shook her head; this was impossible!

    *   *   *

"I don't believe it," Rust breathed as he approached Rizon and the other prisoners and soldiers.

"I told you that we would all survive," Rizon said smugly.

Rust did another head count just to satisfy his shocked mind.

"You didn't escape..." his worst fear had proven false.

"I will stand before the king. Whether this storm likes it or not," Rizon said determinedly.

Rust shook his head in wonder at the man's faith.

"Rizon!" Fate came running up to them, "Have you seen my brother?"

"Yes- I saw Desert pull him onto the beach a few moments ago- there," he pointed.

Fa followed his finger and felt her heart skip a beat when she saw Rave and Desert sitting with their backs to her.

"Rave!" she called, nearly tripping in the sand as she ran to them. Dropping beside her brother Fa wrapped her arms around him.

"Fa..." Rave breathed in relief as he returned her embrace. Letting her pent-up breath go, Fa looked over Rave's shoulder and met Deserts smiling gaze.

"You could have told me he sinks like a rock," Dese said with his all too easy smile.

Fa breathed a laugh and closed her eyes, but she felt her heart tremble as if the ground had given way; she had survived the storm, but surely only fire, ash and death awaited her in Tarva.

    *   *   *

When the shivering survivors of the storm shuffled into the fishing village further south, the captain and all the crew were astounded to find that they were not on an uncharted island, but on Chresacroon- a mere three-day voyage from the mainland and the city of Tarva. The crew and the whole village were baffled at how a ship could sail north-west when such a mighty storm was blowing south-east. Some laughed and called it a happy mistake, but Fa knew better. Fa knew that it was the heart stain, or more properly, it was Eloi who was pulling her closer to Tarva, closer to her doom.

The little Tarven village had welcomed the shipwreck survivors into their homes and barns. They considered it their duty to feed and care for those who washed up from the sea, hoping that others would return the favour should their loved ones ever be shipwrecked. And so, by nightfall everyone was well fed and warmed up and either sleeping in a villager's loft or in their barn. Fate, Rave and the prisoners had been invited to stay in the largest barn, sharing it with a herd of goats. The soldiers took up guard at the doors, but everyone was so exhausted that escape was the last thing on anyone's mind.

Since no one else seemed interested in climbing the rickety ladder, Fa and her brother had the small loft of the barn to themselves, and they curled up in the hay, as the prisoners, including Horizon, settled down below. Along with fishing, the village also raised long haired goats, and they had given goat hair ponchos to the castaways for the night. The ponchos were rough, and the strange fabric made Fa's arms and neck itch- but she was grateful for the temporary gift. She had never seen long haired goats before, and she and Rave watched them for a long time as they bleated at the visitors.

The cottages of the village were similar to what Fa and Rave were used to, only every cottage seemed to have an outdoor oven for cooking, and every structure had a gap between the walls and the roofs, as a way to cool the cottages in the hot summer months. It was through such a gap in the barn wall that Fa could see the sleepy village in the twilight. She could hear the muted sounds of goats and voices all through the village; it must have been a very exciting day for them!

Fa's eyes fell to the cottage across the little street as the door swung open and Confess stepped out. Her braided hair was left down, and she also wore a goat hair poncho- but it didn't make her look any less fierce. Fa couldn't make out the woman's expression- but her posture said it all.

"Do you think I did this?" Fa asked quietly.

Rave propped himself up on his elbow In the hay, and gave her a questioning frown, "What do you mean?"

Unbidden tears welled up in her eyes, but she forced herself to look at him, "Where I go, death and destruction follows."

Rave looked stunned.

"I dreamed of fire; and Eamer burned. I warned Vanished; and he and his men were killed. I went down the river, and the land burned- don't you think that crops and cottages were destroyed that day? Then I dreamed of the storm…" Fa's eyes drifted back out to Confess as she went back inside, "And this happened."

"Fa… that- none of that was your doing!" Rave insisted weakly.

"Rave, I have constant dreams of Tarva burning; if I go there, I *will* bring destruction with me."

Rave sat up and gently took her bandaged hand, "Fa, you see the worst of what is coming- that's what you did for Vanished, and you tried to warn him- it was him- and him alone that chose what happened next."

"You think life follows me?" Fa asked sarcastically, Rave just hadn't faced the truth as she had.

"I think *hope* follows you!"

"What hope is there for Confess?" Fa argued, "She has lost everything! What hope is there for Tarva? For I see only death." 'What hope is there for me?' she added silently.

Rave seemed at a loss, and Fa despaired at the thought that she had won the argument.

"Freedom said that the heart stain was like a guiding hand, that Eloi was calling you to Tarva- to warn them; not to destroy them." Rave's confidence grew, "Grandfather used to say that Eloi fosters life– and that death, true death, comes when people shut Eloi out."

Fa listened, not quite daring to believe him, yet not dismissing his words.

"Where you go *hope* follows. We all survived that storm Fa, all of us! And as for Tarva, destruction is already on its way to the city, but you… I believe your message will offer an escape."

Fa was shocked; Rave wasn't given to deep thoughts about life and Eloi, she thought that he had never listened to their grandfather or parents when they spoke of such things. And yet here he was, telling her that she was a bringer of hope and escape. But Fa couldn't make herself believe him, she didn't know of any escape- the Dream Child had said nothing of hope. But she couldn't tell Rave that he was wrong- he was so certain that he could help her…

"LOOK OUT!" one of the Tarven woman screamed, and Fa heard Horizon gasp.

Scrambling to the edge on their hands and knees, Fa and Rave looked down at the barn floor; Horizon stood holding his arm while the other prisoners all jumped to their feet. Between them and Rizon was a snake! It was the length of Fate's arm and was black with bright red stripes, it thrashed on the floor as if it had been flung there moments before.

Jumping to action, one of the younger Tarven's grabbed a pitchfork and speared the vermin, pinning it to the dirt floor before it could slither away.

"What's going on!?" Rustling demanded to know as he burst through the barn door and took in the scene.

"It was a snake!" one of the women shrieked.

"It came out of the hay and bit Rizon!" one of the soldiers reported.

Fa scrambled to the ladder, and Rave hurried after her.

"I'm alright," Rizon informed everyone and inspected his arm.

Fa jumped down the last four rungs of the ladder and saw two holes in the Garatin's lower arm.

"It bit you!" one of the soldiers said, he was clearly shaken.

"Yes, but I'm alright," Rizon insisted when he saw Fa's worried gaze.

Rust stepped closer to inspect the bite.

"That's a blood viper…" everyone looked up as the owner of the barn stood in the door and looked at the impaled snake, "It bit you?' he asked coming closer.

"Yes, but I'm alright," Rizon repeated.

"Blood vipers are… deadly venomous," one of the soldiers said and everyone took a step back from the still writhing snake.

"What kind of outlaw are you?" the villager asked and peered at Rizon with a mix of awe and suspicion, "Are you… a murderer?"

Rizon was surprisingly silent.

"Why?" Rustling demanded to know.

The villager shrugged his shoulders and took a step back. "Blood vipers are rare on this island, they only seek out guilty souls- they avenge the innocent. Perhaps he wasn't meant to survive the storm, and the snake has finished the job."

"Superstition and folklore!" Rust dismissed the man's warning.

"No, but he's right," one of the soldiers spoke up, "Blood vipers *are* venomous- no one ever survives a bite."

"He'll be dead by morning," the villager gave the grim verdict with a strangely sympathetic look at Rizon.

"I'm alright," Horizon insisted again. "I will not die before my task is done," he assured a rather fearful looking Rust.

"Is there no cure?" Rust looked to the villager, the man shook his head.

"Rust; I will not need one! Trust me, I know what my fate is." He glanced at Fa.

Rust insisted on at least bandaging Rizon's arm, to which the villager shook his head and left, muttering about nursing dead men. Rust didn't seem to know who to believe, but Horizon wouldn't allow a fuss to be made and urged everyone to go to bed and rest, and after the snake had been removed, and with some hesitation to return to the hay, the other prisoners obliged him. They didn't seem overly bothered with the idea of the Garatin dying in the night while they slept. Rust had worried his new hanky and mopped his brow a great deal, before finally laying down close to Rizon. Fate had wanted to sit by Rizons' side through the night just in case- but Rizon wouldn't hear of it, and he made her and Rave return to the loft.

Nevertheless, Fa sat up all night, and peeked over the edge of the loft, watching Rizon till she could see his chest rise and fall with his breath. In the end, all Fate could do was wait for morning's light. All the while she was thinking that she could have warned Rizon if she had slept, and she hated herself for being so useless. If Rave was right and she was meant to warn people- then surely, she shouldn't avoid dreaming! And yet, every time she dreamed, the 'thing' became stronger inside her...

Part Three - Tarva

Chapter 14   The Threshold

The whole village had heard of what happened the night before, including Confess, and she was a little disappointed- although she would never admit to liking the Garatin.

And so, early that morning, the whole of the former crew of 'The Prestige' gathered in and around the barn, along with a good number of the villagers, as Fess stood over Horizon's still form. Fate and her brother were watching from the loft and all the prisoners and soldiers had awakened to learn of the Garatin's grim fate.

"No one survives a blood vipers' venom," a villager said in the silence.

Beside him Rustling mopped his brow, by all accounts it was he who should check to see if the Garatin was still breathing- but Confess didn't have the patience to wait for the nervous soldier to gather his nerve and approach the body.

Ignoring everyone's breathless gaze, Fess nudged Horizon's leg with her boot. There was a collected gasp as Rizon stirred and moaned. He blinked his eyes open to see everyone watching him.

"You're still alive then?" Fess asked with a raised brow, masking her shock and relief.

Rizon smiled and stretched as he sat up, "Just like every morning."

His voice seemed to awaken everyone, and they all started talking at once.

"That's impossible!"

"He should be dead!"

"He must be a sorcerer of the black arts!"

Rizon stood up and rolled up his sleeve to inspect and show off the bite, "Eloi of Garatin has promised that I will stand trial before the King of Tarva. Just as he promised that we would all survive the storm. Until I stand before the king; nothing can harm me."

Unlike other times, no one dared to disbelieve him!

"You are an astonishing man!" Rustling said as he and several others stepped closer to inspect the bite for themselves.

After the astonished voices had died down and before the sailors started to disperse, Fess raised her voice, "Attend to me." Everyone's eyes went to her and she waited till even the villagers had gone quiet, "In case it is not understood; there are no wages paid after a shipwreck." None of the sailors were caught off guard by this, "I wish you all better sailing on your next voyage." The sailors stood about for a moment, then they began to walk away, Desert and the first mate were the only crew members who remained.

"Thank you for your service," Confess said stiffly as she faced her former first mate. Normally she should have thanked him for his 'loyal' service, but they both knew that was a stretch.

"If you should ever captain a ship again, my lady," the first mate looked her in the eye for one of the only times that she had known him, "I advise you to listen to the experienced." His words couldn't have been more cutting than if he had blamed her openly for the shipwreck.

Fess bit her tongue and managed a tight nod, her first mate made as if to bow over her hand the way a man should when bidding a lady farewell, but Fess refused to offer her hand. So, he left without another word, and Fess honestly wished to never set eyes on him again!

Rustling waited till she turned to him and he nodded his head respectfully, "Farewell Cap- my lady."

Fess tilted her head back, "I trust you don't blame me for the misfortune we find ourselves in," she held back a smile as sweat popped out on his brow, 'how did he ever become a soldier?'

"I..." he faltered.

"At any rate, farewells are not quite in order- not yet. I believe we will yet journey to Tarva together, I assume you will be going to the harbour as soon as possible?"

Rust nodded, "Yes, today- you are going to Tarva?"

Fess sighed deeply, "I have some unfinished business to see to. Unless you object to sailing with me?" Traveling with a Tarven soldier would provide her with some much-needed protection.

Fess felt a little cruel for making the man sweat so.

"No! of course not, my lady- ah captain..." he stuttered. Not bothering to correct him on her title- she wasn't entirely sure what her title was anymore herself- Fess turned away and fixed her eyes on where Desert was loitering by the door.

She took a deep breath; she wasn't done with him yet.

*   *   *

Brave sat back in the hay and pinched his eyebrows together; he didn't think that Horizon would die in the night, but he did think that he'd be sick in the morning, or that at least his arm would be swollen. And yet there he was, below the loft, discussing travel arrangements with Rustling! How was it that Eloi protected Rizon, but he and his sister ran into danger at every turn? Was Fa doing something wrong? Was *he* doing something wrong?

It was truly Rave's great growing fear ever since that day on the road from Cinders Grove, that he had failed his sister in some way. That he could help her, if only he was *better* somehow.

He looked up at Fate, she was inspecting her hands again, when Deserts voice outside caught their attention. They hadn't spoken with Dese since yesterday evening- and they hadn't discussed what would happen in the morning when they would most certainly go their separate ways.

They could also hear the voice of Confess, Rave exchanged a look with Fa before crawling over to the wall and looking out through the gap.

"You shouldn't be listen-" Fa began to scold him, but Rave hushed her with a wave; whatever Dese, and Fess were discussing below- it looked intense! Grudgingly Fa crawled up beside him and together they listened.

"You misunderstand me; you have no choice in the matter," Fess said in a low tone.

Desert had his arms crossed and he looked away down the street. "Very well. To Tarva we go," he replied tightly. Fess looked less than satisfied with his response.

"We travel with the good soldier, be ready to leave" she said jerking her head at Rustling, then she walked away.

Dese stood for a moment, Fa could see him take a deep breath before heading to the cottage he had slept in to return the poncho.

"Could he owe her something?" Fate asked as they watched him walk away, but Rave had a different idea.

"Maybe his life- maybe he's been her servant this whole time!" Rave's head reeled at the possibility.

"Maybe... When she found me on the beach yesterday, she specifically asked about Desert- that could explain why she seems to favour him." Fa sat back.

Rave grinned, "I don't think she 'favours' anyone!" It didn't bother him that Desert was keeping a secret, in fact it seemed fair to him! After all, he and Fa hadn't told Dese about the heart stain. Rave settled down in the hay once more, he was pleased that Desert would be traveling with them to Tarva, he had never had a friend his own age before, and over the past few weeks that's exactly what he had come to considered Dese to be. A good friend- no matter what secrets he was hiding, and one more friendly face in Tarva couldn't hurt!

          *   *   *

The depleted group thanked the villagers for their kindness and left the little village, taking the road to the nearest harbour. The day was warm and bright, as if to defy the storm the day before, and the road was easy to walk. Fate walked in silence, unable to shake the feeling that she was drawing closer to the end. Desert however was chipper, and he kept up a mostly one-sided conversation with her and Brave. Fess and Rust hardly said anything, but the prisoners (aside from Rizon) complained about the long walk.

They reached the harbour late in the afternoon but couldn't find a ship that would take them till the next morning, and since no one had money for an Inn, the group camped on the town's outskirts. And so, it was, that the rumor of the shipwreck reached Tarva before the survivors themselves did.

The next morning Rustling, his five soldiers and nine prisoners, Fate, Rave, Desert and Confess boarded a little vessel that was bound for Tarva. They would reach the city the next afternoon. The large channel between the island and the mainland provided enough shelter for boats to sail without overdue concern for storms, but understandably there were several of the group who were nervous to be on a ship again.

The small hull of the ship was crowded, and there weren't enough hammocks to go around, consequently several people were forced to sleep on the cold deck. Fate, Rave and Dese had spread their borrowed, threadbare blankets in a row, with Rave in the middle and Fa next to the ship wall. Everyone counted the minutes till they could disembark the over-crowded ship- everyone but Fa. For her, nothing but dread came with the thought of reaching their destination.

What was she to do once they got there?! At least Horizon knew what his task was- even if it wasn't pleasant, at least he knew!

'If only I had clear instructions!' Fa thought with despair as she leaned against the ship's wall soon after the ship had left the harbour, 'what good is a guiding hand if I can't see it!?'

With a sense of defeat, Fa conceded that the only way she could get answers, was to dream. She allowed herself to become drowsy through the day so that when night came, she felt fairly certain that this time sleep would come easy.

She hadn't told Rave her plan- she didn't have to, he knew just by looking at her. He and Desert sat on the far sides of their bed rolls, Dese was teaching Rave how to tie sailor knots with a bit of rope. As Fa lay down, Rave cast her a knowing glance; he knew that when she woke, she would need new bandages. But that just seemed like the price for speaking directly with Eloi.

Fa lay awake for a few minutes with her eyes closed, listening to whispered conversations around her, until suddenly, she was dreaming.

Fate knew exactly where she was; she was atop the cliff that overlooked the city! Sitting on the cliff edge, swinging one leg over the edge, was the Dream Child. Fa felt an impulse to pull the child back, but she didn't want to touch the child, she knew that if she did, the 'thing' would strengthen inside her. She flinched a little when the child turned and looked at her, and Fa noticed for the first time how sad the child's eyes were, as if they had seen too much.

"Tarva's end is drawing near."

Fa looked up to the city- and gasped, the image would always be with her. Although far off, she could see the city in great detail, every brick, every blossom, every flame… and she could hear the screams.

"Spring will soon be here." The child's voice made the dream change and Fa was standing in the courtyard from her other dream. She looked up and just like before, the guard was standing on the ramparts keeping watch.

"When will the morning come?" Fa couldn't stop herself from asking the question- and still it made no sense! Wasn't it already morning? Was that not the sun casting her shadow before her?

Just as before, Fa didn't get to hear the guards' response, for suddenly she was running down a hallway lined with tapestries large enough to get lost under. At the end of the hall was a great door that made Fa feel incredibly small- and still she ran towards it; it flew open before her, and she was met by a blast of hot air. The room inside was burning; it was the first dream she had, before Eamer burned. But the Dream Child stood in place of the king, with sad eyes brimming over with tears.

"Tarva has shut me out for far too long. This is the fate of all who shut me out."

Fa turned away from the child and was met with her own reflection staring back at her from a mirror. Not with all the words of every language could Fa explain it, but she knew that her reflection was dead.

"Don't be afraid Fa, let me in- before its too late." The child reached out to hold Fa's hand, but Fa jerked away, her hand swinging out and striking the mirror causing it to shatter into ash.

*   *   *

"No, you forgot the second loop," Desert said with a smirk at Brave's feeble attempt at the knot that Dese was trying to teach him. Rave didn't seem to hear him. The sun had set an hour ago, but the ship was too crowded and stuffy for some to sleep, Dese and Rave weren't the only ones who sat awake

"Are you alright?" Dese asked seriously, his voice low so as not to disturb the passengers around them, there was moonlight shining down the hatch, but they were sitting too far back from it to see clearly.

"Huh?" Rave looked at him with a blank expression, then glanced over at the sleeping Fate, the unfinished knot, forgotten in his hands. "Yeah, I'm fine," he began to untangle the rope.

"Is she really your sister?" Dese asked suddenly.

"Yes; of course! Why would you think otherwise!?"

Dese smiled at himself for the idea that had popped in his head, "You two just seem real close- that's all."

Rave looked disgusted at the implication, "No! We... No."

"I'll happily banish the thought then," Dese assured him as he effortlessly knotted his own rope in the knot that Rave was having trouble with.

"She's just been through a lot..." Rave mumbled as he untangled his knot. "It's probably my fault," he added quietly.

Dese narrowed his eyes as he watched his friend, now he was more intrigued than ever; what were the siblings hiding?!

Just then, Fate gasped and clutched her hands to herself, her face twisting in pain. She wakened with tears slipping off her face.

Rave scrambled over his and Desert's blankets to Fa's side, Dese right behind him, "Is she alright?" Dese asked in a hushed but alarmed voice.

"I'm fine," Fa struggled to catch her breath and sat up, wiping away her tears with bandaged hands. "Where's Rizon?" she asked at once.

Rave nodded across the deck to where the Garatin was dozing beyond the shaft of moon light. "Let me rebandage your hands first," he insisted.

Desert frowned; why would her hands need bandaging after sleeping? He had tried asking several times before, why her hands were bandaged- but had never gotten an answer.

"Later- I must speak with Rizon," Fa brushed them aside and went on tiptoe through the sleeping passengers to Rizon.

"What was that about?" Dese asked softly and watched his friend's face closely.

Rave looked uncomfortable, and Dese didn't think he would say anything, but then, "Fa has... prophetic dreams; she sees the future."

Dese leaned back- was he serious?!

"It's true- she saw the storm before it happened," Rave said defensively.

Dese thought about it for a moment, "Why didn't she warn the captain?"

"She probably knew that she'd give her the same face your giving me now."

Dese went silent and looked to where Fa stood before Horizon; what else didn't he know about the fire hair girl?

*   *   *

Horizon sat, slumped against the wall; he had opted to sleep on the floor so that someone else could have a hammock- a gesture that had not been properly thanked, but Rizon didn't mind. Every couple of minutes he dozed off and woke back up again, letting the sound of the sea and the soft murmur of voices lull him to sleep. But he straightened up when he saw Fate making her way towards him.

"Fate- what's wrong?" he asked when she passed through the moonlight and he saw her expression.

Fa knelt beside him looking very grave, "I haven't been entirely honest with you."

Rizon smiled softly, he had guessed as much, "I'm sure you had good reason."

She took a deep breath, "I told you that Eloi is calling me to Tarva through my dreams. What I didn't tell you is what happens when I wake." She hesitated, "I have a heart stain."

Rizon blinked in surprise; he had heard those words before.

"When I wake from the dreams I have burns on the palms of my hands," she explained.

"Not just your palms," he noted, looking at her hands.

Fa gasped; the old bandages she wore no longer covered the burns, they now spanned from her fingertips to her wrists. Fa's face crumpled in a whimper, "They're spreading the closer I get to Tarva."

Rizon took a steadying breath; he knew well the nature of heart stains, but this one seemed different, "And what happens to you when you get to Tarva?"

"I don't know... in my dreams, Eloi takes the form of a child, and this child has made two things clear to me, the first is that I must warn Eloi's people."

"Warn my people?" Rizon repeated with interest, Fa nodded. "Warn the *Nity followers*," he suggested.

Fa blinked in surprise as if understanding for the first time, "*Are there Nity Followers in Tarva?*"

Rizon smiled, "Oh yes! Last time I was here, I met with many who follow the teachings of Eternity." Rizon would have said more, but Fa interrupted.

"Then they're in trouble! That's what my dreams keep showing me."

"You said you keep seeing a storm heading for Tarva in your dreams?" he asked again, he wasn't convinced that a mere storm could cause much trouble- but Fa was very distraught.

"Yes- and that I must warn them by spring!"

Rizon nodded, "It soon will be spring... Let me sleep on this Fa, by morning I'll know what course of action to take. I won't be able to go with you in Tarva," he glanced at Rustling who was fast asleep. "But I do have some friends you could go to. Let me see... in two days it will be a quarter moon, if I remember correctly that means the Nity followers will be meeting in the Pearl Square at sundown. But who could take you there?" he thought for a moment, it had been sometime since he had been in Tarva and he wasn't sure who would still be living near the harbour. "Let me sleep on this, in the morning I'll know who to send you too," he repeated.

Fa nodded, she had calmed down a great deal; she just needed someone with a level head to help her.

"The second thing the child told me…" Fa's face looked uncertain again, "Was that, I am to help you in some way."

Rizon was really taken aback this time; *Her*? Help *him*!? How could this timid young woman prove to be of *any* help to him!?

"I don't know how," Fa said as if reading his thoughts. "The child just said that you would need my help- nothing else." Fa waited for him to speak- to explain what it could mean.

Rizon couldn't begin to even dream how she could help him! Eloi had chosen *him* to speak before the king and tell him the story of Eternity. *Chosen* him, prepared, tested, and called to him, then waited for him to answer. Even when Rizon was blind and hunting down the Nity followers to put them to death- even *then* Eloi was molding and crafting him for this purpose!

How could Fa help him?

*   *   *

None of Fate's dreams could have prepared her for the enormity and splendor of the harbour of Tarva. The water teamed with ships of all sizes, with crew members readying them for sailing; from great big sailing ships anchored overwinter, to small merchant boats with open decks, displaying all kinds of trinkets. From silk dress's to steaming drinks. These water merchants would paddle up close to the other ships and call out their wares in loud unbashful voices. There were small flat ferries, that took cargo and passengers to and from the docks.

There were over a dozen long docks, pointing out into the bay, they all converged back to land connecting to large stone steps that rose out of the water. The steps went up to the left and right around a wall. On the wall was a freshly painted red and gold dragon; the dragon of Tarva.

Great big yellow birds, sea sparrows, filled the late afternoon sky, their voices calling through the air; they dove into the water around the ships and came back up with wiggling fish. The larger vessels were mostly still, their captains and crew still ashore for the winter season but the waterways between these ships were busy with smaller fishing ships and merchants.

Things happened too quickly for Fate's liking, one minute they were below deck, waiting in the stiff hot air with the prisoners, and the next they were being hurried out on deck. The captain of the small ship was talking to Rustling, Confess also stood near by. Fa and Rave only had a moment to take in the spectacular view of the harbour before Rust was waving to them.

"Yes, you will be payed for our passage! I am a soldier, I will keep my word!" Rustling sounded weary as he mopped his brow and pointed to a ferry that had pulled up to the ship. "I've arranged for you two to be brought ashore," he said to Fa and Brave.

"Thank you!" Rave said, as the soldier turned back to the captain.

"Count it as your first bit of Tarven charity," Fess said to the siblings, as a rope ladder was flung over the bulwark. "It's likely to be the last too," she said dourly. "Watch your backs, you could easily end up as slaves again," she warned.

"You're not coming ashore with us?" Fa was disappointed, she would have felt better in the woman's company.

"I'll be going ashore with the good soldier," Fess said, nodding to Rust, who was still arguing. "My enemies might think twice when they see me with a soldier."

Fa couldn't tell if she was serious.

"I may see you again," Fess's voice softened.

"Thank you Fess, for all you've done," Fa said. Beside her Rave nodded his own gratitude (he was still a bit frightened of the woman). Fa was sad to part ways with the fierce sea captain. "I won't forget your kindness to me," she said, hoping that her sincerity was clear.

Her words seemed to touch Fess, and Fa supposed that what she saw was the closest thing to a blush on the woman's face. "If I hadn't lost everything, I would offer you two a place to stay, or passage on 'The Prestige' back to Garatin," Fess said in a bittersweet tone.

Fa offered a smile, who would have guessed it? Fess had grown to like her!

"Is Desert around?" Rave asked looking about the deck.

"He's below," Fess said shortly.

Fa was disappointed- they hadn't got a chance to say goodbye to Desert.

"You'll be alright than?" Fess asked as they moved to the rope ladder.

"Yes, Rizon told us to contact a friend of his," Fa assured her.

Fess shook her head, "You and Rizon, I'll never understand you lot. Off you go- and stay clear of the curfew guards," Fess gave a last warning, as Fa carefully descended the ladder.

A few moments later, Fate and Brave were sitting with some of the ship's crew, as the ferry slowly navigated the cluttered harbour.

"Well... we made it!" Rave said, as he raised his eyes to look at the high cliffs and walls of the inner city.

Beyond the lower ring of the city a yellow cliff rose to a dizzying height, and the rest of the city curved around to the sloped back of this rock face. Perched atop of the cliff overlooking the harbour, with ramparts and towers, was a gigantic castle; red flags fluttered from every pinnacle like a flock of fire birds. The red and gold dragon painted high up on the cliff clearly identified the castle as the Dragon keep; the king's castle.

Fa shut her eyes and ran the namesake that Rizon had given her over in her mind to try and block out her fear. 'Glimmer.... Glimmer....' That was all she had to go on, Rizon told her to ask around the market for a woman named Glimmer, and that she would take them to the Pearl square. 'Horizon...' she thought of the Garatin sadly, would he meet his end in this city? 'I will,' she thought darkly, and wondered what Rave would say if he knew what she was so certain of... a dead reflection and a foreign presence growing inside her.

'Trust me...'

Fa gasped softly and opened her eyes; that was the Dream Child's voice! Fa took in her surroundings to convince herself that she wasn't sleeping- that the Dream Child had really spoken to her while she was awake...

*   *   *

Waiting on the deck, letting the wind and sun wash away her cramped and stuffy night, Confess watched as the ferry carried Fate and her brother to shore. She could hardly believe how much she had come to care for the Garatin maiden. She had come to think of Fa as everything that she herself might have been... if her life had been different. She would hate to see the maiden's innocence and light heart be stolen, the way those things had been taken from herself.

People were wrong about Confess, she wasn't cold, her heart wasn't stone; she was an example of what happened when the world threw a girl down and trampled over her. What a cruel world.

Fess took a deep breath and pushed aside her self-pity and made herself focus on her next task; Desert. She half turned away from the ship edge when something in the receding ferry caught her eye; a dark head popped up from behind some crates. Was that!?

"Desert!" Fess hissed in a mix of anger and surprise, how had he gotten on the ferry!?

Desert met her gaze and flashed her a smile before ducking back down.

Fess opened her mouth- but the ship was already out of shouting distance, she hissed a curse, "The little imp gave me the slip!"

*   *   *

Fate and Brave jumped off the ferry onto the stone platform, they paused to look back at the gigantic eye of the painted dragon. Fa hadn't realized how big it was, the wall before them towered far over their heads. They hurried up the steps and found themselves frozen in place as they looked about the busy harbour courtyard. In front of them, was the promised market, with carts of fish and white sheets supported on poles for shade. People were everywhere, pushing wheel barrels, carrying baskets and exchanging money.

"So, we're just going to start asking for a woman named Glimmer? And hope no one takes offence, and hope we find her before nightfall- and hope we don't get run over?" Rave said as he pulled Fa out of the way of a group of sailors who went running past.

"And hope there's not two 'Glimmers'." Fa added as she watched a woman with three baskets balanced on her head walk pass.

"Yikes! Sounds tedious!"

Fa and Rave turned to see Desert. He was halfway up the steps and was resting his arms on the courtyard stones, he looked up at them with twinkling eyes.

"Where did you come from?!" Rave asked with a half grin.

Dese jerked his head back to the ferry, "I was there the whole time, I just took a nap is all." He winked at them.

Fa found herself smiling; Desert's cocky and carefree presence made the whole city a little more manageable.

"You're not really going to hang about asking for someone, hoping they'll turn up- are you?" he asked doubtfully, as he bounded up the last of the steps.

"Not much else we can do," Fa realized how feeble it sounded.

"Nonsense! You got me!" he said cheerful as he came to stand with them, "This is my home- remember? I can show you around."

"What about Confess?" Fa asked, glancing back at the harbour.

"What do you mean?" Dese asked innocently.

"You know… we…" Rave faltered.

"We overheard you and Fess; we know that you're her servant… or something…" Fa was trying to be delicate, but a huge grin spread across Desert's tanned face.

"What are you talking about!?" he laughed, "I'm not Confess's *anything*! I was just a sailor on her ship— work that I'll now never get payed for!" he led them away from the water and towards the market. "Now what do you say? Shall we begin the grand tour?" he said with fake flair.

Fate and Rave laughed at how wrong they had been; they had clearly misunderstood what they had heard between Fess and Dese. For a moment Fa forced her fears and misgivings aside and let Desert's light-hearted attitude distract her from what she felt; the 'thing' growing stronger now that she was in Tarva.

Chapter 15   Old Friends

The city of Tarva was shaped like a giant sea snail, the top and inner part of the spiral being the Dragon keep on the cliff edge, the rest of the city was built in tiers as it descended the cliff to the sea edge. The end and widest part of the spiral was the harbour, with the sea on one side and the cliff wall rising as a stunning backdrop; the city curling around behind it.

There were four main tiers, each one separated from the other with a wall and portcullis that closed each night. While the city wall ran around the entire outside of the city, only giving way when the cliff rose as a natural barrier and defence. The King lived on the top tier, known as the 'Kings Ring', the nobility and members of the court lived there, and the garrison was also located in the topmost tier. Through the Dragons Gate was the 'Dukes

Ring', where the rich landowners and lords and their ladies lived in grand manors; this was where the only outer city gate was located. Then the 'Dukes Gate' allowed passage to the 'Earls Ring'. This is where the middle class lived in smaller manors, and flat, stone roofed houses. Then came the last gate, the 'Sea Gate', and beyond that, the 'Harbour Ring'. It consisted of a few small manors, but mostly it was filled with ramshackle cottages with thatched roofs, and cargo yards walled in with sharp spikes on top of the walls to keep out intruders. This was where the market was located.

Desert took Fate and Brave into the market, and they wandered around for a time amongst all the stands with strange looking fish, and barrels of clams. There was even a cart of 'winter melons' that grew in the cooler season. Fate was overwhelmed by the busy market and old feelings of claustrophobia came back as people brushed by her. It took her some time to pluck up her courage to approach one of the sellers.

"Sir?" she asked timidly of the woven blanket seller, "Do you know a woman named Glimmer?"

The man shook his head and turned away from her to a customer.

"Hey," Desert said beside her, "You don't need to look for that woman- I told you I would look after you two."

Fa looked past him to Rave, he didn't look concerned with finding Glimmer, and Fa felt her determination waver; maybe she didn't NEED to find Glimmer- but could they trust Desert by telling him that she needed to get to the Pearl square? Would he know of Nity follower meetings?

"Alright..." she said hesitantly.

"Rave- tell your sister that you two are in good hands!" Dese said with a cocky smile.

Rave laughed and looked at Fa as if to say, 'I think we'll be alright'. Fa smiled; searching for a woman they had never met was sounding less and less appealing- it *was* much easer to just stay with Desert!

Just then she looked up and saw Rustling and his soldiers leading the prisoners across the courtyard to waiting carriages. Horizon saw her, he paused and looked around- looking a bit concerned that she didn't appear to have found Glimmer yet. Fa nodded and smiled to assure him that she was alright. He nodded and allowed the soldiers to direct him into a carriage.

Someone else also caught Fa's eye; standing in the center of the courtyard, with hands on hips and looking very cross, was Confess. Before Fess saw them Dese grabbed a blanket and held it up.

"Fate, come here," he called so that all three of them were conveniently standing behind the blanket, "Now this is made from one of *the* best weavers in the city, I mean could Glimmer tell you that? I don't think so." Dese expertly peeked around the blanket to see Fess turn away, "Now, how about we get something to eat?" he asked cheerfully as he folded the blanket and turned his back to the courtyard.

*   *   *

Confess had fumed the entire ferry ride over to shore with Rustling. The soldiers had given her a wide berth, and once ashore Fess had reluctantly parted ways with him and his company.

'So much for added protection!' she thought angrily as she leaned against a wall in a side street and watched the busy market and harbour. She had searched the waterfront for a half hour but had seen no sign of Desert.

'If I were an impish young brat, where would I go?' she questioned herself furiously, she had already spent longer in the Harbour Ring than she had intended! One thing was certain, she didn't care who Desert was; when she found him, she would give him a good pounding for giving *her* the slip!

"I'd recognize the wife of Devotion anywhere," a dangerous voice said nearby.

Fess stiffened and turned to the speaker; it was Endure, a man that both she and her husband had past dealings with. One of the men that had made her wary of coming to Tarva. He was a vulgar man with no sense of morals, and worse still; he never went anywhere alone. Two of his thugs were always close by, today was no exception.

"Hello Fess, you're an interesting breed of cat to find at this time of year," he sneered. Endure was the kind of man who took pleasure in harming small creatures- particularly cats. He had always compared her to a feline- and not the nice kind, but the kind you find in a street corner, with a broken tail and open wounds- inflicted by himself. He had always pretended to be a perfect gentleman when her husband was around, but it was a different story when she was alone. His two thugs smiled at the 'pet' name he had for her, and Fess smothered the old feeling of insecurity that Endure always awoke in her.

Fess planted her feet firmly and raised her chin, as if Endure was a bug on the ground, "What do you want Endure? My dealings with you are done."

"Don't forget what you are 'pet'," he pronounced the word like it was a weapon. "Your husband owes me three hundred gold from our last dealing."

Fess steeled herself, Devotion had told her that he hadn't done dealings with Endure for years - evidently not. But more importantly, Endure didn't sound like he knew about Devo's death; she could use that. "Whatever business you have with my husband does not concern me. I suggest you take it up with him," she secretly held her breath; would the bluff work? What if news had traveled of Devotion's death ahead of her somehow?

Endure smiled cruelly. "I know that look; your hiding something Fess," he said in a patronizing voice, "I don't recall seeing 'The Prestige' in the harbour- do you wish to 'confess' anything?" He thought himself so clever for his wording.

"Perhaps you should go look in the harbour again, I remember how poor your eyesight was, it must be getting worse with age." She turned away into the crowded square and felt the hairs on the back of her neck stand on end as she walked away.

"Tell Devotion that I aim to collect - soon!" Endure called after her.

Fess took a calming breath; she wondered how many other 'old friends' were lurking in the city, waiting for her.

*   *   *

"Get out of here!" a Tarven woman shooed a gray cat away from her doorstep with a broom, above her, swinging on unoiled hinges, was a sign; 'Vision's Boarding House'.

Cats were another thing that was new to Brave and his sister, they seemed to be everywhere! The one the woman chased away, hissed and ran past Rave and Fa while Desert approached the woman easily. She had unkept hair and a hard face.

"You can stop your crying Vision; your favorite waif is back!" Dese spread his arms for a hug. The middle-aged woman looked at him with a frown.

"Well, look what the tide washed in!" her frown broke and embraced Dese with a hearty laugh. Was Dese related to this woman? Rave wondered, if so, Dese hadn't said so.

"What have you brought back from afar?" she asked looking suspiciously at Fa and Rave.

"This is Fate and Brave- my friends," Dese said, inviting them closer.

"I'm not sure about that one," Vision said jabbing her broom handle in Fa's direction, "She looks too much like a witch- and they both look pale enough to be dead."

"They're my friends!" Dese said defensively, "And we're hungry- you can't turn us away! You know I have no other friends aside from you." Dese winked, and Rave smiled at his boyish charm.

Vision narrowed her eyes for a moment, then to Rave's surprise, she cracked a smile, "Alright- come in, the lot of you."

Vision's boarding house was small and cramped, the stairs to the second story were right beside the door, and the main room was crammed with three sets of chairs and tables. At the back of the room was a doorway to a kitchen and beyond that was another door that stood open, an out-door oven could be seen in a little walled in courtyard. Much to their relief, the room was empty, Rave and Fa sat down at the middle table, while Desert followed Vision outside to the little courtyard.

Rave turned his head and glimpsed the two standing beside the strange oven. The door to the street had been left open, and the din from the market could still be heard, it masked Desert's conversation with Vision, but Rave watched Desert's mouth and was certain he said, 'you know I'm good for it'. Rave felt a little guilty for spying and he looked away, only to meet Fate's knowing gaze.

"Didn't you learn anything from the last time you overheard- and misunderstood a conversation?" she asked with a raised brow.

Rave sighed; sometimes he forgot how annoying a big sister was!

The two of them sat in uncomfortable silence until Desert came back. He set a tray with a humble meal on the table. "Here we go- Vision's the best! I've known her for ages!" he said as he pulled up a chair backwards and sat down, resting his arms on the back of the chair.

Rave started eating hungrily but paused when he saw Fate give him a look; she was going to tell Dese about the Pearl square. Rave nodded his approval; he believed that they could trust Dese, after all he was feeding them!

"Desert, can you get us to the Pearl square?" Fa asked as she joined Rave and Dese in demolishing the meal.

Dese swallowed his mouthful, "Of course! I told you, I'll give you the grand tour! But, why the Pearl square?"

Fa hesitated and looked to Rave for help, he shrugged his shoulders as if to say, 'what do we have to lose?' He had told her earlier that day that he had shared a little about her dreams to Dese the night before. She had been a little angry with him for doing so, but he suspected that she was also relieved that *she* didn't have to explain it to Dese.

"I need to speak with the Nity followers... I have a message for them."

"A message?" Deserts hand paused halfway to his mouth, a hunk of fresh bread hanging in mid air, "From Garatin?"

Fa shrugged, tight lipped. Rave supposed that was easier than trying to explain the whole thing.

Desert looked like he was fairly burning up with curiosity, but to his credit he didn't ask further. "The Nity followers are in the Pearl Square eh?" he popped the bread in his mouth and chewed thoughtfully.

Fa nodded, "Tomorrow night. Can you get us there?"

"Tomorrow night? - No problem! That means we're in no hurry!" he exhibited a carefreeness that cheered Rave a fair deal- but he could tell that Fa was still a bit on edge.

"The Pearl Square is in the 'Earls Ring'; I'll just have to get us pass the Sea gate, we can do that tomorrow."

"What do you mean 'get us pass'?" Fa asked carefully.

How like his sister to pick up on Desert's wording! Rave thought.

"All the city gates have guards posted," Desert explained with a shrug, "At the Sea gate they don't stop people from going through- unless you really look like trouble."

"Me and Fa don't exactly 'blend in' too well here" Rave pointed out, with the first of his own doubts.

It didn't seem to bother Dese, he shrugged again. "We'll be fine! – you'll see," he reassured.

Rave was put at ease and thought again how much better everything would be with Desert to help them!

*   *   *

The trio spent the rest of the afternoon and evening exploring the Harbour Ring at Desert's directions. He had shown them his favorite waterfront hideaway; on the most eastern side of the 'Harbour Ring' was a stretch of beach where small fishing boats were pulled up on the sand. They had sat in the sun-warmed sand and waded in the cool water for a time, enjoying the relative quiet.

Then Dese took them to the west side of the Harbour Ring, where they had secretly climbed to the top of a cargo barn and sat on the roof. From there they had a clear view of the cliff and could see the sea sparrows flying up and down, building nests. But better still they had a magnificent view of the waterfall that thundered down the cliff edge from heights above; the water turned to mist halfway, and a sparkling rainbow hovered near the top. Desert explained that it flowed from a lake in the cherry gardens, that was located in the Dukes Ring. Craning their necks, they could see an intimidating stone dragon's mouth at the top, where the water poured from its mouth like white fire.

After their day of exploration in the crowded Harbour Ring, the three returned, exhausted, to Vision's boarding house. Vision had showed them upstairs to a room with six beds, three down each wall. The idea of a shared room would have been strange to Fa and Rave, if they hadn't spent the past month and a half on a ship in close quarters to thirty-some other people. But they were pleased to find that they were the only ones staying that night in the boarding house.

Nudging the door shut behind them, Desert sniffed the air as he did a quick inspection of their room, nodding his approval he flopped down on the bed nearest to the door. Fa tested the bed next to the window, wondering how comfortable it would be compared to a hammock, then sat herself down on the window ledge. Yawning, Rave kicked his worn boots off, he left them abandoned at the foot of the middle bed, then followed Deserts example. The boys talked on and off about the events of the day and what tomorrow would bring, until Dese contentedly fell asleep.

In the twilight of the evening Fa sat on the window ledge, with the shutters open wide, the wind touching her face now and again. She had a view of several crooked streets, and beyond them, the sea shrouded in a gray haze. She sat watching until the Harbour Ring's buzzing activity faded into the constant throbbing of the sea on the shore.

She knew that the Dragon's Keep was behind her out of sight, atop its cliff, keeping watch over the city; the thought of it hung over her like a dark cloud.

Fa unwound her bandages and inspected her hands in the fading light; they were raw, and her skin was torn and blistered. Yellow liquid oozed from her burns constantly, crusting her bandages. Her palms were the worst and most painful- but she had found a way of bunching the bandages and holding her hands in loose fists, and that seemed to ease the pain the most. Several times that day she had grabbed hold of something too tightly and bitten back a cry of pain; she had gotten quite good at masking her discomfort. She couldn't stand the helpless look on Rave's face every time he saw her wince, so she didn't let him see her in pain. She had also noticed Desert's questioning and concerned looks throughout the day, but he hadn't said anything, and she was grateful to him for that.

Fate heard a sound behind her, looking sharply she saw that Rave had risen and was coming to stand by her, a glance behind him told her that Dese was still fast asleep.

"How are they?" Rave asked softly, looking at her hands.

"Sore," she replied, hoping he wouldn't guess just how sore.

"They wouldn't be so bad if only they could get a chance to heal," he said, with a touch of frustration.

"Don't worry; I won't be sleeping anytime soon," she said dryly.

Rave huffed in further frustration, and she knew that he very badly wished he could help her... but he couldn't.

"I just wish it would end..." she confessed quietly, she was so tired of being strong!

"Fa- we made it!" Rave said leaning closer to see her face. "We're in Tarva. We crossed the Neenor sea- we got here! All that's left, is for you to deliver the warning- then your job will be done! You'll have done what the heart stain required; we can go home."

His words caught her by surprise; could he be right? Had she been wrong about her doom?

"Home?" the word felt strange in her mouth- when had she spoken it last? She had given up hope of returning long ago.

"Yes Fa, *Home.* Back to Father and Mother- and Grandfather, just imagine their faces when they hear our story!"

The thought made Fa smile- an honest to goodness smile, "I guess your right; it is almost over."

*   *   *

Confess rolled her stiff shoulders as she approached the fourth Inn that morning, to be fair though, the sign said it was a boarding house, 'Visions boarding house'.

"How quaint," Fess mumbled, and wondered if the beds here were any nicer than where she had stayed.

Inside was a woman sweeping the floor.

"I'm looking for a young man, who may have stayed the night," Fess stated without fanfare.

"Well isn't that nice!" the woman mocked, in a sweet voice.

"His namesake is Desert," Fess persisted, her patience was nearly gone at this point. But her efforts were rewarded; the woman paused just long enough for Fess to notice.

"Can't say as it sounds familiar," the woman lied.

Fess opened her mouth, but a harsh voice spoke from the doorway.

"I heard that you were about, Fess, and I decided to pay you a visit."

Fess tensed as she turned to see Endure blocking the doorway with his two henchmen. That's the trouble with looking for someone; it calls attention to oneself.

"Have you forgotten pet? You can't hide things from me for long."

"Have *you* forgotten that I don't respond well to intimidation?" Fess glared back, glad to see that her sudden venom took the henchmen by surprise, but not Endure, he knew her too well.

"Whatever business you have- take it elsewhere!" the woman ordered and brandished her broom as if a pack of hissing cats had wandered inside.

"Go do your gardening, woman," one of the thugs said, as he firmly shut the street door behind them, "This will be unpleasant to watch."

The woman grunted in anger, but retreated none the less, leaving Fess alone with her enemy.

"My men told me an interesting story this morning- maybe you know it Fess? It's about Captain Devotion and his ship 'The Prestige'," Endure said in his patronizing voice, as he sat down on the steps to the next floor.

Fess watched his men carefully as they split up, going to each side of her, she maneuvered herself smoothly so that her back was against the kitchen wall. The thugs were now forced to circle a table to get to her, they paused halfway, waiting for Endure to give the word.

But Endure liked to watch people squirm, "The story goes like this; that gambling coward of a captain let himself die of sea-fever, then his cheap excuse of a wife lost his ship and all the cargo in a storm off the coast of Chresacroon. And I find myself three hundred gold coins short."

"That's funny," Fess said without humour, "I find that I'm a bit short on money too." She refused to let herself feel the pang of grief at the mention of her husband.

"Fess!" Endure growled with an evil grin, "Is that defiance I see? I think I'll have to teach you again who I am. Do you remember how the lesson starts?" he nodded to his men. They grinned and came closer; they thought beating up a woman would be fun!

Fess rolled her shoulders back; there was a time when she would have cowered in fear of Endure's 'lessons', but that's when she had been a child, defenceless against Endure's cruelties- not so anymore!

Fess lashed out quickly, kicking a chair into the approaching thug on her left. Without pausing to watch the man stumble, she vaulted the table, scattering dishes, and landed between the second thug and Endure. Catching up another chair, she threw it at Endure as he jumped to his feet; it caught him full in the face and he fell back onto the stairs. Fess turned to the second thug; he threw a glancing blow that caught her on the side of her head. Wheeling away she delivered two quick jabs to his side, he yelped in pain and doubled over.

Confess found herself being grabbed from behind by Endure, she kicked and pushed back against the table, but he had her by her right arm and was wrenching it up behind her back. Holding back a scream, Fess was forced to her knees.

"That's it pet," he hissed behind her. "Come here!" he ordered. The first thug came, who had recovered from the thrown chair, but the second Tarven, was still on the floor- she must have gotten him good!

The first thug flexed his hands as he rounded the table towards her, Fess tried to stand but the pain was too much- soon she would be beaten past consciousness!

Not today.

Clenching her teeth, Fess screamed in rage and pain as she stood to her feet in a tremendous show of strength. She threw her body forward, the movement forcing her shoulder to dislocate with a sickening pop!

Endure was startled to find himself holding onto a limp arm, and he let go before he could stop himself. Without slowing her momentum, Fess charged forward and headbutted the first thug in the stomach as he came at her, he stumbled back and gasped for air. Knowing that Endure had come up behind her, Fess spun round- and caught his fist directly on her nose.

Snap!

Fess stepped back as blood dripped from her broken nose and stars danced across her vision, she tripped over backwards on the thug she had head butted. Fess fell and landed on her back, she gasped in pain from her dislocated shoulder, but managed to push herself with a kick and slide a few feet away from her attackers on the smooth floor planks.

Endure straightened and shook-out his hand that he had hit her with, "Get up!" he roared at his two henchmen who were practically rolling on the floor.

While he dragged them to their feet, Fess brought her knees up to her chest and carefully moved her limp arm till it was between her knees. Although it was limp and tingling, she managed to grab her boot and grip it tight. Coughing on the blood from her nose, Fess clenched her teeth for the next part; twisting her body suddenly, she pushed away with her feet- pulling her limp arm with them. A scream escaped her as her shoulder popped back into place. Gasping for breath, she knew that Endure and his thugs would be on her any second. Looking she saw that one thug, the one she had headbutted, was still on the floor, while Endure had dragged the second to his feet and they were now approaching her.

Thinking fast, Fess shifted so that her head and shoulders were under the table behind her, she could see Endure sending his thug ahead of him. Waiting a moment, Fess braced herself and rocked back, catching her legs under the table, then she heaved with all her might, sending the table flying. It struck the thug with a crash, and he fell with it landing on both him and the other Tarven on the floor. Endure dodged and jumped over the obstacle, pouncing on her like a maddened dog. He landed on his knees in front of her and reached for her throat, by his eyes she knew that he intended to choke her until all fight forever left her. But if she had learned anything from his 'lessons' it was to survive.

She grabbed his right wrist with both hands, threw her legs up, struggling until she could get a leg up over his head. From that position, Fess pushed his head to one side until he loosened his grip on her neck, but she didn't let go of his wrist- she twisted it until he gasped in pain. He grasped at her leg with his free hand trying to free himself from her lock. She twisted his wrist and pressed on his neck, forcing him further to the ground, until his face was pressed against the floor.

Fess paused for a moment, glancing back up at his two thugs- they didn't seem anxious to help Endure. She cleared her throat before speaking close to Endures ear, "I'm not your 'pet' anymore." The blood from her nose gurgled in her throat, "I will honor my husband's debts when I am able." He grunted and Fess twisted his wrist even more till he grew perfectly still.

"So, you tell your filthy friends and the rest of my husband's old 'partners', that he may be dead; but I am far from the helpless child you remember. You can tell them that *I*, Confess, did this to you."

She released him and kicked him away from herself. Endure stumbled to his feet and cradled his arm, his two thugs shuffled out the door, and he followed, but he paused at the door, "Watch for me Fess; I'll be back!" he spat at her.

Fess picked up a wooden spoon that had fell to the floor, and whipped it at him, he ducked and it hit the door frame. She heard him running as the spoon clattered to the floor.

Fess squeezed her eyes shut and allowed herself a cry of pain and anger. When she had been but a child, this was not at all what she had imagined her life to be; her husband, the only man who had ever cared enough to pretend to love her, dead. Her entire livelihood, destroyed. Old enemies lurking the streets like sharks smelling blood. And if she couldn't find Desert, then she would have someone far worse to worry about.

Chapter 16   The Dukes Gate

Brave opened his mouth for a great big yawn, Desert playfully cuffed him on the shoulder, "One night on land and you're already a lazy mess!" Dese teased.

"Why'd we have to leave so early?" Rave complained as he stifled a second yawn. Dese had woken Rave and his sister up with the dawn, his enthusiasm for the day spilling out into a great big grin- he had jumped on top of Rave and pushed him off his bed- much to his own amusement. They had wolfed down a breakfast that Dese had somehow paid for (Rave didn't know where he had gotten money). Then Vision had shooed them on their way before the boys had even finished shoving food in their mouths. It was long before Confess got to Vision's boarding house that the threesome had started out towards the Sea Gate.

"We got a big day ahead of us," Dese explained elusively. "We've got the whole of the Earls Ring to explore before meeting the Nity followers at the Pearl Square. Just wait until you see the fountains! You know, Tarva is famous for its fountains."

"Our day will be much shorter if we can't get pass the gate," Fate pointed out, as they turned onto the main street; the Sea gate stood before them. The gate was wide and tall, with the tip of the portcullis poking out from the top like teeth from an open mouth. Over ten city guards with pikes stood around watching the crowd of people who were passing through the gate from both sides.

"Rave calm down!" Dese warned and grabbed the Garatins arm to slow his pace, "They'll only stop us if we look suspicious." He set a confident stride to hide his own misgivings. There were more soldiers on duty than he remembered there ever being. Had he been away long enough for something like that to change? Had there been a riot of some kind?

Melting into the crowd, Dese made sure that the siblings stuck close by him, and he winced inwardly at how much their pale faces and light-hair stood out amongst the crowd of dark skinned, raven-haired Tarvens.

Dese directed them to the center of the gate- furthest from the guards, and as they passed under the gate, Dese saw one of the guards watching them. Dese boldly made eye contact and offered a disarming smile, the soldier looked away. Breathing in relief, Dese led the way out into the main street of the Earls Ring, leaving the Harbour Ring behind them.

Ahead of them was another market; this one was circular in shape, and had red flags fluttering from poles; it looked cleaner and calmer than the one in the Harbour Ring.

As the three of them stopped before the market, Rave jumped up onto a crate to get a better view, "Where to now?" he asked with bright eyes.

Fate pulled him down from the crate with a smirk when someone came to collect it.

"I got a few ideas," Desert said, glancing behind them to the gate. He pressed his lips together in dismay; the guard who had been watching them was searching the crowd, looking for them. Dese narrowed his eyes and craned his neck to see better, when he saw the guard studying a paper posted on the gate wall.

"Oh, that's low," Dese mumbled, as he realized what the paper must be; a wanted poster.

"What?" Fa asked as people pressed around them.

"Nothing- lets start the tour of the Earls Ring, shall we?" he smiled cheerfully and turned away from the gate.

        *   *   *

Cascading, bubbling and shimmering in the morning light, the famous fountains of Tarva did not disappoint! Half a dozen streams of clear water meandered through the Earls Ring, directed this way and that in stone canals built into the streets. Swiftly flowing down hills and steps, flashing tiny rainbows in the sun, the water would then pool in wide shallow basins or ripple over smooth slanted slabs. Sometimes the streams would disappear into underground tunnels only to shoot up a few feet away and splash the cobblestones. In some places, moss and other green slime made the waterways slick, but Fa thought that the green colour only added to the beauty.

In some places, the water would gather in troughs for passing horses, and children could be seen wetting their feet in the streams. After winding through the streets, the little streams ran to the inner wall and disappeared through grates to join the great waterfall on the far side, the thunder of it could always be heard now.

Fate had noticed even before leaving the Harbour Ring that the streets had begun to slant upwards as the city began to climb around the side of the cliff. The slope was so great in the Earls Ring that the city was built in shelves, each manor and house a little higher than the last. Fa also noticed that behind them, a view of the harbour was opening up, and beyond that; the sparkling Neenor. And above them to their left, higher still, was always the great castle, the Dragon keep, shrouded in the mist of the waterfall.

Desert had led them on a tour of the lower reaches of the Earls Ring until noon, when they had climbed higher to where the fountains were numerous and most spectacular. After feasting their eyes on the sight, the three friends had sat down on the edge of a large stone basin, from which the water flowed out into a stream from a drain. Under the inch of water, Fa could see the common design of a dragon in the stone, and on the far side of the basin two children were cupping the water in their hands and splashing each other.

Fa took note of how different the atmosphere was compared to the Harbour Ring; instead of grungy and loud, the Earls Ring hummed pleasantly with activity, backdropped by the waterfall's thunder. The streets were cleaner and there were no thatch roofs, only flat stone roofs on large houses and walled in manors of all sizes.

The three friends were munching on spice rolls that Dese had gotten from a bakery, the golden-brown bread was rich, and they savored the taste. Fate wasn't sure how Dese had paid for the bread, and in the back of her mind she wondered if he had stolen it. She didn't take the thought seriously enough to be concerned though. But she did see the irony of it; in his younger years, her father had stolen food every day. Fa wasn't sure how she felt about comparing Dese to her father, so she placed the thought to one side to ponder later.

Fate smiled slyly to herself when she saw Brave's head turn to watch as two young maidens walked by, 'poor Rave' she thought without sympathy, 'traveled halfway across the world and still hasn't met any young maidens!' This new thought startled her a bit; Rave was growing up! There he sat, his boots worn and growing holes in the soles, his chest and shoulders widening, and she had noticed that his voice squeaked less and was growing deeper… 'how long have we been away?' she wondered sadly.

She let her eyes wander and her mind be distracted by all the strange new sights all around them, from the fountains to the tasty spice roll in her hand, to the spiral towers and busy streets, everything was new to her! She nearly forgot to eat, she was so overwhelmed by it all.

"Is it anything like Garason?" Desert asked sliding closer beside her, Rave was now absorbed in eating and didn't pay them any attention.

"Oh… um…" Fa laughed nervously and looked around again. Dese had heard a very shortened version of their journeys, and she wondered how much more she should tell him. "We didn't really see that much of Garason when we were there."

Dese took a bite from his roll and waited for her to say more.

"We were kind of kidnapped before we saw much of anything," she stumbled on.

"Kidnapped by the slavers?" Dese asked- he thought he had it all figured out!

"No, that came later. We got mixed up with some rebels first, then I fainted… so I don't remember a whole lot of the city."

Dese laughed, "It's just been one adventure after another for you two, hasn't it?!"

Fa laughed sarcastically, "Yeah, adventure!" If she had of looked just then, she would have seen that Desert was watching her with all the attentiveness of an artist!

"Is that when your dreams started?"

Deserts question caught Fa off guard; this was the first he had asked her about her dreams.

"No… the dreams came before Garason. They started when Eamer…" the name stuck in her mouth, so she tried again, "When our home burned." Fa was shocked to find how raw her emotions were when she spoke the name of their lost home. 'that was nearly three months ago!' she realized.

"I lost my home too," Deserts voice took on a seriousness that it didn't often have.

Fa realized that he was about to share something personal with her, and she watched him closely, feeling a new sense of comradery with the Tarven.

"Only, not in the same way," Dese gazed down at his hands and his face turned sad, "My father was a serf, he died shortly after I was born. When the villagers realized that I was cursed, they declared me a lost orphan."

"What's that?" Fa asked, hating herself for interrupting his story.

"It's like an old tradition, to protect the village from the cursed child; they disowned me and my mother and divided our possessions among them."

"That's awful!" Fa breathed, the unjustness of the whole thing made her angry.

156

"My mother and I were thrown out, and we weren't permitted to rejoin the community until I proved that my curse was lifted."

"Have you?"

Dese actually laughed, "No, I guess not! But people in the city don't care about the 'lost orphan curse'."

He smiled easily again, like it was all a joke, but Fa saw through his mask. Who would have thought that such a beautiful city could hold such ugliness? Or that such a carefree person could hide such... sorrow.

Dese continued, serious once again, as if he wanted to get the whole conversation over with, "My mother died when I was young, more of the curse no doubt. And that's how I lost my home- but I've been alright, and I'm sure that you'll get your home back some day."

The thought warmed her, reminding her of Rave's words the night before, but something Dese had said was nagging at her, "You don't really think that you are cursed... do you?"

Desert smiled and shrugged, "Nah; of course not!" he glanced deviously at her out of the corner of his dark eyes, "Not unless you've put a spell on me."

It took Fa a moment to switch from serious to jesting, "Oh, because I'm a witch- right?" Fa shook her head with a smile and looked away, "And what 'spell' would I cast on you?"

"What do you think?"

Before Fa could look and see the glimmer of something new in Deserts eyes that betrayed his teasing for something more, Rave stood up and spoke.

"When do you think the Eternity rebels will be at the Pearl Square?" he asked Dese.

Fa looked to Dese for the answer and realized how intense his gaze on her was. But she didn't allow herself to blush or look away, but met his gaze head-on, refusing to show her emotions.

"Don't call them 'Eternity rebels' Rave," Dese said smoothly as he returned Fa's gaze evenly, "That's what the outlaws call themselves. The *Nity followers* will be at the square just before sundown, after the day's work is over. We got lots of time to see the rest of the Earls Ring."

Breaking their gaze Dese shoved the last of his bread in his mouth and stood up, telling them where he would take them next. As he talked, Rave accidently stepped in the nearby waterway. Dese laughed as Rave shook his boot of water and complained that his foot was soaked.

Fate sat watching, thinking of the glimmer she had seen in Desert's eye, 'when did that start!?' she wondered, 'and what will I do about it?'

*   *   *

Rustling mopped his forehead with a new hanky and tucked it away inside his tunic as he made his way through the stone halls of the garrison in the Kings Ring.

He had done it! He had delivered the nine prisoners to Tarva, against all odds; he had dealt with reluctant sea captains, unsure passage, he had braved storm and shipwreck. And after all that, all he got was a curt nod from the captain of the guard, and a few pats on the back when the other soldiers heard his harrowing story. For some reason, Rust had expected a little more after all he had been through.

Some men would have gone straight home, told of their bravery to their family and kicked back next to a warm fire- but not Rust; he dreaded returning home to his little manor in the Earls Ring. He had been away for three years, and in that time, he had received only two letters from home. A letter from his sister telling him that she had had another child, and a letter from his mother informing him that his aged father had passed on. But Rust did not mind the minimal contact, he had enjoyed it! During his three years in Garason he had lived in garrisons with other soldiers, and had found that he much preferred that, to living in a manor, and seeing to mundane household chores. And now that his father had passed, the responsibility of the family manor would fall completely to him- a burden he most certainly did not want.

He had been in Tarva for nearly two days and one night, and still he had not gone home, yet he now thought that even going home to face his mother would be preferable to his current task.

Upon delivering the other prisoners, Rust had self-appointed himself to see to Horizon's needs. He felt that he owed the Garatin something, if it hadn't been for Rizon, then who knows what would have become of them in that storm?

But the news that Rustling had for Rizon, made Rust wish he had gone home the night before. He had a feeling that the fiery-heart and ice-gazed man would not take the news well. Still, Rust supposed that it was best

158

if *he* told Rizon the news, then he might be able to stop him from doing anything rash.

'I'll start with the not-so-bad news,' he decided with a touch of irony, for what else could he do; there wasn't any good news to share.

Horizon had spent the night in a private room in the soldiers' garrison, under guard (even though he insisted that it wasn't necessary) and he now sat on a bench in the hall, his gaze was fixed on a patch of blue sky through a small window; he was waiting for news on his future.

"Well?" Rizon asked with a warm smile when he saw Rust coming, "What is my fate to be?" he was making light of what he surely knew was a bleak future.

Rust absent mindedly took out his hanky and worried it till it was a knot of wrinkles, "As you predicted, your audience with the King will not be for some time yet, the captain of the guard thinks it could be as long as a year before the King will grant you a trial. Until such time as you are granted an audience, you will be assigned a guard, and forbidden to leave the city walls, you will be permitted to acquire land or a house within the city limits." Here Rust paused, that was all he was required to tell the prisoner- but he knew that he owed him more.

"Be warned though, there is a heavy tax on any foreigners who own property in Tarva, if you are not careful, you could end up working as a slave to pay off debts until your trial."

Horizon nodded his thanks for the warning and smiled confidently, "I have many friends who will welcome me into their homes and look after my needs- have no fear, and the time waiting will afford me the chance to finish my work. You should believe by now that no harm can come to me before I see the King."

Rustling marveled at the man, "I think I am beginning to believe you; either Eloi is real, or you lead a charmed life!"

Rizon gave him a knowing smile as if celebrating an early victory at winning Rust over, and Rust was content to say nothing more on the topic. Rust took a deep breath; It was time for the bad news, "As for meeting the Nity followers in the Pearl Square this evening- I think it best that you don't. They... aren't the friends you mentioned... are they?"

Rizon stood, turning very serious. He fixed his icy blue eyes on Rust, "What's happened?" he demanded to know.

Rust winced, "I've been told that the Nity followers will all be arrested at the Pearl Square tonight."

"What!? Why? There are no laws in Tarva against them!"

Rust couldn't meet his friend's gaze anymore, "The King has just recently passed a new law, it's being made official tonight," Rust explained delicately, "It states that the Nity followers are not permitted to meet in public, and anyone who has information on meetings, past or future, are being called to come forth and name any, and all participants."

Rizon was still- very still.

"If you went to the Pearl Square tonight, you would be arrested with all the others, and that would jeopardise your... 'work'." Rust forced himself to look back at Rizon's face.

"The law hasn't been made public yet?" Rizon didn't seem to have heard the last part, "You mean that tonight is a trap for the Nity followers? I must warn them." Rizon stepped past Rust, his face full of determination.

Rust felt his face heat up and his heart rate increase, the words he spoke didn't seem to come from him at all! "I can't let you go Horizon."

Rizon paused and looked back at him, and Rust felt that he would burn-up from the Garatin's gaze- but Rust refused to back down; he was doing this for Rizon's own good. "I shouldn't have told you at all- I knew you would react this way. I am a soldier Rizon! I *can not* allow you to warn them. And I will guard you all night to make sure that you don't, if that is what I must do."

Horizon was silent for a moment as if trying to will Rust to change his mind. "What punishment is there for breaking this new law?" Rizon asked at last.

"I don't know." It was a half-truth; Rust had heard that the Nity followers would spend weeks- maybe months in jail, before the King would pass judgment on them- and there was no word on how harsh that judgment would be. "Please forgive me for this Rizon, but I am doing it for your own good."

"It's not my future that I am concerned for!" Rizon said with an edge of trepidation, "Among others- I sent the maiden Fate to the Pearl square!"

*   *   *

The Pearl Square was a few streets away from the main city street and was near to the outer wall, the square was circular in shape and dipped down like a crater. Stone benches were built into the steps that led down to the center, where an O-shaped bench was placed so that people could sit and address the crowd. Around the perimeter of the Pearl Square were canopies of yellow dyed cotton, that cast a ring of shadow for those who did not wish to sit closer. It was the perfect place for celebrations, city proclamations, or a gypsy show.

Brave, Fa and Dese arrived at the Pearl Square as the setting sunlight was flooding the area with golden rays. They sat down under the canopies and waited for the Nity followers to arrive.

Throughout that day, Rave may have missed the glimmer in Desert's eyes whenever he looked at Fa, but Rave hadn't missed how light-hearted and happy Fa was. As they sat side by side waiting, Rave felt content; his words of comfort the night before had gotten through to Fa, he wasn't totally useless! Fate was on the mend; their journey was almost done. When the Nity followers arrived, Fa would deliver the warning of the storm. Perhaps then, he, Fa and Dese would help them escape the city. And then… he and his sister would go home; free of the heart stain. Maybe they would even drop by Freedom in Cinders Grove on their way by- wouldn't she be surprised!

Rave was a little concerned with how they would find their parents; surely, they wouldn't be in the same place after all this time! Rave pushed the troubling thought aside to deal with later, and instead thought of Desert; what if Desert were to come with them?! 'He has no family,' Rave reasoned, 'and he wants to see the world!' it was perfect! Rave was about to suggest his idea when Fa stood up; it was dusk, and for the past few minutes people had been gathering on the steps below. Now there were about two dozen Tarvens sitting in the square, and another handful across the square standing about greeting one another.

Desert began to say something, afterwards Rave could never remember what it was that Dese said, for it was at that moment when the shouting began. A young Tarven man came running up to the group across from Rave and the others, he was pointing behind him and shouting franticly. Down on the steps the Tarvens stood up to see what the commotion was about.

"SOLDIERS!" the man shouted in a breathless warning, that came too late.

Soldiers poured out from where they had been hiding in side-streets, and converged on the Pearl Square, and the scene erupted in chaos.

*   *   *

Fate stood in shock as the Nity followers began running in every direction, trying to escape the Pearl Square, while the soldiers gave chase.

Desert jumped to his feet, "Come on- RUN!!" he said backing away.

Rave scrambled to his feet and looked around franticly; the soldiers hadn't seen them yet- but they soon would!

"There- go there!" Dese pushed them towards the closest street.

Before running, Fa chanced a glance behind them; the soldiers had caught nearly half of the crowd, throwing some to the ground and rounding up others.

Rave led the way as they picked-up speed and darted down an empty street dark with evening shadows. Halfway down the street Rave glanced over his shoulder past Fa and skidded to a stop. Fa looked too; Desert remained at the street entrance, watching the square.

"Desert!" Fa hissed, "Come on!" her fear was mounting with every second; to be arrested seemed to fit all too well with their other 'adventures'.

Desert hesitated a moment then turned to them, "Keep going!" he urged and ran to them. Fa didn't need anymore prompting, as soon as she saw that Dese was coming, she took the lead in a headlong run, and chose a number of small streets that zigzagged away from the Pearl Square. They ran until the noise of the soldiers died away, and their breath was ragged.

Reaching a wall ahead of the boys, Fa sagged against it and heaved in air, she peered pass the wall into a large street of the Earls Ring; it was silent. It was as if the neighborhood had sensed the soldiers and gone indoors, shutting windows and blowing out candles.

The boys reached her side, panting and looking behind them to make sure they hadn't been followed.

"What was that about!?" Rave gasped after a moment, Fa looked to Dese, fearing that she knew the answer.

Desert leaned against the wall and covered his face with both hands as if his head ached, "I don't understand…" he whispered- he was clearly shaken, "When I left the Nity followers were free to do as they wished- but those soldiers, I heard them; they were arresting them because they were meeting in public!" he turned away, running his hands through his raven hair- and the siblings saw him for the first time, at the end of his rope.

"Where will we go?" Fa breathed as she realized that, once again, her hopes had been scattered like seeds in a field, ready to grow a harvest of fear and doubt.

"We can sleep out here- tucked away somewhere… can't we?" Rave suggested, trying to be strong for the others, but Dese turned back to them and shook his head gravely; he seemed to have gotten over his shock and dismay.

"The curfew guards will be out soon- they'd find us, and instantly connect you two with the Nity followers. We *have* to hide somewhere- preferably somewhere outside of the Earls Ring."

"What about the gates? Don't they close soon?" Fa pointed out.

"I can get us past them," Dese said confidently.

Fa wondered how he planned to get them pass guarded *and* closed gates- but at that moment she would have trusted him with anything.

"Ready?" Dese asked after a moment.

Fa pushed off the wall and cast Rave a concerned look through the thickening darkness; he was giving her the same kind of look. They both nodded.

Brave turned and started walking back the way they had come, south towards the Harbour gate- but Dese had turned north and started to carefully cross the street. Neither of them noticed the other's direction. For a moment, Fa wasn't sure who to follow, and stood looking back and forth like a lost child.

"Desert!" she called softly.

Halfway across the deserted street, Dese paused and looked back at her, Rave did the same.

"This way!" Dese waved.

Feeling a little embarrassed, Fa sprinted to his side, but Rave didn't move.

"The Harbour Gate is this way!" Rave said, dangerously loud, and hooked his thumb over his shoulder.

"We're not going back th-" Dese cut his words short abruptly when a pair of curfew guards on their horses turned a corner onto the street, they were walking slowly and hadn't seen the two youths through the gloom- yet.

Desert clutched Fa's arm and pulled her back, shrinking into the shadows on the opposite side of the street from Rave! Rave panicked and darted up to the edge of the street, barely remaining hidden.

"Stay there!" Dese hissed and waved his arm to emphasize.

The approaching guards heard the hiss and stopped just before the hiders and looked around. Dese and Fa silently shrunk back, Rave mirroring them on his side of the street.

"It's an early curfew tonight," one of the guards announced into the night, "Go back to your homes!" he barked. The other guard searched the darkened streets- his eyes halting uncertainly on Dese and Fa's hiding place.

It was involuntary- Fa couldn't stop herself; when the guard's eyes paused, even though he still couldn't see them clearly- she flinched, as if to run away.

The guards' eyes caught the movement, "HALT!" he ordered and tugged his horse towards them.

Fa bolted away down the street- with Dese on her heels, leaving Rave to shrink further back.

The clatter of horse hooves was bearing down on them as Fa and Dese ran into the shadows, their hearts pounding. Up ahead the street dead-ended in a short wall, a garden lay behind it, and another street beyond- if they could just get over the wall, they could escape!

They reached the wall- but the guards were right behind them. Fa and Dese pressed themselves against the wall as the guard's horses reared up into a halt- much too close for comfort.

Before anything else could happen, Dese lifted both hands to his mouth and took a deep breath; his shrill whistle split the night. As if on cue- as if they had been trained to respond in just such a way- the horses reared up and brayed, their riders were completely unprepared and struggled to stay astride.

Fa and Dese didn't hesitate, they turned and heaved themselves onto the wall, Fa risked a moment to look back- but Brave was gone. Fa dropped into the garden, trampling spring growth, Dese dropped down beside her and they scrambled across the garden rows to the opposite wall. Dese gave Fa a leg up and she rolled over the wall and dropped to the empty street on the other side. Jumping up after her, Dese paused on top of the wall just long enough to flash a cheeky smile at the guards who could do nothing but watch as their quarry escaped.

Dropping down beside her, Dese led the way as they darted down dark street after dark street, the light had completely gone, and Fa had lost track of how far they had gone. Twice more they narrowly missed running headlong into more curfew guards, but Dese seemed to know what he was doing, and Fa managed not to give themselves away again.

At last Desert led Fa to the inner wall of the city, on the far side was the Cherry Lake and gardens, the waterfall's roar filled the night and masked their heavy breathing. They stopped in what looked like an old unused square, a fountain sat in the center, but the water that had once gushed from it was long gone. The square was closed in on three sides and lay deep in shadow from the walls around it.

"I'm going to leave you here while I find Brave… alright?" Dese asked after he had given the square one look over. Fa looked about nervously; she didn't want to be left alone- but she knew that Dese could look faster without her.

"I'll be alright," Fa nodded, trying to sound confident.

Dese looked like he only half believed her. "Stay in the back corner there… I'll be back soon with Rave." He hesitated one last time before darting away.

Watching him go, Fa backed into the darkest corner and lowered herself down against the inner wall. Hugging her knees to her chest, Fa took a deep breath- had she been holding her breath again!? 'Not good' she scolded herself, fainting was about the only thing that could make this night worse! The night closed in around her and in the emptiness a nagging fear pounced on her, suggesting that Dese would not return, that he would slip away into the night, saving his own skin. But she quickly battled the fear with the fact that Dese had been a solid and good friend; there was no chance he would abandon her!

She made an effort to steady her breathing and closed her eyes. Lifting her head back to rest against the wall, Fa opened her eyes- and blinked in surprise as something soft brushed her face. Looking down she saw something on her knee; picking it up Fa squinted her eyes through the dark to see what it was.

It was a cherry blossom petal. Fate's heart thudded as she looked up in horror; a branch of a cherry tree was hanging over the wall above her, and it was in full bloom…

In a flash, images of her dreams filled her mind; the city of Tarva, pink with cherry trees. Freedom's voice played in her ears, "You must hurry' the woman said, and you must, for cherry tree's bloom in the spring, and winter will soon come to the Neenor…'

A night wind stirred the tree above her, and more petals drifted down onto her.

"I'm too late…"

*   *   *

Braves' legs wouldn't stop shaking and his ears were filled with the sound of his pounding heart trying to breakout of his chest. He crouched in the shadow of a manor wall and watched the Dukes Gate; the portcullis had been lowered early and guards were patrolling both sides with blazing torches that made Rave shrink back further.

Rave searched the surrounding streets with his panicked blue eyes, but he could find no sign of Desert or his sister.

'She's safe with him' he tried to console himself, 'but what if they were caught!?'

After the guards had seen Fa and Dese, Rave had retreated, keeping himself from sight, as soon as he saw Dese and Fa escape, Rave had turned and ran. He had gotten a little lost but had eventually found his way to the main street with its babbling fountains and waterways. Staying in the shadows, and only once glimpsing more curfew guards, Rave followed the street upward till he reached the Dukes Gate. He had decided that that was the best place to find the others again- but they weren't there!

Rave would never forgive himself if Fa was arrested!

"Rave!"

Rave looked back down the main street to where the whisper had come from; Desert was poking his head out from behind a wall. With a sigh of relief and a cautious glance at the guards, Rave darted to Desert's side.

"Where's Fate!?" Rave asked, his stomach twisting inside him.

"Don't worry! I left her in a safe place- come on." They glided along softly away from the gate.

"The portcullis- how will you get us past?" Rave asked grabbing Deserts arm to slow him down.

"Leave that to me," Dese replied.

Chapter 17   The Grand Duke

"*How* will you get us past the Dukes gate?" Brave asked again as he and Fate followed Desert through the dark streets, going parallel with the inner wall, "And shouldn't we go back to the Harbour Ring anyway?"

"Trust me, I know what I'm doing- and keep your voice down!" Dese warned and cast a wary look about. The waterfall was now too far away to properly mask their voices.

"But how will you get us past the gate?" Rave repeated in a much quieter voice.

"The inner wall wasn't built as a line of defence," Dese spoke in hushed tones, seemingly ignoring his question, "It was designed solely to separate the common folk from the nobility."

Fa, who followed last, was having a hard time focusing on anything but the blooming trees, and her own despair.

"Years ago, I found a place where you can climb the wall without being seen by the gate guards." Desert stopped as the alley they were going down dead-ended; in front of them was the inner wall, to their left was a much lower wall of a manor, and on their right, was the Dukes wall.

Fate looked up at the Dukes wall; it was four and a half times her height. How were they going to climb THAT!?

"There's a place to put your foot right... here." Dese touched a stone that jutted out a bit from the rest, "You have to get your right foot on it, other wise you won't be able to get your left foot on the next hold. Now, see how the inner wall bumps out a little? You gotta brace your back against it and push up as you climb." Dese demonstrated by climbing halfway up, pointing out foot holds as he went- he made it look easy!

"Look out for this hole here," Dese fitted his fingers into a hold near the top and shimmied up further, until he could reach the top with his hands. Before pulling himself completely up, he peeked over the edge. Then he heaved himself up and lay face down on top of the wall, "Alright Fa, you come next- can you manage with your hands?" he asked, as if just remembering.

Fa smoothed down her bandages and nodded. She had a bit of trouble at first and Rave had to give her a leg up, but soon enough, Dese was reaching down to help her up beside him. His grip on her wrist made her grit her teeth in pain, but she didn't say anything.

Once on top, Fa had a view of most of the Earls Ring, since it all sloped down from that point. Further along the wall, Fa knew the guards would be watching the gate, but it was too dark to see that far. Fa paused in surprise when she surveyed the other side of the wall; she had expected to see the cherry garden, but instead she found herself looking into the private courtyard of a grand manor, who's wall jutted out into the gardens themselves.

'We'll have to crawl along the wall back south to get into the gardens,' Fa realized, she thought that would be a little risky- just what was Desert's plan?

After a four-foot gap from the wall, there was the thatched roof of the manors stable, Fa looked but she didn't see anyone about in the courtyard.

When Rave was atop the wall beside Fa, Dese raised himself up to a crouching position and checked once more to make sure that they were still unnoticed.

"We're going in there?" Fa asked uncertainly when she saw where Dese was looking.

"That's right, I've done it lots. There's a place to hide in the loft of the stable; we'll be safe there." Dese pointed to the thatched roof, "Now, we have to land in that spot, there's a supporting beam underneath- anywhere else and you'll fall through and wake someone. Watch me." Dese gathered himself up and jumped, clearing the gap, he landed on the thatch roof with a soft thud. Steadying himself with his hands, he stepped aside a little to allow room and turned back to Fa and Rave.

"Alright Fa, jump exactly where I did." Dese instructed in a hushed tone.

Fa nodded and raised herself up to her feet, judging the distance she prepared to jump. But with an abruptness that shocked Fa cold, a memory filled her sight, so much so that she could taste the smoke again.

She was standing on top of her trunk with her father and brother looking down at the ground, with the hungry crackle of flames behind them.

'Quick now!' Fa's father placed a hand to her back. Fa didn't hesitate further, stepping out, Fa stretched her arms out as if hoping to grow wings and leave this waking nightmare far behind her, she jumped.

And her hands burned.

Rave jumped up and grabbed her arm to keep her from falling off the wall as she teetered precariously.

"Easy- Careful!" Dese reached out as if he could steady her from where he stood.

Fa gasped for breath, "I'm alright!" she assured them. After a moment Fa jumped, but she came up a little short, her right heel going through the thatch with a crunch. She lost her balance and teetered backwards, Dese caught hold of her just in time, saving her from falling through the gap. He searched her face, as if trying to understand what had distracted her. She returned his gaze; did he guess how close to breaking she was?

When they were all safely on the roof, and no one had been awoken, Dese pulled back a patch of thatch big enough to drop through. Below they could see the loft, piled high with dry, inviting hay. One by one they dropped below, landing with a soft rustle.

Fa's nose tickled with the scent of horses- she had forgotten how she missed the smell, it had been so long since she had ridden- were her parents taking care of her horse in her absence?

Dese put a finger to his lips. "There'll be stable boys sleeping below," he warned in a whisper.

Fa looked but they were completely surrounded by hay (was this hideout made by Dese in the past?). A shaft of dull starlight, from the gap they had come through, made it just barely possible to see each other's face.

"What do we do now?" Rave whispered as Dese sat back in the hay wearily.

"We'll be safe here tonight," Dese sighed.

"And tomorrow?" Fa couldn't see what they could do after what had happened in the Pearl Square.

"We'll figure that out then," Dese covered his face as if trying to hide from their situation.

"We'll find more Nity followers- they can't all have been arrested today!" Rave said optimistically, "You can still deliver the warning."

Fa nodded, glad that the darkness hid her downcast face; she found no comfort in his words. She had failed; arrived in Tarva too late...

Rave didn't pick up on Fa's behavior and lay back in the hay, "What a day!" he breathed.

Dese lay back as well and shut his eyes wearily. "Welcome home," he whispered.

Crouched in the pale shaft of light, Fate watched as the boys drifted off into an exhausted, peaceful sleep, leaving her alone with her thoughts. For she couldn't sleep here- not now! Looking around Fa could only imagine how quickly a fire would spread in the hayloft, and the smoke would creep down her lungs...

With a spike of anxiety, Fa banished the thought before it could fully form; there would be no sleep for her- even if she desperately wished she could, she knew that as soon as she did, she would have another dream, her burns would grow, and the Dream Child...

But staying awake no longer kept the child and the 'thing' at bay! Fa apprehensively unwound her bandages and peered at her hands in the pale light; the burns had definitely grown. Her heart stain had grown while she had been wide awake!

Fa bit her lip and held tears back, 'What am I to do!?' she questioned- but there was no answer. 'It's all wrong!' she thought in frustration, the Nity followers had been arrested for merely meeting in public!

'They couldn't have been the Nity followers!' the thought gave Fa pause, 'at least not the ones I was meant to warn! The Dream Child had said to warn *my people*, but there wasn't any Garatins in the Pearl Square- only Tarvens. Fa tried to think it through with a sleep deprived mind; perhaps there are Garatin's somewhere else- in hiding! She thought with a touch of hope, but it died quickly when she thought of the blooming cherry tree.

"I'm already too late..." she whispered aloud, hoping that it wasn't true, and yet believing it was.

*   *   *

Morning sunlight grew in the common room at Vision's boarding house, dust floated through the golden beams and the sounds of the Harbour Ring waking up grew to a dull din.

Confess woke when she heard whispers at the door; it was Vision with a neighbor, they were sneaking a peek at the woman who had made Endure and his thugs run away like scolded children.

Fess had momentarily passed out after her fight with Endure and awoke to Vision bending over her. Although the woman had not been helpful earlier, she had insisted that Fess stay as long as she needed to recover- free of charge.

170

"That man is a constant menace to me and many others!" she had said as she half dragged half supported Fess up the stairs, "But since you beat him blue- I don't expect I'll see him for a while in this neighborhood- too embarrassing!" she had said gleefully.

Fess had collapsed face down on one of the beds and had drifted in and out of consciousness throughout the rest of that day, sometimes she woke up enough to fear that Endure would come back. But Vision had assured her that if he did, she would send him on a wild goose chase. Indeed, Vision had been very helpful to Fess, she had cleaned her up, reset her broken nose, and adjusted her arm so that it would rest easy on the bed.

Opening her eyes, Confess shifted and felt her body stiffen- but it wasn't too bad, she heard the whispering at the door stop and she assumed that they had retreated. Fess carefully rolled over, taking care not to move her injured arm too much, and slowly swung her legs over the side of the bed. Vision had removed her boots, Fess wished that she hadn't; it would take a lot of effort to get them back on.

Sitting still for a moment, Fess tested her arm, rolling it forward; it was sore and stiff, but it felt like she had set it properly. Next Fess touched her nose and was pleased to find that Vision had washed away the blood; her nose was swollen, but it felt straight. Gliding her fingers back, Fess knotted her tiny braids at the crown of her head; there wasn't time to re-braid her dark hair (although she really did need to soon), she needed to leave. The longer she stayed, the more chance there was that Endure would get over his embarrassment and make good on his parting threat. And more than that, the Harbour Ring was a dangerous place for her to be, and she was in no shape to fight off anymore 'old friends'.

Once she had gotten her boots on, Fess stood with a stifled groan. 'Time to deal with my old problem' she thought wearily - the problem with the namesake of Desert.

*   *   *

Desert peeked out of the stable into the courtyard; it was empty, but he knew that it wouldn't be for much longer. The three friends had sat snoozing in the loft till late morning, when Desert saw the stable boys go elsewhere, he and the others had left the safety of the loft and descended the ladder.

"Alright, this way," he said over his shoulder to Fa and Rave. They followed him out into the morning light.

A strong hand clamped down on Desert's shoulder, "Sneaking around, are we?!"

*   *   *

Every inch of Brave told him to run- fight! Anything but just stand there!

A manor guard had been walking along the stable wall when Desert had led them out into the open. Now all three were firmly held by their arms by two guards who pulled them across the courtyard.

Rave's heart skipped a beat when they were directed away from the manor gate and towards the main door of the imposing manor. He had been hoping that they would just be thrown out on the street- but if they were being taken inside...

"The Grand Duke will have something to say about this," the guard who held onto Deserts arm said, as the main door was opened. Dese didn't respond, nor did he struggle, he was looking more and more solemn with every step.

'Don't struggle' Rave told himself as panic fought to take control, 'Desert knows what he's doing- he's probably done this before, he's got a plan'.

As they were led up the steps into the manor, Rave glanced at the guard who held him and Fa; he had a stony face, and his grip was unyielding. They entered a room with a large circular fireplace in the center of it, with low benches around it. They turned left under a great arch and went up a flight of stairs, tapestry's glittering with gold thread hung on the walls, and the floor was carved of smooth black stone. Rave thought about what the guard had said... Grand Duke- that sounded important!

'What kind of punishment is there for sneaking into the stable of a Grand Duke?' Rave wondered nervously, as they were pulled along at a quick pace after Desert and the other guard. 'Imprisonment? Whipping!?'

The thought of someone laying a whip across Fate's back made Rave go hot all over with rage; he wouldn't let them harm her! But even if he could get free of the guard- he would need Desert's help and Dese didn't look like he was going to be doing any fighting!

'Trust in his plan!' Rave reminded himself, 'He must have a good plan.'

They turned right down a wide hallway that was lined with framed paintings of stuffy looking men and women, turning away from a large sweeping stair, they then took another left and went up a shallow flight of steps. The steps led out onto a low balcony that looked out over the manor wall into the Cherry Gardens where the little lake could be seen amongst the flowering trees. Half of the balcony was shaded by a trellis that supported tangled vines, curtains of dark red hung to the sides and were stirred by a gentle wind. A half circle of wooden chairs with beaded pillows was arranged to look out at the view. Standing in the center of the chairs, in a strong stance with hands on hips, was the Grand Duke.

Rave looked around for an escape, feeling the urge to run- but it was useless; running would only make things worse, he realized with new maturity. He and Fa were released, and they stood next to Dese in a sulky line before the Grand Duke. Glancing over he saw that Desert didn't look scared- he looked annoyed!

'How often does this happen to him!?' Rave wondered and looked back to the Grand Duke- just how important was a Grand Duke? He wondered and tried to gage how angry the man was. The Tarven's gray hair still held a hint of black, it was cut just below his jaw line, and was smoothed back, curling at the ends slightly. Streaks of silver shot out from his temples, he wore a close-trimmed beard that made his jaw look sharp. Rave noted hopefully that he had kind dark eyes- but his face was otherwise stormy, as he studied the three misfits before him. His eyes searched Fa and Rave briefly before settling on Desert.

"They were found sneaking out of the stable, my lord," one of the guards spoke then stepped back- blocking the only exit. The Grand Duke didn't speak, his eyes were boring into Dese, without exhibiting shame, Dese refused to meet his gaze.

Fate felt that it was up to her to explain themselves, but unlike Rave, *she* had an idea of how important a Grand Duke was- she just had no idea how she was to address him!

"My lord… um," she floundered when he turned his eyes sharply on her, "My lord, Grand Duke." She started over, feeling slightly more confident, "My brother and I," she gripped Raves arm, "and our friend, were only looking for a safe place to rest- we meant no harm! We have taken nothing, and only slept in your stable loft, we had no where else to go-"

The Grand Duke cut her off sharply by looking to the right; A woman was standing leaning against the railing, she had been momentarily hidden by the curtain.

"These are the two you spoke of?" the Grand Duke asked in a clipped tone.

Fate started in surprise; it was Confess! Fa's mind reeled 'What is she doing here? What does she have to do with the Grand Duke?' Fa couldn't make sense of it and stared in unbelief.

"Yes, my lord, they are," Fess replied calmly, and for a moment she met Fa's confused gaze, but she looked away, offering no help.

The Grand Dukes eyes darted back to Dese, "Desert- what lies have you told these two!?"

Fa and Rave looked at their friend in astonishment, but Dese refused to meet anyone's gaze, instead he shrugged his shoulders. "No harms been done," he grunted.

The Grand Duke looked like he would explode, "You disobeyed orders from your captain and ran away once you landed!" he said flinging his arm in Fess's direction. "Then you went about the lower rings, galivanting for two days without a thought of telling me that you had arrived back in Tarva! Confess sent me word- said that you were missing; I sent men out looking high and low for you!"

"And you put out wanted posters I noticed."

Fa was surprised by Desert's insolent reply.

He dared to look the angry Duke in the eye, "I suppose you had those made for just such an occasion!"

"Indeed, I did. I had hoped that I wouldn't need them after your voyage, I believed that your time away would mature you- obviously, I was wrong!" The Grand Duke took a menacing step towards Dese, his face red with anger- Dese clamped his mouth shut.

The Grand Duke closed his eyes and breathed through tight lips, as though ashamed for losing his temper.

Fa took a step back from Desert… he had lied…

When the Grand Duke spoke again, his voice was calm and heavy with meaning, "And when you did deem it time to return, you skulked about the manor like a common thief, and what's more, this time you dragged two innocents into your games. *I* will be the judge of what harm you have done."

Rave reached out and gently pulled Fa away from Dese a little more; he lied!

In frustration, the Grand Duke turned away, holding his hands behind his back, "I should throw those two in the tower!" he said impulsively.

"Even a rich man can't afford to be cruel," Desert quoted the Tarven proverb with a touch of spite- he was clearly unafraid of the Duke.

The Grand Duke turned around and glared at Dese for a moment before snapping his fingers, "Escort these two Garatins to rooms and put a guard on their doors, they are not to leave. I've had enough vagabonds wandering the grounds for one day." He added with a touch of sarcasm.

To Fa's heart stopping horror, Rave stepped out in front of her like a human shield, "I and my sister won't be staying," he said firmly.

"Rave!" Fa hissed harshly; she knew that it was not the kind of invitation that you could refuse, "We gladly accept your hospitality, my lord!" Fa added quickly, hoping that the angry Tarven wouldn't be offended by Rave's outburst. To her relief, he only looked mildly surprised by Rave's protest, then he waved for them to be led away.

Fa caught Confess' gaze for a moment, Fess nodded slightly as if to apologize- but it was not Fess that Fa had a grievance with!

"It's alright Rave, you'll both be safe here," Dese assured them as they were escorted down the stairs- but he had eyes only for Fa.

Fa turned away from him coldly- she couldn't look at him! But Rave on the other hand, shot Dese a look that said it all.

*   *   *

There was silence on the balcony, and Desert's heart sank as Fate and Brave disappeared.

"I Invite you to stay as my guest," the Grand Duke said turning to Confess after a moment, "It's the least I can do after having this scamp as your charge."

Fess nodded her thank you, she knew better than to refuse, and took the hint; she left the two alone on the balcony.

The Grand Duke waited till she was gone before speaking again, although he sounded calm and indifferent, Dese knew he was far from it.

"When word reached here that 'The Prestige' had sunk off the coast of Chresacroon, I feared I would never set eyes on you again!"

Dese gritted his teeth.

"Evidently your brush with death didn't make you long for the comforts of home."

Dese refused to meet his gaze and rejected the nagging feeling of guilt.

"Desert I warned you that there would be a price to pay the next time you did something of this nature. You're not a child; you have responsibilities!"

"And what punishment do you deem appropriate?" Desert insolently asked with a touch of sarcasm; this was not at all how their reunion after months at sea should have gone, "A night in the tower perhaps?" he dared.

The Grand Duke turned away and threw up his hands in annoyance, "I don't have time for this; I have been summoned by the King- a summons that I am now *late* for! Guard!?" he called sharply, and one of his guards appeared on the stairs.

"Escort him up," the Grand Duke ordered with a dismissing wave of his jewelled hand.

"My lord?" the guard hesitated, "Where?"

The Grand Duke smiled broadly and Dese knew he was in for!

"I heard it from his own mouth; he wishes to stay in the tower!"

Chapter 18   King's Fool

The Grand Duke of Tarva was a title that Thrive had been working towards for most of his life, he had inherited the title of Duke from his father, but the title of *Grand* Duke had to be granted by the King. And Thrive had won the coveted title after his trip across the Neenor to Garatin, on the King's business; that was fifteen years past, since then he had earned the respect and loyalty of many, including his liege lord; Triumphant the Great.

Thrive was a tall and slender man in his mid sixties- although no one would guess it to look at him, he walked with a straight back and steady stride, only becoming winded after long flights of stairs. He had a close-cut beard of mostly gray, and his hair was smoothed back, and although it still held a hint of black, it had gone mostly gray with the silver streaks on his temples. Deep crow's feet wrinkled the corners of his dark brown eyes as a testament to how much of his life he had spent smiling, but now laughter was far removed from his face, and the mischievous gleam in his eyes was absent.

"I warned him," Thrive muttered under his breath, as he thought of Desert locked in the tower. Thri gritted his teeth and determined to deal with the issue better after his summons; now he must focus on the task at hand.

He readjusted his dark blue cape so that it cockily hung off one shoulder and walked confidently through an inner courtyard of the King's castle, known as the Dragon Keep. As he went through the halls and courtyards, he passed guards who stood to attention, and maids who curtsied low. Large tapestries depicting battles hung from the walls and open windows were letting in a stiff breeze.

The King had summoned him that morning, and even as important as he was, Thrive knew that it was unwise for even him to keep the King waiting- and he wondered how irate the King would be since Thrive was indeed delayed.

The King had grown increasingly unpredictable since the death of his only child, a young son, a month earlier. Yet his majesty was not distraught with grief as one would expect, but instead had become disturbingly lighthearted, and had delighted in the entertainment of gypsies and fools. It had become a high-class scandal amongst the nobility in the upper rings, whispers of why the King didn't mourn the loss of his son grew louder with every day.

But Thrive's cautious ears did not listen for whispers about the king, but rather for whispers about himself. Although he had many friends amongst the nobility, there were a number of lords and dukes who had long been hoping to witness- or orchestrate his downfall. They hungered for the power that came with the title of Grand Duke, they believed that he was weak- but Thrive had come to a head-to-head with many in the past years, and 'weak' was not a word that described his dealings with those who crossed him.

Added to his own position of being the second most powerful man in the Tarven empire, Thrive also was a long-time favourite of the King, having earned his respect and even friendship over years with wise dealings and shrewd advice.

But Thrive had grown up knowing that the refined so called 'sophisticated' life of nobility, was in truth a dangerous, and at times vicious game. A game in which the rules could be changed at anytime by a king who had, of late, proven to be alarmingly unpredictable.

Considering all this, Thrive took a deep breath as he approached an impossibly tall set of carved wooden doors with oversized silver rings. Two guards in ceremonial armor, who stood guarding the doors, saluted Thrive smartly by pounding their right fists over their hearts, then pulled the doors open. Thri waited till the doors were fully ajar before entering the King's council chamber, taking that time to scan the room and make note of who else the King had summoned- and who he hadn't.

Inside were a dozen other dukes, lords and knights; essentially, a room overstuffed with power. They were standing about the council chamber, and all looked as the doors opened for Thrive, among them he noticed that his chief adversaries were also present; Duke Command and Lord Mountain. The two were dangerous apart from each other, but recently they had seemed to grow closer- Thrive found it very concerning.

But the King himself- was absent from the gathering.

The council members all pounded their fists over their hearts as he entered, and the doors were shut behind him.

"We are graced with the Grand Duke's presence after all!" Lord Mountain said, with heavy sarcasm.

"My lords." Thrive chose to ignore Mountain's remark and addressed everyone, offering a lazy smile.

"Of course, you realize, Lord Mountain," Duke Command spoke up with mock sincerity, "That the Grand Duke has many matters to attend to- such as issuing wanted posters." His words came as little surprise to Thri, Duke Command had been trying to undermine him for years, and making cheap jabs was common for him, but there were others who saw through his mockery.

"You insult like a child, Duke Command!" one of the other Dukes glared at Command openly, he gripped his gloves in one hand, perhaps ready to throw them down in a challenge- Thrive wasn't the only one who was a target of Command's insults.

Thrive stepped forward with a suave air, "My lords, enough with such words- we are in the King's council cham-" he cut short his peace-making, and everyone looked up and around at the deep baritone voice that had broken out in song from the hallway that only the King entered by. They stood silent and unnerved at their King's voice.

"OH, how they come! The jolly, meek and glum. And they ask- nay they cry!"

A second voice joined in, "Mighty King! We are faint and weak and ain't got noth'n to eat!"

"And my answer doth come even nigh they speak…" the voice faded off as if the poorly written lyrics had been forgotten, then the King burst out aggressively, "And I said- NO! HAHAHAHAH!" his laughter boomed into the room as the two singers emerged from the hall.

Here, before his councillors, dressed in fine silk and bejeweled heavily, singing and laughing like a common drunkard, was THE most powerful man in the world. He had his arm slung over the shoulder of his most recent favorite fool, and the two of them stumbled in laughing hysterically.

This was the worst that Thrive had ever seen the King in public- and it left him feeling terribly embarrassed for the King. In the past month the King had been reduced to this! Triumphant had once gained the title of 'Great' through his cunning and sharp mind, what had happened to that man?

Triumphant was in his forty's, he was a bit below average height, with a stocky build. He had a mane of black hair and a rounded short beard, his fingernails were clean and short, except for the smallest finger on his right hand whose nail stretched out a full two inches. His many large rings slipped up and down his fingers, including the one with his royal seal, a testament to having lost weight recently.

Half supporting the King was the fool with whom the King had taken an obsessive liking to. He wore a brightly coloured costume with bells sewn into every seam, including those in his bobbing hat.

Triumphant took a deep breath and straightened up when Thrive stepped up close.

"Well!?" he asked with a grin, "Tell me Thrive- what do you think of my fool? I've named him Thrive."

Thrive was well accustomed to the King's little games; Trium had long found it humorous to try and shock a response out of Thrive, asking and doing odd and unexpected things then waiting to see how Thri would respond. But his 'games' had grown increasingly outrageous after the death of his son.

Aware of not only the King's watchful gaze, but also the rest of the nobles, Thrive smoothly raised a brow, "I am glad for your sake, my King, that he is a better singer and fool than I."

"Well said!" Triumphant growled. Those who knew him well, knew that, like a cat, the King growled when particularly pleased.

Thrive watched and felt a prick of unease, as the King's gaze went past him to the others, and looked a bit shocked to see them, then his face flattened out. He waved an arm in dismissal to his fool, and Thri noticed the King's mood shift dramatically from jolly to serious and level-headed.

Triumphant moved to his giant throne-like chair and sat down. "Well my lords, let us begin," he said, like it was a rehearsed line, that he had memorized for similar situations.

Thrive steeled himself for what was to come and took his seat.

The council table was in the shape of a half moon, the flat end facing the King who sat two steps up in his throne-like chair, on the step below him, Thrive sat on his right in a slightly less impressive high-backed chair. The other lords and dukes sat about the table with a clear view of both the King and the Grand Duke. A wide space opposite the king was left open so that he was the first face anyone would see when they entered the large doors. Around the curved table were twenty-three chairs, each one had a shield with a lords' family crest hanging on the back. A little under half of the chairs were empty that morning. The King was often selective of whom he summoned to meetings, using it as a way to snub his advisers who had displeased him.

Thrive was the only one who had not been rebuffed in this manner in the past few months, clearly distinguishing him as the King's most trusted adviser.

The mood of the others was severely dampened by the King's strange entrance, and all were relieved when Trium seemed to take on a more serious and appropriate air for a king.

"You all know of what transpired in the Pearl Square this past evening?" Triumphant asked in a stern voice as he scanned the faces before him. Everyone was silent; news of the arrests and new law had taken everyone by surprise.

One of the minor dukes- who was always quick to flatter- spoke first, "His majesty made a very bold and decisive move, I admire him for it."

It was law that in a council meeting, no one could address the King directly- unless the King spoke directly to them. He also used this as another way to snub, summoning yet refusing to address some lords for months at a time.

"Thrive," Trium pronounced heavily, "Don't be coy now- what say you!?" he demanded.

Thri took a moment to respond- favourite or not, he knew he walked on the edge of a blade, "I think you have made your intentions clear, my King, yet I fear how the people will respond." Thri held Triums gaze.

"What do you mean?" Trium narrowed his eyes; a danger sign- or it use to be.

"I fear the people do not understand your reasoning's for outlawing the Nity followers, my King. I fear that it will incite panic in the common people, they may fear that even they are not safe." Thrive watched the King closely, waiting for his reaction, wondering if he had gone too far. But the King leaned back and was silent.

"Try as you may, Thrive." Everyone looked to Lord Mountain when he spoke, "We all see through your weak words; your sympathy for these-"

"WATCH your tongue Lord Mountain!" the King barked without warning, cutting Mountain's words short, a few jumped and looked up startled. Mountain swallowed hard and met the King's angry gaze fearfully.

"The Grand Duke is *the* only one here who has offered any useful advice for months! He is the only one I trust..." He scowled down at Mountain, "Watch whom you accuse!"

181

Everyone was silent again and Thrive daringly made eye contact with Lord Mountain; that man was testing him a little too much.

"Thrive," the King said with a heavy sigh, "Is there any truth to this accusation- this question of your loyalty?" He didn't look at Thrive but continued to scan the other men, as if wanting to prove them wrong with Thrive's impending denial.

Thrive knew that his words must not cast even a shadow of a doubt. "You are my sovereign; I would not dare question you my King," Thrive stated clearly, a twinge in his heart the only thing that belied his words.

"I do not wish to hear anymore such 'talk' of my most loyal Grand Duke!" Triumphant warned, then sat back lazily, "I shall consider your concerns Thrive, but we must also consider the rampant crime in the lower ring in connection with the Nity followers- my Lord Quest, what say you?"

Quest was one of the few lords who lived in the Harbour Ring. He cleared his throat, "Indeed there have been crimes centered around the Nity followers; horse thieving, bandits and other things of that nature. I believe that once the Nity followers are rounded up, the crime will end, my King."

"What evidence is there linking the Nity followers to these crimes?" one of the Knights inquired, he was known for his justness and Thrive counted him as an ally.

"We have many witnesses," Lord Quest replied.

"All of whom would gladly see the blame placed on anyone but themselves," the Knight pointed out, and there was a murmur of discord.

"Crime has always existed, in the lower ring, and always will." Thrive rose his voice above the others, aware of the King watching him, and how risky his words were, "And might I add, that the Nity followers are known for their high moral code and distaste for crime."

The King seemed to ponder this for a moment, and others were emboldened by Thrive's words.

"The Grand Duke speaks wisely, perhaps the King should reconsider his ruling on the Nity followers."

"I will *not* reconsider!" Trium snapped and Thrive set his jaw in defeat; he knew the tone that the King used, and he knew what it meant.

"The Teachings of that pale faced *Eloi-man* have infested my domain for far too long!" Triumphant grew red in the face, his level-head vanishing, "His teachings have brought rebellion and insurrection to Garatin and other countries under my rule for years! I will suffer a dead man's empty words no

longer! He who said I was a plague on the lands! NO! I *will not* 'reconsider'!'"
he changed his voice to that of a mocking child, and spat, his raised voice
making some flinch, "I want every last Nity follower smoked out and brought
to the Dragon Keep dungeons to await my judgement!" Suddenly, as if
exhausted, the King flopped back in his chair and whimpered a sigh, "Thrive-
I grow tired, carry out my orders; sweep the city and fill your own dungeons
as well, I shall decide a fair punishment later. Now leave me."

Thrive stood, bowed his head and pounded his fist over his heart,
"As you wish, my King."

*   *   *

"The Grand Duke gave orders that you are not to leave your
chambers until his return," the guard outside Fate's door explained, he looked
a bit wary of her, like he expected her to try and run past him- but Fa didn't
think she'd get far if she did.

"I just want to speak with my brother!" Fa pleaded- was that so
unreasonable!?

The guard sighed, "I can not allow that." He looked like he wanted
to push her back into the room and pull the door shut, but Fa planted herself
firmly.

"May I then speak with the Grand Duke?" she didn't really want to
speak to him again- but what other choice did she have?

"His lordship left the manor some hours ago, I do not know his
plans- now, if you would?" he gestured for her to step back into her room.

With a frustrated sigh, Fa stepped back and closed the door before
he could lean in and get it himself, it closed a bit louder than she had expected
and she felt bad, knowing that she was acting like a child. Taking a breath Fa
turned back to look at the room she had been confined to for the past two
hours. She had spent the first hour sitting somewhat patiently on a stool,
watching the door, and then she had resorted to pacing the room, too
nervous to try opening the door, until a few moments before, only to find
that it was guarded. The chamber was larger than her old loft room back in
Eamer, and its furnishings made her feel like a thistle that had been dropped
by accident onto a silk pillow. There was a wood framed bed with a thick
mattress and unworn blanket. In one corner was a changing screen hiding a
brass tub. A tapestry on the wall had the crest of the Grand Duke, and in
one wall was a small window with a glass pane. On either side of the door
were wall scones that held large yellow candles, there was another candle by

the bed in a holder (all were unlit), surprisingly, it was the candles that astounded Fa the most about the room! Her family had only ever used one candle for their house- and had used that one sparingly.

What Fa didn't know was that her chamber was meant for servants of visitors and was really quite a modest room in comparison to most!

Looking to the window where the late morning sun came through, Fa walked up to it for the third time, and pressed her face against it to try and get a better view; but the glass was thick, and it distorted the view. Then Fa noticed an iron latch, glancing back at the door, she gingerly lifted the heavy latch; the window swung in.

Excitedly Fa poked her head out, hoping to see a way to climb out, or at least be able to call for Brave- his chambers could be right next to hers. Fa looked down and was instantly overcome by a wave of dizziness; she was four or five stories' up at least!

Swallowing, Fa stepped back and steadied herself against the wall, giving up her plan, she waited for her head to stop spinning.

'What a mess we're in this time!' she thought in despair, then anger, 'All because we trusted Desert! He lied...'

Fa thought back to what he had told her the day before about being an orphan, tears sprung to her eyes; he had been lying to her the whole time- possibly even mocking her! Did he think it was all a joke? Had it been a game of his to see how many lies she would swallow!? Fa pushed away from the wall and blinked back the tears bitterly; what a fool she had been! She started in surprise when the chamber door opened; Fa looked up hoping to see Rave.

"Confess!" Fa said in surprise as the curt sea captain waited for the guard to close the door behind her before stepping closer. Although Fa had noticed her earlier on the balcony, she now realized the dreadful shape that Fess was in; although clean, with her hair washed and unbraided for the first time since they had met, Fess walked with a limp, and her right arm hung by her side a bit stiff looking. Her forehead boasted a purple bruise, her nose had a cut across the bridge and was swollen.

Fess nodded and looked around the room casually, "I didn't expect you and your brother to find your way here."

"Fess- what happened to you?" the words left Fa's mouth before she could think better of them.

"My husband died, and my ship was lost at sea, I'm surprised I don't look worse!" she replied sarcastically, "Not to mention the young man I was supposed to deliver to the Grand Duke gave me the slip."

"You knew who Desert was the whole time?" Fa asked, feeling more betrayed.

Fess twisted her face, "The Grand Duke entrusted my husband with the young scamp, just one more debt I inherited when he died. It wasn't prudent to tell the crew who he was; it was hard enough keeping him out of trouble when they didn't know."

Fa thought back over the sea voyage with this new information; Confess' supposed favouritism of Dese suddenly made sense. Fa remembered the conversation that she and Rave had overheard; Desert had lied to them about that too!

Determining to forget about Desert, Fa pressed her lips together before asking, "Fess can you help me? I and Brave really meant no harm and only wish to leave, but the Duke won't allow us to-"

"*Grand Duke,*" Fess interrupted to correct, "He is the Grand Duke of Tarva. And, no, I don't think I can help. The Grand Duke was a friend of my husbands- not me, today is the first I have ever met him. I doubt he would listen to me on the subject of your release."

Fa felt like she physically shrunk with disappointment.

"Don't worry yourself, Fa." Fa blinked in surprise at how tenderly Fess spoke; she hadn't realized the woman cared that much about her. "You and your brother are safe here- safer than you would be out there," she nodded to the open window- had she guessed that Fa had thought of escaping?

"This city isn't safe for your kind, including Horizon," she said airily and walked past Fa to close the window, letting the latch fall back into place with a click. "I doubt the King will grant an audience to anyone that he has already declared an outlaw."

Fate's mind reeled as she thought of Rizon; she hadn't considered what the new law meant for him. He may have arrived too late.

'What if I'm also too late?' she considered- not for the first time, 'What if it wasn't a storm I was meant to warn about, but instead the king's new law? And I was one day too late- all because Desert was giving us a tour!'

"Can you at least arrange for me to speak with my brother?" she asked hopefully, she wasn't entirely sure they were safe; if the Duke- Grand Duke, discovered that she and Rave were Nity Followers themselves...

Fess turned back to her from the window, and studied her face for a moment, "I'll see what I can do."

*   *   *

Brave had the same idea that Fa had about the window, only he wasn't disturbed by the height. He was standing on a stool, leaning halfway out the window, mapping out a route, when a noise at the chamber door startled him. He jumped, hitting his head on the window frame, wincing in pain he ducked back inside and stepped off the stool just as Confess entered the room.

"Where's my sister!?" he demanded to know, hoping that Fess wouldn't notice the open window, he had asked the guard outside earlier the same question- and gotten no answer.

Fess raised her chin, unimpressed with his insolence, "I've arranged for you to speak with her. I'll escort you to her chambers."

Rave looked past her and realized that she had left the door open, Rave went quickly to the door, anxious to see Fa, but Fess reached out and stopped him as he walked past her.

Her left hand gripped his forearm, and she grunted in pain when he tugged slightly- but her grip did not lessen. Rave found himself looking up into her battered face.

"Don't try to escape; it would not be wise," she enunciated each word heavily and held his gaze with her hard eyes.

Rave swallowed and managed a tight nod, in the back of his mind he wondered if she practiced being so terrifying.

Confess led him out into the hall, her intimidating presence alone made Rave forget about running. Instead he contented himself with memorizing the way to Fa's chambers; it was a longer walk than he thought it would be, but he silently repeated their route to himself until he felt sure he could do it alone.

The guard at Fa's door exchanged a nod with Fess and let Rave pass, just as the guard at his door had done. He felt Fess' gaze bore into his back as she planted her feet in the hallway and waited.

"Are you alright!?" Rave asked as the door was shut behind him, Fa glanced at her hands before nodding.

"You have new burns," Rave guessed.

"I got them last night," she admitted quietly, even though it was impossible to be overheard through the thick door.

"I didn't think you had slept!" Rave said in astonishment. He thought that she wouldn't sleep until the whole thing was over.

"I didn't... it happened when I was awake," she said fearfully.

For a moment Rave didn't comprehend her words. "Oh," he said after a moment, "Well that's great news! The heart stain spreads, and you don't get any rest! I guess Freedom didn't think to mention the possibility!" he said ill temperedly. But he knew that he wasn't really angry at the Cokhawken woman, but he couldn't say the namesake of the person he was *really angry* at.

"I'm alright," Fa assured him.

But Rave didn't believe a word; the dark smudges under her eyes seemed to grow by the day.

"What was the... 'non-dream' about?" he asked. He always felt uncomfortable when she described her dreams, but he needed to help her in whatever way he could- and if that meant listening, then he would listen, but this time he didn't have to.

Fa shrugged and sat down on the edge of her bed, "Nothing really, I don't understand it."

Rave sighed and glanced at the window- maybe hers would be easier to climb out of! But he despaired of the idea when he thought of Fa's newly burnt hands, 'She could barely climb that wall last night- and that was before she got the new burns!' he thought drearily, but thinking of the night before made him think of Desert- and those were unwelcome thoughts!

"What are we going to do?" he asked, and immediately regretted it; Fa had no more of an idea than he did- he should be the one looking after her, not the other way around!

"I don't know..." Fa sighed, "I don't know what we can do! Other than wait and hope the Grand Duke will let us go. Confess won't help us."

"Yeah, I figured that! What is she doing here anyway?" Rave said, nervously glancing at the door, fervently hoping that Fess couldn't hear them.

Obviously reluctant to talk of Desert, Fa explained what Fess had told her.

Rave took a moment to digest what it meant, then he got angry all over again. "If I see him again, I'll..." Rave turned away angrily.

Instead of scolding him, like he was used to her doing, Fa just sat silently- it made Rave even angrier!

'That liar! That....' Rave struggled to find the right name to fit the betrayal, but gave up, 'He lied to us for months- and hurt Fa so much she doesn't even try to defend him! If I see him again...' Rave wasn't sure what he would do if he saw Dese again- but he'd do something!

"We need to come up with a plan of what to do," Rave said, gaining control of his emotions after a moment, "If we could see Horizon maybe he could help!"

"I'm afraid I'm too late Rave... I'm afraid my warning is much too late!" Fa whispered.

Rave winced inwardly; the last time they had this discussion, he had convinced her that their troubles were almost over! How foolish that sounded now.

Chapter 19   Guest of Honour

Confess approached one of the low benches in front of the fire in the main entrance hall, called simply enough 'the fire hall', she suppressed a groan of pain as she lowered herself down onto the bench. She felt less out of place here, than she did in her own chambers, despite living in a manor all her life, the Grand Duke's manor made her feel uncomfortable. Perhaps she would have felt different if she wasn't living on someone's charity, but with no money and no ship and many enemies, she didn't have many options. Indeed, if one was to be alone and destitute, having a Grand Duke as your only friend wasn't so bad. Even still, Fess felt trapped, and that made her irritable.

She put a hand to her right shoulder and gently rolled it, she felt the muscle catch once and her fingers felt a little numb; she would be feeling the pain of Endures 'lesson' for a long time yet. Looking up across the fire, Fess made eye contact with a pageboy who was walking through the hall, he awkwardly looked away and quickened his pace. Fess found it slightly amusing how intimidated people were of her- like Fate's brother and sometimes Fa herself. Desert on the other hand refused to flinch or bend to her will- as was demonstrated in recent events. She supposed his up bringing could be blamed for his strong will and lack of respect; what could one expect, being raised by the Grand Duke? For the Grand Duke was someone who would *never* flinch at her hard gaze- and nor would Fess try to make him do so.

She wondered how friendly the Grand Duke and her husband had been, even though Devotion had not mentioned it, they must have been close, for why else would the Grand Duke entrust Desert to her husband?

Just then a voice from one of the halls that opened up on the fire hall, made Fess sit still and listen.

"-the supplies won't last much longer, my lord; there are a lot of people. They'll start to go hungry by tomorrow night," the voice said, and a pair of footsteps came closer, but stopped before coming out in the open.

"Of course," a second voice said wearily, Fa recognized it as belonging to the Grand Duke, and she tensed, wondering how private the discussion was.

"I want a large amount of supplies sent- enough to last a week, hopefully by then the heat will have died down."

"It will prove quite difficult to transport that much without drawing attention, especially from the kitchen servants, my lord."

"Leave that to me, I have a plan. In the meantime, make arrangements to transport everything."

Confess inhaled sharply when she realized that the conversation was over and that his lordship would step into the hall soon. Turning away, Fess pretended that she had been finger combing her hair before the fire.

"My Lady Fess," Duke Thrive exclaimed, as he entered the room.

Fess smiled stiffly and stood even more stiffly.

"You should be resting my lady!" he said stopping short and looking knowingly at her stiff arm as she somewhat clumsily curtsied.

"That's not necessary, my lord."

Thrive narrowed his eyes as he stepped closer, "You must let my healer see to you."

Fess wondered how far she could push back, "Thank you my lord, but I am quite well."

Thrive smiled shrewdly, "Then you are well enough to attend a banquet later this evening- I shall make it in your honor!

"No, I-" Fess realized too late how she had cornered herself.

"A small banquet- I insist!" he smiled.

Fess knew that it would be unwise to push further; she nodded her consent.

"Very good then! There is also Desert's homecoming to celebrate!" he said with a note of sarcasm, "I trust that my Garatin visitors haven't tried to leave?"

"I took the liberty of convincing them otherwise," she said, thinking that she would need to rest before attending any banquet.

"Excellent! The three misfits will all join us at the head table, it will be quite festive!"

Fess noted for the first time how tense he seemed to be, not angry like he had been earlier on the balcony, but tense. 'His summons from the King must have gone poorly' she surmised and wondered what the conversation that she had just overheard was about.

"I look forward to hearing of the voyage, until this evening, my Lady," the Grand Duke reached for her left hand and bowed over it smartly, before striding away.

*   *   *

Fate carefully smoothed out her new clean bandages and glanced at the guard out of the corner of her eye; what did people think of her bandages? Did they know that she had a heart stain? Fa had a sudden urge to hide and couldn't trace where the feeling came from.

Fa stood outside her chamber, the guard standing beside her as they waited, looking up Fa saw Brave coming down the hall with his own escort. After Confess had taken him back to his chambers, Fa had sat on her bed and watched as the morning sun rose higher, it was then that she realized how badly her hair and clothes stunk of saltwater. Deciding to make the best of their situation, she bathed, and washed her old tunic and trousers. Her clothes really were in bad shape, and after looking around she had found a sewing needle and thread in a cabinet, she had spent some time stitching up holes and seams.

When she had done all this, a maid servant had come to her chambers to tell her that the Grand Duke had invited her to a banquet that night, the maid also presented a dress for Fa to wear. Fa was completely bewildered but couldn't get the maid to tell her anything more. Fa figured since she was all clean and washed up that she might as well wear her own clothes, and had declined the dress, the maid had hesitated, then nervously glancing at Fa's fire hair, had left.

As Brave approached, Fa saw that he had, like her, washed and apparently refused any banqueting clothes that he had been offered.

"Do you know what's going on?" Rave asked under his breath, when he reached her.

Fa brushed her clean hair away from her face -maybe she should have tied it back- and shook her head.

One of their escorts led the way down the hall, and the other one followed.

"Stay close beside me," Rave whispered as they passed from torch light to torch light along the hall, "We might get a chance to escape at this banquet."

Fa glanced over her shoulder at the guard following them and remembered Confess' words. "I'm not sure we'd get far," she answered, as they descended a flight of steps.

"Do you think the Duke will punish us in front of everyone?"

Fa could here a note of panic in his voice. "Peace! We'll be all right." Her words belied her own fears, 'What if we see Desert at the banquet!?' she thought suddenly, 'What will Rave do!?' She surprised herself by wishing that Rave would lose his temper and hit Desert if they saw him, the thought wasn't like her at all, and she buried it with effort.

They were escorted down more stairs and hallways than Fa remembered climbing, and she was thoroughly lost, astounded at the size of the manor; if it weren't for the high ceilings and large windows Fa would have felt claustrophobic again. Fa hesitated when she heard voices and general merrymaking coming from a large room ahead of them, but the guards led them out into the banqueting hall without slowing, giving Fa and Rave no time to fully take in the scene.

The large domed hall was well lit by open fires, with turning spits of roasting meat and low wooden chandeliers with flickering candles. A troupe of performers with flutes and mandolins were playing a light-hearted tune as a crowd of fifty or more people stood about admiring the roasting meat or sat on benches talking loudly. Three rows of heavily adorned tables were set up where servants were busy bringing and arranging trays of steaming bread rolls, mountains of stacked cheese and cooked fish. At the far end of the hall, on a dais, was the head table, servants were most busy here, placing the best trays until the table was full.

Standing in front of the table, waiting, was Confess with an expression of granite. Fa had to look twice before realizing who it was; the brittle sea captain had donned a dress of dark mauve with trim and wide belt of gray blue. Her hair had not been re-braided and was done up so that it fell down her back, a gray blue silk band holding it in place. The cut of the dress did less to hide and more to accent her wide strong shoulders, and what with her bruised temple and puffy nose, she looked more formidable than she did feminine.

Fate met her gaze, and the corner of Confess' mouth turned up ruefully at Fa's own choice of wardrobe. As they were led towards the head table through the crowd, Fa felt terribly self conscious and wished that she had tied her hair back, at the very least! The only 'banquet' that she and Rave had been to, had consisted of laying blankets out over the grass and eating their father's latest hunting kill. Even Brave looked a bit uncomfortable.

Their escort stopped before the dais, but before Fa could say anything, a trumpet sounded, and all eyes turned to the lord of the manor; the Grand Duke came striding through the merrymakers smiling and greeting as he went. He wore a simple enough tunic, but his blue cape and gold chain made up for it, as well as the gemstones he wore on his fingers.

Fate thought she saw a flicker of amusement when he saw her and Rave. He stopped short before them, Fess dropped a stiff curtsy (her arm still looked stiff after the days rest) and Fa made Rave follow her in a clumsy bow.

Thrive spread an arm and smiled, "My young guests from across the sea, allow me to properly welcome you to The Ducal Manor."

Fa was speechless- 'did he call us guests!?'

Thrive continued as he mounted the dais and bowed over Fess's hand, "Come and join us, I look forward to hearing of your travels!" Fa couldn't tell if he was serious or not.

"A 'small banquet' you said my lord," Confess said as she took her seat at the right end of the table.

Fa and Rave were directed to sit at the left end of the table.

"But of course!" Thrive said innocently, "These fine folk are just my household!" he raised his voice to be heard over the noise of the merrymakers, "I want to be remembered for being a generous man!"

A cheer went up and goblets were raised to him. Fess smiled ruefully and raised her own goblet in the toast.

Fa and Rave sat nervously on their shared bench, but the Grand Duke remained standing, as if waiting for someone. Fa decided then was as good a time as any.

"My lord- I apologize again for this morning." Fa was emboldened by the Grand Duke's festive attitude, and hoped that he would simply let them go, "I and my brother will leave just-" she was cut off promptly by a wave of the Duke's hand.

"Nonsense! You can not leave now- the guest of honor has not yet made an appearance- with the exception of yourself my lady," he said, turning to Fess with a little bow.

She still had a slight smile hovering over her face- she must think something was humorous- Fa couldn't think what though! For she was having a hard time determining if the Grand Duke was sincere or if every word was laced with sarcasm to mask his festering anger over what she and Rave had done. Fa decided that although he seemed nice enough, that he also had a cruel streak.

"Ah, and there he is!" Thrive announced the presence of Desert to the hall, "The young man with a fantastic story to tell of all his vast adventures!"

Desert didn't look like he appreciated the fanfare, and quickly made his way towards the head table. Fa noted with cynicism that his disguise of a sailor had been replaced with the wardrobe of a rich, entitled Tarven nobleman- although Fa was sure that there wasn't a trace of nobleness about him. Fa turned away when he sought out her gaze as he drew closer.

'What a cruel lie!' the bitterness and betrayal welled up in her again, and she sensed Rave tense beside her.

"Fate, Brave..." Desert said but stopped when they both coldly refused to meet his eyes.

"I trust your day was restful, Desert?" Thrive asked innocently and waved to a high-backed chair at his right-hand side.

Desert mounted the dais and circled the table behind Fess, all the while glaring at Thrive. He sat down heavily without a word. Thrive raised a brow at his sullen behaviour, "Let the feast begin!" he announced and sat down.

Fa was relieved to find that due to the seating, she could avoid eye contact with Desert completely!

The banqueters sat down, and for the most part paid no attention to the head table and the tension that mounted there throughout the meal. Finding that they were hungry, Fa and Rave followed Fess' example and filled their plates from the assortment of trays and platters, most of the food they had never seen before, and some they avoided gingerly. Servants stood close by to fill their goblets, but they remained silent, and the siblings soon forgot they were there.

All the while Fa felt Desert's gaze seeking her out, pleading her to look at him- but she was stalwart in her decision not to.

"So, Garatin- I assume that is from where you hail," Thrive asked, when they had all filled their plates.

Fa wished that he had remained silent.

"That's right, my lord," Rave answered tightly.

"Oh, I think we can dispense with formalities," he said airily, "Since you are such good friends of Desert!"

Dese shifted his jaw, but still said nothing.

"My namesake has been Thrive for far longer than my title has been Grand Duke."

There was a moment of silence as everyone considered how Fate and Brave would *never* address the Grand Duke by his namesake!

"I have been to Garatin myself once- many years past," Thrive said thoughtfully, as he chewed a piece of roast pheasant. "Why come to Tarva?" he asked innocently enough- but Fa was wary of answering, she exchanged a look with Rave- but he didn't offer any help.

"We traveled with Horizon," Fa realized too late how unwise it was to mention that namesake.

Thrive raised a brow, "That is the second time today that that namesake has come to my attention, do you speak of the Garatin rebel who just arrived?"

Fa nodded her head and wondered where her careless words would take her.

"And I understand that you had him aboard your ship," he stated rather than asked, as he turned to Fess.

Fa realized that he must have already known that she and Rave traveled with Rizon- since he knew that they were all aboard The Prestige. 'Was he testing us?' she wondered in alarm and determined to speak with more caution.

"Your voyage must truly have been eventful then!" Thrive said as his goblet was refilled. "The namesake of Horizon must have been heard in every castle, cottage and farm throughout the Tarven empire in the past ten years. The man creates controversy wherever he goes. Now he awaits the King's judgment."

Fa grew hopeful; he didn't sound disapproving of Rizon. "We very badly wish to speak with Rizon, my lord," she ventured.

"Oh?" The Grand Duke paused and arched one brow, "Do you have 'business' with him, that you so urgently need to speak with him?"

Fa felt frozen- had she misread him completely!? 'I could say we're his servants' the thought crossed her mind, but she decided that saying so would not be helpful- so she remained silent as if she had miss-swallowed her food.

"It's not wise to associate with such a man in these times," Thrives tone was light, but considering what had happened in the Pearl square, Fa wondered if the Grand Duke really was as unconcerned as he sounded.

"Now, tell me of how the three of you met!" he said looking at Desert by his side.

Dese glanced at Fa, but she looked away.

"A ship is a small place," Dese replied, tight lipped.

"Indeed," Thrive murmured, and Fa felt his knowing gaze.

They sat in silence for a time, listening to the performers play their instruments above the noise of the banqueters.

"I can't tell you how grieved I am about your misfortunes my lady," Thrive said solemnly, looking at Fess, "Your husband was a good man."

Fess did not reply, and Fa noticed how her smile had long since disappeared.

"'The Prestige' was your husband's only ship?" he asked.

Fess set down her fork and sat back. "You are correct, my lord. He did, however, have many debts. Now if you'll excuse me; I really must retire to rest."

"As you wish, my lady," Thrive said, standing to his feet and bowing slightly as Fess stood. "You are welcome to my hospitality for as long as needed- I insist that you stay at least until you are recovered."

Fess nodded, and curtsied before making her exit, and Fa considered how, unlike the first mate aboard 'The Prestige', or the other sailors, the Grand Duke genuinely treated Fess like she was a lady.

"Alas, I have things to attend to and must also leave," Thrive said, turning to his table guests, "I'm sure the three of you have much to discuss. Tomorrow I will hear in full why you have come to Tarva." He gave Fa a look that told her he didn't believe her explanation.

"Are we prisoners here!?" Rave demanded to know, standing to his feet just as the Grand Duke had begun to turn away.

Fa nearly choked on her food and watched the Tarven's face apprehensively.

A lopsided grin came to Thrive's face, "Well I can't have you running about the Dukes Ring causing trouble!" He turned away and stepped off the dais, then added over his shoulder, "There are much worse places to be held 'prisoner'."

Rave sat down heavily and huffed as the Grand Duke walked away, while Fa just breathed a sigh.

"I might be able to get you to Horizon," Desert offered quietly.

"We've had enough of your help!" Rave snapped.

Fa tried to ignore him, but it proved very hard to do.

"I know I mislead you- but there are worse things to lie about!" Desert said leaning as far over the table as he could, as if getting closer would make things better, "I know how you feel-"

Fa couldn't take anymore, she stood to her feet suddenly, "You said that before." her voice was oddly hushed, as if she couldn't get enough air. "I'd like to go back to my chambers now," she said to her escort, who had come closer when she stood.

He nodded and let her lead the way through the banquet. He grabbed a leg of meat as he went, while the other escort stepped closer when Rave stood to his feet to follow Fa.

Dese jumped up, "Rave please! Can't we just forget about this?! Fa still needs to speak with the Nity followers- I can help with that! I'm not the enemy here!"

Rave stood with his back to Dese, but he turned to look at him, and as he did, he didn't see an enemy- just a good friend whose company in this strange place was sorely missed. Rave felt his hot head cooling; maybe holding a grudge about this was a bit childish.

Chapter 20   Cracks in the Vessel

"It's so dark- I'll light the candles for you miss," the maid servant said briskly.

Fa looked up at the candles by the door; the room was dark, the sun had set long ago and only a bit of starlight came through the window.

"No! No thank you." Fa said hurriedly.

The Tarven girl who was about the same age as Fa herself, paused, glanced at Fa's hair, then nodded. "Anything else I can do?" she asked kindly and went to the window to close it- why did everyone keep closing the window?

"What are all the wagons in the courtyard for?" Fa asked. Over the rooftop she could get a glimpse of the manor courtyard below, blazing torches revealed several wagons.

"Awe that's his lordship, miss," the girl said with a smile, "As if giving us a banquet weren't enough, he sends out wagons of food."

Fa thought it was a wonderful thing to do, and her liking of the Grand Duke grew quite suddenly, "Where do they go?"

The girl shrugged, "Someplace." She turned back around and shyly glanced once more at Fa's hair, "I'll be off now."

She left, and through the momentary open door, Fa glimpsed the guard still standing outside her door; there would be no escaping! She hoped that Rave wasn't foolish enough to try.

Stubbornly, Fa went to the window and reopened it, she caught her breath as her hand smarted at the action; her burns now stretched from her fingertips to her wrists, the worst burns being in the center of her palms.

Sighing heavily, Fa sat down on the bed. 'When was the last time I had a full night sleep?' she wondered wearily, 'How many days have we been in Tarva?' Her thoughts felt fuzzy, like she couldn't focus, and the longer she sat the more her body felt- so heavy!

"Too long" she answered herself out loud, when she remembered the blooming cherry tree; was there any point in finding the Nity followers now?

'Maybe the worst is yet to come' the thought gave her anxiety, and her eyes darted to the window and the clear starry sky, 'Maybe I am meant to warn of a storm, and I still have time!'

Her thoughts scattered this way and that, trying to make plans, trying to think of what she would say to the Nity followers, thinking of how angry she was with Desert, than trying to organize her stray thoughts.

The longer she sat, the heavier her limbs and eyelids felt, and the slower her thoughts became. She was warm, in a new clean dressing gown, the maid had also left a shawl, and Fa had wrapped it about her shoulders, soon her resolve to stay awake slipped away. Fa slummed back on the bed, she was dreaming a second before her eyes were even closed.

'I don't belong here' was the first thought that crossed her mind when she realized where she was, her mother had described this place to her in great detail and she knew it at once. It was where every Garatin heart turned in reverence; she stood before the inner doors of the Vase in Garason.

The large black double doors opened of their own will, and without her permission, Fate's feet took her forward, passing into the inner chamber, where The Vase itself was kept; only a select few were ever allowed to stand where she now stood.

The doors shut behind her, and Fa was alone, looking up at the dais where the Vase sat on its stand; the man-made home of Eloi. It had broken when Eternity died, but from its shards, a low bowl with a narrow mouth had been crafted, fragmented images painted in gold were scattered about its cream surface. The craftsmen who had recrafted it probably meant to capture its original beauty, but the tiny gold figures were twisted and disjointed, making the Vase a pale mockery of what it had been. Stuffed in the narrow mouth was a white silk cloth.

Before Fa had fully taken in the scene, the Vase began to crack- its old crack lines widening and a blinding light from inside began to shine through. Fate's heart thudded as she heard the fire hardened clay splinter bit by bit; she knew that the very presence of Eloi dwelled inside. She knew that she shouldn't be as close as she was, but her feet kept moving her forward- what would happen to her if she came into direct contact with Eloi!?

Unable to stop her feet, Fa turned her head aside as the light became stronger, "I don't belong here!" she whispered fearfully; compared to the pure *good* that Eloi was- she was just a wicked child, meddling in things she shouldn't!

"Don't be afraid." The voice came from where the Vase had been a moment before- it startled her, and her feet stopped; she looked before she could think better of it. A man stood on the dais, he was Garatin, he had a strong and kind face, his blonde hair hanging over his blue eyes; he was in great pain. His tunic was torn, and his hands clutched at his rib cage were his tunic was stained a deep red, his face was bruised badly, his right eye was puffy, and his lip was bleeding. Through a tear in his sleeve, Fa saw a red brand on his shoulder, marking him as a slave.

He swallowed back blood and watched her with sad eyes, "The Vase was only ever meant to be a temporary vessel," his voice was raw and halting, betraying the pain he was in, "it served its purpose well enough for a long time, but its use ended when I came." With great effort, he stepped off the dais towards her, he stumbled, his steps uncertain.

Fa *felt*... she felt the stirring with in her, this time it was slight, gentle- yet still not her, "I don't belong here..." she repeated- she wished she could run away, for deep within she knew who the man was- and it frightened her beyond understanding. But her feet remained planted.

He came to stand before her, gathering his strength he reached out and touched her face tenderly, the way her father had done on her last birthday. Blood from the mans finger smeared her face and she caught her breath at its warmth.

"Have you wandered in the dark places so long, that you don't know your own home when you feel it?" he asked, and it really seemed like the thought saddened him. Fa was speechless; Eamer was gone- wasn't it?!

She gasped and stepped back when she saw that his skin was cracking- like the Vase had done, and the light shone through.

"Your breaking!"

*   *   *

Brave sat on the edge of his much too soft bed; on it he felt like a rock sinking into a marsh- what a horrid death it would be to suffocate in his sleep because his bed was too soft! He had sat there for a half hour after the banquet, thinking about what Desert had said, and the more he thought, the less angry he was with Dese for his deception.

Something that his mother had said came back, 'Forgiveness is the first step to selflessness'. If that was true, Rave surmised, then holding a grudge was the first step to self-destruction. Rave frowned; such abstract thoughts made his head hurt!

"Brave?" Rave jumped a little when he was pulled from his thoughts by his sister's voice. Apparently, the guards would now escort them to each others' chambers.

"Fa? What is it?" Rave stood up, he could see that she was distressed.

She glanced about the room, making sure they were alone. "I dreamed again," she whispered.

Rave's eyes darted to her hands, and he stepped closer to see the new damage; but the bandages still covered the burns.

"I didn't dream of fire this time," she said, as if that explained why there were no new burns, "I don't understand why." She shrugged and held up her hands a little.

Rave shrugged and sat back down on his bed- it still unsettled him how soft it was, "I won't complain if you don't get new burns."

Fa sighed and sat down beside him, "I dreamed... I dreamed I saw Eternity."

Rave was still for a moment, "Really!?" for the first time he was envious of her dreams!

She nodded, "I was in the fort in Garason- in the inner chamber, I could see the Vase!"

A smile crept over Rave's face- what could be wrong with *that* dream!? "What was it like!?"

Fa looked a bit disgusted that he thought it was a great thing. "It was wrong!" she insisted.

He wiped the smile from his face.

"The Vase was *wrong* and twisted! It was breaking, right before my eyes! And then Eternity was there- standing where the Vase had been."

"Did he say anything?" Rave tried hard to keep excitement from his voice.

Fa hesitated, as if trying to decide if it was too personal to share. "He touched my face and told me not to be afraid," she said numbly.

"What do you think it means?" Rave thought about her task, and decided that he understood what it meant- but did she?

Her face crumpled in exhaustion, "I don't know." She leaned to one side and buried her face in the bed, "I don't know what I'm meant to do now!" her muffled voice lamented.

Rave sighed, he wished he had better advice than just 'don't be afraid'! A lot of good that would do her now! She needed a firm plan, something doable!

But Rave had no plans to give her.

*   *   *

The noise of the banquet reached Desert's ears as he wandered the halls of the manor, he had been trying to find the right words to explain things to Fate- and Brave. He knew that this whole mess was of his own making. 'If only I had told them sooner!' he thought back on all the moments where he could have told Fa and Rave the truth.

Dese looked up, and turning a corner, coming towards him- was Fate! She was dressed for sleep, her bare feet chilled on the stone floor and a shawl about her shoulders, her fire hair had been braided in a loose braid down her back. A guard walked behind her, escorting her down the hall. She paused when she saw him, then quickened her pace, intending to pass him.

"Fa please, let me explain!" he begged, and instead of blocking her way, he took up step beside her, "There just never seemed like a good time to tell you-"

Fa stopped abruptly and faced him, "Never a good time to tell us that you're the son of the Grand Duke of Tarval?" her voice was calm but accusing.

Her escort stifled a snort of laughter, Dese shot him a glare, and Fa continued.

"Apparently you had plenty of time to lie to me though." The fact that she was calm- not waving her arms or raising her voice- made her words sting even more. Dese pressed his lips together; he felt thoroughly scolded- and embarrassed that the guard was watching the whole thing!

"You told me that you were an orphan- your time at sea must have made you forget what the word means! I trusted you..." the betrayed look in her beautiful eyes broke his heart, "I trusted you, and you were mocking me the whole time."

"I *wasn't* mocking you!" he insisted- he needed her to believe him! "And I didn't lie about being a lost orphan!"

Fa took a breath as if bracing herself for more lies- but she was listening!

Rave glanced at the guard, "Would you mind stepping back?" he gritted, the guard smirked, but took five steps back, not quite far enough for his liking but it would have to do. He looked back at Fa; would she believe him?

"Thrive is not my father," There, let the truth float around in the open air for once!

Fa's sceptical face froze in surprise.

"The truth is- I don't even have any relation to him at all! He took me in as a ward years ago, after my mother died; what I told you was true… I just left out some things."

Fa waited for a moment, searching his face, she even glanced at the guard. "A ward? I don't know what that means," She said at last.

Dese was relieved; this he could explain! "I'm not his son; I won't inherit a title from him. I'm just under his protection." It surprised him how much the words cut him.

"He was angry with you on the balcony- the same kind of angry that my father gets with Rave," she pointed out, with a lingering note of scepticism.

Desert shrugged and chose not to think too deeply about it, "He's always expected me to act like his son- to play the role of the Grand Duke's son. But I'm not- I never will be nobility."

Fate seemed to digest his words and Dese felt a bit of hope from her expression.

"So…" he ventured, "What do you say fire girl?" he said with a tentative smile, "Friends?"

She sighed, "I'll think about it."

Dese bit his lip and nodded; that would have to do for now!

He watched her walk away, feeling hopeful and beat-up at the same time. As her escort passed him to follow her, he smirked, and Dese glared at him in return.

*   *   *

Desert closed the heavy door behind him and took a deep breath, before him through an arch, sitting by a fire, he knew that Thrive was waiting. Dese had always felt like a naughty child when he was in Thrive's chambers- maybe he always was.

Thrive was sitting by the fire, his feet propped up, a book with a moth-eaten cover in his hands, he looked tired. Dese had gotten one of the guards to tell him that Thrive's summons from the King had not gone well and Dese wondered just how bad it was.

"I need to speak with you," Desert said quietly, after he'd gone through the arch and stood in the firelight.

Thrive looked up briefly before returning to his book, he turned a page calmly. "You wish to speak? What a pleasant surprise," he said dryly.

"Fate and Brave are Nity followers."

203

"Well, that is unimaginatively typical of Garatins," Thrive said, without looking up.

His aloofness irked Dese. "I'm sorry- alright!?" he burst out.

Thrive closed his book with a dusty thud and leveled his dark eyes on Dese.

"I'm sorry I caused you concern when I didn't contact you when we docked; it won't happen again."

"Do you give your word?" Thrives voice was still annoyingly calm.

"What?"

"Give me your word," Thrive repeated, with heavy meaning.

Dese stared back at him, the words refusing to form in his mouth.

"I don't know why this is so important to you- it's not like I'm being groomed for your title; I will never be nobility!" he repeated what he had said to Fa only moments before and saw a flicker of something cross Thrive's face. Was it remorse, regret- shame?! Dese couldn't tell, anymore than he could distinguish the emotions he himself felt on the topic. "I will never be a Duke- much less Grand Duke," he stated, and felt his throat contract.

"But you could be more than a deckhand," Thrive said.

All Dese could hear was disappointment, and it cut him deeper than he would have thought possible! Oh, the sweet relief that had been his while he was away sailing, with enough leagues behind him to forget how much of a failure he was.

There was a long moment of silence; Dese stared at his feet feeling like a child being scolded, and Thrive gazed into the fire, no doubt wishing he could burn away his shame over Desert's short comings.

"As Nity followers- are Fate and Brave safe in the city?" Dese asked, after long minutes filled with the wood snapping in the fire.

"They will be; under my protection," Thrive said wearily.

"Is the King likely to change his ruling on the new law?" Dese asked hopefully.

"Considering his state of mind today- I would not make any plans on him doing so," Thri said heavily.

"Has the King gotten worse while I was at sea?" He knew that Triumphant the Great wasn't the best King- but he had heard he had gotten worse after the death of the prince. That had happened a few days before Dese had set sail from Tarva- how had things gotten so bad, so quickly!?

Thrive didn't answer Dese- he didn't need to.

"What about... your friends- is there any chance of meeting with them? Or... have they all been arrested?" Dese asked fearfully.

Thri considered his answer before speaking, he stood up and went to place his book on a shelf. "Not all of them, some have fled the city, others are in hiding." He turned and looked at Dese, the darkness and firelight casting his face into deep contrast, "Why do you ask? You've never been terribly interested before about the Nity followers and their meetings."

His words stung; of course, Dese cared about the Nity followers! The teachings of Eternity were as much a part of his life as Thrive was... he just wasn't as involved as others, but after the events of his voyage; the storm, Rizon's snakebite...

"It was a long voyage with a lot of strange happenings- and just because I've never been outspoken, doesn't mean I'm not 'interested'," he defended himself.

Thri was skeptical- he needed more of an explanation.

"Also..." Dese hated himself for adding the next part, it discredited his first reason and made him sound foolish, "Fate needs to speak with them."

"Ahh," Thrive said, patronizingly, "A lovely maiden, that explains all."

Dese could feel his knowing gaze.

"She has a message for them," Dese said tightly.

This interested Thri and he arched a brow. "A message from the Nity followers in Garatin?"

It peeved him that he couldn't give a real answer; Fa hadn't really told him, so he shrugged his shoulders, "She said it's an important message."

Thrive thought for a moment, then he went to the fire and threw another log in from a silver stand near by, in so doing momentarily turning his back on Dese. "As I said; the Nity followers are, understandably, in hiding, arranging a meeting would be impossible."

"You don't know where they are?" Dese asked stepping closer- that couldn't be true!

"I am the Grand Duke!" he said turning to face him again, the fire behind him left his face in shadow, "Hiding wanted outlaws would not be fitting to my station. And even If I knew their hiding place, I would not risk the Nity followers discovery by letting their location be heard by the wrong ear. Not everyone in this manor can be trusted."

"Including me!?" Dese was hurt and offended.

Thri looked like he would try and deny it, try to make his words sound nicer.

"No, it's all right!" Dese beat him to speaking. "I understand; I'm a very irresponsible deckhand!" he said bitterly, he spun around and left with his ears burning and a sour lump in his throat.

*   *   *

Thrive sat down heavily as Desert shut his chamber door firmly and covered his face with his hands.

"Excellent!" he muttered irritably, "I should teach on the street on how to raise a ward!"

He closed his eyes and leaned back. All his life he had been told and believed, that he was skilled with words, 'a silken tongue' some had said, but sometimes he wondered if they were right at all.

"Desert…" he whispered with despair.

Chapter 21   Mischief

"The message?!" Fate asked, her heart thudding in her ears. After Fa and Rave had been served breakfast, the Grand Duke had summoned them. With trembling nerves, they had been escorted to a room with more books than Fa thought existed in the whole world. The Grand Duke stood with hands on hips, and had briskly wished them a good morning, then had asked her what 'the message' was.

"Desert told me you had a message from Garason for the Nity followers, what is the message?" Thrive waited for her response- but Fa was speechless, she glanced sharply at Desert who was standing to one side, leaning against the wall, he offered her a weak smile.

"Don't be alarmed," Thri said when she hesitated, "I won't be imprisoning anyone for being a Nity follower."

Fa glanced at Rave for help, he shook his head slightly. He thought the same as she did; this was too risky.

"I'm not sure that the message is meant for you, my lord," she said, feeling her heart quicken sickeningly, "It's for the Nity followers." She was determined not to let him intimidate her into telling him.

"What do you take *me* for?"

His question startled her. "What?" She forgot about his title.

He smiled, it transformed his whole face and calmed Fa's breathing. "The reason I won't be arresting Nity followers is because I am one myself, have been for many years, ever since my voyage to Garatin." He turned his back and sat down, Fa took the opportunity to hiss at Desert, "Why didn't you tell us!?" she knew that Thrive no doubt heard the hiss- she didn't care though.

Desert shrugged his shoulders and smiled slyly, "Guess I was under your spell."

Fa didn't have time to say anything more, Rave squeezed her arm, and she turned back to face Thrive.

"Not everyone in my service knows this," Thrive said, glancing wearily at the closed chamber door, "So do try and keep it to yourselves." Here he gave Dese a look heavy with meaning, "Now, who is this message from- or am I not allowed to know even that?"

Fa was calmed by his tone and relaxed approach, but was he ready for the answer to his question? She decided to tell him and judge by his response whether or not to tell him the message, "It's from Eloi." She watched his face.

Thrives eyebrows shot up, and she heard Desert stand up straight. "How intriguing!" Thri murmured, "And you are certain that I can not hear this message?"

Fa glanced at Rave to see what he thought, he still looked a bit uncertain, but he shrugged. Fa took a deep breath.

'Don't be afraid Fa', she couldn't tell if the Dream Child's voice really spoke, or if it was only a memory.

"I have dreams of the future," she began, and was reassured to see that Thrive didn't balk immediately at her words. "They aren't clear, and they don't come in order… But I know that something bad is coming to Tarva. A storm off the sea maybe. I was only told to warn Eloi's people."

Thrive took a deep breath and leaned back, lost in thought, "I see."

'Is it over?' Fa wondered with an unreal feeling, 'Have I done what the heart stain required? Will Eloi let me go home now!?' Fa had expected something to happen when her task was done, but her hands were still burnt, and there was silence in the library.

"I understand now why you wish to speak with Horizon; he is usually the one with messages from Eloi," Thrive said, standing to his feet. "I shall find out if it is possible to contact him. Now I have a great many things to do today," he said, walking to the door. Opening it, he called to Fa and Rave's escorts who had waited outside.

"The Garatin's are free to roam the manor as they wish," he turned to Fa and Rave, "I urge you; stay here in my manor where you are safe." With that he left.

Fa felt Desert's gaze, but she purposely kept her back to him- she wasn't ready to speak to him yet. Glancing at Rave, she too left, thankful that the guards didn't follow her; she needed time to think. She wasn't worried about Rave leaving the manor now that they were free to; she knew he wouldn't leave without her.

She frowned and looked down at her hands; was she free of the heart stain?

*   *   *

"On the contrary, my lord, you have been very kind to me, and I will not soon forget your hospitality," Confess bowed her head in a rare show of respect that she did not give to just anyone. She had waited in the fire hall, knowing that the Grand Duke would pass by that way some time that morning. "But I must take my leave now, I hope to find work, perhaps in the Earls Ring." At this point Fess's pride was so desolate that she hardly felt the prick of humility- hardly, but she still did.

"If that is your wish," Thrive said politely, "However please consider an offer first, my lady."

Fess shifted; perhaps her pride wasn't in as bad a shape as she thought, for she balked at the thought of working as a maidservant in Thrives manor. She believed she could stomach the work somewhere else- but not here! "My lord?" she asked apprehensively.

"You are a sea captain- are you not?" he asked with a hint of a challenge.

Fess blinked, "I haven't proved to be a very good one." Where was this leading?

"I disagree!" Thrive said taking a step back, his bold voice filling the fire hall, "You ran The Prestige' through a mighty gale, and although the ship was lost- not *one* of your crew or passengers was left in the sea."

Fess considered his praise and wondered if it *was she* who had anything to do with the safety of her crew. Wasn't it Horizon who had promised they would all be safe? Or rather… Eloi?

"I know few would think me wise, but I believe you are a fine captain, despite it all. I want to offer you a position on one of my merchant ships." Thrives eyes twinkled playfully.

Was he serious!? A sea merchant of the Grand Duke!?

"I currently have a ship in need of a captain, what say you?"

"My lord, I…" Confess' mouth had gone dry; could this really be happening to her!? Wasn't her story one of disappointment, failure and defeat? Could it also be one of hope?

"Think it over, I'll send word to the ship's first mate to expect you- you can look her over before giving your answer. 'The Lady Loyal' is in the harbour now, undergoing spring repairs. Now, I must be about my day." Thrive bowed slightly and walked away with a slight smile.

He was gone before Fess realized that she hadn't thanked him! Fess sat down heavily on a bench before the fire and tried to process the last ten minutes of her life; she knew that the Grand Duke was a good man- but this!? Was it pity? Did he pity her!? Fess shoved the thought aside; her desire was stronger than her pride in this case. She knew of the ship Thrive had spoken of- she had seen it before, but never imagined that it could be hers!

'The Lady Loyal' was a twin hulled, five-mast beauty of a ship! Fess remembered that her hulls were made from rich red wood that gleamed and made the waves around it glow with warmth. The thought of captaining such a ship- in the service of the Grand Duke, was almost too much to hope for...

Fess forced her starry-eyed thoughts to come to a halt; surely, she wasn't worthy of such a position! But Thrive thought she was... did she deserve his trust? Fess felt a desire rise in her- so strong it was sickening; she *had* to prove her worth- perhaps to Thrive, but more to herself.

"*What are you doing here!?*" a secretive voice hissed somewhere close by. Fess tensed and strained her ears to listen.

"You told me you would help!" a second voice said slightly louder- slightly more frantic.

Fess stood up silently, unlike last time, neither voice belonged to the Grand Duke, and Fess felt a prick of unease at the tone of the voices. She looked around, trying to determine which dark hallway the hushed voices were coming from.

"I told you to stay where you *were!*" the first voice hissed again, he sounded angry, for Fess could tell they were both men, and she was fairly certain which hallway they were in. She cautiously approached the arch, her boots making no sound. She stopped when she was close by and pressed herself against the wall to listen.

The first voice continued in a more hushed tone- he obviously didn't want to be overheard. "Coming here is much too dangerous! Don't you know *he* lives here!? Did anyone see you?" he cut himself off, afraid he had spoken too loudly. Then there were footsteps and Fess realized that they were retreating farther down the hallway. Fess pressed her lips together; if she stepped into the hall- would they see her?

"Confess?" a soft voice said behind her. Fess spun round and nearly struck Fate with a blow that might have broken her jaw. Fa was alone and looked frightened by Confess' response. Fess forcefully jabbed a finger at her own lips and willed the girl to be silent. Fa froze obediently, her face quite pale, and Fess turned her ear back to the hall; they hadn't been heard, and the voices had continued the conversation- but they were too far away to hear.

Taking a risk, Fess stepped into the hall; it was ill lit with only one torch further away. It led down some steps, and had several smaller hallways leading off it- the main one led to the stables. Fess was conscious of Fate silently following her as she went down the steps, like a child afraid to wander far from safety; Fess didn't mind if she remained soundless. Fess paused when they reached the bottom of the steps; she could here the voices again.

"Do as I say- and nothing will go wrong! Do you understand!?" the first voice was speaking again, they had stepped into one of the smaller hallways and were quite close. Fess directed Fa to step back, and together they listened as the first voice gave instructions, "Go to the stables, if asked say I sent you; wait for me there."

There were hurried footsteps, and Fess put out her hand to keep Fa as far back in the shadows as she could, they watched as a Tarven man dressed in the clothes of a servant emerged into the main hall. He didn't look their way but instead walked down the hall, apparently obeying his orders to go to the stables. They heard another pair of footsteps, and the other man emerged. He watched the second man disappear towards the stables, then he turned towards the fire hall and hurried up the steps; none the wiser for the two women pressed against the wall in the shadows. Fess had a good look at the second Tarven man as he passed by and her face darkened; it was Valor, Thrives head guard! It appeared that Thrive had misplaced his trust.

"What's going on?" Fate asked when the last echoes of footsteps had died away.

"I intend to find out," Fess replied, her mind working on double time.

"Is the Grand Duke in danger?" Fa asked, following Fess' line of thoughts exactly.

"Is your brother near by?" Fess asked instead of answering. Fa shook her head.

Fess hissed in frustration, "You'll have to do then." She marched down the hall towards the stables.

"Shouldn't we tell someone?" Fa asked nervously as she hurried to keep up.

'At least she's wearing sensible clothes,' Fess thought as she glanced at Fa in her trousers and boots. "No, that was the head guard; if he's plotting something against the Duke- no one can be trusted till we know what's happening."

"We're going to follow them?"

"Yes, I'll need you to go for the Grand Duke if we uncover something foul." Fess hoped the girl wouldn't turn flighty and useless under pressure.

"This could be a misunderstanding," Fa pointed out, proving that she had a good head on her slim shoulders.

Fess paused before going through the door that would take them out to the stables; what if this *was* a misunderstanding? She questioned herself. Could she be over reacting? No; Fess knew what people looked like when they were keeping a secret, and Valor the head guard was keeping a big one. And if the head guard of the Grand Duke was keeping secrets; then there was much cause for caution.

*   *   *

Desert watched Fate leave the library, his mind working quickly, while Brave lingered in the room, looking about himself awkwardly.

"I think I can get you and Fa to the Nity followers," Dese said boldly.

"Really!?" Rave asked hopefully, yet still sceptical. "What about the Duke?" he asked, glancing at the door.

Dese grinned mischievously, "What about him?"

A smile crept across Rave's face as he understood Desert's meaning, but it faded, "But aren't all the Nity followers arrested?" he lowered his voice.

Dese glanced to the open door himself and lowered his own voice, "Not all of them." He grinned when he saw his friend's excitement grow.

"You know where they are," Rave whispered and stepped closer.

"I know how to find out." Dese only wondered briefly if he really could follow through on his statement.

Rave's excitement was dampened suddenly, as if he remembered that only last night the two of them weren't on speaking terms, "What about the Grand Duke?" he asked again. He seemed a lot more cautious since coming to the Dukes Ring- or was it since he had been betrayed?

Dese shrugged, hoping it was reassuring, "He may be able to arrange a meeting with Horizon- but Fa wouldn't need to see him if she could get to the Nity followers."

Rave thought about it and Dese feared that he was losing his enthusiasm.

"Look," Dese reasoned, "Thrive might be able to get Fa to Horizon- but he won't if he thinks it's too dangerous. But Fa *needs* to warn the Nity followers; right?"

Rave nodded reluctantly.

Dese smiled confidently, "So let's make it happen!" He watched as Rave thought about it.

"How?" he asked and Dese knew that he had convinced him.

"Follow me." Dese smiled; if he could pull this off, then Rave would really trust him again and he would get his friend back- and... Fa might forgive him too.

He led Brave out through the halls and back up several stairs, all the while keeping a sharp eye out for Thrive. When they were nearing Thrive's chambers Desert saw Thri's manservant coming towards them.

"Good morning Contrast! A fine day don't you think?" he greeted cheerily as they approached each other; he had to be careful around Contrast, he knew Dese well enough to sense when he was up to mischief.

Contrast bowed his head and gave the boys a wary look, "Master Desert." He failed to comment on the quality of the day.

"Rast- did Thrive go out for the whole morning?" Dese hoped he sounded casual.

Contrast moved as if he was anxious to go about his work, "I believe his lordship has gone to make arrangements for the Queen's banquet- it's fortunate that you returned in time to attend, assuming you won't be spending anymore time in the tower."

His tone was innocent- but Dese knew better. He resumed walking and flashed a smile over his shoulder, "Who can say what the Duke's next whim will be on my quarters?" he asked flippantly. He was pleased to see that Contrast continued on his way with only a rueful smile and no trace of suspicion.

"Queens banquet?" Brave asked when Contrast was out of earshot.

"Yeah," Dese explained absently as they reached Thrives chamber door. "For her birthday; there's a banquet every year." He stopped and made sure that the hallway was empty, "Alright, this is Thrive's chambers. Contrast was going the other way so we should be safe. If we get caught by a maidservant or someone- just act like we're meant to be in there... alright?"

Rave looked pale and a bit frozen in place, "We're going in *there*!?"

Dese smiled confidently and pushed the heavy door open. Stepping in he glanced through the arch at the room beyond; it was empty. Brave followed him and closed the door firmly behind him, he looked around with wide eyes.

"What are we doing in here?" he asked in a fearful whisper.

Dese waved his arms about the chamber and walked about confidently, "Taking a risk! Relax!" he laughed at the look on his friend's face.

Rave cautiously joined him, only he was looking around as if expecting the Grand Duke to be hiding somewhere. "What are we looking for?" he hissed after scanning the room three times.

Dese smiled cockily and moved to look at a beautiful painting of a white castle with fluttering flags, it hung in a little alcove in the wall. "This," he said feeling suddenly confident again.

Chapter 22   Old Words

The main city street outside the Ducal was respectfully busy with people, carts and mounted horses. In the same way that the Earls Ring made the Harbour Ring seem loud, vulgar and dirty, so the Dukes Ring made the Earls Ring seem commonplace and dull by comparison. The Dukes Ring was all castles, ramparts, arches and gardens. The people on the street at this late hour in the morning were mostly servants on their way to market. Riding in carriages, women in beautiful headdress could be glimpsed. Men in silk capes rode fine horses, and the soldiers and guards looked less ready to chase people. Maid servants followed their mistress and young men in page attire hurried about on errands. There were even stable boys who were paid to keep the streets clean after the horses!

Confess and Fate waited outside on the street, until Thrive's head guard, Valor, stepped out with the suspicious Tarven by his side. Fess watched them from across the street with a sharp eye. The two men turned left without hesitation- going further into the Dukes Ring, even Fa was taken by surprise by this, surely if they were plotting something foul- they would go to the Earls Ring… unless this plot involved more dangerous people than they had first thought.

Seemingly undeterred by this troubling thought, Fess led the way and followed the two men at a safe distance. It was easy enough to follow the two men through the streets, although they walked quickly and were obviously nervous, they didn't suspect that they were being shadowed. Fa noticed that Confess seemed quite comfortable following people, and she wondered, not for the first time, about the fierce woman's past.

A thought struck Fa with a spike of anxiety, "Fess!" She hissed, her feet hesitating, "What if they are leading us into a trap?!"

Fess did not slow her step or show any sign of second thoughts, "Let them try." She dared with unwavering tenacity.

Fa's heart raced with growing apprehension, and she glanced backwards wondering if she could turn back; but the Grand Dukes manor was left far behind. Swallowing her second thoughts, Fa hurried to stay close behind Fess.

Ahead, the crowds grew and became louder as they neared the Dukes market that was centered in the middle of the main street; to the left, great stone arches opened to the cherry gardens.

"Keep your eye on the guard, I'll watch the other one." Fess ordered as their quarry entered the market, "We'll lose them too easily in there- keep your eye on the perimeter," Fess said anxiously, as the crowds obstructed their view.

The next few minutes were spent in strained silence as Fa and Fess neared the market and tried to keep the two men in their sights. They were jostled by the crowd, and their progress was slowed to an agonizingly relaxed pace. Soon they lost sight of the two Tarvens, and Fa was ready to give up- but Fess forced her way deeper into the crowds and scanned over everyone's heads till she spotted the two men again.

"What are they doing?" Fess wondered aloud as Fa came to her side again and followed her gaze.

Valor hung back in the open, while the other man went to the back of a covered wagon. Fa watched in puzzlement when the man beckoned to a boy of five or so. The boy jumped from the wagon and embraced the man, then the boy and man turned back to Valor and the three of them began to make their way out of the market, towards the gardens.

Fa looked to Fess, but even she seemed baffled by this turn of events. "Come on, we can't lose them now," she said, with a single-minded determination.

*   *   *

Brave did a double take when Desert turned sharply and disappeared into the wall, "What-!?" he exclaimed as he jumped forward and realized what had happened. In the side of the alcove there was a narrow gap, just big enough for a person to pass through turned to one side. It was completely hidden from the rest of the room and could only be seen if you stepped up close to the painting.

Desert stuck his head out and grinned, "All castles have secret rooms and passages." He explained, "This is Thrive's secret study!" he ducked back in before Rave could respond.

"Secret!?" Rave squeaked; the wrath of the Grand Duke was not something he wanted to experience!

"Come on Rave!" Desert's voice echoed out to him.

Rave took one more nervous glance at the room, then followed his friend. The passage was narrow and dark, the kind of place the Fate would loth to go into. The cold walls turned sharply to the left, then opened into a small windowless room. Desert was lighting a lantern that hung over a desk and chair in the center of the study. Its light illuminated a bookshelf against the back wall, and several trunks on the floor lining the side walls. The desk was neatly stacked with books and writing paper. An ink well and feather pen sat ready, as if waiting for their master's return.

The simplicity of the secret chamber afforded a unique glimpse into Thrive's nature, that the rest of his chambers did not.

"If Thrive knows where the Nity followers are hiding; this is where he'd keep that information," Dese said, scanning the room as their eyes adjusted to the lighting. "I only know about this place because I found it when I was little…"

Rave's fear evaporated, and excitement took its place; he was in the secret study of a Grand Duke! Rave's smile widened when he thought of the scolding that Fa would give him when she found out.

"Look for a map… or letters," Desert instructed, as he began to sort through the papers on the desk.

Rave had a fleeting doubt about how successful their mission would be. 'Do people write down where their secret hideout is?' he wondered doubtfully, but he began to search just the same.

While Desert searched the desk, Rave took notice of a series of little alcoves in the walls, each one holding something different; an hourglass, a little black urn, vials full of powders and a small wooden box. Rave was instantly drawn to the box- it looked important somehow. All fear of being caught was forgotten as he picked up the box; it was the size of a large book and had a carving of a horse with flowing mane and tail. The lid opened smoothly on little hinges, and Rave caught his breath as something fluttered to the floor, kneeling, he realized that it was a little folded paper.

With growing excitement Rave unfolded the paper to discover it was a hand drawn map! Rave scanned the map but found he couldn't make sense of it. It wasn't a map of the city at all… it was a simple layout of a castle- as drawn by a child, there were names scribbled down, but since Rave had refused to learn; he couldn't read it. But he did notice how yellowed and worn the folds were, and he decided that the map was too old to be what they were looking for. There were two other things in the box; one was a very old, very dry and yellowed white rose. The second was a ribbon bound letter; the ribbon was a deep royal blue, and it held the letter closed in a neat bow.

"Find something?" Dese asked as he leaned over the desk to look at Rave, who was still kneeling.

"It's a letter," Rave said, as he stood and placed the box on the table. The ribbon pulled off smoothly and the letter opened revealing deep creases.

"Whats it say?" Dese asked, as he replaced a stack of books that he had flipped through.

Rave sighed, "I can't read." He handed the letter across the desk to Dese; it was the first time in his life that he wished he *could* read! Already he could hear Fa's voice, 'if you only let Father teach you how'-

"Spring has come for the first time without you- and the cherry blossoms have surely faded without your presence..." Dese read aloud the first few lines, seemingly uninterested in Rave's confession.

Rave waited for Dese to read more, but his friend read the rest silently with a strange expression, "It's a love letter..." he said after he had finished, "To 'Lady Loyal' from Thrive when he was young- I didn't know Thrive was ever in love!" he said in wonder.

"Do you know her?" Rave asked, as he looked again at the dried rose in the box. He had a hard time imagining the Grand Duke being in love.

"No, it says that she left Tarva. I've never heard Thrive speak of her!" Dese seemed a bit shaken by the letter but Rave lost interest and spotted something else that looked promising; a trunk on the floor with leather binding.

"What about this?" Rave asked as he approached the trunk.

Desert clumsily retied the bow and returned the box and its contents to the alcove, "That? those are just my old things. Just keepsakes that Thrive's been holding on to, he brings it out every birthday and insists on telling the same story about each one." Dese explained with an eye roll.

But Rave's curiosity was piqued, and he knelt to open the trunk; inside was a child's outfit and a woman's dress- and something else. "What about these?" Rave asked holding up a large bundle of letters tied together with twine.

"You won't find anything in th-" Deserts words stopped when he saw the letters, "I've never seen those before!"

*   *   *

Fate and Confess split up when the came to the Kings Monument; it was an elaborate courtyard with the cherry tree garden on either side and the cliff face of the mountain at its back. The Dragon Keep loomed far above, birds flew to and from nests in the cliff face as the sun banished all shadows from the courtyard below. The courtyard was filled with arch ways and pillars, stone statutes of past kings sat on platforms interspersed with stone dragons, making it impossible to see clearly from one side to the other.

The two women had followed the three Tarvens from the busy street into the much less crowded gardens and were forced to slow their pace lest they alert their quarry. When the came to the lake they joined many others on the bridge that crossed the narrowest part of the lake; they nearly lost sight of their quarry, but caught sight of them on the other side, where they went on for a few more minutes through more trees. Passing through the blooming trees was almost more than Fa could bear, and she was relieved when they came to the Kings Monument and left the trees behind them.

But Fess had quickly seen the risk of losing the Tarvens amongst the arches and statues, so she sent Fa one way and had gone the other way herself, giving Fa the instructions to walk slowly and to not let the men catch her watching them.

Fa didn't like the thought of being separated from Fess, and again wondered about turning back. But as Fess disappeared to the left, Fa took a deep breath and forced her feet to take her right.

She skirted the monuments, all the while watching the men from the corner of her eye as they went through the center. The little boy suddenly glanced her way! Fa snapped her gaze away and stared at a statue of a king with sad eyes. She forced herself to stand still, hoping she didn't look suspicious, but it felt like the sad eyed statue was staring back at her, and she found it hard to meet his gaze. When at last she tore her eyes away, the boy and two men had kept walking, and she resumed her stalking, keeping them ahead of her and to her left.

'Are they here to meet someone?' she wondered as they neared the cliff face. Carved into the cliff were even more arches and statues, with countless tunnels behind them, so that you could wander through looking at the stonework from all sides. The statues in the cliff went back two and sometimes three deep, providing the perfect opportunity to lose anyone who might be following you. The thought struck Fa as the three men entered one of the arches and disappeared behind a large statue of a dragon with spread wings.

Fa hurried closer and met Fess in the middle of the courtyard.

"Where did they go!?" Fa asked in bewilderment as they watched the many tunnel entrances; the three Tarvens did not emerge.

Fess hissed in frustration, then wordlessly led the way to the arch where their quarry had last been seen. Peering into the semi dark tunnel, they saw nothing but dust floating through the beams of sun. Stepping inside Fess went to the back, past two more carvings where it was almost completely dark. The cold stone of the mountain began to seep into Fa's skin as she followed hesitantly, her claustrophobia slowly rearing its panicky head.

Fess breathed a curse when she reached the back wall and stooped down to inspect the ground.

"What is it?" Fa's voice was scarcely a whisper.

Fess stepped out of the way to reveal a rough-hewn hole in the wall, large enough for a person to crawl through. Fa felt her heart tremble with more than her fear of tight spaces, she felt the heart stain. The presence inside her grew to a throbbing, stealing her breath and clouding her thoughts. A deep, familiar foreboding also grew, like a childhood nightmare that she couldn't quite explain, and could only remember bits of it, like broken glass cutting her mind to shreds. It was like a damp fog that had been stalking her footsteps for... Fa wondered if it had in fact always been there. It was a darkness- nay, a *threat* that had pursued her across the world, and Fa could see only one possible ending; it was an image in her mind... a pile of ashes.

"I thought the kings blocked off these tunnels decades ago!" Fess thought out loud and stooped down to look inside the hole.

"What is it?" Fa was having a hard time concentrating on her voice.

"An ancient ossuary, miles and miles of tunnels and caves- a labyrinth under the mountain." Fess explained as she tried to see through the darkness inside the hole, then she looked up at Fate's blank expression, "Old catacombs; tombs." She summed up and brushed off her hands.

"They're hiding in old tombs?" Fa asked in timid horror, she didn't know a dark tunnel could get worse!

Fess raised an unimpressed brow, "You afraid of ghosts?"

Fa shifted her feet, it was more the thought of stumbling in the dark over old bones wrapped in rotting cloth that made her squeamish, "are you sure they went in there?" she asked looking around, hoping to see the three Tarvens somewhere- anywhere but inside the tunnel!

Fess returned her gaze to the hole, "They went in there all right- I can see torch light. This doesn't look good for the Grand Duke's head guard; only outlaws, smugglers and traitors would have reason to go in there now," she hissed another curse then looked back up at Fa.

"Are you coming?" she asked briskly.

Fa's eyes darted to the hole, then back to Fess' face; everything inside her balked at the idea of going inside that hole... but there was something inside that was not *her*, it pushed and swelled against her.

'Don't be afraid Fate'

Fa nodded her head, and Fess looked momentarily impressed, "Keep quiet; sounds will carry far in there. We'll have to be careful not to get too close to them- or they'll see us. And careful not to fall too far behind- or we'll be lost in the dark." Fess bent down and disappeared inside the hole.

Fa glanced back at the sunlight and open air, then followed.

*   *   *

Desert counted and found that there were nearly twenty letters, all neatly folded, each one written in Thrive's smooth hand, but the first letter didn't begin with who it was addressed to- it just began.

'Six weeks at sea is much too long for anyone- I hope it is something you will never experience!'

The letter went on to describe the weather through the voyage and condition of the ship, all things that Dese knew well and he almost lost interest, until his eye snagged on something at the end of the letter.

'Strange that I should think of your namesake- given my surroundings, but I think of you all the time...'

At first Dese thought it was another love letter- and it was, just of a different kind, as Dese realized with a start when he read his namesake.

'Desert, I know that it is not logical that I should write to you, I doubt anyone would understand why a Duke should care so much for his serf and her son- I don't think I understand it myself! But your mother has always been dear to me, from the first, I thought of her as my baby sister- oh how tongues would wag if anyone in the court read this letter- but despite what they say, I don't have any relation to you or your mother!

But when I first held you- tiny babe that you were- I might as well have been your uncle- or father, for all the tears I wept! You, Desert, are a joy that I did not foresee, and it pains me to think that no one will ever understand... I also can't bear to think of how old you will have grown by the time I return to Tarva.

But when I do return, I'll be made Grand Duke- I know the title means nothing to an infant- but I will be able to make sure that you and your mother are properly cared for, let the court frown and disapprove- but I swear I won't let them stop me from bringing you both into my care for good! As Grand Duke, only the King could keep me from doing so- and I doubt he would care! And I don't care what the village

221

says about that idiotic 'lost orphan curse', it will take more than a 'curse' to keep me from caring for you both properly!'

Desert had to pause, for he found that his eyes had misted over, 'This letter' he realized, 'must have been written only short months after my father died!' Thrive, the Duke, was writing letters to a child not even five years old! But Dese knew how this story ended; a Grand Duke returning home to find the son of his beloved serf- was alone. More tears came to his eyes when Dese realized that Thrive's promise in his letter to care for him and his Mother was only half kept; his mother died before Thrive even boarded the return ship for Tarva.

"Well?" Brave asked, bringing Dese back to the present, "What do they say?"

"They're letters that Thrive wrote to me," Dese replied, as he stealthily wiped his eyes.

"But you've never read them?" Rave asked with a frown.

"I was just a babe when he wrote them- he must have written them on his voyage to Garatin… after my father died. I guess Thrive just… never gave them to me." He felt a stab of guilt for reading them without Thrives knowledge but pushed it aside.

Rave showed more interest at the mention of his home country, and Dese moved on to the next letter, reading out loud, but skipping over any parts that were too personal. He noticed that in this letter, the writing was different- shaky as if someone was constantly bumping Thrives elbow. He skipped over the beginning of the letter and read aloud the next part.

'The rest of the voyage was for the most part uneventful- I do hope that for the return voyage, the crew will double as good company! I am happy to say however, that two weeks ago we finally landed in Larsanne. I shudder even now thinking of the place, I doubt Lord Contrast would do a good job of lording over anything. I left Larsanne a little over a week ago, and in that time, have traveled north along the eastern shore of the Neenor Sea. I've passed through several tiny fishing villages and past many farms, but not one inn to be seen among them! I've never slept on the ground so many nights in a row before, I do believe I'm starting to feel my fifty-one years.'

Dese smiled, he had never seen Thrive in such an unguarded and open way, it was like he was talking to Thri before he knew what a disappointment Dese would turn out to be. He kept reading aloud.

'The land here on the coast is beautiful- even if the roads are atrocious- but the villages are quite poor and I fear the people have suffered mistreatment at the hands

of the rich, I suppose that here, that just means Tarvens. I only now just encountered a child, a Garatin girl, I expect she was only a bit older than you are now. She was afraid of me- I do hope that when I return you won't be afraid of me.

When I arrive in the city- Garason- I'll speak with Ambassador Sinister (how would you fancy that namesake?) I will speak to him of the problems I see here on the coast- living so far away he probably doesn't know. But I don't expect we'll see eye to eye, I've heard many a report that Sinister is a ruthless man. I do not look forward to meeting him!'

Desert continued to read, going through the third letter that spoke more of his travels before reaching the city, Rave listened with interest; their mission was forgotten.

*   *   *

"He's been well behaved, hasn't made any trouble- but he won't shut his mouth!" the Tarven soldier complained.

Rustling managed a smile as he worried his hanky; he wasn't really listening to the soldier, he was trying to think of what he would say to Horizon after the mass arrests at the Pearl Square.

"We moved him to private chambers he talked so much!" the soldier continued, "He can't stay here much longer Rustling, barracks are no place for long-term prisoners."

Rust nodded, forcing himself to answer coherently, "Yes, I've come to take the Garatin with me." He turned to go to Horizons chambers.

"Where are you taking him?" the soldier asked curiously.

"My manor," Rust replied, without turning back, he didn't need to see the soldier's face to know that he disapproved- everyone would disapprove of his idea, including his mother! But he hoped that Rizon wasn't angry enough with him to refuse. Rust could protect the Garatin, keep him out of trouble, if he had him at his manor- but would Rizon cooperate?

"Private chambers!" Rust commented as he let himself into Rizon's chamber, "They must think you are rich." He hoped his light-hearted jest would set the tone for the conversation, and he nearly held his breath as Horizon stood to greet him.

"Rich- or very annoying, these soldiers don't seem much interested in theological debates!" the Garatin replied lightly, with only a hint of sarcasm.

Rust breathed a sigh of relief; that was one of the things he liked about the Garatin, you never needed to wonder if the man was hiding something, or holding a grudge, for Rizon would always come right out and say whatever was on his mind. Rizon had obviously forgiven him for keeping him from warning the Nity followers, just knowing that, made Rust want to sit down like he would after a long hard day.

"You have been well?" he asked and absent mindedly wiped his forehead of the perspiration that had gathered there.

"Indeed, I have- but I worry for my friends," Rizon said, with a serious tone.

Rust didn't need to ask which 'friends' and he avoided commenting on the matter.

"I've made arrangements for... more permanent accommodations, since it doesn't seem likely that your trial will be in the near future..." Rust cleared his throat; they both knew that it could be years before Rizon got his 'fair trial'.

"Where, may I ask, will I be staying?"

Rust shifted nervously- would Rizon agree to come with him? "I know it is not- protocol, but I consider you to be a friend..." he looked at Rizon, who was waiting patiently, 'oh just come out and say it!' Rust scolded himself. "I hope my manor will be acceptable to you."

Rizon smiled, "What more could a man ask for than to be a guest in the home of a friend?"

Rust nodded gratefully and wondered for a moment if it was necessary to clarify that Rizon wouldn't exactly be a 'guest', more like a prisoner with privileges, but Rust realized that Rizon was well aware of his position.

"Let us be off then- I'll have your things sent for." Rust glanced about the room for Rizon's personal things before remembering that they were shipwrecked, and that Rizon didn't have 'personal items'.

Leading the way out into the hall, and back to where the soldier was sitting at a desk, Rust tucked his hanky away. "I am taking custody of the Garatin prisoner," he officially informed the soldier, who had already gotten the appropriate papers ready, including hot wax to seal the documents with Rust's own ring.

"Shall I prepare an escort for you?" the soldier asked as Rust took off his ring and stamped it in the wax. Rust glanced at Horizon, and hesitated, his waxed ring hovering above the transfer document. "No, that won't be necessary," he said at last, making his trust of Rizon clear.

After finishing with the paperwork, the two men went down to the stables, where a horse was saddled for Rizon, then they started out for Rust's manor in the Earls Ring.

The ride through the city, was pleasant in the mid morning, and the Tarven and Garatin didn't bother with conversation as they rode down through the rings from the barracks in the Kings Ring, to Rust's manor in the Earls Ring. It took an hour to reach the manor, and they arrived at about the same time that Fate and Confess took to the streets in pursuit of Thrive's head guard.

Rustling and Horizon rode into Rust's humble manor courtyard and dismounted, leaving their horses for the stable boys. No sooner than they did, a page boy came running from the main doors, behind him came another man that Rust didn't recognize.

"Master Rustling," the page said breathlessly and bowed, "This is Golden, the household steward of the Grand Duke." The page's voice trailed off when Rustlings eyes widened.

Sweat popped out on Rust's brow all over again and he felt rather than heard himself stuttering, "G-Grand Duke!?" he bowed at his waist and searched his mind for a reason why the man who ran the household of the Grand Duke- should have come to him!

He glanced nervously at Rizon with a horrid feeling that it had something to do with the Garatin. "How- what can," Rust dapped his forehead with his hanky that was suddenly in his hand and started over, "How can I be of service to you?" he asked with another bow of his head. A soldier of his rank would not show such respect to a household steward of just any man, but even the household steward of the Grand Duke- servant though he was- was an important man.

Golden was a slim man, his long hair had gone mostly silver and was held back with a black tie, his clothes foretold of his status, and he held himself with dignity.

"I am here to escort Horizon to his lordship the Grand Duke; my master wishes to speak with him." Golden cut straight to business.

Rust looked to Rizon- but saw that he was as surprised by this turn of events as he was!

"Certainly- shall I accompany him to his lordship?" Rust asked after a moment, it's not like he could have said 'no, he can't go'.

Golden looked at Rizon and arched a brow, "No, I don't believe that will be necessary, but I must insist on leaving now, his lordship has a great many things to see to today."

Before Rust knew it, Rizon was riding off with Golden, on the promise that he would return in a few hours. Bewildered by the abruptness of the whole thing, Rust was across his courtyard and halfway up his manor steps before he realized that no one could have known where to find Rizon... Rust frowned and turned to look- but the two men were long gone.

"Page?" Rust called out with a rising sense of something... wrong. "When did Golden arrive here?"

"Just before you arrived- he did not wait long my lord." the page answered.

Rust frowned anew; he hadn't told anyone of his plans to bring Horizon to his manor- how had the Grand Duke known where to find him!?

Chapter 23   Understanding

"We're lost!" Fa breathed, as panic welled up inside her, nothing could be seen in the total darkness that had engulfed them! Fa felt funny in her head and realized that she was holding her breath- she let it go, her gasp echoing in the empty darkness.

They had been following the Tarvens with their flickering torch at a safe distance, sometimes walking in darkness because the torch bearer had gone around a corner. It was hard and nerve wracking, knowing that even a slight stumble would make an echo and give away their presence, but they had successfully been following for nearly a quarter of an hour, when the torch bearer turned another corner. Fate and Confess had hurried ahead, only to find darkness around the corner, with not even a glow from the torch in the distance; they were lost!

"They were just here!" Fess hissed in disbelieve, "They couldn't have gone far- feel along the walls for a passage!" she instructed, her voice sounding eerie in the darkness, but Fa couldn't move, her lungs wouldn't bring in enough air, and she found herself panting.

"Fate!" Fess reached out and roughly found Fa's shoulder and shook her, "Calm down! -"

She cut off her own words when they were both momentarily blinded as torch light suddenly flooded the tunnel. Surprised and frightened voices spoke all at once.

"Who are *they*!?"

"Grab them- quick!"

Fa found herself being pulled towards the torch light and blinked in surprise as she was pulled through a wooden door to a lit passage beyond. Just before the door was shut Fa caught a glimpse of a painted symbol on the door; it was a white five-pointed flower. Fa and Fess were held fast and surrounded by a group of Tarven men and women, the men were old, and all were frightened looking, one of them held a torch up and peered at their faces.

"Unhand us!" Fess demanded in a warning tone, she didn't struggle, but her face was murderous. To Fa's surprise, they were released- but a bolt had been slid across the door and they were well surrounded; they had no where to run.

"Who are you!?" one of the women asked, fear plainly displayed on her face.

"Confess, and Fate- who are you?" Fess sounded much more intimidating.

"How did you find this place?" one of the men, who was less intimidated by Fess, questioned with an air of authority.

"First answer me!" Fess demanded and stepped in front of Fa, as if protecting her, "Who are you? - Rebels? Outlaws? Who!?" she faced them down in a fierce stand off, her shoulders and fists tensing.

"They're Nity followers…" Fa realized, and all eyes went to her; she knew by the silence that she was right.

"What?" Fess hissed, obviously still on edge.

"You're Nity followers!" Fa said in relief, her emotions flying away in all directions, "I've been trying to find you since we arrived in the city!" She could hardly believe this turn of events!

"Who are you?" the woman asked again, her voice a bit calmer but still mistrusting.

"I'm a friend of Horizon – from Garatin," she explained hopefully- but the door keepers still looked sceptical.

"We haven't received word from Horizon; how did you know where to find us?" the old man asked cautiously.

Fa faltered; what could she say?

"It was by accident I assure you," Fess spoke up, she still looked like a wild dog ready to lunge out, "We followed someone; thought they were acting suspiciously."

The door keepers glanced behind them to where the tunnel slanted down, and there watching the proceedings was Valor- Thrive's head guard!

"You were followed by just the two of them?" the man asked Valor.

Valor nodded. Fa found herself holding her breath again, as she worked out what must have happened; Valor must have realized in the tunnel that he was being followed, and when he ducked inside the door, he would have had just enough time to tell the door keepers, who then jumped out and grabbed Fa and Fess. Did the Grand Duke know that his head guard was involved with hiding Nity followers?

"Who are they?" the door keepers asked.

"Guests of his Lordship," Valor answered, looking Fa and Fess up and down; he did not look pleased to see them.

"Does *he* know they are here?" one of the door keepers asked.

Valor scowled, "I should think not!"

"Please," Fa interrupted, "I'm a Nity follower myself- I'm a friend!"

"And you?" one of the door keepers asked, nodding to Fess, but she refused to answer.

"Take them down to the storage cave, and tell the others what happened, we'll have to decide what to do with them later."

Fa was thankful that Fess didn't resist as they were led down the tunnel away from the door. Now that Fa could see the stone tunnel clearly in the troch light, Fa realized that it was a very old tunnel indeed. They descended uneven steps and passed by several tunnel entrances. They also passed by a few more Tarvens who watched the procession without comment, and Fa wondered how many Nity Followers were hiding in the tunnels, and her hope began to grow- if only she could gain their trust and convince them she was a friend!

Fa hesitated when the wall on their left opened into a little, long alcove; old cave paintings of kings long gone covered the alcove wall, the colours faded, and edges chipped. The kings looked noble and brave. She remembered that Fess had called the caves catacombs, Fa shivered, and she quickened her step to keep close to their escort.

"Have you brought news from *him*?" Fa heard one of the door keepers ask Valor quietly, the two of them had fallen behind the others a few steps.

"Yes, *He* said he would try and contact Horizon- but if the Garatin doesn't come soon then we must assume that he won't be coming at all. *He* must remain very cautious in these times."

Their voices lowered and Fa couldn't hear anymore, she wondered who the '*he*' they were talking about was- could it be the Grand Duke? But only that morning Thrive had said that he didn't know where the Nity followers were hiding- had he lied?

Fa and Fess were led into a small cave filled with sacks and barrels. "Keep them from leaving," one of the door keepers instructed to the other, then left.

Fa felt her heart sink as Valor also left; how long would they be kept here? She glanced at their guard; he was younger than the others- just a boy, and his eyes reminded her of Desert. Desert would know what to do.

Fa sat down heavily and looked down at her hands. The excitement of her discovery began to ware off, and Fa felt anxiety building up in her; what if they didn't trust her? What would she say to them if they did!? The message? She somehow knew that telling Thrive the warning wasn't enough. No, she had been clearly instructed to warn Eloi's people... but she didn't see any Garatins on their way from the door, only Tarvens.

'This isn't right' she thought with growing unease, 'I don't belong here' she thought over and over, each time she did, the statement became a little more solid in her mind, till it seemed impossible that she could be wrong.

Confess leaned against the cave wall and through the flickering torch light watched the young guard with narrowed eyes. More than once the young man shifted nervously under Fess' gaze, but to his credit, he didn't abandon his post. Fa made eye contact with him a few times, each time he quickly looked away as if ashamed to be caught looking at her.

They waited for an hour in this way, and Fa began to fear that they had been forgotten, then they heard voices and footsteps hurrying towards them.

"Fate!?" Horizon exclaimed as he stepped inside the storage cave.

Fa jumped up, and felt herself breathe easy, the Garatin's presence was the next best thing to Rave's.

"These two are the intruders?" Rizon asked turning to a Tarven who stood by him, the man nodded, "The young maiden said you knew her," he explained.

"I know them both!" Rizon confirmed, stepping forward. Fess pushed off the wall and gave Rizon a wary look.

"This is Confess, the sea captain I sailed with, and this! This is Fate..." Rizon hesitated, and Fa wondered what he would say- or wouldn't say. "She ah... has a message; a very important one," he said at last.

Fa felt her self-confidence grow a little at his words, yet her many doubts remained.

"That's all well and good, but what about the other woman?" the Tarven said, giving Fess a mistrusting look- she glared back at him.

Rizon took a deep breath and smiled at Fess, "Confess, I realize what you must be thinking- finding outlaws hidden in the city- but after all we've been through; don't you think you could let these poor people be?"

230

Fess sighed and shrugged, "I have no wish to get involved- you may count on my silence."

Rizon nodded and smiled- the others still looked unsure.

"Now- I think it's time you met the others- and delivered the warning, hum?" Rizon waved for Fa and Fess to follow him, he led them back out and through the tunnels, their escorts still following.

"I can't tell you how relieved I am to find you here," Rizon said as Fa hurried along beside him, "When I heard about the Pearl Square I feared the worse- is your brother all right!?" he asked as if just remembering Rave, he paused and searched her face.

"We all escaped- but it was close," Fa assured him, and they began down the narrow passage again, with Fess a few steps behind.

"Who's 'we'? Where have you been these past few days?" Rizon asked curiously.

Fa sighed, "Desert- he's ah… a ward of the Grand Duke, who is a secret Nity follower, and has been very good to us. I and Fess feared that Valor was up to something and followed him- I had no idea we would find our way to the Nity followers!"

Rizon smiled and shook his head, "The Grand Duke! Sorry, hold up, you have been staying with the Grand Duke!?"

Fa smiled and shrugged her shoulders, she supposed she had forgotten how powerful Thrive was.

Rizon nodded, "All right, Desert is the Grand Dukes ward," he glanced back at Fess before continuing, "It seems Eloi was well prepared for you."

This thought seemed very strange to Fa, and she pushed it aside to deal with later, instead she wondered that Rizon wasn't surprised that the Grand Duke was a Nity follower.

"You knew the Grand Duke was a Nity follower?" Fa asked, watching his face in the flickering light.

Rizon smiled mysteriously, "Indeed. It was his household steward who got me here today- don't tell anyone though." He gave her a wink, and Fa marveled; the Grand Duke, his captain of the Guard- AND his household steward were all Nity followers!?

"Now, I assume you haven't delivered your warning yet." Rizon didn't give Fa a chance to do anything but nod, "We mustn't waste anymore time then, I'll have a word with Cherish- she's more or less in charge, and you can give the message!" he said briskly.

"Rizon..." Fa felt the presence inside her fighting for more power- but Fa fought back, "I don't think I can; I'm not sure the message is meant for... *them,*" she said, hoping he wouldn't need further explanation. Images of watching the city from the cliff top flashed in her mind, she had almost lulled herself into believing that her troubles were almost over, but were they? If there were no Garatins here- what was she to do!? Who was she to warn?

Rizon was silent for a moment, then he stepped off into the entrance of another tunnel and waved for the others to go ahead. Fess hesitated, but then went ahead to what looked like a larger cave. Fa swallowed hard and watched Rizon's face; oh, how she wished that he would tell her that he would handle things from here on. She was the wrong person to do this, she shouldn't even be in Tarva! Rizon was clearly the better choice as a messenger, so why had Eloi chosen her!? If it *was* Eloi... the thought sent a wave of unease through her, leaving doubt in its wake; did she know for certain that the Dream Child was Eloi? Could Eloi's presence fill someone with... fear? Surely the Dream Child was something other than Eloi.

Rizon was watching her face, "When there is only silence, it is easy to forget that Eloi is still there," he spoke knowingly, the way someone does when the have felt as you do.

Fa looked at him apprehensively; she didn't want him to tell her to be strong! She wanted he to say that he would be strong *for* her!

"You must remember Fate, that Eloi called *your* namesake," he said firmly, as if he could read her thoughts, "You have been led here for a reason. Your dreams- your heart stain; they have a purpose- same as you. Eloi chose *you*, and that was no mistake."

"But... look at me!" Fa held out her bandaged hands and felt a lump in her throat; she didn't want to be strong anymore! "I don't belong here!"

"Fate, you have answered the call of Eloi; you are *exactly* where you belong!"

The resemblance to her latest dream was striking and it made Fa want to cry, for she realized that her path had already been chosen for her.

"Come; see the people of Eloi," Rizon said, and led her to the larger cave that Fess, and the others had entered a few moments before.

The cave was much larger than Fa had expected, and her claustrophobia eased away as the cave roof opened above her. Loose stone and gravel covered the cave floor, flat in some places and piled high in others, natural pillars wide at the top and bottom and narrow in the middle were scattered randomly throughout the chamber, holding up the roof. Torches were burning across the cave, flickering into the dark corners where large toads hopped out of sight. Strange twisted shadows were cast on the rough walls and moisture dripped from above. Blankets, barrels and crates made makeshift tents and scattered among them were over eighty people; women with white hair and canes, mothers with babies on their hips, children playing and old men holding up torches to see the newcomers. There were very few young men, as a testament to how many had been rounded up in the arrests; these were all that was left of the Nity followers. The thought made Fa's skin tingle... but they were all Tarvens- not a single Garatin among them.

"I don't think Eloi is prejudiced on who he calls his people, do you?" Horizon waited a moment then went to speak to Cherish- the woman in charge.

*   *   *

Desert had read aloud several more letters, both boys oblivious to the passage of time. The letters told of Thrive's travels, and the many troubles he encountered along the way, each one equally filled with Thrives good humour and sarcasm. The boys had been most interested in the letter that told of Thrive's visit with the Tarven Ambassador Sinister, but now on the sixteenth letter, Dese had detected a weariness in Thrive's tone, as if he could no longer pretend even in the letters that all was well.

The letter spoke of corrupt lords and dukes, Tarvens who dealt out punishment on the weak and innocent all too swiftly, and Garatins who turned a blind eye on the needy all too often.

'-*Quite honestly, Desert, I have grown tired of all the boasting and excuses. While the people wait for justice their lords sit about growing rich on their taxes! Truly, my route through the country must have taken me to THE most inept and unsuitable men to ever govern over anyone. I refuse to believe that all Garatin nobility are the same- there must be some honest men and women out there, but then, with the example that the Ambassador has set, I suppose it is fool hearty to hope for a shred of decency among the nobility.*'

Desert paused and looked up at Rave, who was leaning against the desk listening, "Is Garatin really as bad as it sounds?" he asked.

Rave shrugged, "We lived in the eastern wilderness."

Dese smiled at his friend's lack of knowledge, then continued to read.

I've been trying to come up with an appropriate report on my findings about Sinister- but I simply don't know what I'll say to the King about his favourite ambassador. For truthfully, I can think of very little favorable things I could say about Sinister's method of running the country, however my list of things he could do better gets longer with each passing day!

And that brings me to another thing, my dear Desert, if you are ever given the opportunity to let a blood thirsty man have free rein to arrest and imprison anyone he feels like; lock the mad man up and throw away the key instead! I know it sounds ridicules (it sounds absurd to me and I can only imagine how it would sound to a child like yourself) but that is exactly what the good Ambassador has done! Everywhere I go I am witness to the absolute carnage (I can not think of a better word for it) that the mad man in question has left in his wake of terror. I speak of the Garatin Horizon- I hope that when you are old enough to read this that man will be long gone- he has been given unquestionable authority to hunt down and arrest what he no doubt deems to be dangerous rebels, I call them harmless and simple idealists. He arrests whom he pleases, without thought to the chaos that it ensues- there have even been deaths over this- these are peasants whose only crime is that they believe differently than the Garatin leaders do- and they have been killed for it, without a trial!

I have no doubt, that unchecked, this mad man will begin the war for Garatin all over again. He seems quite skilled at creating division.'

The letter ended, and Desert looked up with a frown, "It can't be the same Horizon... can it? I mean- no!" he assured himself, the thought of the kind Garatin he had gotten to know over the voyage as the same man spoken of in the letters- was too absurd to believe!

But Brave was silent for a moment, with a look that said he knew better. "I think it is the same man," he said at last, and Dese let his mouth hang open in disbelief.

*   *   *

"Alright, Fa," Horizon beckoned Fa over to where he stood with Cherish at a higher point of the cave.

"Brothers and sisters!" Cherish called out, her surprisingly strong voice echoed back, and everyone turned their attention to her, even the children paused in their play to listen.

"This maiden is a friend of Horizon, and she has a message- a warning from Eloi to us, let us listen."

Fate hung back, her heart pounding and her nerves a wreck; she had never spoken to so many people at once before! And she didn't even know what she would say to them! Why was this up to her!? She wished that Brave was with her- or even Desert. How strangely fitting that she should come all this way, to stand alone.

"I can't…" she said looking hopefully at Rizon, his face was kind, but his eyes were stern.

"Deliver your message, Fate," he encouraged simply but firmly.

Fa swallowed hard, then nodded, again feeling that this path that she walked, was one she could not run from. She stepped forward, and Cherish and Rizon stepped back, leaving her alone in the flickering torch light, with eighty pairs of eyes watching her- waiting in silence. Fa noticed that even Confess was watching her, with feigned disinterest.

Fa took a deep breath; this was what she had come to Tarva to do… wasn't it?

Chapter 24   Unspoken

'-Raise the tax, a day in the stocks, a night in the dungeon- the amount of times I have heard those words in the past month is astounding!'

Brave listened to the defeated tone of the seventeenth letter and thought of the man who had written it, so many years ago.

'For the first time since landing in Garatin, I have encountered an honest to goodness, good lord- one who deserves his title. And yet, although he is good and fair to his people, there is still a division- a contempt and fear that I can see in the eyes of both Tarvens and Garatins.

'Young Dese, perhaps one day you will read all these letters that I have written to you,'

Rave's throat unexpectedly tightened as Desert read; the love that Thrive displayed for Desert was clear and tangible throughout the letters, and Rave was overwhelmed by an ache in his soul. He longed for home; to hear his mother's voice, to know the safety of his father's embrace. Rave swallowed away the lump and listened as Dese read on.

'- but I sincerely hope that you never fall prey to the unjustness and brutality that I have seen in this country. Even at your tender age you have already seen how Tarvens treat one another,'

Rave felt slightly uncomfortable- the words sounded very personal, but Dese didn't seem to mind, and Rave could only just here a small catch in his friend's voice to betray his own emotions.

'- but the way Tarvens treat the Garatins, is shameful. The Garatins treat us like barbarians, and it is well deserved, for we act like barbarians. I didn't want to believe my people could be so brutal, but we are. My King (may he reign forever) has done little to win the hearts and loyalties of Garatins. Sixty years ago, we marched in as victors taking our prize. Since then, I had thought that Garatin had merged with Tarva and had become Tarva- but that is far from true.

The king will dub me Grand Duke upon my return, should he be pleased with me. But I will have little peace of mind, for I see little that I can do to change this situation.

No, I fear that the change this country needs can not come from me- or perhaps any Tarven for that matter. Such a change must come from within, and I doubt that could happen with Tarva bearing down on the country the way it is.'

Desert was silent for a moment as he folded the letter, "These letters could be considered treason against the glory of Tarva…" he said dully, as if realizing what exactly he held in his hands.

*   *   *

Treason was also the word running through Confess' mind; how could the Grand Duke support and hide wanted outlaws!? He had so much to lose if the wrong person were to find out… or the right person.

The thought of selling her new-found information only caused Fess a small twinge of guilt, as she watched Fate address the crowd. This kind of information would repay her debts and then some!

Fess noticed how Fate trembled as she spoke, her voice hardly loud enough for everyone to hear.

"Eloi has given me many dreams, none of which I fully understand," Fa faltered, and the crowd shifted, "But Eloi has made this very clear to me; you are all in great danger."

"What kind of danger?" someone asked with a hint of scepticism- and Fess didn't blame them! Dreams that tell the future? - it sounded ridiculous! Just then Rizon caught Fess's eye, and she retracted her last thought; some dreams were very reliable!

Fa looked a little helpless, and Fess cringed; how awful it must be to live in such uncertainty and fear all the time!

"I saw a great storm…" Fa offered, her voice sounded none too sure, "a storm coming towards the city- a great storm off the sea."

There was a murmur through the crowd, "Some storms have been known to flood the Harbour Ring- was this one big enough to do so?" someone asked.

Fa swallowed and seemed to sense that she didn't sound very certain, Fess saw her straighten and her face hardened a little.

"All I know is that Eloi wouldn't bring me across the world just to tell you to bring in your washing from a rainstorm!"

Fess was impressed by her sudden confidence, so too was the crowd.

"I'm telling you; something terrible is coming- worse than what's already happened! I don't know for certain if it is a storm-"

The crowd seemed to scoff a little again at her lack of conviction, and Fa took a deep breath, "I was told that something terrible would come with the spring- and the trees are now in bloom! I'm warning you; something is coming!" her voice trembled a bit, it had the right effect on the crowd- for they went silent.

Rizon and Cherish ushered the girl off the platform and towards where Fess leaned against the cave wall.

"Wait here, Fa, I'll speak further with them," Rizon assured the girl. Then he and Cherish went off with several others and held a hurried and whispered meeting.

Fa sat down and sighed.

"A warning message to the Nity Followers of Tarva, *that's* what brought you across the sea?" Fess asked.

Fa smiled bashfully, "That's right."

Fess shook her head, "You and Horizon, with all your dreams; I'll never understand you lot." She breathed. Yet despite her tone, she believed what Fa had said, and her mind began to make plans to leave the city. Only problem being; where would she go?

To Fess' surprise, Fa lay down and curled up, closing her eyes peacefully.

"Long day?" Fess asked sarcastically.

"I can't believe It's finally over; I can go home now," Fa replied, without opening her eyes.

*   *   *

'*Desert, one day you will be old enough, and I will tell you the story of a courageous young lady, and her mother- who was noble and fearless.*

I must apologize for my last letter, I had despaired of my quest and all but given up- not a very good example, is it? But just a few days ago I found the change that I had thought impossible, and I found it in the most unlikely of places. I found hope in the wake of a mad man's disaster, I found a new future born from fire. I found it all in the little village of Fray; a tiny place, one step to the left or right off the road and you might walk right past it! As I almost did.

The lord of the manor was truly mad! And I had given up hope of doing any good (he was impossible). I admit that I gave up and left, I saw what a horrid monster he was, and I walked away. Then SHE came after me- a wondrous woman indeed- she forced me to see that someone had to do something, that I had a duty to set things right.

If I had not gone back, I would have missed it; a young Tarven lady, giving up everything for Garatins she had never met! She risked her life to protect the innocent. And I have been inspired to do the same.

238

First, I'll start by taking care of that idiot in Hawthorne- I don't know who I'll replace him with, but anyone would be better! And I'll do the same for the rest of Garatin! I won't just turn a blind eye on my journey back; I will set things right! For I have been shown, that change can happen, and it starts with me- and someday, with you, little Desert, of that I have no doubt.'

Desert finished reading the last letter and felt his spine tingle with awe and excitement. He had heard people speak of Thrive's reforming work in Garatin- but had never given much thought to it!

What an incredible legacy Thrive had left behind! Desert swallowed and placed the letter back with the others, it was a legacy that Desert fell short of… No wonder Thrive had never shown him these letters!

*   *   *

With mild apprehension, Fate realized that she was dreaming; she sat on the edge of the sea cliff, her legs dangling over the side where thousands of feet below the sea frothed and churned. She jumped and pulled back a little when she became aware of the Dream Child sitting beside her. The child looked hurt at Fa's reaction but didn't try to move closer.

"You did well Fate," the child said.

"I can go home now?" Fa held her breath, hardly believing that the time had come at last- but her heart sunk when the child hesitated and gazed across the water. Fa followed her gaze to the city far away- but suddenly found herself in the city itself. She stood in a street of the Earls Ring, it was deserted- but she was not alone. Fa felt the presence there with her- stronger and darker than ever before.

Panicked, she broke into a run, not daring to look behind her at the thing that had stocked her across the sea, the thing that had driven her from her home to a strange place, the thing that would not be satisfied until… until she was cold.

Fa looked up at the Dragon Keep- and caught her breath and nearly stumbled to a stop; the castle was aflame! Ash began to rain down on her- smudging her face and clouding her vision. Her feet stopped without her consent and Fa looked down to see her reflection in one of the fountains; she was pale and wide eyed with fright.

Then, the thing came up behind her and met her gaze through the reflection, Fa stared in muted horror at the face in the water; it was her own.

"You're not done yet," a voice, not her own, boomed from inside her.

Fate sat bolt up right and gasped for breath as her hands sizzled and smarted with new burns. Confess looked down at her with a curious look from where she'd been leaning against the cave wall. "You are an odd woman," she said, with a raised brow as Fa panted and looked about, till she remembered where she was.

Everything looked the same as when she fell asleep- but Fa felt un uncomfortable passage of time, as if she had wasted too much of it.

"I need to leave!" she insisted and franticly stood to her feet, pain from her hands making her gasp.

"I'd like to leave too- assuming we haven't seen too much," Fess muttered and looked over to where Rizon was still speaking with the leaders and elders. Fa ignored Fess and everyone else who gave her strange looks, as she stumbled towards the meeting, her face pinched in pain and anxiety.

"Rizon!" Fa's strained voice put a halt to the meeting, "I must leave now- please, I can't stay here!" Rizon and the others looked surprised, but Fa refused to explain herself.

"You've had another dream," Rizon guessed when he saw how she held her hands.

Fa felt a stab of guilt that was followed up with uncertainty; should she tell them of her latest dream? No, she couldn't tell anyone- until she could make sense of it herself.

"Please; I *must* leave now," she insisted.

"Alright, alright," Rizon soothed, "Here, lets get new bandages on your hands, and then you and Confess can be escorted back through the tunnels." He said the last part as more of an order to the others, who looked like they still weren't sure they could trust the surly sea captain.

Fa managed to sit still as two women rebandaged her hands- although they looked curious, they didn't ask any questions. While this was happening Rizon drew the meeting to a close.

"That's all the discussion there is time for, my sisters and brothers, I too must return- less Rustling grows suspicious," here he waved for Golden, who Fa recognized as someone else from the Grand Duke's household. "Please; do not hesitate to put into action the plan to leave the city, as you heard yourself- the danger is coming! And above all; hold fast! This path that Eloi has set at our feet *must* be walked to completion."

His last words twanged in Fa's ear, like a discorded note on a harp; was Eloi at all aware of the desolate 'path' that she had been forced to walk?

Things moved quickly when Rizon finished speaking, he bid farewell to Fa, afterwards she couldn't remember what exactly he had said, for to her everything passed like one of her grim dreams. Then she and Fess were escorted back the way they had come. When they came to the door, their escorts made Fess give her word one last time to keep silent, but Fa wasn't paying attention, nor did she take much note of their passage through the dark tunnels. But she did take note of the torch their escort held, and she stood as far from it as she could, the horrid thought grew in her that when they emerged into the sunlight, something would be on fire.

But it was only with mild relief that upon coming out into the late morning, they found everything as it had been, for next, Fa feared for Rave; what if the Duke's manor was aflame!?

Fa knew that she was walking too fast, and that Confess was waiting for an explanation for her strange behaviour, but not a word was spoken as the two made their way back through the streets to the Ducal. But Fa couldn't slow herself, nor could she calm herself; she needed Rave! If he was taken from her…

'*You're not done yet*' the voice from her dream seemed to echo in her mind of its own volition, and a dark premonition of what it meant was beginning to dawn in her heart.

At last the Grand Duke's manor came into view as they turned a corner; there was no angry flames or pillars of smoke, and yet Fa still couldn't calm her racing heart. Fa entered through the side, smaller gate without trouble, Fess was a few paces behind her, and at last Fa found that she could slow her feet.

What would she tell Rave? That they had been wrong? That she would not be returning home anytime soon- if at all!?

Something oddly familiar about the courtyard and the way the shadows lay, made Fa look up to her right at the manor ramparts; there was a guard patrolling along the wall. Fa stilled her breath; she knew this moment- she had seen it before in a dream back in Cinders Grove!

'*When will the morning come?*' Was what she had asked in her dream, but she hadn't heard the man's reply.

Fa stopped as she looked up at him and felt her heart tremble; he was singing an old folk tune softly to himself, and as Fa watched, the wind picked up his voice and carried it to her ears. At the same time, he glanced down and met her gaze. Fa felt a sickening reassurance grip her, like marsh mud swallowing her cold feet. She could do nothing but listen to the single line of the guard's song that the wind had caught.

"...The morning comes, but the darkness will soon return..."

Fa's breath abandoned her, and her legs betrayed her. As she fell to the paving stones; Fa knew in her soul that the darkness was coming for her.

"Fate!? What's wrong with you!?" Confess' voice sounded far away, and Fa's vision began to blur as her lungs failed to draw breath. A screaming pain struck her head, and Fa felt like she was still falling...

Confess firmly shook Fa by her shoulders, and the force made Fa gasp for fresh air again, her vision cleared, and she felt the courtyard stones beneath her burning hands- would they ever stop burning?

"I need to find Rave!" she gasped.

*   *   *

Desert ran his hands through his raven hair, as Brave replaced Fa's bandages; this was the first time that Dese had seen Fate's burns and the reality hit him hard, that, added to his already spinning head full of old letters and the news that Thrive was actively hiding the Nity followers, made Dese want to sit down and simply breathe.

When Fess had carried Fa into the west hall where Brave and Dese were taking lunch, there had been a rush of activity, that included dismissing any servants who were about. After drinking some water, Fa had insisted that she was fine, and implored Fess not to call for Thrive's healer. Seeing that she had recovered, Fess had left them, and Rave had insisted on seeing Fa's new burns. Fa had related to them what had happened that morning, leaving out nothing but the details of her dream, and ending with the fact that she couldn't return home until her task was truly done.

Now, with Fa's bandages back in place, and lunch forgotten, Rave sat down and huffed his unhappiness.

"I still don't understand," Rave frowned, "What more are you to do?! You warned them- what else is there!?"

Desert turned to see Fate's face, she looked ragged and exhausted, "I know what I am to do, it's what my dreams have been about from the very first one, I just didn't see it."

"What was your first dream?" Rave asked and Dese listened closely.

"I dreamt on the morning Eamer burned..." Fa paused and Dese saw the sorrow on both their faces at the mention of their lost home.

"I dreamt of a king, in a burning banquet hall. I saw his crown fall."

The hidden meaning of the dream sent shivers down Desert's spine; did Fa know what she was saying!?

Fa looked grieved, "I didn't understand Rave- I thought I did, but I've misunderstood every dream from the start! The warning isn't just meant for the Nity followers!"

Rave licked his lips, his voice was calming- but it didn't have an effect on his sister, "You said that the Dream Child told you to warn the Nity followers."

Fa shook her head, "I was told to warn Eloi's people- I just thought that meant the Nity followers- I thought it meant Garatins! I didn't understand." She was becoming more frantic by the second.

"Wait," Dese interrupted and Fa looked up at him, "Who are Eloi's people if not the Nity followers?" Dese asked, trying to get a handle on Fa's scattered explanation.

"Everyone!" Fa breathed, as if she was only then fully understanding it, "The warning is for everyone; everyone in Tarva is in great peril! And I might be too late to warn them…"

Dese wet his dry lips, as he began to understand; when he had first heard her warning earlier that day, he had brushed it aside as something that didn't affect him personally, not so anymore.

"So… what are you meant to do?" Rave asked hesitantly.

Fa waited a moment before answering, "Everyone needs to be warned; I think I must speak to the King."

Desert turned away and covered his mouth; small wonder Fa carried a cloak of sorrow about her! She had seen the end of Tarva in her dreams! And the only way to warn everyone was to speak to the King!?

"Fa, do you realize what your saying?" Dese asked, trying hard to keep his voice even, "Not just anyone can speak to the King!" 'It's impossible!' he added to himself.

"He's right Fa," Rave agreed, "Even Horizon thought he'd have to wait for months for his trial! And besides- what would you say to the King? You don't even know for certain what's coming!"

"I don't know," Fa closed her eyes in weariness, "But I know that I must try!"

They were all silent for a moment and Dese racked his brain for some way that Fa could see the King- or another way she could warn thousands of people in the next few days, he came up with nothing- but he wouldn't give up.

"Look, we'll figure something out later- I promise!" Dese said firmly, he was aware that if he could make it happen, then Fa just might fully forgive him, and that thought spurred him on. Maybe Thrive could help, but that thought was bogged down by a great many other things; things that he needed to discuss with Thrive when he returned that afternoon.

He frowned and wondered how he would begin the conversation, 'So Fa thinks the whole city is in danger and she needs to speak to the King, face to face and she told me that your hiding Nity followers- you know, the ones you said you didn't know where they were. Oh, and why did you never show me those old letters in your secret study?'

Dese cooled his rising anger and thought better of mentioning the last part.

*   *   *

Confess made herself comfortable in Thrive's private library and waited two hours for his return, interrupted only by a servant bringing her lunch. Fess thought long and hard over the events of that morning and the previous evening, until, with narrowed eyes and a bit of admiration for Thrive's cunningness, she realized the truth. The conversation she had half heard the night before had been about the Nity followers running low on supplies, and Thrive, who apparently hadn't gotten to be so powerful on name alone, had come up with a reason to have a grand banquet, where he would order more food than was necessary to be made. He had then sent out the extra food on wagons, as nobility are wont to do, but instead of sending the wagons out to his serfs or into the Harbour Ring, he had sent them to the cherry tree gardens, where under cover of dark, the food had gone to the outlaws.

Fess waited patiently and planned carefully what she would say to the Grand Duke, until she heard Thrive's voice in the hall.

"My lady!" Thrive greeted her as he closed the chamber door behind him.

"Grand Duke," Fess stood and nodded coolly.

"My captain of the guards, Valor, told me that lady Fate collapsed in the courtyard earlier."

"She has recovered, my lord," Fess took note of the fact that Thrive had already spoken with Valor, and that he must already know what Fess intended to speak to him about, "I suppose the realization must have shocked her," she said casually, watching for his reaction.

Thri raised a brow, "Realization of what, may I ask?"

"That the Grand Duke is involved with hiding outlaws from the King, under his very nose."

"Outlaws?!" Thrive's voice was calm; he was probing her to find out exactly how much she knew before admitting to anything- he was very cunning.

"I overheard your man Valor, I feared I had stumbled upon a foul plot against you my lord. I and Fate followed Valor to the caves beneath the Dragon Keep."

"Indeed?" Thrive continued to disclose nothing, and Fess began to fear that she was in over her head- but there was no backing down now.

"We were met with hostility to say the least, that is, until they learned that we were *your* guests," Fess watched him closely.

Thrive nodded as if listening to a report on everyday household affairs, silence stretched between them and Fess wondered how quickly things could get ugly.

"Have you been to see 'The Lady Loyal' yet? Or have you had no time to consider my offer?"

'Ah, that quickly' Fess took a deep breath, well now she knew, time to clear things up, "My silence can not be bought, my lord." she informed him crisply, "But you have no need to try in this instance. I have no desire to get involved, and I only wonder why you would risk discovery and worse, all for these outlaws."

"I believe in their cause," Thrive watched her, "And I don't believe in executing the innocent."

Fess noted how his words still weren't a confession.

"Surely after seeing them, you don't think they are dangerous outlaws- or do you in fact have a fear of old men, women and children?" Thri raised a sarcastic brow.

"What I saw was a small army; and they did not seem harmless to me," Fess pointed out stubbornly.

"Did they threaten your life?" Thrive asked pointedly.

Fess was forced to admit (if only to herself) that even when they thought she and Fate were spies or worse, the Nity Followers hadn't made any threats on their lives.

Thrive saw her answer and smirked, "If you wandered into any other outlaw camp- do you think they would spare you? OR let you go just on your word that you wouldn't betray them?" he drove home his point.

Fess felt like wincing- but she would not allow herself to be that weak. "Dangerous or not," she half conceded, "They are still wanted by the King- if your involvement was discovered; you could lose your head," she warned.

"And I thought you didn't want to get involved!" Thrive sat down, showing a disregard for her words.

"If I am to captain one of your ships- I want to be certain that I won't sail into harbour one day and find my liege lord has been executed for treason," Fess defended herself and sat down, all too aware of her still healing body.

"Truly, your concern is appreciated, my lady," Thri dipped his head, "But I would rather your concern be turned into action. You saw the plight they are in, if they heed Fate's warning, then they all must be smuggled out of the city- and soon. Help them."

His challenge came as a laughable surprise to Fess- but there was no mirth in her, "Everything I have ever touched in my life, has turned to ash." She thought of her mother dying, her father rejecting her, her years of mistreatment at Endure's hand, her husband's cold body and "The Prestige" in flames. "I am the last person you should ask to help." As she said it, Fess wondered if it was even wise for her to captain 'The Lady Loyal', wouldn't that just end the same as everything else she touched?

Thrive's twinkling eyes turned suddenly sad, "You forget, they have already lost everything, it is only by the efforts of people like you and I that they have any chance of survival, or any hope of a future. The Nity followers live out the teachings of Eternity; they believe in peace, forgiveness, honesty and grace- quality's that have become much too rare in our world. They have become victims of the powerful, and face annihilation in Tarva- how, I find myself asking- how could such an evil go unchallenged? The answer, is that people like you and I, do nothing."

Fess was silent.

*   *   *

Thrive took a moment outside his chambers to mentally prepare himself for what waited inside; having already spoken with Confess a few minutes before, and Valor, the captain of the guards, AND Golden, his household steward. From the three of them, Thri had fit together a near perfect picture of how that morning had .gone. And he could guess quite easily that Desert had some things to say- Thri didn't expect the conversation to be pleasant.

Stepping inside his chambers, Thrive saw Dese draped over a chair waiting for him; he did not rise.

"Golden and Valor tell me that you've had an eventful day, and it must have been, for you to be here; two visits in two days, what a treat!" he said dryly- it was the only way he knew how to start an awkward conversation.

"You told me that you didn't know where the Nity followers were hiding." Deserts temper could be heard rising in his voice.

Thri choosing to ignore it and hope it wouldn't develop into a shouting match. He removed his light cape and tossed it aside.

"I recall you saying that it wouldn't be wise for you to be involved!" Dese now sounded a bit insufferable!

Thrive hated it when Dese quoted his words back to him. Thrive sighed and sat down heavily, facing his ward with a weary face.

"So, I did, and I meant it too. Discovery would most certainly mean my death, and many others would pay the same price; secrecy is vital." Thrive looked hard at Dese, he looked away.

"Fa thinks her warning is for everyone," Dese said at last.

Thrive sighed, he had been told about the girl's message in great detail by Golden.

"Yes, I've made arrangements for the Nity followers to be smuggled out of the city by some of the servants on their way to the summer manor inland. I fear the process will be quite slow, suspicion will arise- especially if I left for the summer manor so early in the season, but I have work yet to do here... I would send you to the summer manor- if I thought you would go." He looked up at his ward, with a shred of hope that Dese would agree- then he might be out of harms way.

But Dese didn't speak, nor did he make any movement to suggest that he would leave.

"I thought not..." Thrive mumbled, and the two sat in silence for a long time.

Desert felt like the silence was soaking into him, making his limbs heavy, he wished he could speak. He wished that Thrive would say something- anything. But the silence grew between them like an unwanted friend who had become too comfortable.

"Who is Loyal?" Dese broke the silence when it became unbearable, with the question that had been gnawing at him since he had read the old letter.

Thrive looked at him sharply. "How do you know that namesake?" he demanded to know tightly- too tightly.

For a moment Dese considered telling Thri about his discovery- but Thri's face was too tense, "Your ship." Dese said, "Your ship 'The Lady Loyal', who is she named for?" he asked innocently, being careful not to glance in the direction of Thrives secret study. Thrive's face turned from agitation to weariness.

Thrive pushed himself up out of his chair and poured himself a goblet of water from a pitcher. "A woman I grew up with," he explained shortly, but refused to meet Desert's gaze.

"You were in love with her." If Dese had any doubts about his statement, they were all forgotten by the sad look on Thrive's face.

Thrive took a sip of his water before answering, "That's right."

"What happened to her?" Dese asked, thinking of Thrive's long years alone.

"She was betrothed to another in Garason."

Desert's lips parted as he felt a pang of identification, "She sailed away?"

Thri looked at him and narrowed his eyes as if seeing right through Dese, "Just as the lady Fate will soon do."

"You didn't follow her?"

"No; she was betrothed to another, and I had a future here in Tarva, as you do."

Desert stood and turned his back on Thrive, and on the new direction of their conversation. He went to a window to let the fresh air cool his face. He didn't want to repeat last night's words and be reminded of all his obvious shortcomings.

"The Queen's birthday banquet is tomorrow evening, it's one of the reasons I can't leave the city just yet."

Thrives sudden subject change gave Dese a grand idea!

"It will be an excellent opportunity for you to show yourself in a good light to the court, time to put a deckhand's life away and aspire for more."

If Desert's mind hadn't been working over-time on his new plan, then he would have paused at Thrive's tone; for he did not speak out of disappointment or shame- but hope, and maybe even pride!

"Will Fate and Brave be extended an invitation?" Dese didn't dare turn to face Thrive, lest he see through his plans.

Thrive hesitated, "If they behave themselves, and exhibit more grace than they did at last night's banquet, I see no reason why not- being my guests and all."

Dese turned and flashed a smile, "They'll be bowing and scraping before the King; I promise!"

Thrive gave him another weary look, "They won't be getting close enough for that."

His words did nothing to discourage Dese, and for another moment there was more silence between them, where certain words should have been said, but weren't.

Chapter 25   The End Drawing Near

Desert decided to keep his plan to himself until the next day, and it was just as well, for Fate needed the rest of the day and night to calm herself. She spent the night sitting at her window gazing up at the dark sky, hoping to catch a glimpse of a star, but the sky was dark with clouds, and Fa wondered it they were the beginning of the storm that would destroy Tarva. A nagging doubt also grew in her that night, one that questioned what she really knew; if she had been wrong about who she was meant to warn- wasn't it also possible that she was wrong about what she was warning against? She thought back on all her other dreams, nearly all of them came before a fire... but not the last three, was she somehow gaining control? She liked to think so, perhaps, by strength of will she could regain control, and escape the thing that was hunting her!

But this was all wishful thinking, and Fa knew it. She was like a child who had misbehaved and was trying to make-believe that she wouldn't be reprimanded; although she may make-believe it- she ultimately knew that it was not true.

This was simply the morning, and like the guard had unwittingly said, Fa knew that the darkness would soon come back for her.

Confess was another who did not rest that night, she lay awake thinking of what Thrive had said, and in the twilight of the evening she went to the window to see some of the manor servants departing the courtyard. Fess knew that they would be smuggling Nity followers out of the city as they went on there way to Thrive's summer manor, and she also knew that it would take weeks to safely smuggle so many people. She was not certain that they had that much time. Fess felt a momentary prick of guilt at not helping- but she ignored the feeling. Surely Thrive would be caught, and no matter how noble his intentions; he would pay a terrible price.

Fess only momentarily considered the fact that she had accepted Fate's warning, it was not such a hard thing to believe once she thought about it. Tarva was on the brink of disaster, perhaps the terrible future that Fate foresaw was the downfall that Tarva would suffer if the Grand Duke's treason was found out. Such a thing could bring the empire to its knees- especially if the people had lost faith in their King! Yes, Fess could see the future plain enough for herself! The only question remaining, was 'what would Fess do?'

At dawn Confess rose and left the manor of the Grand Duke- but her decision was still unmade. If she left the city on foot, she wouldn't get far without money, and it wasn't likely that anyone would hire a woman on their ship, especially if the news of her last voyage had spread.

Escape by land and sea were both out of the question... unless she took up Thrive's offer of captaining 'The Lady Loyal'. She suspected that the ship would also be smuggling Nity followers out as soon as they got the right papers from the harbour master to leave. Although not ideal, it was her only hope of an escape.

Fess made her way down through the city to the Harbour Ring, she was stopped at the Dukes Gate, but when she said she was on the Grand Duke's business, they let her through. The streets began to fill as the sunlight drove away the night shadows, and with the sea sparrows over head, it was easy to believe that all was well.

She kept a sharp eye out for Endure or any other thugs, but she saw no sign of trouble as she made her way down to the docks. When she reached the seashore, the sun had risen high enough to light up the ships in the harbour with golden light, and every wave glittered so as to nearly blind. Fess searched the ships in anchorage until she beheld 'The Lady Loyal'; the sight took her breath away.

'The Lady Loyal' was the only ship of the Grand Duke's that was in Tarva and was quite possibly the jewel of his entire fleet. She was a five-mast and twin-hulled ship, both hulls were crafted from gleaming red wood that made the water around them glow with warmth. New white sails were neatly furled on the tall masts, and the words 'The Lady Loyal' were painted in gold on the stern of both hulls.

Confess was lost in awe as she beheld the ship that could be hers. As a young woman, younger than Fa, Fess had sailed on ships disguised as a boy, and had fallen in love with the sea, but when she married, she was forced to give up that joy... until Devotion died. The circumstances of captaining a ship for the first time had made it a very bitter thing indeed, but as Fess gazed at 'The Lady Loyal', her heart longed for the freedom that she had discovered out there. Being a woman would always make being a sea captain difficult- but it was a price that Fess considered inconsequential in comparison to the freedom and power of charting her own course through life. She could forget all the men who had tried to control her. Sure, her last experience as a captain had not ended well- but she was certain she could make it work- and the second chance she needed, was all hers for the taking.

'If Thrive sent word to the ship's crew about me, it's possible that they would obey my orders...' Confess let the line of thought play itself out; she imagined herself going out to the ship, pretending that she had indeed been made the captain. She could probably set sail and leave the harbour far behind before the harbour master even noticed.

'The crew would never do so without an order from the Grand Duke though,' Fess realized the hole in her plan before her hopes were raised.

The only way she could escape the city on 'The Lady Loyal' was -no doubt- by smuggling Nity followers out, she thought ruefully, and that would not exactly be an 'escape'.

Fess turned away and found that her heart was not truly in it; she couldn't leave the city yet- she needed answers!

Why!? Why did so many people risk so much to help the Nity followers- didn't they know it would all end in ultimate failure?

Why did Horizon persist in his 'work' when he had lost everything!? He had been arrested- and was doubtlessly bound to spend the rest of his life in a dungeon! And yet still he carried on... how could he find the strength- or hope, to carry on when his life had turned to ash.

Fess set her face as she headed back up into the city; she needed to know, and she would not leave until she understood.

$$*\qquad\qquad *\qquad\qquad *$$

"Tonight!?" Fate repeated Desert in astonishment. She and Brave were on their way through the halls, on their way to breakfast, when Desert had intercepted them and shared his plan with barely contained excitement.

"Yeah! I know it's a little short notice- but it's perfect!" Desert explained. "The Queen has this banquet every year, the whole city will be banqueting all day!" he leaned closer and lowered his voice secretively, "Thrive will probably be sneaking more of the Nity followers out while everyone is celebrating." He grinned as if it was all great fun. "And, you two will be able to attend the banquet at the Dragon Keep, being guests of you know who. It will be tricky- but we should be able to get close enough to his majesty to deliver your warning to him and his advisers! I told you that we'd figure something out!"

"A banquet?" Brave asked, he was uncharacteristically refraining from picking up on Desert's enthusiasm and instead was being quite mature about the whole thing, "Like the one a few nights ago?" He and Fa had never really been to any other banquets and didn't know what to expect.

Desert shrugged a shoulder, "Sort of, only this one will be outside in the Dragon Keep's gardens- and there will be a LOT of court members." He didn't look like he looked forward to that aspect, but his eyes got bright again as he looked at Fa, "And by this time tomorrow…"

"It will all be over…" Fa finished Desert's line of thought, only she didn't smile; for her, it really would be over.

Brave's serious face broke into his familiar smile, "I can't believe we'll be going home soon!"

Fate saw how Desert's own smile faded at the thought.

"It will soon be over," she murmured, and thought of how Brave would be going home… but not her.

There was an awkward silence between them as their three, very different emotions hung over them.

Desert cleared his throat as if clearing the air. "Well, lets eat some breakfast before they think we're not coming and feed it all to the dogs," he said lightly.

Rave looked concerned. "They wouldn't really do that- would they?" he asked nervously- no doubt thinking of his empty stomach and the fifteen-minute walk to the banquet hall.

Desert laughed as they began to walk, "Oh- don't say anything about this to Thrive," Dese warned with raised brows, "He would *not* approve!"

Fa nodded solemnly; she wouldn't allow anyone to foil their plans!

Desert went on as they walked in a row of three down the hall, "We can work on what exactly you're going to say to the King, and how to address him, and how low down to bow." Here he playfully jabbed at Rave, who's stomach had growled, "And soon we'll have to start getting ready!" he added airily.

"Start getting ready?!" Rave asked with a frown, as they descended a flight of stairs.

"Yeah! We'll have to get a wardrobe picked out for you two," Dese took the opportunity to slyly look Fa up and down, she was still wearing her tunic and trousers- she pretended not to notice his gaze.

"And do something with that mop!" Dese tussled Rave's blond brownish hair, and Fa noticed how long it had gotten again.

"Well that can't take all day!" Rave pointed out as he flattened out his hair again.

Desert laughed, "This is the *Queen's* banquet! You'll be going before the King of Tarva! We can't look like we just jumped off a hay wagon!" Dese continued to poke fun as Rave persisted to argue that it couldn't take them the whole day just to get ready for a banquet.

Through it all Fa was quiet and allowed herself only a small smile at their antics. She wondered if she was getting a glimpse of who- and what Desert was; the ward of a Grand Duke, confident and free spirited, someone who knew his way around the royal court, and knew how to behave before a king. Fa quite suddenly decided that she liked this Desert more than the scalawag, lost orphan, deckhand she had first met, perhaps it was because she was seeing Dese as he truly was- and not as he pretended to be.

*   *   *

Rustling sat down heavily; had his life always been this stressful!? Or had it started when he met Horizon? Rust decided that it was the latter.

When Horizon had returned the day before, an hour and a half after his departure, he hadn't said anything about his visit with the Grand Duke, and quite honestly, Rust was afraid to ask. He was afraid because he knew that Rizon wouldn't lie to him, and he also knew that Rizon had not gone to see the Grand Duke- at least that's what he suspected, and if he never asked, then it could forever stay a speculation.

Horizon seemed to sense this, for he hadn't said anything about it either. Unfortunately, Rust's aged mother was not so silent. She had made it quite clear to him- on several occasions- that she was very unimpressed at having a 'Garatin criminal', as she called him, living within the same walls as her. Rust had endured his mother's complaints for as long as he could, then had escaped to his private study; not even noon, and he was already seeking refuge from his day.

"I won't let him leave these grounds again unless it is on the king's business!" Rust muttered, thinking again of Rizon. But it was no use, if the Grand Duke 'sent' for Rizon again, there was nothing Rust could do about it!

There was a nock at his door, Rust groaned; not even ten minutes to himself!

A page cracked the door open and peeked in. "You have a visitor, my lord," the page said nervously.

Rust dabbed his brow with his hanky that was suddenly in his hand, "Send them away." He waved his hanky in dismissal.

"Oh- I..." The page stuttered then stepped aside as the door was pushed open all the way. Rust sat up straighter, first in outrage- then in shock; Confess came striding in with a confident air.

Rust jumped to his feet and gave a little bow and simultaneously reached out for her hand before snatching it back again, a lady captain was so confusing! "Lady- Captain Confess!" he stuttered as she came to stand before him. "What a surprising... surprise," he ended lamely, and once again considered how tiny the woman made him feel.

"Not 'captain'," Confess reminded him, "not at present anyway." Her words were only just loud enough to be heard.

Confess looked about the room lazily, and Rust noticed that she had a bruise on her forehead, and her nose had a healing cut across the bridge. 'I'm sure I don't want to know' Rust thought ruefully- he was confident that who ever gave her the cut and bruise- looked much worse.

Rust made an effort to straighten his shoulders- it only made him feel slightly less like a child in the woman's presence, "I assume that you are not here on a whim." Rust doubted that Fess *ever* followed through on 'whims'.

A corner of Confess' lip turned up, "Just so, I understand that Horizon is here in your manor."

"How did you know that!?" Rust asked on edge- did everyone know!?

Confess raised one of her brows at his slightly over the top reaction. "Is it meant to be a secret? I made inquiries at the barracks, I may have dropped the namesake of the Grand Duke once or twice to get things moving," she explained nonchalantly.

Rust flinched and looked at her warily, "The Grand Duke?!" What did she have to do with him!? Could this be yet ANOTHER plot to get Rizon out?

"That's right," Fess' words ironically interrupted his thoughts, "I have been his guest these past few days."

Rust dabbed his forehead again; this was too many brushes with such a powerful man to be comfortable with!

"I wish to speak with the Garatin- if that is acceptable," Fess said and waited.

Rust gave her another wary look, "Where?" he half expected her to say that she was to escort Rizon to the Grand Duke's manor.

Fess gave him a blank stare, "Wherever he is. Assuming he is decent."

Rust blinked; did Fess just crack a joke!? It was hard to tell since her expression remained stony. "Ah..." he hesitated, was this another one of Horizon's schemes?

"Is it acceptable?" Fess asked, her brow going even higher.

Looking into her face, Rust suddenly found it comical to think that Confess, of all people would be involved with Nity followers. Why, she thought it was all nonsense! As if she would ever be the type to be given over to Eloi and follow Eternity! She was no collaborator with outlaws!

"Yes, of course- page!?" Rust called, and the page poked his head back inside the chamber, "Escort, er, Lady Confess to Horizon's chambers."

As Confess was being led away, Rust smirked to himself; he couldn't believe or imagine that 'no-nonsense', fierce woman as a gentle hearted Nity follower.

*   *   *

"Confess! I didn't expect to see you- but I am pleased," Horizon was smooth speaking as always, as he greeted Confess. He sidestepped the fact that they had seen each other only yesterday in the caves, and Fess thought it wise not to mention it either; anyone could be listening. Fess noted that his chambers were comfortable and spacious- obviously the good knight Rustling didn't treat him like a prisoner, although there was a guard on his door.

"How has Tarva been to you these past few days?" Rizon asked courteously.

Fess thought of her stiff body and bruised face, "I've been treated better."

"Oh?" Rizon raised a brow, "I thought you were a guest of the Grand Duke!?" he asked innocently.

Fess took a breath through her nose and measured him with silted eyes; maybe he had a point.

"Any progress on... your mission?" Fess asked, she didn't want this discussion to be centered on her, and on how bad- or good life was being to her. To her the answer was clear; life was VERY bad! Leave it to the Garatin to turn her world view on its head though!

Rizon let the conversation change without a struggle. He sighed, "I am still waiting to hear back from the Dragon Keep- they haven't even formally acknowledged my arrival in Tarva! Apparently, the King is in bad shape though- or so the rumors say. But... you're not here to ask about my 'mission', are you?"

Fess turned away and ground her teeth- of course he could turn the conversation back to her! What *was* she doing here anyway!?

"Why are you here!?" she found herself asking him the question with a bit of an explosion.

Rizon didn't look startled, "Why am I where?"

"Here! In Tarva, in Chresacroon, in Nirin, in Garatin- anywhere! You've traveled the sea many times before this, doing...- what ever it is that you do! And everywhere you go- even before you were arrested- people wanted you dead, more attempts have been made on your life than on some of Tarva's past kings! And yet you persist on your... 'Mission'! Why!?" Fess was startled to hear how frustrated she sounded, and even more surprised to realize how much the whole thing bothered her!

"You've been asking around about me," Rizon noted quietly.

It was true, she had asked at the barracks, she had even stopped in the market on her way here, and everyone had a different story to tell about the man who couldn't be stopped.

"They say you've been doing this for years," she tried to calm herself, "and that this is not the first time you've been arrested. But this is the first time that you'll likely die; but still you don't give up..." Fess' voice lowered to a whisper as she tried to keep her voice calm, "Why is it, that no matter what you face, or how much you lose; you survive- and fight on!? What kind of strength comes from failure?" Fess realized with a pinch of vulnerability- that she wanted the strength that Rizon had.

"I 'fight on' because I believe in the future that Eternity promised," Rizon's voice was gentle. "There is an evil in this world that will choke out everything that is good and true. As long as there is breath inside me; I will fight that evil. And when I stand before the king; the entire Tarven empire will hear that there is hope."

Confess blinked; was that it!? Half of what he said made no sense to her! She expected more than just... *hope*! "What hope?" she demanded at last, "The Nity followers are coming to their end; even if they can escape the city, they will be hunted down throughout all the lands after the king's decree.

Even those in Garason won't be safe for long. Everything that your Nity sacrificed for, will come to ash!"

"We need not fear disaster of any kind," Rizon argued, his voice becoming passionate. "For us, the end is not what it once was; not since the death of Eternity. For out of death- he began anew. Yes- I say we have hope! Despair, failure- even death comes to nothing in light of what Nity can do, for he has the power to restore what we believe to be lost. The only question remaining is; will you let him do so?"

Confess made no movement; she knew nothing of restoration, only of pain, and loss. She had never known anyone to *give* her anything: no, the only one she trusted to restore her life- was herself.

*   *   *

Desert tugged at the bottom of his tunic and flattened out the dark blue silk across his broadening chest. His tunic was a rich one, trimmed in silver with a wide black sash about his hips, and a black silk cape hanging from silver fastenings at his shoulders. Black pants and gleaming boots finished off his wardrobe, while his raven shaggy hair was only mildly tamed back with oil; he cut a handsome figure.

Dese had dismissed his manservant a few moments before and now stood alone before a mirror in his chambers, satisfying himself that he looked the part of the ward of a Grand Duke. He took a few extra moments to gaze back into his dark eyes; this was the last time he would dress this way. His gaze drifted across the mirror to where he could see the reflection of his desk behind him, and the blank sheet of parchment that lay on it. A feather pen and ink well sat close by- all untouched since he had placed them there four hours ago.

He knew that he needed to write the letter- but although his mind was made up, he couldn't think of the right words.

'I'll have time later," he told himself with a deep breath. 'But not much time' a voice in his head seemed to warn him; if all went as planned then Brave, Fate and himself, would be aboard a ship bound to Garatin by midnight. They didn't know this plan- no one did, but it would work.

Dese looked back at himself and went through his plan again; after Fa delivered her message, then Thrive would no doubt send her and Brave and hopefully himself back to the manor. But instead of the manor, they would go down to the Harbour Ring- the Grand Duke's carriage would be able to pass through the city gates after sundown- he hoped.

258

He glanced to where he had hidden his bag of packed provisions, he would need to send a page or someone to bring the bag to Vision down in the Harbour Square. Dese worriedly thought of Fa and Rave; they would need a change of clothes too. Hurriedly, Dese stuffed two more pairs of his simple tunics and trousers into the bag. The real trouble would be convincing the carriage driver to take them down to the Harbour Ring; hopefully they would be driven by Justice, Dese knew that he could easily bribe him.

Dese had considered telling Fa and Rave of his plan earlier, but he hadn't fully thought it through then, and he knew that Fa had enough to worry about. They probably thought that the Grand Duke would see them off on a ship the next day or something, but no, in order for Dese to go with them, they needed to slip away tonight- and Dese *was* going with them. He had carefully tucked a pouch of gold coins under his tunic to pay for passage on a ship. They wouldn't be able to get far until the weather turned good for sailing in a few weeks, but they would at least get to Chresacroon. He didn't trust Vision enough to send the money in his bag. Thrive would probably send men to look for him- but he might not think of the Island of Chresacroon, and the island was big enough to hide if Thri did think of it.

Thrive…

Dese turned back to his desk and the waiting letter- he had to write that letter now. But what could he say!? With a deep sigh, Dese made himself pick up the pen and dip it in the ink…

> *I know it's no use me asking, but don't look for me, trust me; Tarva is better off without me. I've gone with Brave and Fa.*
>
> *I'm sorry Thrive, I'm just not like you, I don't have a future here, and I never will. If you were me- if your life had been like mine- wouldn't you have gone after Loyal? I suppose not; but I could never be as logical or as brave as you. I must go.*
>
> *I'm sorry, I realize how disappointing I must be- but on the bright side you won't have to endure it anymore. Thank you for all you've done for me, and for my mother, you tried your best, I'm sure she would understand that, she would also understand that I just wasn't meant for court life.*
>
> *Don't worry, I'll be happy, and one day, I'll try and repay you properly for all you've done for me.*
>
> *Desert.*

Dese looked over his words and failed to see how pitiful he sounded. He shook some powder over the ink then blew it away. Folding up the short letter, he addressed it to Thrive, and left it on his desk. Then his mind went to the letters addressed to him in Thrive's secret study; could he get them without Thrive noticing?

Dese decided that there wasn't enough time, besides, he didn't think he would ever forget those tender-hearted words so full of hope- on second thoughts, Dese decided that having the letters with him would make him feel much too guilty! Best to leave them where they were, forgotten, and hopefully, Thrive would one day also forget about the massive failure that had been his ward.

After instructing a page to deliver his bag to Vision's Inn, Desert left his chambers for the last time, and shut the door on his former life, 'Time for a new one' he thought with a deep breath and a shiver of excitement. He continued to run over his plan as he made his way through the manor to the main balcony where he'd agreed to meet Brave and Fate before they left for the banquet.

As Desert reached the entrance to the balcony, he stopped and stood in wide-eyed awe, all thoughts eclipsed in his mind by a single, glimmering thought; Fate.

Fate was alone and stood at the balcony railing with her back to Dese, the low evening sun glinted on her long hair, making it look more like fire than ever. She was wearing it out down her back, and the soft wind touched and teased the gentle fire waves, as well as slightly lifting the hem of her dress.

"I'm speechless!" Dese breathed aloud.

Fa turned at his voice and Dese felt like the wind was knocked out of him as she returned his gaze. Dese hadn't really wondered how the Garatin maiden would look in a gown- he had already thought that she was stunning!

Fate's dress was of the new Tarven fashion, with a stiff corset and small puffed sleeves around the shoulders that flowed out into thin bell shapes that ended at her wrists. The skirt had two layers, the first matched the corset and upper sleeves in a deep forest green and ended just below the knee to reveal the second skirt that went all the way to the floor. It was a soft smoke gray that matched the lower sleeves. The embroidery on the corset and hem were a mix of gray and a greenish yellow. Her hair was held back from her face in two braids, secured behind her ears by bronze combs. Fa had new white bandages on her hands, but they didn't take away from her exotic, stunning beauty.

Dese found himself staring shamelessly.

"Pardon?" Fa asked, her pale face void of emotion. Dese wanting nothing more in the world, than to make her smile.

"You're beautiful," he made himself walk up beside her confidently, ignoring his trembling heart.

"Thank you," she said quietly, then she looked back out over the railing to where the sun was glinting off the Cherry Lake in the gardens, the murmur of the city drifted up to them on the breeze, but she didn't seem to take pleasure in the sight.

"Are you nervous?" Dese asked as he leaned his back against the railing to better look at her face, "Because you shouldn't be! Confidence is always imperative when you don't know what your doing- that's how I do it!" he grinned and was rewarded by a slightly rueful smile on Fa's part.

"I'll remember that."

Her smile faded when Dese gently took Fa's bandaged hand in his own. "And tomorrow; a ship to Garatin," he said, hoping to bring the smile back.

Instead, Fa refused to look at him and took a deep halting breath, "That's right."

'I'm coming with you' the words were on the tip of his tongue- but he decided that the timing wasn't right, 'I'll surprise them later tonight' he thought, 'When they get on the ship, I'll jump on too, and say, I've always wanted to see Garatin- do you think your parents will like me?' Dese grinned at the thought.

But when he looked back at her again... she *needed* to know how he felt!

        *   *   *

Fa stood as still as she could, completely aware of Desert's hand holding hers, and his eyes always on her face, the best she could do was pretend she didn't notice. 'Please- let the moment pass!' her mind begged, 'Don't say another word!' But even if she had said it out loud- it wouldn't have stopped Dese.

"I've never met anyone like you Fate. Saying you've cast a spell on me isn't quite right; I know exactly what I'm doing."

Fa held her breath and still refused to look at him, she knew that if she did, she would not be able to resist the calling of her heart.

"I think I would have fallen over dead if you had stayed angry with me for one more day!" Dese went on, his voice imploring her to look at him.

Hoping to lighten the mood and break the moment, Fa tried a joke, "I haven't actually said that I forgive you."

Desert was silent- and it was worse than his words, Fa turned to face him; it was a mistake. The longing and pleading in his dark eyes was tangible! Fa felt it would be cruel if she didn't say the words out loud, and the last thing she wanted was to hurt Dese. "Of course, I forgive you!"

Desert broke into a smile, then he leaned forward, but instead of a kiss, he rested his forehead against hers, in a most tender gesture of his feelings.

Fa felt that if she looked into his eyes for another second that she would fall in, and never find her way out again. She closed her eyes and let her heart thump out of control inside her. She didn't need him to say it out loud, her heart had known for days now; Desert loved her, and she...

Oh, how cruel life was! If this had been another life, a different story, she would have allowed herself to fall -forever- into his loving gaze, it would be amazingly easy. But not this life- not now! She couldn't- just *couldn't* allow those feelings in, she had already gone too far!

'I am the girl of fire and ash' she reminded herself painfully, 'I am not meant to be loved, I am not meant to have this. My end is coming.'

She knew that anyone close to her might also suffer her end, just as Eamer and 'The Prestige' had burned, so would anyone else who was too close to her. Brave, and Desert must *Not* be allowed to be close to her when the end came, not physically, and certainly not romantically.

Dese didn't know it- but she was saving his life.

"Fate, Desert? The carriage is waiting for us," Brave called.

    *   *   *

Rave trotted up the steps to the balcony and looked up to see Desert and Fate standing close beside each other. Rave failed to notice just how close they were, or how Dese quickly stepped away.

"Are you ready?" he asked in a serious tone.

"I am," Fa replied without a tremble or hesitation.

Before Rave turned away, he saw Dese hang on to Fa's hand a moment too long as she went to follow Rave. An inkling of understanding began in Rave's mind.

Rave led the way down to the fire hall, then out into the courtyard. As he went, Rave marveled at how drastically things had changed over the past few months! Here Fate was, on the other side of the sea from her beloved home that she had never wanted to leave, preparing to speak to the most powerful man in the world; and her voice didn't even tremble.

And Desert!? When they had first met- Rave did not like the carefree, cocky Tarven- not one bit! And now he considered him to be a close friend- the only true *friend* that Rave had ever had. And Dese was apparently quite close to Fa too. Rave didn't want to think about just how close the two might be, and chose to smother the feeling of jealousy, mostly because he couldn't tell if he was jealous of his best friend taking away his sister- or of his sister taking away his best friend.

And then there was himself, Rave caught a glimpse of his reflection in a window as he passed by; what a strange reflection- who was the stranger looking back at him? As foreign as his own reflection looked to him, Rave also felt that the boy who had dug up his grandfather's dagger and ran away into Garason- wasn't *him* either. Rave wasn't sure what had happened to that boy, for he had become someone else entirely- as was evident from his reflection. That boy had been self-centered, and childish, unaware of how big the world was, and how small in comparison he was. What a silly boy he had been.

Earlier as Rave was dressing for the banquet (in finer clothes than he'd ever thought he would wear) he had noticed for the first time that his chest was broader than it had been, and there were prickly hairs on his chin! Even now in the fire hall, he noticed that he was now taller than Fa- hadn't it been just a few days ago when she could scold him from a foot above him!?

Things were changing indeed.

Chapter 26   Intrigue

The courtyard of the Ducal was neatly arranged with a single carriage and a large escort of mounted and armed guards, headed by the head guard Valor, they were not entirely for the sake of ceremony. The horses shifted impatiently, and groomsmen and stable boys held the horses ready, while everyone waited. The Grand Duke emerged from the main doors and stood for a moment to look over the waiting procession. His lordship would be impossible to miss in a crowd that night due to his striking wardrobe. He wore mostly black, with thick silver embroidery embellishing his shoulders and chest, a striking red cape hung from his shoulders, he had it draped over one arm. Not a hair on his head was out of place, and his beard was trimmed close, giving his jaw the appearance of a sharp point.

His dark eyes flickered over the courtyard, then a smile spread easily, giving the signal that he was pleased. He walked down the steps towards his horse, a gray dappled mare of high breeding, she wore a decorative silver chamfron down her face, fashioned to look like dragon scales, as well as silver greaves, fastened on her lower legs. Thrive nodded to his groomsman and stroked his mount's neck with affection.

A moment later and the Grand Duke turned and smiled broadly as three more figures appeared at the main door and descended the steps. Fate came first, her face pale, held in cold determination- but it could easily be mistaken for lady-like aloofness.

"My lady, you are a vision!" Thrive complimented courteously, with a shrewd side glance at Desert, who was a few steps behind.

Fa bobbed the curtsy that she had been made to practice all that afternoon by a handmaiden, then allowed Thrive to bow over her hand (he was careful with her tender hand). Thrive straightened and nodded to Brave, who had cleaned up impressively, then his eyes went to rest on Desert, whom he seemed to critique. Desert stood and bore his gaze, with an air of formality that the siblings and Thrive no doubt noticed. Thrive didn't seem to know how to correct the stiffness of the interaction, or at least he didn't try.

"The carriage will bring you three to the banquet- I'm afraid I may get caught up in some ceremonial foolery, I trust you will present yourself appropriately when you arrive," he half asked, half instructed Desert.

"Bowing and scraping," Dese promised and flashed his smile, he then led the way to the carriage, where a footman was holding the door open and ready.

Thrive, allowed himself a small rueful smile before going to his horse.

"He won't be riding with us?" Brave whispered to Dese, as Fate was helped into the carriage first.

Dese nodded. "As part of the court, its customary for him to ride a horse to this sort of thing," he explained, as he climbed in and took his seat across from Fa, Brave sat next to him. "If he had a son and heir, then he would ride with him," Dese added.

Rave did not miss the fact that Dese was hidden away in a carriage, instead of riding on horseback with the duke.

Soon, the procession was underway, and they rolled out into the street with much fanfare in the early evening's light. The ride to the Dragon Keep was mostly quiet inside the carriage, with only a few attempts at conversation by Dese, who as always, seemed to be treating the whole thing like one great adventure.

But Brave found he couldn't laugh, or respond much to his friend, his head was too full of worry for his sister. Every time he looked at her, he got a sickening feeling, like he had forgotten something important, and he would ultimately fail her- again!

'This will soon be over,' he tried to sooth himself, 'Then Fa will be free, and we'll go home,' the thought only brought with it a strange sense of anxiety. Words like 'over' and 'free', somehow sounded menacing to Rave. He looked at Fa again- she was impossibly calm! It reassured Rave a little to see her so, 'She knows what she's doing'.

*   *   *

Lord Mountain smiled proudly as his six-year-old son rode his pony up to a stable boy, his smile turned rueful as his son snobbishly ordered that his pony be taken care of.

"A fine rider he'll be one day," Duke Command noted, as he trotted his steed up next to Lord Mountain, "Not unlike my sons at his age." Duke Command had two sons who were now lords of their own manors and had ridden ahead and were now ordering stable boys about themselves.

"What a pity not all can share in our pride," Lord Mountain's voice was sarcastic, and Duke Command followed his gaze. The Grand Duke came riding through the Dragon Keep's open gate and portcullis into the grand courtyard. It was teaming with activity as stable boys hurried to lead horses and carriages out of the way and members of court stood about with puffed out chests and flashing jewels- each one trying to outdo the other, but none were as impressive as the Grand Duke.

The Grand Duke's fine horse high stepped fashionably to the center of the courtyard, his fluttering red cape catching many envious eyes. His escorts dismounted their own steeds and stood to attention, but for all the flashing silver and sharp looking escorts, the absence of a son riding at the Grand Duke's side was glaringly obvious to all who cared about such things.

"Yes, his painful lack of an heir is precisely what I intend to speak to his Majesty about tonight," Duke Command said, as they watched Thrive nod to his fellow lords. He and Lord Mountain were obliged to bow their heads in respect- they did so with much spite.

"My lord? What plans have you made?" Lord Mountain inquired quietly.

Duke Command smiled deviously as Thrive dismounted, "I may have a foothold from which I can remove the current Grand Duke from power, and we would both benefit from that, my friend."

"Indeed, we would, my lord," Lord Mountain watched as Thrive's poor excuse of a ward stepped from a carriage that had pulled up; Mountain smiled.

*   *   *

The king's gardens were perched on the edge of the cliff facing the sea, with only a wall and rampart between the cherry trees and the thousand-foot drop. The Dragon Keep's walls looked down on the garden from many windows and arches, and a fresh breeze off the sea refreshed the banquet guests as they gathered in clusters in the many small courtyards or walked the flower lined paths that twisted this way and that. Elegant cherry trees in bloom shed their flower petals to carpet the paths, and all around there were bushes trimmed to look like ships in full sail, or dragons with arched wings. Every tree and bush were in full bloom, and thick perfume filled the evening air. Paper lanterns were hung in the trees or on poles to light up the paths when the setting sun bowed away completely, in the meantime, guests could climb the cliff wall and watch the sunset over the sea in all its splendor. From such a height, the ships in the harbour looked like children's paper ships that they might float on a pond. In one of the small courtyards there were flute players and other musicians, who kept up a playful tune throughout the evening.

Lords and their ladies stood about and greeted one another with snobbish tilts to their dark heads, proud fathers introduced their sons, the younger ones would soon be sent home, having only come to be shown off. Young maidens were introduced to potential suitors, and young men gathered together to compare hunting stories and brag about their newest horses.

Fate followed Thrive into the midst of all this, with Brave close at her side, and Desert a step behind Thrive. Thrive introduced Fa and Rave to whomever they approached, but Fa and Rave hardly spoke, only bowing and curtsying when necessary. Everyone was very polite (too polite for Fa's liking, and she suspected that it was all pretences at kindness) but everywhere Fa went she could feel curious eyes following her, as if everyone knew there was more to her than just 'a guest of the Grand Duke'.

Fa didn't allow herself to feel uncomfortable from their lingering glances, and instead focused on her mission- so much so that the beauty of the gardens was lost on her.

"Earl of Wavecrest, my ward, Desert, he is the one I spoke of at your banquet." Thrive introduced Dese to a man with a round belly. Fa noticed how Desert was forcing a smile and didn't seem interested at all in the exchange with the Earl. Fa and Rave stood silently by as Thrive chatted with the Earl for a few moments. When the conversation was over Thrive glanced towards one of the courtyards where a group of important looking men stood about.

"Alright, you three are free to wander on your own, I have some business to see to," he said, with a meaningful look at Dese. "Stay out of the way of anyone who looks important," he instructed.

Dese flashed him a smile, "Like I always do!"

Thrive sighed but allowed Dese to lead Fa and Rave away down a path, he wondered briefly if Desert shouldn't in fact, be by his side, so he could be presented to the members of court, instead of hiding in a back corner of the garden. But he dismissed the thought; there would be time later for good impressions. And his conversation with the royal clerk, was best done without Desert present.

Thri set his eyes on the royal clerk, he was standing in the courtyard, looking extremely bored. It was a bit unusual to see the clerk at such an event, the man was a recluse- but it was fortunate; Thrive hadn't been able to speak to him for weeks, and now that Desert was home, there was a sense of urgency.

Thrive approached the royal clerk and nodded his head in greeting, while the clerk made a short bow.

"My lord, Grand Duke," he made some attempt at small talk, but the clerk wasn't adept at such things, so Thrive did him the mercy of getting right to the point.

"I trust you have had time to go over those documents I gave you last we met?"

The royal clerk gave a long nod before speaking. "Indeed, I did, your lordship, I assume you still wish for my sanction on the issue," he said delicately.

Thrive appreciated his lowered tone, "You are correct, the sooner the better, I'm sure you understand."

"Oh yes, of course; we all want our children to be secure in their future." The royal clerk hurriedly said, "I just wonder if- in light of recent events- perhaps it would be best if this was delayed, your lordship, till a... more stable time." He glanced about, perhaps nervous that they might be overheard.

Thrive smiled, hoping that it would calm the man, "I see no reason to wait, he has been my ward for over ten years, surely that is long enough. Unless you think the King will find fault with the arrangements?" Thrive secretly held his breath.

The royal clerk operated under the king, and although many transactions could be done without the King's involvement- or interest, the King could put an end to anything he did. Thrive feared that in his present state, the King just might deny Thrive's request for Desert- even if it was perfectly legal.

The royal clerk balked at the suggestion, "No, no, no!" he shook his head, "I doubt the King would care..." he stopped his words short and stared at his shoes for a moment; both men knew that the King had not payed much attention to any request or transaction that the royal clerk had dealt with over the pest few months- even the past few years!

"It's just... the court members might not approve of your ward inheriting your title- forgive me your lordship!" the clerk apologised hastily, Thrive nodded for him to continue- although he had a good idea of what he would say. "The boy- young man, Desert- that is, has not exactly instilled confidence in the court about his abilities to handle the responsibilities of being a Duke." He glanced nervously at Thrive- afraid of how he would respond.

Thrive threw him off by smiling, "Were any of us responsible at his age? Indeed, I believe there have been many a young heir that has disgraced his father, yet they still inherit a title."

The clerk smiled ruefully, no doubt thinking of any number of incompetent young lords and earls.

"I have confidence that Desert will grow into a fine young man- given the opportunity," Thrive said, his voice swelling with pride, "And since when did a Grand Duke need the approval of the court to manage his own household?"

The clerk bowed again, "Just so, your lordship! Quite right!"

"You will sanction the adoption?"

The clerk nodded vigorously, "Without further delay, your lordship, and gladly- I have been looking for an excuse to leave this function early, I shall attend to your request directly!"

Thrive smiled, relief filling him, "You have my thanks, royal clerk." He bowed his head, and the clerk bowed in return then hurried away, no doubt to a cluttered chamber with a large, equally cluttered desk, where he would add his seal to the adoption papers of Desert.

Thrive took a deep breath as he watched the clerk disappear through a door into the Dragon Keep. 'Duke Desert' Thrive tried out the title in his mind, and imagined Dese growing into the kind of man, that Thrive hoped he himself had set as an example. A good man, fair and compassionate; exactly the kind that Tarva sorely needed. He also thought of how and when he would tell Desert, he had withheld his plans in fear that the adoption would be denied, but now... now Desert could hold his head high in the court, with the title of Duke awaiting him.

*   *   *

Looking up along the path, Fate noticed a group of young men and maidens, about her age, she just vaguely noticed how she seemed to be the only one with her hair worn down her back. The group of them turned to look as Desert came up the path with Fa and Rave, and some of them snickered, while others stared rudely. Desert smoothly turned away down a separate path, avoiding the group entirely, he seemed to guess Fa's thoughts.

"Just a bunch of blueblood snobs," he said, not caring if his voice carried to the group of 'bluebloods'. "They've never accepted me, just like the rest of the court." The last part he said much quieter, and Fa thought she detected a hidden longing in him.

They walked down the path for a small way until they came in sight of another courtyard, this one had more women- who wore flashing jewels in their dark hair.

"When will the King come?" Brave asked as he searched the courtyard in vain for the, as yet, absent monarch.

"Soon, he likes to wait till everyone else has arrived," Dese said easily as he brushed a cherry flower petal from his shoulder. He then laughed when he saw Rave's agitated state, "Relax Rave! Everything is going as planned! When the King comes, we'll try to be the first to his side, then Fa can give her message, and it'll be over! Here sit down- you both are way too nervous!" He directed Fa to sit on a stone bench nearby.

Although she was calm, Fa sat down without comment, but wondered if Dese should be the one sitting when she noticed a tremor in his hand. It touched her to think that he was trying to be the calm one, when really, he was just as nervous as Rave.

Brave took a deep breath and looked around again, tugging at his tight collar, "Where will the King come from?" he asked, obviously still agitated.

The boys didn't seem to notice how quiet Fa was, and as she watched, they grew more and more agitated, while she just grew calmer; her time was coming.

"I'm not sure," Dese said as he craned his neck to see through the trees to where a door from the castle could be seen. "There's a few places he could come from- he might even have trumpeters to announce him, if he's in the mood for it."

The boys paced for a few minutes, while Fa just sat, until Dese ruffled his own hair, ruining the styled look. "I'll go down to the main courtyard and see if the King has come yet," he said and hurried away.

Fa watched him go with an oddly melancholy feeling- as if she feared that was the last she'd see of him.

"I'll go back this way and see if the Kings come over there," Rave said after a moment, and turned back the way they had come.

"Rave?" Fa called him back; she was glad they were alone, what she needed to say had to be said in private.

"What?" Rave asked half stopping and looking at her with raised brows.

Fa hesitated, she knew she needed to say it- but the words seemed to retreat in her mind. "Be careful Rave," she said at last, intently returning his gaze, but he misunderstood and gave her a weird look.

"Of course!"

"I mean it!" she insisted, feeling her throat tighten.

Rave smiled reassuringly, "It's almost over Fa; we'll be going home soon." He turned and jogged away down the path, leaving Fa alone.

"Goodbye Rave..." Fa whispered sadly, and the wind sent a curtain of cherry blooms down on her. She sat for a long moment in the silence that followed, the setting sun's red light filling the gardens. She held her breath as a strange sensation filled her; it was like something was rising within her- something that was not a part of her at all. The presence that had been fighting for dominance inside her since... Fa suddenly understood that it had always been there, waiting and growing in power, until Fa was too weak to hold it at bay. It felt foreign and yet frighteningly familiar, complex, but suddenly horribly simple.

She could feel it growing- flexing, and she no longer had the strength, or the desire to fight it.

"Don't be afraid Fate."

Looking up, Fa was not surprised to see the Dream Child standing on the path before her, she knew that she *should* be surprised though, for she was certain that she wasn't dreaming, and yet there the child was.

"There has never been a moment when you were alone, and there never will be," the Dream Child promised.

Fa resisted the child's voice for only a moment, before giving in and completely trusting the child's words. As she did so, Fa felt the thing inside her swell and reach out to the hidden places of her heart, filling every corner of her being. Fa was becoming less, and *it* was becoming more.

"I'm ready," Fa said at last, and the child smiled and held out a hand. Taking the hand and standing up, Fa noticed that the child's hand on her burns didn't hurt. The child led her down a third path that seemed to appear out of nowhere. As they went, Fa became less aware of her surroundings, and found herself nearly intoxicated by the presence inside her- or was it coming from the child?

The garden around her seemed to change and transform, its beauty growing tenfold, until it was breathtaking, the red light gave way to a bright golden light, and Fa's heart nearly broke inside her for the unmistakable feeling of coming home.

Quite suddenly Fate was alone again, the garden had gone back to the way it was before, leaving a dull ache in Fa's heart that she would have for the rest of her life.

She stood in the center of a wide, empty path that she didn't recognize, although she could hear the crowds further down the path, there was no one in sight. The Dream Child was gone too, and the presence seemed to have retreated inside her; why!?

"Hello, have you lost your way?"

Fate turned to the voice that had spoke behind her; there stood a richly dressed woman with an entourage of handmaidens and guards a few steps behind her. The woman had a round jawline and a wide mouth, her raven hair was piled atop her head, then cascaded down her back. Her dress was deep red, accented with black silk. She looked like she had lost weight recently and there were dark smudges under her warm brown eyes, a curious smile hovered on her lips, almost disguising the sadness that hung over her like a mantel.

Fa's eyes darted to the delicate, golden crown resting on the woman's head, and felt her knees tremble.

"Her Majesty, Elegance, Queen of Tarva and wife of Triumphant the Great," one of the queen's escorts announced, when Fa failed to respond in anyway.

Fa masked her surprise by dropping into a deep curtsey, until she could feel her knees on the path stones. "Your Majesty!" Fa breathed and kept her face downward, her heart pounding.

"Who are you child?" the Queen asked, her voice kind. Fa risked a glance around the Queen's skirts but saw no sign of the King.

"Fate, Your Majesty, a guest of the Grand Duke."

"Rise Fate," the Queen invited. Fa stood on shaky legs and faced the queen, returning her gaze without quaver. "I have never met anyone who looks the way you do! Where are you from Fate?" she asked, her eyes were constantly drawn to Fa's hair.

Fa swallowed; why had the Dream Child led her to the Queen and not the King!? "From Garatin," Fa replied, forgetting to address the Queen properly. Some of the escorts shifted, and one of the guards looked to the Queen to see if she demanded an apology for such rudeness, but Elegance did not take offence- instead she laughed, a sweet tinkling laughter.

"What a charming girl! And quite lovely- wouldn't you say so?" she asked turning to an older handmaiden beside her.

"Indeed, Your Majesty, like a fairy from the old songs," the woman said, looking at Fa's hair.

Fa suspected that she meant 'witch' not 'fairy', but Fa hardly gave it any thought, her mind was racing nearly out of control. What was she to do!? Deliver her message to the Queen instead of the King?

"My Queen," a voice said, from behind Fa.

Fa froze as the Queen's escorts all bowed low- but it was not their reactions, nor the look on Elegance's face, nor even the voice that made Fa freeze. For with the voice came a reawakening of the presence inside her.

Chapter 27   Just a Girl

"My lord, Grand Duke!"

Thrive turned and forced a smile, most of the banqueters had moved elsewhere, and now Thri found himself alone with his court enemies- with no hope of a graceful escape; he would have to stand his ground. "Lord Mountain, Duke Command," he nodded to both men, and was suddenly put on guard; they seemed… confident, as if they knew something that he did not.

"Did I see young Desert here with you?" Mountain asked with a malicious grin, "You must be so proud of all your son has accomplished!"

Thrive tilted his head back and narrowed his eyes as if having trouble identifying a strange insect- but he understood when Duke Command joined in.

"Tut tut, Lord Mountain!" Command mockingly reprimanded, "One would think that you've forgotten; our Grand Duke has *no* son. If he did, I trust he wouldn't be as much a disappointment as his ward."

In Thrive's younger years, when he was more prone to anger, he would have struck Command until the Duke blacked out- then he would have gone to work on Mountain. But over the years, Thrive had honed his strength in his whit and silken tongue, until he could make men cower before his words as if he brandished a sword.

Thrive smiled thoughtfully, "Of course!" he breathed, "I always assumed that your lordships got to where you are now, by the sheer power of your heritage, now I see that it was by cheap words and cowardly insults aimed at those you are afraid of. My, how the world has changed!" Thrive's twinkling eyes hardened to granite, "Between us, your lordships, I suggest that you prepare for battle; when war comes, you'll want more than bribed allies and ranks grown weak from corruption."

There were few things that could have pleased Thrive more than to see the uncertainty and fear on the faces of Command and Mountain; they obviously had miscalculated how dangerous the Grand Duke could be.

"Good evening," Thrive said pleasantly and turned his back on them, he silently swore to deal permanently with the two later. He reminded himself that he no longer need fear for Desert's safety from the two vipers of the court- and others like them, for now, Dese would have the protection of his title.

As he walked away, Mountain and Command seethed in anger and wounded pride.

"One day I'll have his head on a spike!" Command gritted.

     *   *   *

Thrive did not look back as he walked away, soon he found himself approaching a growing crowd on the path- but instead of laughter and a general buzz of conversation, the crowd was nearly entirely silent. They parted enough for Thrive to see who was at the center of the crowd, and when he did, he froze in disbelief and fear. On the other side of the crowd, Brave and Desert did the same, and everyone fairly held their breath. In the center of the crowd was the King and Queen, and their attendants; between the monarchs stood Fate.

The presence inside Fa had leapt back up and filled her instantly at the sound of the Kings voice, giving her no time to fear for her own safety. The Dream Child was also back, and stood beside her holding her damaged hand, but still Fa had no words to speak! It was as she feared; she didn't know what to do.

"My Queen," the King ignored Fa's clumsy curtsy- indeed he didn't seem to see her at all, and instead addressed his wife with a crooked smile, "I must say- you do not look well! Have you been crying again?" he jeered, and

Fa winced inwardly at his cruel tone. Beside her, the Dream Child flinched and squeezed her hand slightly.

"Ele!" The King now spoke loud enough so that everyone in the growing crowd could hear, "You really must stop grieving; your son, the prince- is dead!" his tone was crass- prideful even! "He will never be greater than ME!" he whispered with eyes full of… triumph.

Ele looked as shocked as everyone felt at the King's statement, then she looked about at the crowd, "Trium please! - he died but a month ago!" Elegance whispered fiercely, her embarrassment and shame clear to all.

Triumphant smiled cruelly, and ignored her plea, "And who is this?" he asked, his dark eyes falling on Fa, with a smugness and confidence that only a King could get away with.

And then it happened; the Dream Child spoke- not to Fa as she had expected, but directly to the King! Fa only stood there and listened, bearing the gaze of everyone, at least… that's what she thought she was doing, but to everyone else, it was she who spoke to Triumphant the Great.

"Do you think me blind, that I haven't seen what you've done to my world?" Fa's voice was cold and flat, yet throbbing with raw energy, Brave hardly recognized it as hers! As she spoke, Trium's face drained of colour, and he stared at her like he had encountered an enemy he thought was long dead. "Do you think me deaf, that I wouldn't hear the cries of my children?! Do you think me weak, that I could not stop you? Did you think there would be no reckoning for your evil?! Yet even now I would redeem you, Triumphant the plagued, even now Tarva is not without hope. There is yet time; return to me, for I-"

Fa's words- or the child's words, were cut short when the Kings face went red and he exploded, spitting and hunching his shoulders, "DEMON! WHO ARE YOU!?" he demanded.

Fa returned his murderous gaze without fear, her face pale and her eyes suddenly looked sunken and sorrowful, "You know my name."

"Fate?" Elegance stepped forward uncertainly and reached to touch her shoulder but jumped back with the rest of the crowd when the King roared, veins in his neck standing out like cords under too much pressure, "SILENCE! I will hear no more of your treasonous words! GUARDS! Take the demon to the dungeons- gag her if she utters but one more word!"

Fate lost hold of the Dream Child for a second as she was set upon by more guards than was necessary. The crowd erupted in gasps and hushed oaths, and they all jumped back as the King stormed off, pushing aside anyone who was unlucky enough to not have moved fast enough. The guards hurried away next, jostling Fa amongst them, and she only had a brief glimpse of Brave, all the while the Dream Child, apparently completely unseen, scurried along beside her, narrowly avoiding being trampled by the guards.

*   *   *

"FATE!" Desert's voice failed him and was drowned out as the crowd erupted in a strange hush of whispered voices, Dese watched in shock as Fa was led away. The Queen also made a hasty departure, and the banquet guests became considerably louder. Fate's namesake could be heard repeated over and again, connected with things like 'demon?', 'Garatin witch' and 'Who did she come with?'.

More guards came and created a barrier to the door the King had gone through and began ordering the guests to disperse. Dese was in so much shock that he forgot that Brave stood beside him, that is, until Rave grabbed his arm.

"There!" he pointed to Thrive who looked to be in as much shock as Dese.

Desert darted to Thrive through the muttering and thronging crowd who began to push and shove as the guards began to enforce their exit. Rave was close on his heels as he reached Thri's side.

"Thrive- do something!" Dese begged.

Thrive grabbed his and Raves shoulders and pulled them along the path away from the guards, glancing behind him, he spoke quietly, but his voice held an edge, "There's nothing to be done!" he walked quickly, "Rave-cover your face," he instructed and pulled Rave's hand up over his pale face. Desert nervously glanced around, understanding the peril Rave was in if someone decided that he too, needed to be arrested. Rave held his hand up and shielded his face as if the sun was too bright- but the sun had long since set, and soon the darkness would aid in hiding Rave's features.

"She's safe enough for the moment," Thrive lowered his voice as they entered the Dragon Keep on their way to the front of the castle where they could escape. Servants and attendants looked up questioningly, no doubt wondering why someone would be leaving the banquet so early- they would soon find out! "I will try and speak to the King to plead for her release, but I doubt he will grant me an audience tonight."

Thrive's pace was exhausting to keep up with, but already Dese could hear the crowd coming up behind them. He had doubts about how much success Thrive would have in pleading for Fa's release, hadn't Thri said just two days ago that The King had gotten worse to deal with? And the King certainly didn't look like he was likely to forgive Fa her words. Dese was beset with guilt; it had been his plan to get Fa here- he didn't know *this* would happen though!

Thrive glanced behind them again. "I must get you two away from here," he muttered, and Dese wondered if he had misspoken; surely, he meant get *Brave* away from the Dragon Keep... surely, *he* wasn't in danger here!

They went the rest of the way through the castle in silence. Reaching the large front courtyard, Thrive called sharply to the stable boys to bring his carriage around. There were a few agonizing minutes while the horses were hitched back up. In those precious moments, more of the banquet guests also came out into the courtyard and ordered for their carriages and mounts- soon it would be impossible to make a hasty retreat!

The carriage was hitched up in record time, and soon rumbled up.

"To the Ducal," Thrive instructed the driver, "As swift as you may." He turned to his mounted guards, "Bring my mount- and Valor," he said to his head guard- who no doubt was beginning to understand the situation, "I do not want to be stopped at the Kings Gate." Valor nodded smartly with a serious expression.

Desert nearly pushed Rave into the carriage, and Thrive came after them, he immediately drew the curtains, casting the interior of the carriage into an oppressive gloom.

Valor's voice could be heard calling, 'Make way for the Grand Duke!', then the carriage rolled forward with a lurch. Before long Valor's voice could be heard hollering for the Kings Gate to be opened. Dese held his breath and peeked through the curtain, but the Gate hadn't been closed and they rumbled through the gate without slowing- now they were truly away from the Dragon Keep.

*   *   *

"THRIVE!? GET IN HERE!" Triumphant bellowed.

The court fool who had been renamed after the Grand Duke, took a moment on the other side of the King's chamber door to prepare himself. The King had been raging and ranting for an hour after the interrupted banquet. The light of the sun had long since faded, and the castle gardens were now empty of guests. No one had dared go near the King's chambers, and then, Triumphant had summoned the fool.

Provider, as his namesake had been before the King had christened him Thrive, pasted on a wide smile and pushed open the chamber door, dancing out into the King's large chamber. Trium stood near the middle of the room and watched without comment or discernible expression.

Vider halted before him with a comical jump and bowed low, wondering morbidly if this was the last time he would do so. "Here to please, my lord and king!" he remained bowed, flinching slightly when Trium touched his chin with his hand and raised him.

The king's previous long pinky fingernail had broken and left a jagged edge. He looked at him long and hard, his face taunt and stern, Vider held his breath and felt sweat bead down his back under his brightly coloured fool's costume. Then, suddenly, like a dam breaking, Trium's face broke into a near whimper.

"Thrive..." he breathed, "You are the only one I *can* trust!" he sounded like a child who had just discovered how the world worked.

Provider let out a sigh- but swallowed it back; he knew how swiftly the king's mood could shift when he was like this, and he knew from experience that it didn't take much to push him over the edge. "How can I serve you, my king?"

"I can't trust anyone else! Only you Thrive!" Trium whispered secretively, "I have plans-" he glanced about the room suddenly, as if afraid that someone was there.

Vider also looked about, but he knew that no one dared come near the King when he was in such a mood. "I believe we are alone, sire," he said, hoping he didn't sound patronizing.

Trium looked at him with wide, uncomprehending eyes, and Vider wondered if he could really see him at all.

"Yes... Alone," Trium agreed at last.

"What plans were you speaking of, my king?" Vider prompted, he felt confident that he had the King under his control; what would the rest of Tarva say if they knew their King could be controlled by a fool?!

Triumphant stared blankly for another half minute. "The Harbour Ring- it's a mess- a disgrace!" he said at last, as if there had been no pause at all. He turned away and didn't seem to care about the volume of his voice anymore, "I'll rebuild it with splendor after the accident! It will be a wonder to behold, and I will be revered as the greatest King of Tarva! Nay- of the world!"

Vider couldn't keep a quiver from his voice as he spoke his next words, "The accident- sire?"

"SHHH!" Trium scolded harshly and spun around to face Vider, jabbing his finger against his lips, "They might hear you Thrive! And you know how jealous the council members are of you! And there are others…"

It occurred then to Vider, that the King may have forgotten which 'Thrive' he was he was! If he thought he was speaking to the Grand Duke, then that would explain the topic; it was a strange thing to discuss with a fool!

"May I ask, what others, my King?" Vider asked delicately, half wishing he hadn't asked.

"The rebels!" Trium said, as if it was obvious. "They sent that girl- that *demon*, to kill me! Poison me…" Trium pulled his cape about him protectively and looked suspiciously to where a turned over tray and a gold goblet lay on the floor. Red wine had spilled out into a puddle, the thick carpet soaking it up; it looked blood stained.

Provider jumped a little when Trium clamped his hand down on his shoulder. "Do you know they tried to poison me!?" he asked, apparently having forgotten that he had already told him so. He leaned closer and smiled, "I can trust you though! Can't I Thrive?"

Vider swallowed hard and nodded solemnly, the king giggled and went to a chair where he flopped down and sighed, closing his eyes he seemed to fall asleep. It was then that Vider also noticed, that the king had taken off his many rings, and had discarded them to the floor; priceless rubies and diamonds laying about like so much waste.

Trium giggled again, at who knows what twisted thought. Vider had never seen the King this bad- and he had certainly never seen anyone act in the same way. Something was horribly wrong with the King… and there was nothing Vider could do about it!

*   *   *

While the court fool dealt with the king's mad ravings, the real Thrive was on the other side of the Dragon Keep, in the outer chambers of the Queen. He had intended to send Golden to the Keep, or even go himself to try and find out what was happening to Fate, but before Thri could do so, he had received a royal summons- but not from the king as he had expected with a mix of hope and dread, but rather from Queen Elegance.

"Explain Thrive," Elegance said firmly as soon as she had dismissed her maids. She had changed from her banquet gown, into a slightly less extravagant dress.

Thrive took note of how worn and tired her face looked; she was not doing well.

"Who is she?" Ele held his gaze, and Thri bowed his head- he had always known that she was a strong woman.

"Fate is a guest of mine- she is just a girl, who has been through much, my queen," he said carefully, he had a hope that she would help- but he must choose his words with care; the truth might be too much.

"That is not an answer Thrive!" Ele said sternly.

"She is just a girl," Thrive repeated, looking up at Ele, "My queen, I swear she is not a threat to the king- or anyone!" he said calmly, his voice compelling her to believe him.

Ele still looked sceptical. "Trium called her a demon... that may be a bit far- but you can not deny that she spoke as if one possessed!" she looked a bit frightened; black magic and witch craft was nearly unheard of, and had begun to fade into wild stories and fables, but there was always the fear that it would return.

"She is not a witch, my queen," Thrive said slowly, pronouncing each word. "She is just... ill and must be cared for!" Thrive could find no other way to say it, it was one of those odd occasions where he couldn't think of the right words! For he couldn't come clean and tell the truth about Fate, to say that she was a messenger of Eloi from Garatin, with a message apparently of utter doom... it might be better to say she *was* a witch! "Please, she is just a girl, I swear the king would never hear of her again if she was released! Perhaps if you were to speak to him on her behalf, together we could sway the king's mind and save her." His tone came close to begging- but he didn't care!

Elegance turned her head to one side, as if protecting her face from something too hot. "No Thrive. You alone know how strained my relationship is with the king. I do not want this girl to come to harm- but I *can not* ask any favors of Trium; he will not grant them if they come from me." She swallowed hard and looked truly frightened, "I will not give him what he wants- I will not give him a reason to eliminate more of the royal family."

Thrive anxiously glanced about to make sure they were alone, and he dared take a step closer to her, "Your majesty- I implore you to be careful with your words!" he warned in a lowered tone.

Ele's eyes teared up, and she looked like someone who was tired of hiding, "Thrive, I know now. His words tonight…" her voice dropped to a ragged whisper, "My son is dead- and he did it! I know it; he had his own son killed! No don't argue! You were the one who first questioned the circumstances of his death- and now I know the truth, and the rest of Tarva should know it too!"

"Your majesty- PLEASE!" Thrive breathed, reaching out he touched her arm, hoping it would remind her that she *had* to be strong. He knew that not even she would be safe if others heard her speak against the king in such a way.

Elegance blinked her tears away and held her head up higher, Thri removed his hand. "If you are to save the Garatin girl from the kings judgment; you must do it alone, old friend, for I would be of no help."

Thrive took a deep breath, that was the answer he feared. "So be it," he bowed his head, "I will speak with the king in the morning, perhaps his anger will be forgotten by then. Please, see that Fate is looked after and protected; she is not well."

The Queen nodded her head, "I will do what I can."

                    *   *   *

Brave and Desert had paced in Thrive's library until their feet ached, then they had sat and held their heads in their hands until their anxiety built so high that they were forced to their feet- and they began to pace again. Every time a servant walked by the door the boys looked up, hoping to see that Thrive had returned with Fate- they were always disappointed.

Rave kept running over everything through his head, over and again, until his head throbbed; was there something he should have done!?

"Oh!" he gasped and stopped pacing, Desert looked over at him, and Rave covered his face in shame as he realized the truth, "She knew this would happen!"

"What?" Dese asked with a frown of anger- or was that just Rave's own guilt?

"Why didn't I *listen* to her!?" Rave pulled at his hair as he remembered Fa's last words to him, "She told me to be careful- because she knew she wouldn't be there to keep me out of trouble; she was saying goodbye! And I didn't *listen* to her!" he crouched down where he was as if in great pain.

'I failed her...' he thought in shock and defeat, 'all this time- all the *stupid* things I've said and done, and when she needed me... I was too afraid to do anything! I should have stopped her- I should have done something...'

"I should have stopped her..." he whispered.

Desert turned away and ran a hand through his raven hair, his own heart heavy with guilt and blame. "Thrive will be able to help her," he stated, but it did not offer comfort for either of them; they had both failed Fa, and now, she was alone.

*   *   *

The guards were rough and unfriendly as they escorted- or dragged, Fate to the dungeons in the lowest levels of the Dragon Keep. Twice Fa tripped on the hem of her smoke gray skirt, she heard stitches rip, the guards didn't wait or help her regain her balance, but instead pulled her along till she found her own footing. Their gloved hands on her upper arms left bruises, and she could feel her burn blisters opening and dampening her once clean bandages.

'Alone' her mind kept saying over and again... but not entirely; the Dream Child was still with her, scampering along with the guards, darting out of their way. Fa could feel the Child's gaze always on her. Every time they passed by a torch mounted one the wall, Fa squinted and shied away from it, as if its mere existence burned her.

When they reached the dungeons, one of the guards took up a torch- which Fa flinched away from, gratefully taking note that there was no wood to catch fire, only cold stone. The dungeon warden, who had an equally cold face, led them down a hall of cells with iron bar doors, there wasn't enough light to see if they were full or not. They stopped halfway down the hall and shoved her into a cold cell. Fa tumbled in and turned to see the impassive warden lock the iron bar door with a bone key. Without a second glance at Fa's frightened face, the guards and warden returned the way they had come, taking the torch with them. The light from the torch receded, only a dim gray light remained, the kind that seems to grow darker every time you try to focus your gaze.

The cell was just barely wide enough for a person to lie down in, and just deep enough to be able to sit at the back of and be forgotten. Three walls were made of stone, and the back wall was wet and slimy from an underground river, that left the fourth wall of iron bars and a rusty hinged door. There was a small pile of old straw against one of the dry walls and a dead rat in the far corner.

Fate stood in the center of the cell and listened to the receding footsteps of the guards, slowly loosing control of her breathing as panic set in; she was alone- except for the Dream Child who stood beside her.

"Don't be afraid Fa-" the Child began to say.

Fa jerked her hand away, "GET AWAY FROM ME!" she surprised herself by screaming, her frightened voice echoing in the darkness. Her surprise wasn't because she was angry, but that she wanted to scream about it; the feeling wasn't like her at all. But she didn't care.

"I've done *everything* you asked! I left my home, my *family*- my whole country! And still that's not enough for you!?" Tears were now streaming down her face, and she didn't care if the warden down the hall was listening. "This is my reward!? After everything I've done? The King will *kill* me for *your* words!" the flow of tears from her eyes shocked her and her tightly balled fists stung as sweat entered her opened burns.

The Dream Child said nothing and only watched Fa with large eyes- it infuriated Fa further.

"After everything that I've sacrificed for you- you still want *more*!? I know now- I see you and what you've been doing; you've been rising inside me from the beginning. Growing- demanding more and more- choking me out like..." Fa searched for the right word, when she found it, it scared her, "Like a *demon*! Twisting me into a tool of your destruction and death! Well I've had enough!" she screamed and took a menacing step forward so that she loomed over the Child, "I warned the Nity followers- I tried to warn the King; I'm *done*! Do you understand!? *Done.*"

The Child took a step back, but still did not speak.

Fa shook her head bitterly, then felt her knees buckle under her. Frustrated, completely used up and done with pretending to be strong, Fa allowed herself to collapse face down, onto the dirty straw, the folds of her gown billowing around her. She wept then, and bitterly mourned all that she had lost, doing nothing to control the broken sobs or flow of tears.

She wanted to curse Eloi- yes *curse* him, for pushing her from her gentle nature to a breaking point of anger and bitterness. She wanted to regret everything she had ever tried to do for the Dream Child, she wanted to go back to when her life was *right*. But Fate didn't have the strength of will to do anything but weep.

At last, months of tormented, sleepless nights, forced her body into an exhausted sleep, and when she dreamed- mercifully; the Dream Child was gone.

Fate dreamed she was a little girl again, when the only thing that burned in her was wonder. She dreamed she was running through the Byla grasslands, with her copper hair streaming behind her and white star flowers under her bare feet.

Then a heart stopping roar came from the sky, and she felt the earth shake beneath her as if in pure fear. Looking up, Fa saw the glorious sun fall from the sky and crash into the meadow, the sky went dark, and the land was cast into scarlet shadows as the sun smoldered in the grass.

Running forward, Fa went straight for the fallen sun, with disregard for her own safety, she had but one thought; restore the sun to the sky! Little Fa fearlessly approached the burning sun, unencumbered by the choking smoke and fumes. Stooping down, Fa tried to pick up the sun, but jumped back with a cry of pain and shock, she held up her hands; they were badly scathed and blistered, smoking themselves like the sun.

Suddenly, as if from her failure, the land around her burst into flames, and little Fa's heart filled… with fear.

"You can not do this alone Fate." The Dream Child was suddenly standing a few paces to her right, in the burning grass, and Fa was all grown up again, her face wet with tears.

Fa held out her hands, "I can not do this at *all*! I'm just a girl!" 'let me *be*' her mind begged.

The Child's face softened in sympathy, "You were right Fa, I have been rising up in you; I've been chasing you across the world, but you have been running from me for that same distance. Won't you let me in yet? There is *so much more* that I planned for. Destruction is *not* your fate; you were meant to be hope… I meant you to be a beacon of life renewed- for the whole world to see! Let me bring an end to this."

Fa grew still with longing.

Peace... no more fighting, no more running. Let the fire turn to ash; let the end come.

Fa looked down, the burning grass and fallen sun were gone, and in their place, was a still, mirror like pool. It held a perfect reflection of herself- only her reflection was dead. Her skin was parchment white, and her copper hair blew in the restless wind, lifeless eyes gazed back into her own, and Fa understood at last.

Death; were Eloi had been leading her from the beginning. Where- at last, she could *rest*. Fate's journey end had come- and yet, Fa was still afraid!

"Fear," The Dream Child said close beside her, "Was never meant to be part of who you are."

Fa closed her eyes and breathed deep, thinking of all she had never done, everything she had ever hoped for, all her dreams that had never come to be, and never would... exhaling, Fa let them slip away, and embraced full surrender.

Fate fell forward into the water, she felt no panic as she sank, only a tight squeeze of her hand, a reminder that even there- she was not alone.

The girl of fire, turned to ash.

Rachel Lang   Heart of Ashes

Chapter 28   Tarva the Prideful

Across the frothing Neenor sea, at the edge of the sprawling Cokhawk forest, on a dark rutted road in Cinders Grove, Freedom, returning to her cottage from 'The Cokhawks Feather' dropped her basket and placed a hand to her heart.

"Fate..." she breathed in dismay.

In a field glowing with star light, not far from the village and keep of Fray, Imagine paused in his journey, his vision blurring for a moment. A woman with cinnamon eyes, who was riding to meet him with her escorts, paused in confusion as he placed a hand to his head as a bittersweet wave rolled over him.

Farther still, in an island castle on a wide balcony overlooking a strange sea, an old man gasped and gripped the railing. "Oh...." He breathed and tears sprung to his eyes; it was an old sensation, but he remembered the touch of the heart stain.

In Rustling's manor in Tarva, Horizon sat down heavily on the side of his bed and closed his eyes as his vision grew fuzzy. 'What does this mean!?' his mind searched for an answer but came up empty.

*   *   *

The morning after the Queen's birthday banquet the sun rose, just as it always had, defying all the despair of the night before with its shafts of firelight. In the early morning, before the shadows had been truly chased away for another day, the Grand Duke's carriage carried him, Desert and Brave swiftly through the streets to the Dragon Keep.

Thrive had not wanted to take Dese and Rave with him but had realized that he couldn't have stopped them from coming. But he had made them promise to do as he said, and not to draw attention to themselves. The boys had soberly agreed- Thri thought that they would agree to anything, so long as they could go with him.

'They believe Fate will be returning with us' Thri thought as the carriage rumbled up the main street, he wanted to believe the same... but knew that there were no guaranties. That's why he had an escort of two dozen of his most trusted guards, surrounding the carriage, including Valor. He had instructed Valor on what to do if things went wrong. The only thing that truly concerned him was what Dese, and Rave might do. Thrive looked at them as the carriage entered the Dragon Keep's courtyard.

286

"Desert, listen carefully," he said, with one last attempt to impress on the two young men the gravity of the situation. "Asking the king to release Fate to me, could prove to be the moment of vulnerability that my court enemies have been waiting for." Thri held Desert's gaze long and hard, Rave's presence nearly forgotten. "If the king... if this doesn't go as planned- you must be on guard! My men will be loyal to you, and Valor will take you back to the Ducal at the first sign of trouble."

Desert listened without comment, he looked startled- overwhelmed even! 'Good' Thri thought with a sadness, 'He's starting to realize what this could all mean'. Thri swallowed, and his heart ached as he looked at Desert's face; there was so much that he had hoped Desert would do- becoming a target of the likes of Duke Command was not one of them.

"I understand," Desert said at last.

But Thri doubted that he did. The carriage had come to a stop, and Thri pounded on the side of the carriage, the door was opened promptly.

"I should have left you both at the Ducal," Thrive muttered as he stepped from the carriage. Desert and Brave got up to follow, but Thri halted them with a raised hand. "No, you both will stay here."

Both the boys opened their mouths to protest, but again Thri cut them short, "No; you both agreed to do as I said. If all goes well, I will return with Fate shortly, if not then you must make a hasty retreat."

"But-" Dese tried again to protest, but Thrive would not allow him to do so, "Give me your word that you will do as I say," he said heavily. The words were familiar, and both Dese and Thri remembered the last time he had asked for Desert's word- Dese had refused to give it then.

"Give me your word, Desert."

Dese sighed and sat back down. "You have it," he mumbled.

Thrive hesitated only a moment to memorize Desert's face one last time, then he closed the carriage door firmly and turned to the driver, "As soon as Valor returns, or if you sense that anything has gone wrong- you take them back to the Ducal; understood?"

The driver nodded, his face set.

Thrive set out then, with Valor and six guards marching behind him. Thri held his head high as he entered the Dragon Keep, and walked with confidence, his cape billowing behind him, not an inch of him betraying his doubts.

But he was only halfway through the main hall before a page called him to a halt, Thrive felt his heart skip a beat with fear.

"My lord Grand Duke?" the page bowed low, "The King has requested your presence in the council chambers."

Thrive paused... he had expected to spend at least a half-hour requesting a presence with the King... and now a summons to the council chambers? Something was not right. Thrive exchanged a look with Valor, then followed the page. As they neared the council chambers Thri turned to Valor, he knew that it was unusual for someone to have so many guards follow them about the Dragon Keep- but surely subtlety was not a strong friend anymore.

"Wait outside," Thrive instructed Valor in a low tone, "If things do not seem right; get Desert away and safe."

Valor nodded, then with a deep breath, and a confident resetting of his head, Thrive motioned to the two ceremonial guards to open the tall double doors, and he entered the council chambers.

Within, Triumphant The Great waited alone, and when he saw Thrive, his face lit up.

"Thrive! You always come when I call!" he beamed.

Thrive relaxed; Trium looked well, with apparently no ill effects from his 'ravings' the night before, and what's more, he was in a *good* way. Everything would be alright. Thrive bent on one knee till it touched the floor and brought his right fist over his heart in an extremely formal greeting- he knew Trium liked that kind of over the top display, and it often helped to placate him.

"My King, I am your servant," Thrive stated elegantly, then rose to his feet.

"You remember what we discussed last night?" Trium asked hesitantly.

Thrive frowned; he had not spoken to the King at all at the banquet, "My lord?"

Trium growled his pleasure, "Thrive! You can always make me laugh!"

Thri smiled stiffly and shifted his feet, his first assessment had been dead wrong; the King was not improved. Indeed, Trium's gaze was unfocused, and a silly grin hovered on his face as if he might burst out in laughter at any moment.

"I've already given the order- our plans…" Trium laughed, the kind of laugh that unnerved, "My most trusted men left to do my bidding before the sun even rose! The son…" his smile drifted, and he stared at Thrive- perhaps without really seeing him. "The son… your son- or mine?" he whispered, "what happened to him?" he sounded confused and Thrive reached out to touch his forearm- the King was worse- much worse!

"My King? What plans?" he hoped to move on from the sensitive subject of 'sons'.

Trium's happy smile returned, "I've summoned everyone- all the lords! The whole table must be filled, all the chairs." He walked over to the large council table, the one that had not had all its seats filled at one time in decades.

"They will *all* hear of our clever, clever plans!" he announced happily.

Thrive took a calming breath- there was still a chance of success in saving Fa, the King seemed open to suggestion. But he had to do it quick, for the others were coming- and if Trium spoke true, then everyone was coming; every lord, Earl and Duke, perhaps ones that hadn't been summoned by the King in their entire lives! And they were all coming to hear these 'plans', that Thrive knew nothing about, all of them, including Lord Mountain and Duke Command. So, he must be quick about saving Fate.

"My King, what a grand idea!" Thri played along, "Perhaps it would be best to get some other- smaller matters out of the way before everyone else comes. The matter of the Garatin girl perhaps?" he smoothly suggested.

Triumphant's smile froze and he stared blankly at Thrive, "The girl?" he asked, as if he had never heard of such a thing.

"Yes sire, the girl. I propose that I take her back with me to the Ducal, so that she won't bother you further."

"Yes…" Trium's gaze drifted to an empty space behind Thrive's shoulder, "We must… hold a trial," he said in a distant voice.

"I don't think that would be necessary-" Thrive's attempt was cut short.

"A TRIAL!" Trium burst as if just remembering something that had been hugely important a few moments before but had been forgotten since. "Of course- we must… the girl…" he added in a frightened whisper, then he whirled around and shouted, "GUARD!?"

Thrive felt things slipping from his control- but he could do nothing, and Trium was suddenly holding his wrist- tightly, his broken fingernail digging in uncomfortably.

"Bring the Garatin girl here for her trial- at once!" he ordered. The guard ran off to do his bidding, and Trium went to stand by the large arched windows of expensive glass, ignoring his throne-like council chair, and choosing to gaze out at the gardens, and beyond to the city. Thrive tried to speak, but Trium hushed him the way he would a grandchild- if he had any, and then had stood silently, forcing Thrive to wait anxiously.

Thrive grew more anxious as the lords and dukes began to arrive, they all bowed before the King, and nodded- or bowed to Thrive, then took their place at the council table, until all twenty-three chairs were filled, including Lord Mountain's chair and Duke Command's. But Triumphant did not move or show any response, forcing the gathered nobility to awkwardly sit in silence and whisper as much as they dared to one another. Thrive stood a few paces away from the King, and ignored Command's and Mountain's eyes, all the while fearing what would happen when Fate was brought in. Thrive's only mistake was not to wonder or fear what was already happening.

*   *   *

This time, only one guard was sent to fetch the Garatin girl, and he whished that someone else had been sent; he hated the dungeons, the cold dank air seemed to seep into his bones and leave him achy for hours. He had another reason for not wanting to be there; he had been there the night before, and had heard the girl screaming at no one, and then sobbing, the kind of sobbing that makes a father want to comfort, no matter who the weeper is. It had greatly unnerved the guard. But he had been ordered by the king to bring her, and like his comrades, he *couldn't* disobey the king!

'A witch' had been his first thought when he had seen her fire hair and pale skin, and he had dreamt the night before of the stories he had been told as a child, the ones with witches who had fire hair and ate children who were naughty. Of course, the stories were rubbish… but the fire hair did give the guard pause.

The guard approached the cell gingerly with the warden who held a torch high and close to the rusty bars; the girl's body was laying on the straw, face down with her back to the door. The guard expected her to awaken when the warden loudly unlocked and opened the door, the hinges screaming- but the girl didn't stir.

"Get up! The King is giving you a trial!" he called, aware of the rare circumstance of getting a trial so quickly; she did not move. Cautiously, the guard stepped inside, the stench of mold and other unsavory things growing stronger, still she did not stir. Her face was hidden and her fancy dress about her made her look like a wilted flower, one of her pale hands was laid out on the floor, old bandages did little to cover a nasty burn on her wrist.

The guard nudged her hesitantly with the tow of his boot; she didn't move.

'She's dead!' he thought in surprise, and a touch of fear.

Then, she woke, and lifted her head, shakily, her unnatural fire hair half veiling her chilling face. The look in her gray-green eyes reminded him of when his newborn daughter first opened her eyes- it wasn't right! The guard stepped back, his hand gripping the hilt of his short sword- could he cut her down if he needed to?

"I'm not done yet," she said calmly.

*   *   *

Fate walked confidently, yet with light steps, she knew her old bandages were dirty and didn't cover her new burns, she also knew that she was on her way to speak to the King again and might not come away this time; but nothing could shake her confidence! She was Fate, she was the girl of fire and ash. She was the girl that Eloi had chosen to lead the way, she… she was the beacon that would light the fires of hope. And she knew the fate of Tarva; she knew what must be done.

The guard walked close behind her and a little to one side, he seemed afraid of her, and only grabbed her arm to steer her around corners- maybe he sensed that she had no intentions of running- not that she'd get far anyway. As they neared the council chambers, with their large carved wooden doors, Fa took note of a group of guards- who wore a different symbol on their chest plates, she recognized them as belonging to the Grand Duke. She also made eye contact with Valor, Thrive's head guard, it made her wonder if Brave and Desert were near by, the thought was only a passing one. As she passed Valor and he watched her, he had a peculiar look on his face; he saw *it*. The guard saw *it*, but didn't understand *it*, but Valor looked like he understood; she had undergone a change- a rebirth!

She was more than *just* Fate now. She could *feel* the energy and raw power inside her, she and the Dream Child, she and *Eloi* had become one. And the harmony and perfection were intoxicating! She didn't feel like she was walking at all! But rather gliding along the stone floor.

Then, Fate, the daughter of Destination and Treasure, entered the council chambers of Triumphant The Great. All the lords and dukes looked up and stared at her as she entered, Thrive was standing at one edge of the council table and turned to her, his eyes begged her to be careful. And the king... he was also not in his seat. The King of Tarva, with his black mane of hair, wild about him, stood at the window with his back to the room.

Fate went to stand a little behind the King, turning her back on the lords, ignoring Thrive's gaze; they were not the one she had come to speak with.

Triumphant The Great turned slowly, pivoting on his feet until he faced Fate. All the while Thrive stood to one side, perhaps hoping to step in to shield her- but Fa already had a protector. Triumphant lowered his eyes to look at her, and Fa made no movement to bow or even nod. He had summoned her to give her a trial, but she had come to give him a second message- a second chance.

"Do you know who I am?" she began, and the room suddenly went incredibly still, no doubt waiting for the king's wrath at not being properly addressed. But Trium only stood as if frozen.

"Yes... I know you," he whispered.

"And yet this is the first time you have ever listened to my words."

Trium's face changed to an ugly snarl and he hunched his shoulders like a dog, "You have no authority to speak to me here- I AM THE KING!"

Fate knew that he would respond that way, but it still saddened her heart, "For years I have tolerated your ignorance, for years I have waited for you to return to me." Just as Fa shared in Eloi's power, now she shared in Eloi's stifling grief and heartbreak, and a tear slipped from her eye, "I can do so no more." Fa looked past the King and through the window to the city beyond, only now being lit up with the sun's growing light. She spoke in a strong, yet sorrowful voice full of authority, "Oh great city of Tarva, strong and powerful I have allowed you to become. Like a plague you have gone through the lands, conquering those you were meant to protect, turning your back on those you promised to stand by. Your enemies have learned to fear your name, and they flee from even your shadow, on the battlefield you are rivaled by only the long dead ancients. Your wealth grows with each year and your chokehold on my garden tightens." Fa's eyes shifted back to the King, and he flinched at her gaze.

"But your king sits upon a crumbling throne, for I have long since eroded your foundations from beneath you while you were too preoccupied with your riches to notice; your days are numbered. Your end is upon you, your pride will be the last link in the chains that will bind you, and you *will* fall by your own hand. So, I have spoken, Oh great Tarva, the prideful." Fa turned to the table of lords, once again ignoring Thrive's alarmed gaze, she addressed them all, "The warning has been given- heed my words and the cost may yet not be so high."

The room was silent, and everyone looked on in shock as fearful tears spilled from the king's eyes.

"This is an *outrage!* Your majesty you can not allow this witch's false words of prophecy to mar this great city!" Duke Command said with a snarl jumping to his feet, several others joined him- all shouting their rage and anger at Fate's words. The room erupted and Fa's confidence was shaken. Thrive looked on helplessly, and Fa took a step back from the angry nobles, then felt the King lay his hand heavily on her shoulder.

She turned and looked up into his much too close face and glistening eyes.

"I will show you true power," he whispered with an unsteady voice.

"She must die for such words, my king!" someone demanded.

"No! Please your Majesty-" Thrive's voice was drowned out- but his enemies heard him. All further words were cut short and everyone looked up in surprise as the council chamber doors were burst open loudly and a guard stood there panting, he bowed low- nearly collapsing.

"Sire forgive me! But the Harbour Ring- is on fire!"

Chapter 29   The Harbour Ring Burns

Valor and the other guards were nearly run over by the messenger who went bursting into the council chambers. The guards at the door stepped inside to hear the news, and forgot to close the doors, allowing Valor to see and hear everything that followed. The first thing he did was put a hand to his sword and search for Thrive. But he didn't relax when he saw him and gestured for his men to ready themselves; he didn't know what would happen, but he was on edge and sensed that things were not right.

"Fires!?" one of the lords at the table exclaimed and jumped to his feet, "How many?"

The guard who had delivered the news gulped for air and shook his head, (he was young, and looked nervous to be before all the lords), "No one can say, my lord, they sprang up at dawn and are spreading quickly."

Several of the lords were on their feet now and were going to the window- still in disbelief, "Look! You can see the smoke!" one of them pointed.

Several of them swore, and everyone went to the window to see for themselves.

"Something must be done, my king!" Lord Quest said in alarm and everyone looked to the King, who had been strangely silent.

"Men from the garrison have already been sent-" the guard began to say but was cut off.

"I want all my men pulled *out* of the Harbour Ring at once!" Trium ordered sharply.

No one spoke, and it was then that Valor noticed that the maiden Fate was standing close to the King but seemed to have been forgotten- except by Thrive who was slowly inching towards her, perhaps in the hope of sending her out to Valor.

"My king?" the guard finally asked what everyone else was too frightened to.

"We know nothing of these fires!" Trium stated with a haughty tilt to his head, he seemed to have switched rolls to that of a cautious, wise King, "I will not risk my men to what could be the beginnings of a revolt! I already know who started these fires; it must be the rebels- The Nity followers! HA!" His startling burst made several men jump, "What do you say to that Thrive!? 'A high moral code' indeed- they mean to burn my city to the ground! They are a threat to us- and there is the proof!" he flung his hand at the window, where, from its lofty view point, you could see over the castle gardens and walls to where the city sprawled by the sea, thousands of feet below. Large clouds of smoke were rising from several different areas of the Harbour Ring.

Valor's eyes skipped tensely to where Thrive stood his ground boldly (he still was not within reach of Fate), "You have said it yourself, my King, we know nothing of these fires. We must not be too hasty to pass a verdict, indeed the only thing we should be hasty in is dowsing the flames." He turned to the other lords, "They could be the accidents of drunkards for all we know-" his sensible words were cut short by the King who had gone red in the face.

"They are *not accidents!*" Trium huffed.

"Your majesty," Duke Command spoke up, and Valor tensed even more, "If it is a question of who the culprit is- I say look no further!" He pointed at Fate and took a menacing step towards her, Thrive took a stealthy step to partly shield her.

"She even has hair of fire!" someone joined in and looks of fear passed over the room.

"My lords, are we not too civilized to put stock in childhood fairy-tales and witch stories?" Thrive's voice was confident but his eyes begged for the others to agree with him.

"She had a hand in this!" One of the Dukes pointed a finger at the maiden, "Was she not *just* making threats against our king and this mighty city!? She is in league with the Nity followers!" there was a burst of agreement from the others, and Fate shrunk back.

Lord Mountain's voice rose above the others- the emergency in the Harbour Ring apparently forgotten, "I will go one step further my King; who has harboured this witch! Who has defended the Nity followers at every turn? *Who* has been known in the past to shelter those *scum!?*" he didn't need to point a finger, for everyone knew of whom he spoke.

Every eye turned to the Grand Duke.

"Why," Duke Command continued with a snarl, "He does not even have a *son* to pass on his title to- there has never been one so *unfit* to be at the king's side than he!"

Valor watched on, one hand on his sword hilt, the other held out to stop any of his men from acting hastily; Val knew that this was a moment locked in time, one that he would remember forever. Either his lord and master would walk away from this, or he would not, and Val knew that there was little he could do to tip the scale in either direction.

Thrive stood proudly, not giving his enemies the satisfaction of seeing him squirm under their accusations. The others around Thrive took a few steps away from him, as if wary of being to close when thunder struck, or in this case, the king. But to everyone's surprise, Trium stood still.

"Thrive...?" he breathed, as if still processing what he had just heard.

"My King-" Thrive tried to speak.

"SILENT!" Triumphant bellowed, everyone held their breath as the King slowly walked up to Thrive, going so close that their toes nearly touched. Thrive was the only one who saw Trium's broken smile and teary eyes.

"Thrive," Trium's voice was hardly above a whisper, and no one accept Thri could hear what he said, "This is better than our plan; you have betrayed me!"

Valor saw Thrive shake his head slightly and heard him say, "No, my King, I have not."

Trium closed his eyes and swayed backwards. "Hush now," he soothed, then turned his back and waved his arm to the growing number of soldiers who had entered the room from a back door. "Take this traitor," he shouted as he ambled back to the window, "and the demon girl to the dungeons! The rest of you leave me- AND *no one* is to send men to the Harbour Ring! It could be a trap! And we can't lose men over this can we?" he laughed, his voice turning gleeful, "I want soldiers down at the Harbour Gate- send the whole garrison! Lower the portcullis; no one is to go in- *no one* is to come out!" he waved his arms in demonstration. "Understood!?" he asked of the captain of the guards, who stood to attention, his face betraying no emotion.

Valor made a fleeting eye contact with Thrive as he and Fate were set upon by several guards (they made no move to struggle)- no words were needed to belay Thrive's final order to him.

Valor backed away from the council chambers, his men hesitantly following, "Back to the carriage!" he ordered in a low voice. "The Grand Duke's ward must be returned to the Ducal and protected at all costs!"

*   *   *

Confess glanced over her shoulder as she made her way on foot, at a quick pace through the Earls Ring, the Harbour Gate only a few minutes away. Events were progressing just as she had predicted- and she didn't even know what was happening up in the Dragon Keep! After her frustratingly, thought-provoking, and soul-searching discussion with Horizon the day before, Fess had returned to the Ducal (she had no where else to go) and had made her decision concerning Thrive's offer. Because the Grand Duke was at the Queen's banquet, Fess had gone to Golden, the household steward, and had told him that she had accepted the Grand Duke's offer.

To her surprise, Golden had nodded as if he already knew and had promptly produced a paper with a heavy seal on it, told her to present it to the first mate of 'The Lady Loyal', and that he would recognize her as the captain.

It had all happened so fast, Fess had to take a few minutes in her chambers to realize what she had done; the paper in her hand made her a sea captain again... true she would not be free to sail where she wished or to deal with whom she pleased, but she had little doubt that Thrive was a good master to sail under. She slept well that night, oblivious to what happened at the banquet. But she had awoken early, before dawn, anxious to go down to the harbour and see the ship... *her ship*. It was then that she had learned what had happened the night before. Fess had felt an impulse to go to Thrive and question him on what he knew in regards of Fate but Thrive left the Ducal to go to the Dragon Keep before she could do so. She had told herself it was for the best, she had become too attached to the girl anyway. 'Fate will be fine' she reassured herself to ease her conscience, 'Thrive will secure her release'. But although Fess believed this, she didn't think the Ducal would offer much protection- not with everything that was happening. She had watched with trepidation as Thrive set off from the courtyard with the captain of the guard and a group of tense looking guards.

Not long after, she had gotten the news of the fires in The Harbour Ring. Any hesitation that she had felt about what she was to do evaporated instantly; this city was dammed, and there was no chance that she would go down with it.

She had set out on foot; the Dukes Gate had only just opened, and the sun's light was only now shedding its light to the streets. Her plan was to board 'The Lady Loyal' and move her away from danger- if it hadn't already been moved. And since she was now captain (she touched the paper with the heavy seal that she had tucked inside her leather vest), she could simply sail away... if Thrive came out of this 'storm' unscathed then she would have saved his ship, and if he didn't...

Fess pushed the thought aside, her conscience told her that she was being cold- but she didn't care. She was the only one she was concerned about taking care of- she didn't care what Rizon had said the day before, she didn't *care* anymore; it was her turn to come out on top!

She was making her way through the deserted market (a sure sign that things were bad) the Harbour Gate just ahead, when she heard the sound of running feet behind her, she looked over her shoulder and saw the king's soldiers running towards her- and the gate.

Fess bolted, her booted feet pounding the stones, she vaulted over an abandoned handcart and dodged the constant stream of people who were coming through the gate from the Harbour Ring. Fess reached the gate and skidded to a stop on the other side, just a few moments before the soldiers; her instincts had been correct. As soon as the soldiers reached the gate they spread out in a human wall, pushing back with their spears anyone who tried to get through. Fess watched in stony silence as they lowered the portcullis with a crash, blocking off escape through the Earls Ring. The group of peasants who had gotten to the gate too late, realized what had happened and they rushed forward on the portcullis, shouting and begging to be let through. But neither the soldiers nor the gate yielded to their pleas, and Fess turned away. She knew that the soldiers would not open the gate, no matter how much they pleaded, she could guess who's orders they were acting on, and she could guess the punishment if they disobeyed.

Confess turned away and looked around her for the first time; the street was half-full of people who were smart enough to know that they should get out of the ring, but not quick enough to have done so. There were no fires nearby, but the sea breeze was still, and smoke was growing thick in the air, and ash occasionally drifted by on heat currents, smudging frightened faces. Fess went ahead to the market, like the one in the Earls Ring, it was deserted, and groups of looters could be seen going from stand to stand. On her way, she passed by a cottage that had recently caught fire from a spark a few cottages away. The thatch roof burned first, then the fire fell to the rest of the cottage- Fess knew that there would be nothing left of it in a quarter of an hour.

The fires had started in the western side of the Harbour Ring, but were now spreading to the east side, mercifully, there was not even a breath of wind, so the fires weren't spreading as fast as they could, and that gave the people a chance to escape- or to loot. The majority of people on the west side had already escaped into the Earls Ring, but the people on the east side had thought that they would be safe- and now were trapped. Fess could see no organized effort to dowse the fires- or even to control where they spread. Even with no wind, Fess estimated that the whole Harbour Ring would be burned to the ground before noon. And the inhabitants could only maneuver around the most dangerous spots- if the thickening smoke didn't kill them... the only other option was to escape by boat.

Ignoring the bands of looters, Confess jumped atop a crate in the market to get a better view of the harbour. Although she had hung her hopes on escaping on 'The Lady Loyal', Fess was astonished and enraged to see, through the wisps of smoke, that the Harbour- was still full! Didn't they see that no help was coming!? Didn't they recognize the danger to their vessels!? Even if they were safe for the moment, the higher the sun rose, the more chances there was of the wind picking up and carrying sparks to the unprotected ships.

Fess jumped down to the paving stones and ran for the stairs down to the docks, even as she did so, others were also running for boats- but not many- they still believed that their king would save them. There was a longboat tied up to the dock close to the stone platform, and Fess jumped in, noting where 'The Lady Loyal' sat in the Harbour; it would be a long row out to her- especially by herself, but that did not deter her.

"Are you going out to a ship?" Fess looked up; coming down the stairs was a woman with tangled hair, hanging off her skirts- nearly causing her to trip, were four children, she held a babe in her arms and the oldest of the scared children was a boy of twelve or thirteen.

"Please," the woman sobbed, "I don't have money- but please let us board with you. Our cottage is gone, and the smoke is choking my little ones!" she begged, the twelve-year-old glanced behind them as another cottage went up in flames.

Fess hesitated for a moment, thinking of how the woman could have stolen a longboat (as Fess was- in all honesty- doing herself) but instead the woman was asking- begging to be let aboard!

"Alright- get in," she consented. The family rushed forward gratefully, coughing as they climbed, one at a time into the rocking longboat.

"We make for my ship, 'The Lady Loyal', there-" Fess pointed then moved the oars into place. "You'll have to help me row," She instructed the oldest boy, who nodded and moved to take up an oar. Two of the children were in the boat, while the mother with her infant and two other children were still on the stone dock, the mother was handing the babe to her daughter in the boat. Fess watched, anxious to be off- then she looked up and caught sight of someone she truly wished was *not* in the Harbour Ring.

Endure and his thugs were walking through the courtyard- no doubt looking for their next cottage to loot, Fess ducked out of sight, "Get in- quick!" she hissed, and the other two children jumped in- making the boat rock precariously. But Endure had seen her, he stepped to the edge of the courtyard, eight feet over the docks and peered down at her and grinned wickedly.

"Just the cat I wanted to skin!" he leered, "Bring her up!" he ordered, one of his men ran to the stairs and came jumping down- obviously he hadn't been one of the ones she had beat up.

The mother undid the rope holding the boat to the dock and jumped in- but Fess saw that the thug would reach the boat before they could get away! The thug reached down and grabbed the boat edge, while up above another thug was on his way. Roaring in anger, Fess ignored the rocking boat and jumped to the back of the boat, the mother and children ducking down as she landed behind them, practically on top of the mother, and face to face with the thug. Fess gripped the sides of the boat and swung her legs up, delivering a startling kick to the thug's chest- he lost hold of the boat and staggered back, while the boat shot out and away from the dock.

"ROW!" Fess barked at the boy as she scrambled back through the family and took up her oar. Endure stood at the top of the wall, with the painted dragon beneath him- both seemed to scowl at the departing longboat, he spitted curses at her as she slipped away.

Confess smiled at him; that was the last she would ever see of him. She watched him for a few minutes as she and the boy rowed against the waves, the distance much too slowly growing wider, till at last Endure left the docks and disappeared into the smoke with his men. Fess let out a breath that she didn't know she had been holding and set her strength into rowing- she had to be careful because the boy couldn't row as strong as she could, and they kept veering to one side. But after twenty minutes they reached the side of 'The Lady Loyal'. By that time many more cottages had caught fire, and the smoke had thickened until Fess and the family couldn't see the shore clearly, but the air over the water was much clearer and the children stopped coughing.

Fess called up to the ship, and they let a ladder down after they heard that she was from the Ducal, Fess tied the longboat to the rope and climbed up, helping one of the youngest children go before her while the others followed.

Safely aboard, they were met by the first mate, who looked at them with suspicion, and Fess watched him closely.

"I am Confess, I believe the Grand Duke told you to expect me."

The first mate raised his brows and looked her up and down again. "I didn't expect you now though," he said evenly.

Fess could feel the crew staring at her, and she wondered how much they knew about her, she had a sudden fear of seeing her old first mate aboard- but he was no where to be seen. She pulled out the somewhat crumpled paper that Golden had given her the night before.

"I believe this will explain things," she handed over the paper, the heavy seal weighing it down. The first mate hesitated to take it and when he did, he only looked at it briefly before bowing slightly, he straightened and called the crew to attention. "Captain on deck!" he said loudly, the crew gathered on the deck, stamped their right foot in synchronization and bowed, but they still watched her curiously.

"I have invited this family aboard," Fess gestured to the woman and her still frightened children, "Now," she said, anxious to get on with things, "Weigh anchor and move the Lady out of the Harbour at once!" she ordered sharply.

A few of the crew flinched, but there was no more movement; this was her first test- could she make them obey her?

"The Grand Duke said to remain in the harbour-" The first mate began to say doubtfully, but Fess cut him off- there wasn't time for this!

"The King has blocked off the Harbour Ring and left the fires to burn and spread as they will; there will be nothing left by nightfall. When the winds pick up none of the ships in the harbour will be safe. Disregard what the Grand Duke has previously ordered; I am the captain now- so *weigh anchor!*" she stepped forward and met the man's eyes with her fierce gaze; he hesitated a moment more.

"Hoist the anchor! Bring out the sail! Cut that longboat lose!" the first mate bellowed out the orders.

Fess took a deep breath and looked back at the smoke shrouded shore; Tarva, had seen the last of her!

*   *   *

"Why have you come to me?" Queen Elegance asked as the king's fool bowed low before her, she had nothing to do with the new fool, was his

301

real namesake Provider? This was the first time she had ever even met him, and yet he had boldly come to her in the late morning.

Provider raised himself up and twisted his silly hat up in his hands as he spoke, the bells jingling softly as if unaware how serious the moment was. "My lady, you know I am loyal to the King…" he bowed again, and hesitated.

Ele frowned. "Speak freely," she encouraged.

"I can not stand by silently in the face of what is happening- not when the innocent are being blamed for…" he stopped again and glanced about her chambers, they were the only two there, but he still needed encouragement.

Ele smoothed out her face, thinking perhaps that she looked too severe. "I assure you Provider, you are safe to speak freely before me, what do you mean by the innocent being blamed- I have not heard this, do you mean the fires? Who are being blamed?"

He swallowed hard and spoke in a near whisper, "The Nity rebels my Queen- they say it is an uprising, and that is why the Harbour Gate has been sealed off… but… I heard it from the king's own mouth- he told me- he *ordered* the fires to be lit!" he sucked in his breath, as if afraid of how the words sounded- and indeed they were dangerous words.

Ele did not doubt them for even a moment. She turned away, her mind racing; her husband ordering the lower ring to be burned, the Nity followers being blamed, the Grand Duke in prison for high treason! How could Trium order the burning of his own city!?

"You have done well Provider," she said evenly, betraying nothing of what she felt- never had she felt so old as she did then. "No one will know that you have spoken to me, you will have my protection."

He bowed, and understood that she meant for him to leave, he did so quickly with much bell jingling, leaving her standing alone in her chambers.

Ele closed her eyes and breathed; too long she had stood by and played the complacent wife and delicate queen. Too long.

"Maid?" Elegance called, and one of her handmaidens came running in from another room- but Ele did not worry that she had been eavesdropping- she knew for a fact that her maid was loyal to her- she couldn't say that much for the other maids or guards, "I need a message sent to the Manor of the Grand Duke."

*   *   *

302

Rustling wiped his forehead for what seemed the hundredth time that horrible morning; it was turning into a stifling day! Midday and already the sun was hot enough to make someone want to run for shade- and there wasn't even a breath of wind as a respite.

"What is happening Rust!?" Horizon demanded to know as he was escorted into the manor courtyard where Rust stood beside a waiting carriage.

"The City is no longer safe for you- I'm moving you outside the city walls- far away! And the way the fires are spreading, it's a good idea to leave the city!" Rust said as he tucked his hanky into his belt.

"How bad are the fires?" Rizon asked, as he glanced over the manor walls to where a wall of smoke could be seen- dangerously close. "No one will tell me anything!" he stopped on the manor steps and refused to go further.

Sighing in exasperation, Rust waved his arm in the direction of the waiting carriage, his mother had already gone ahead out of the city, along with his sister and her family- the fires were getting too close to the Sea wall for comfort! "The Harbour Ring is lost, and the Nity followers are being blamed," Rust explained hurriedly, hoping that Rizon would get inside the carriage if he told him what was happening. "The Dragon Keep's prisoners from the Pearl Square are doubtlessly being taken to the executioner as we speak! I doubt I could stop them if they came for you- especially now that the king has turned against his own Grand Duke!"

"I can not leave them," Rizon said stubbornly, planting his feet firmly against his escorts tugging at his arms.

Rust stepped forward and grabbed his arm himself, "No! You can not *help* them- that is what you can not do!" he said, shocking himself at how forceful he sounded. "Now get in the carriage! Tomorrow, or the day after, *maybe* you will be able to help whoever is left- but not if your dead yourself! So, get in! before the king sends men for you!"

Rizon gave in- and looked none to happy about it, before he stooped his head to get inside the carriage, Rizon glanced again to the billowing smoke; he would return to Tarva one day, he silently swore, and he *would* speak before the King!

Chapter 30   To Thrive

The captain of the royal guard entered the king's chambers without knocking- he belatedly wondered if he should have. "Your Majesty! I bring grave news," he reported, as he bowed on one knee and pounded his heart with his fist. Normally he would have stayed in such a position, with head bowed, until the King gave him permission to rise, but the captain didn't have time! He looked up and to his dismay, saw the King sitting on the edge of a wide and tall open window, with one leg hanging over the other side. A large book of the 'History of the Kings of Tarva' sat in his lap, opened to the last page; the one that told the death of the last king, Triumphant's father. The captain also noticed that the king wore a ceremonial cape and rich tunic, like he would for a knighting, complete with his heavy golden crown- it sat crookedly on his mane of black hair.

"Sir!" the captain of the guards jumped to the king's side, intending to pull him from the ledge and the perilous drop to the castle gardens below.

But Trium held up his hand to halt him from touching him, the first acknowledgement he had given of the captain's presence.

"Have you ever seen anything so... perfect!?" Trium whispered in awe, as a sudden gust of wind refreshed the hot air and blew the king's hair out of his face.

"Sire!" the captain begged, yet still the King would not look at him. "My king, I ordered that your ships be moved from the harbour, but because of your earlier order, some of the captains could not get to their ships in time; I'm sorry to say that 'The Dragon's Wing' was too close... and has been lost." The King made no response at the news of his best ship lost in the flames. "If you would lift the order and open the Earls Gate- then..." The captain faded off as he realized with dread that he could feel the wind cooling his face... the *wind* had picked up.

"Look! Look there!" Trium flapped his arm and pointed excitedly like a child, "It's so beautiful!"

With dread, the captain turned his gaze on the burning ring below, and his heart plummeted; with the newly lifted wind, the fires had jumped the Sea wall and several cottages had caught aflame! The Earls Ring... was lost.

Trium giggled, and the captain turned away, half in shock and half in disgust that he had put his faith in such a king. He walked to the chamber doors, his ears burning- never before had he considered acting in such a way without an order from the king- but he *had* to do something!

Behind him, Triumphant The Great tore out a page from the history book, one that told of his father's great deeds as king, and Trium released it into the wind and giggled with delight as the page floated for a moment on the wind, then spiraled down.

*   *   *

"With the wind picking up off the sea, there is little chance the fires will burn out, and there are enough thatch roofs in the Earls Ring to keep the fires going. I estimate that the fires will reach the Dukes wall by sundown- perhaps much sooner," Valor explained to Desert, as they stood in the grand hall.

Nearly every maid, page and guard were gathered there, waiting anxiously to hear what they were to do. Brave also stood near by, while Dese was trying hard not to be overwhelmed; he had never taken on duties such as this- he had never thought he would need to!

"We must evacuate then," Dese said, hoping he sounded authoritative, "Have the stable workers prepare every carriage we have and line them up in the courtyard ready to go. Scullery workers, pack one wagon's worth of provisions- make that two wagons!" those he had ordered set off in a hurry, none of them seemed to question his right to take charge. Dese then turned to Thrive's manservant, "Contrast- pack as many of the Grand Duke's documents as you can find, don't forget the one's in his secret study!" if Contrast was surprised that Dese knew about the secret study, he didn't show it, "And protect them with your life." Dese held his gaze to make sure Contrast knew how important it was.

Contrast nodded, "It will be done, master Desert." He then called two pages to him and left.

Desert looked at the rest of the household and swallowed; they were all waiting for him to tell them what to do! "Golden, prepare the household to leave within two hours, we will make for Thrive's winter manor inland. Pack only what will be needed- I will see to it that we have enough to survive. Send messengers to the duke's serfs outside the city, tell them to flee, or meet the caravan on the north road in three hours. Valor- send men to the Ducal gate to ensure against looters- and get their mounts ready to escort the carriages out." Even before he was finished speaking, the room began to empty, with much noise and clamor, the panic beginning to rise.

After he had given further orders to his men, Dese lay a hand on Valor's shoulder, pulling him aside. "I have a special task for you," he said quietly, "Take only your most loyal man with you- tell no one else and go to the treasury. Take two large chests of gold to the dungeons and bury them in the third cell on the left. And take enough money to get us to the winter manor- then bar the treasury door. And if there is anyone in the cells- release them and put them to work emptying the household."

Valor nodded solemnly, then left to do his bidding, as he went a page came running up to Desert with a letter in his outstretched hand. "Master Desert! A message from the Dragon Keep!" he said breathlessly.

"Thrive!?" Desert asked hopefully.

The page shook his head, "The Queen!"

Dese took the letter, and the page ran off. Brave came to stand by his side as Dese tore open the letter- it didn't bear the royal seal. Dese read it through quickly, his eyes nearly skipping over words in his haste, he read it a second time aware of Rave watching from over his shoulder.

Dese crumpled up the letter and tossed it into the hall fire.

"What did it say!?" Brave exclaimed.

Dese had forgotten that he couldn't read. He pulled him close excitedly, "The Queen said to wait at the bottom of the Princes Road, an hour before sundown."

Brave frowned, "Wait for who?"

Desert grinned, "Who do you think?"

*   *   *

Confess entered the captain's cabin and shut the door behind her, the hot mid-afternoon air had been diminished out in the open sea, but the smoke from the city could still be seen on the coast- it might even be visible from the island of Chresacroon. Although the season of bad sailing was only just ending, and it would not be wise to set sail on a long voyage for another two weeks, the sea was calm, and the blue sky clear. Fess aimed to find safe anchorage in a sheltered bay further down the east coast.

Fess looked about the cabin and wondered who the previous captain had been, 'It wasn't a woman, that's certain!' she thought with a touch of pride. She ran her hand along the captain's desk and felt the sway of the waves beneath her as 'The Lady Loyal' sailed along the coast.

'I made this happen…' she thought to herself with a smile.

"You think you got here alone?"

Fess spun about at the little voice behind her; it was one of the children she had invited to stay aboard. She scowled at the child, what did they mean? "You're not meant to be in here," she half heartedly scolded and turned her back.

"You were not placed here without reason; Fate and her brother- and Desert, they need you!"

Fess frowned- what nonsense was that!? "How do you know those- " she turned, but the child was gone, and the cabin door was still shut- how had they slipped out so quietly!?

Setting her face, Fess stormed out onto deck; she would not tolerate such foolishness aboard *her* ship! She marched up to the main mast where the family was huddled about, her boots thudding on the deck- but she stopped short; the woman, with the babe in her arms was asleep, and her other four children were sound asleep around her... they didn't stir in the slightest at her approach, and now that she could see them, she saw that none of them were the child she had seen moments before- and Fess knew that there were *no* other children aboard.

Who had she spoken with in the cabin?

*   *   *

Fate paced her cell; four steps, spin, four steps spin. There was no way to tell the passage of time in the dungeons, so Fa had no idea how long she had been waiting after she had seen the King, but it felt like ages. It had been in fact, all day, and now it was only an hour before sundown. Fate also hadn't a clue of how bad the fires were, if the dungeon guards knew, they didn't raise their voice enough for Fa to hear them discuss it.

Thrive was in the cell opposite hers, and he had only said a few words the entire time they were there, enough for them both to express that they were both sorry for each others' circumstances. But for the most part, Thri had sat at the back of his cell where the torch light down the hall couldn't reach him.

The awesome power and perfection that had filled Fa earlier, had faded away into a not quite tangible feeling. She knew that she was not alone, that Eloi was still there- inside her, but somehow and for reasons she did not understand, the 'presence' had retreated deep inside, and her old familiar fear was fighting to take hold again.

'What will the king do to us? Why hasn't he sent someone yet? Has the city burned like I foresaw? Is everyone dead!? Will I die now- truly die, now that my task is done?' There seemed to be no end to her tormented questions- and no comfort was to be gained from the cold slimy walls of her cell. After all this time, and how far they had come together, not even Rave was there with her... how fitting that she should be alone.

'You have never been alone' a whisper in her head reminded her, and she breathed deep the truth that she clung to.

Fate stopped pacing and listened; someone -more than one- was coming down the hall towards her cell, the light of a torch growing with each step. A woman in a long dark cloak and raised hood came to stand in between Fa's and Thri's cells, her face was hidden, and beside her was a handmaiden, a guard and the dungeon warden with his ring of keys in his hand.

The woman pulled her hood down, revealing raven hair and sad brown eyes.

"Your Majesty!" Thrive exclaimed, jumping up to kneel at his cell bars, while Fa could only stand and stare in surprise.

"Grand Duke," Queen Elegance said stooping slightly to reach through the bars and touch Thrive's hand. "I am sorry this should happen to you," she said solemnly, then she turned to Fate.

Fa dropped a clumsy curtsy, her mind reeling with what was happening.

"Release them warden," Ele said quietly.

"My Queen... I..." the warden stuttered, obviously reluctant, and not sure what to do.

The queen's guard pushed the warden suddenly to Fa's cell bars menacingly, his strong forearm pinning him across the chest.

"Do as I say, warden," Ele instructed firmly.

The warden nodded vigorously, and the guard released him. The warden unlocked both Fate's and Thrive's cell doors then stepped back, hanging his head.

Fate and Thrive eagerly stepped from their cells and Thrive again bowed low to Ele.

Ele looked behind her wearily, "There is not much time, someone will surely have noticed me coming here, and I can not say who is still loyal to the king- mad though he is. A page waits at the top of the stairs, he will lead you through the servant passageways to the courtyard. The gates have been closed, but I have arranged for a port door to be left open for the next twenty minutes, from there you must go on alone. Do not take the main road, take the Princes Road to the Cherry gardens, at the bottom, your Ward," she looked at Fa again, "And your brother will be waiting for you. Then I advise you to flee the city." She fell short of saying forever- but surely Thrive could never return to Tarva.

Thrive stood up straight and pounded his heart with his fist, "My Queen, you are a valiant woman. I know you have risked much in freeing us. You will *always* have an ally in me."

Ele looked profoundly sad, "The time of allies is over- truly, the time of Tarva is over…" she led the way to the stairs, the other dungeon guards watching silently. "The Harbour Ring is all but ashes now, and the fires leapt the Sea wall hours ago. You must hurry, my reports say the fires are now approaching the Dukes wall and have already begun to burn the Cherry gardens; you must leave by the Kings Gate. I myself will be leaving the city soon" she sighed and stopped as they reached the foot of the stairs, "You alone, Thrive, have been a friend to me, I wish you well." She turned to Fate, "This city has stood for ages, against all manner of enemies, and now she will fall at the hand of her own king. I understand now, Fate; you tried to warn us."

Fate swallowed hard.

"Go now," Ele urged.

With one last bow of his head, Thrive led the way up the stairs, taking them two at a time, Fa was only just able to keep up- but she understood the urgency; the port gate would only be open for another twenty minutes!

The page was waiting for them halfway up the stairs, where a servant's stair jutted off to the left. Wordlessly he led them up the servant's stair; here, Thri made Fa go before him, so that he went last. She realized that this was to protect them from an ambush from behind. But they met no one on their rushed journey through the servant passages- probably another design of the Queen; Fa's regard of her grew with each step.

At last they reached a small door that led out into the courtyard, it was deep in shadow from the setting sun, and was mostly empty.

"There," the page pointed to the open port door across the yard.

Thrive nodded his thanks and the page went back the way he had come. "Alright, are you ready?" Thri asked, looking at the heavy skirts of Fa's banquet dress.

Ignoring decorum, Fa took the front of her skirt and tucked it into her belt, allowing her to run (a bit more freely) in the loose-fitting underpants, she was grateful that she had wore her boots to the banquet. She nodded to Thri.

"Two hundred paces down the road there will be a second smaller road to the right- that's the one we want," Thri said, looking at the sentries on top the Castle walls, "Go!"

Fa and Thri broke out into the courtyard, their foot falls seemed to echo alarmingly loud, but they were almost at the port door- Fa could see the street outside!

"HALT!" Fa nearly stumbled in fright at the sharp yell!

"Keep going!" Thrive pushed her through the port door and slammed it shut behind them- they didn't pause to hear their pursuers, but started down the empty road, away from the Dragons Keep. On their left and right, great manor walls rose to wall them in, and Fa stumbled again on her skirts, without slowing her pace, she tucked more of her heavy skirts into her belt.

Thrive pointed to their right, where a smaller road split off and slanted down. From the opening in the manor walls, they could see the city below clearly in the sun's red light; it was aflame under a heavy cloud of smoke that glowed red. This was the sight that had haunted Fa's dreams for months.

"Halt!" the voice called again, Fa risked a glance over her shoulder; half a dozen royal guards were running after them, they held cross bows, but as they held them up to shoot, Thri and Fa ran down the Princes Road, and the guards were forced to continue their pursuit.

Thrive and Fa nearly tripped as the narrower road angled down towards the Cherry gardens, a steep cliff on their right, growing shorter with every step.

"Keep going!" Thrive encouraged again, his breath growing ragged.

     *   *   *

It had taken longer, much longer than expected to empty the Ducal, and it was an hour and a half to sunset when Desert and Brave had at last sent the last carriage and wagon on its way. For a moment Dese had stood in the empty courtyard, looking up at the suddenly lonely looking Ducal.

"It'll soon be time," Rave said anxiously, "How long will it take us to get to the north end of the gardens?"

Instead of answering, Dese nodded, "Help me close the gates."

Together, the boys pulled the mighty gates closed, it was then, out on the street, that they realized just how close the fires had come in the afternoon. The fires had crept along at a slow but steady pace through the Earls Ring, the fountains in the street offering only a small amount of protection for the fleeing occupants, it seemed as if Tarva was too prideful to admit defeat and run- not until the flames were near engulfing the once mighty manors and castles. The flames had leapt the Dukes wall in places- but the real danger was the gardens; the fires had spread to the Cherry Gardens and had torn through them, eating up bush, tree and flower. By sundown the whole garden would be gone, and the Cherry Lake and waterfall left in smoke and ash.

The streets of the Dukes Ring were mostly empty, and the boys ran like mad through the deserted city, reaching an entrance to the gardens with little breath to spare. There they stood for a moment and looked on in horror; in a few more minutes the path they needed to take would be engulfed in flame!

"Come on!" Rave shouted, choking slightly on the smoke, and he led the way along the path, their feet pounding the earth.

"There!" Dese pointed, ahead was the shore of the Cherry Lake, and as if waiting for them, there was a flat bottom ferry. "The fires haven't gotten to the other side of the lake yet- we can boat across!"

The ferry was small, but sturdy, and there were two very long poles that both boys used to push their way across the narrow lake, they could barely touch the bottom in the middle but out there they were free of the smoke. Twenty agonizingly long minutes later, they reached the west shore.

"Look!" Rave pointed to their left, although quite a distance, they could see that the fire had jumped the lake where it was narrowest and was burning up the trees already.

"The paths to the north are still clear- we can still get out through the Kings Gate," Dese said, as they jumped from the boat onto the grassy shore- they could feel the heat of the fires. In another hour the sun would set on Tarva, leaving it to burn through the night.

Desert chose the path that joined up with the Princes Road, and the boys arrived at the bottom of the cliff a few moments later, panting and doubling over.

Running his hand through his hair, Rave searched the trees for any sign of Fate. "Where are they?!?" his voice sounded shrill to his own ears.

"There! On the ridge!" Dese exclaimed excitedly and pointed further up the road.

Fate and Thrive were running, pell-mell down the road- but they were not alone.

"They'll have to jump down the ridge…" Dese realized, and the boys ran along the bottom of the ridge, looking up, till they found a place that wasn't so steep, "HERE!" they shouted and waved.

*   *   *

Thrive stumbled and ducked as another crossbow shaft came whistling pass, clattering along the road ahead of him.

"HERE!" he looked to his left and saw Brave and Desert at the bottom of the sloping ridge, ten feet below, half hidden by the flowering trees.

"Jump down the ridge- quick!" he shouted at Fate, as he skidded to a stop and glanced behind him; the guards were closing in fast.

Fa stepped to the edge of the road, and paused uncertainly, as the edge eroded under her slightly- but then she saw her brother.

"Rave!" she called determinedly.

THWACK!

Thrive arched his back and fell to one knee, a breathless cry of pain slipping from him as the back of his richly embroidered tunic was dyed red around the shaft of a protruding arrow.

"THRIVE!" Fa screeched in horror, but Thri hardly heard her, he found himself falling forward without his consent. His dark eyes searched out Desert below.

Dese… the unexpected, unmatchable joy that he had found too late in life… what a shame he had never told Desert how proud he was of him! What a fine young man he would be- that's all Thri had wanted to give Desert; a chance to thrive.

THWACK!

Chapter 31   The Fate of Desert

"No…" Desert breathed as a second arrow struck Thrive in the back of his neck, Thri fell and disappeared from sight.

Fa screamed and with a small landslide, ran and jumped down the ridge, making it difficult for anyone to follow her. Rave caught her, and immediately propelled her farther back into the trees, away from the pursuing guards and their flying arrows.

"Desert! Come on!" Rave shouted at Dese. An arrow thudded into the ground dangerously close to Dese, but he stood frozen looking up at the road.

Dese felt Rave pull him from behind, "We have to run!" he knew that Raves voice was close behind him- but he had a hard time grasping onto that reality.

"Dese!" Fa called.

Desert turned then and began running; he did not look back.

Fa took the lead, her fire hair streaming behind her, Rave, with a fierce look of determination on his face, followed on her left, while Dese fell behind on her right. Their booted feet pounded the garden path, sending cherry blossom petals billowing around them. Ahead of them a huge pillar of smoke rose, and the horizon glowed red from the flaming city below.

As they ran, they veered away from the cliff and the pursuing guards, but that steered them towards the growing fire, ash blew across their path, and Dese realized that they were going south! Their only escape was behind them, to the ferry or the Kings Gate- there was nothing ahead- only fire.

The roar of the fire grew closer and they turned a corner in in the path; ahead of them, the path forked, one doubled back towards the cliffs, and -for the moment- was clear of fire. But the path ahead of them looked like a tunnel of flames, the trees were engulfed and dripped sparks, while the smoke billowed and churned.

"Wait!" Dese called as he slowed, trying hard to make himself think clearly, he looked behind him, but there was no sign of the guards, either they had gotten lost, or were satisfied with the body of… Dese couldn't finish the thought anymore than he could say the words.

Fa hadn't slowed- perhaps she was in as much shock as he was.

"Wait!" he screamed more urgently when he saw the blazing limb of a tree that hung over the path ahead of Fa; it was about to fall! The branch fell across the path- just in front of the Garatin siblings.

Fa skidded to a stop just in time, as the sparks from the branch flared up and reached for her. Rave also managed to stop but he lost his balance and fell. Dese grabbed his arm and pulled him to his feet, and lay a hand on Fa's shoulder, "We can't get out that way-" he stopped to cough on the smoke, "It's a dead end!"

Fa covered her face with horrendously burnt hands (how did she manage?) and coughed, "Where are we?" she asked, even as Dese was backing away.

"The bridge across the lake is just there- but the far shore is still burning- we have to go back." He insisted- maybe Thri wasn't dead, maybe they could go back and get him...

"The King's monument!" Fa exclaimed to his surprise, "Come on!" she called and darted off the forked path.

"Fa!" Rave called after her, but she didn't stop, the boys ran after her- but she was faster than both of them and they didn't catch up with her until she had reached the courtyard full of stone arch's, pillars, statues of kings and stone dragons. At the back of the yard was the cliff, where at the top, sat the Dragon's Keep, the sun's light on its walls was almost gone, replaced by a red glow.

"Come on!" Fa encouraged and ran off again to the cliff.

"What is it?" Rave asked as he and Dese struggled to keep up to her, as they weaved and swerved through the stone monuments.

"There's an entrance to the caves- where the Nity Followers were hiding- in there," she said, as they reached the cliff face. It was riddled with carved doorways and arches.

"Where?" Dese asked breathlessly.

"One of these arches- look for a pile of rocks- there should be a hole to the tunnel behind," she instructed and then rushed in.

Dese hesitated to look back, the path they had come on was now in flames; they had no retreat.

They searched for a few long moments in the near dark when Rave called them over, "Is this it?" he pointed to a hole at the back of one of the arches; it was completely dark inside.

Fa nodded and swallowed hard, and Dese remembered how she wasn't good with tight spaces- but the fire was closing in.

"Come on!" Dese bravely dove into the hole, he scraped his back on the stone and he felt it shift slightly, Fa followed and last was Rave. But as he came through, the rocks shifted more and collapsed after him, leaving the three in total darkness.

*   *   *

Fate blinked in the sudden darkness, the settling dust stung her eyes- but at least they were out of the smoke.

"How did you know about this?!" she heard Rave ask, close beside her.

"It's how I and Fess got in. The Nity Followers were hiding in caves much further in- hopefully they are all gone now."

The three were silent for long minutes as they caught their breath after all their running.

"Well, we can't stay here," Rave spoke, "I guess we'll have to follow the walls and hope we find an exit near the Kings Gate."

Fa winced when she remembered the labyrinth of tunnels under the mountain, her claustrophobia rising, "It's no use Rave, there will be plenty of other exits- but we are sure to get lost before finding any!"

Whatever Rave was about to say, Fa would never know, for a voice called out in the darkness!

"Who's there!?" the three blinked as a torch appeared further down the tunnel, held by a woman.

Fa gasped; it was Cherish- the leader of the Nity Followers that she had met before!

"Cherish!" Fa called stumbling to her feet, her hands were badly burnt after her last sequence of dreams, and she cradled them close. "It's me- Fate, what are you still doing here!?" although she was relieved to see the woman, she was also dismayed.

Cherish took a moment to look over the tired dusty faces. "There wasn't enough time for everyone to get out," she said, looking behind them at the now blocked entrance. "Last night the king's men found three of the tunnel entrances- they knew better than to send men in, so they blocked them off. I had hoped to find this entrance… useable." Fa could hear the weariness in the older woman's voice and see despair in her eyes.

315

"You couldn't get out that way anyway- the fires have reached the gardens," Rave said quietly.

Cherish heaved a sigh, "I see. We better go back to the caves then."

"How many are still there?" Fa asked.

"Forty-three, including myself."

Fa felt sick, "I warned you all to leave!"

Cherish gave her a look that a mother might give to scold a child, "It's no easy task to smuggle one hundred wanted men and woman out of the heart of a city." She glanced at Desert, who had been quite silent, "The Grand Duke had made arrangements for the rest of us- but we have not heard from him…" she sounded like she could guess why.

"He's dead," Dese croaked, and they were silent.

After a moment, Cherish led the way through the tunnels, with the expertness that comes only from countless journeys in the dark. It seemed like hours, but they were soon inside the cave where Fa had delivered her warning message. There, waiting about in clusters, were the rest of the Nity followers. Most of the families with young children were gone, but there were many elderly men and women, some too weak to walk, and all had a hollowed out and tense look to their eyes.

Cherish went straight to one of the only young men, "The king's monument is closed," she mumbled to him, but Fa caught her words and observed the look of dismay on the young mans face.

"That only leaves the harbour!" he said quietly, "But even if we could get this lot down there- who knows if the ship will even be there!"

"What ship?" Dese spoke for the first time since entering the tunnels, Fa watched him with concern.

"The Grand Duke," Cherish explained in a low tone, "Promised us passage on a ship- but that was two days ago, and we heard all the ships have moved from the harbour."

"What's the name of the ship?" Dese asked.

"'The Lady Loyal'"

"I know that ship! It's captained by the first mate." Only Fa saw the flicker of doubt on Desert's face, but she didn't comment. "I know the first mate- if he was ordered to stay in the harbour to await passengers- he wouldn't disregard those orders unless… unless the Grand Duke told him to, or if he was ordered by a captain. Even if he moved the ship to safety, he would stay in the mouth of the harbour until he knew for certain that you weren't coming. When were you meant to board the ship?"

Cherish narrowed her eyes, "last night... or tonight- but those plans were made before the fires started."

"He'll still be there," Dese assured.

Fa looked to Cherish- what would she do?

"Alright, get them up- make stretchers if we have to for the older ones- no one gets left behind," she said to the young man, then she turned to address the crowd, who had been watching anxiously, "We take the harbour tunnel- I am assured that the ship *will* be there. But we must hurry!"

Fa felt her heart flutter as the cave erupted into action; they were going to make it!

*   *   *

There were forty-six people who left the cave, five of them were carried on stretchers, and one little old woman was even pushed along in a wheel barrel. Cherish, Rave, Fa and Dese were leading the way along the tunnel that would take them to the Harbour Ring. "Quite close to the docks," Cherish had assured them.

Twice, as they hurried along, they came close enough to the surface to hear the fire raging on. And for twenty minutes they went so deep that the air grew warm, this was where the tunnel passed under the lake. Then once, as they were passing under the Earls Ring, they went through the deserted half caved-in remains of a manor cellar. Then they went past an old well with a gapping hole in its wall, smoldering debris had fallen in, and that part of the tunnel was filled with smoke.

When at last they reached the end of the tunnel, they saw that the trap door had been half burnt through. Going ahead, one of the men shrugged his cloak over his head and stood underneath the trap door, then he heaved himself up, pushing against the weakened door with his shoulders. Sparks and smoldering wood rained down on the Tarven as he broke the door, then he was lit up in pale starlight.

Brave was the second one out, he stood beside the Tarven and surveyed what was left of the Harbour Ring in the silvery starlight; the trap door came out in the remains of a barn, that now was little more than a pile of smoldering rubble. All around in every direction, charred structures of cottages and inns could be seen standing in the night like old tomb stones. Red hot embers could be seen in several places, and a few of the sturdier

317

buildings were still burning. Rave could even see where the market had been, now it was a charred clear spot on the road. And to the north, beyond the Sea Wall, the city glowed a hellish red. Ash and smoke drifted past in the night air, making those who climbed out of the tunnel cough and cover their mouths.

Along with the smell of smoke, the air was thick with the stench of burning pitch, Rave choked on the smell and his gaze was drawn to the Harbour of which he had a clear view. The waters were lit up by the city's red glow and the silver light of the stars, but the sight was far from welcome. The harbor was littered with the burning debris of ships of all sizes, from small row boats to large ships, the largest one sat out in the mouth of the harbor; it was half sunk, and still burning. The restless wind blew the debris about, creating dangerous obstacles to any foolish enough to try and pick through them.

Desert came up behind Rave, with Fa following him, while the other Tarvens came up behind them to witness the tragic scene.

Dese stepped forward and searched the waters, panic and despair mixed on his face; for there was no sign of 'The Lady Loyal'.

"No!" he breathed "It's not here!" he tore at his hair in frustration, as the wind blew ash along the feet of the stranded Nity followers. "NO!" he screamed in anger and kicked aside a piece of charred timber.

Rave closed his eyes- he didn't have enough energy to feel angry, just defeated.

"We're trapped?" an old woman asked in a panic-stricken voice as she climbed from the tunnel.

"Where will we go!? We don't have enough provisions to last another day in the caves!" an old man shrieked and began to shake with fright. Cherish tried to calm him, but more and more people began to panic.

Rave turned to look at the city- perhaps they could go back… his thought drifted away like the endless clouds of smoke, only the Dragon Keep and parts of the Dukes Ring remained untouched by fire. Surely the king's men would be trying to dowse the fires soon. Forty-six Nity Followers weren't likely to go unnoticed for long, and if they were being blamed for the fire, they would all be killed on sight by the soldiers- or mobbed by anyone else who they came across! With a feeling of absolute failure, Rave looked to Fa, she would need comforting no doubt- but Rave hadn't a clue of what to say to her.

But as he looked at Fa, it was Rave who found comfort; Fa was looking across the harbour waters, her hair and dress smeared with ash- but her face was alight with… hope!

"Look!" she whispered, Rave and Dese looked to where she gazed, and there, outlined in starlight, rounding the sheltered cliff walls of the harbour, came a ship! Lanterns glowing, and sails spread- 'The Lady Loyal' was coming back for them.

*   *   *

"I'm coming with you," Desert said casually, as he lowered himself down to sit beside Fa on the foremost dock from shore.

The group of Nity followers had flagged the ship and then had gone out on the docks as far as they could, leaving the smoke, ash and despair behind them. They could see two longboats coming for them from 'The Lady Loyal'. They seemed to be having some difficulty navigating in the dark through the still flaming debris of the other ships, but they were coming, and that had calmed the hysteria. Whoever was captaining 'The lady Loyal' had not risked coming very far into the harbour, for fear of the wind picking up sparks and setting the ship to ruin, but even so, they were still at risk.

"What?" Fa asked softly.

"I'm coming with you and Rave- however far 'The Lady Loyal' will take us, then on to the next ship that's going to Garatin."

"Really?" she breathed, he could tell that she still hadn't fully grasped what he was saying, he grinned at her bewilderment.

"But what about…" Fa glanced behind them at the city.

Dese didn't follow her gaze, and instead looked down and picked at a scab on his hand (when had he gotten that?), "There's nothing left here for me…" he said quietly, forcing himself to accept the truth, "I won't inherit the title of Duke. The king will probably revoke Thrive's title anyway…" he swallowed hard, the shock hadn't quite left him yet, and even saying the words didn't make them sound true, they were just words.

"This place was never my home," he said, with a deep breath looking up and around, "I never had a future here, it was never my… fate." He looked at her quickly, half wishing he hadn't said those words, and half wishing he had said them long ago. What would she think?

She met his eyes for a moment, then a tiny smile touched her lips, "You're coming with me."

Dese grinned. "I'm coming with you," he confirmed, "No more goodbyes." Afraid the moment would pass, and he would waste it, Dese leaned forward and rested his forehead against hers, listening to her hesitant breath, and just rested there. He wanted nothing more than to slip his hand into hers as they sat there, but he knew that her hands were too burnt.

Then, the girl with fire hair shifted and brushed a light kiss on his lips.

*   *   *

Pulling back, Fa smiled, a bit self conscious at her own boldness, but found that she didn't care; let Tarva burn on, for she, the girl of fire and ash was beginning anew. And she now knew that hers was not a destiny of fear and destruction- not at all!

Her smile deepened when she saw a slight blush creep over Desert's face, he may have leaned in for another kiss, but a voice called out.

"Ahoy! How many are you!?" a rower from one of the longboats called as they drew near enough to be heard.

"Forty-six," Cherish answered, "Three are children, and several can help row."

"Right, we'll take two trips- no one panic, we'll get everyone!" the sailor assured as they pulled up to the dock, and the group of people surged forward eagerly.

It took quite some time to load up the longboats, and longer still for them to go back to the ship and return. Fate, Rave and Dese were in the last boat to leave and Dese helped row their way back. Fa could feel his gaze several times and she fought to keep a blush from her own face.

Above the stars shone brightly, as if trying to banish the awful scene of the city burning from the hearts and minds of the survivors.

"We made it!" Rave sighed in relief as their longboat approached the ship.

"Not yet," Dese reminded, "Port side- watch it!" he yelled in warning as a particularly large floating debris loomed up beside them, seemingly out of no where. It had been a fishing boat at the beginning of the day, but now it floated low in the water, charred black and still burning at one end. The mast pointing up like a jagged broken spear.

Brave and one of the sailors managed to push the skeleton of the boat away, and it drifted off into the darkness.

Two rope ladders were hung over the prow of 'The Lady Loyal', waiting for them as they rowed up to the towering side of the ship. The Nity followers climbed up first, the older one's with much difficulty, but somehow, they managed, it made Fa feel foolish.

"I... I can't climb that," she admitted when it came to her turn. Halfway up the ladder, she heard Rave make the sound he made when he felt like an idiot- probably because he had forgot about her hands.

But Desert didn't seem phased by this. "Send down a rope! We got burn injuries!" he hollered up, and sure enough a looped rope was thrown down. Fa slipped it over her head and shoulder, and with Desert's help was able to sit in it like a swing. With only a bit of difficulty, Fa was pulled up, and Dese and the other sailor climbed the ladder, leaving only one sailor in the longboat below. Rave met her at the top and helped her over the bulwark.

"Burn injuries- I should have guessed it was you."

Fa looked up at the harsh, yet still somehow, friendly voice.

"Confess!" Fa exclaimed, and she heard Rave gulp in fear. Fa couldn't be sure in the dark, but she thought she saw a faint smile touch the hard woman's face.

"Hello Fate, glad to see you survived your forewarned disaster."

"Not all of us did," Fa said, hoping she could say it before Dese reached the top of the ladder, "The Grand Duke is dead."

An audible gasp went through the crew on the deck, and Fess for the first time looked truly shocked. "I see," she said after a moment in a business-like tone.

Just then Desert topped the ladder, but instead of stepping onto the deck, he perched himself expertly on the bulwark with practiced balance, as if he was hesitant to step foot on Thrive's favourite ship.

"Desert, glad to see you as well," Fess said tightly, without really looking at him.

Fa remembered the long hours that Fess had searched for him when they first docked.

Dese nodded. "Captain," he greeted simply, as if it were impossible for her to be anything but.

The first longboat was being hauled up on a series of pullies, and was currently dangling in the darkness behind Dese, framed by the red light of the city.

As they stood there, a wind from inland touched their faces.

"Leave the second longboat behind!" Fess ordered, "and get this ship moving!" she thundered, and the crew jumped to action. In the bustle, a sailor lost hold of one of the ropes that held the dangling longboat.

The boat dipped and swayed out.

"Look out!" Fess barked.

The boat swung back in and clipped the back of Desert's head just as he turned to see what was happening.

"No!" Fa reached for him with her burned hands as Dese teetered on the bulwark for a moment, a stunned look on his face- then he fell backwards into the dark.

Fa lunged forward and clutched at air. Leaning over the bulwark, Fa was just in time to see Desert collide into the floating debris they had nearly crashed into earlier. His right shoulder hit the broken mast, the tip broke and in the dark Fa couldn't see if it was stuck in his shoulder or not. The boat broke apart as Dese hit the deck, then he sunk into the black water.

"GET HIM!" Fess barked to the sailor who was halfway up the ladder. Without hesitation, he dove into the water.

Franticly, Fa tried to climb over the bulwark- but Rave held her back, "You can't swim Fa!" he hissed in her ear and she went still.

Together they scanned the dark waters below for a moment that lasted an age, until the sailor popped up again; he was alone.

"No sign of him!" they heard him shout up.

A breathless whimper escaped Fa and Confess cursed.

A gust of wind blew again sending a burst of sparks from a nearby wreckage dangerously close to the ship.

"MOVE!" the first mate roared, but Fa couldn't hear the crew burst into action, she couldn't hear anything, just the echo of the crash Dese had made when he fell. She knew Rave's arm was around her, but she couldn't feel any warmth from it.

Desert...

Chapter 32   Fate

Brave knelt in front of Fa as she sat below deck, he searched her face seriously before speaking. "Fess said that she'll wait in this cove for a week, and if the weather holds, then she'll take us east..." he stopped talking when he noticed that Fa only nodded.

It had been two days since they fled from the city, in that time Fess had sailed east along the coast, wary of getting caught in any storms, until they had found a cove to wait in. There was a small village nearby, and since the disaster of Tarva, they were eager to sell their fish to 'The Lady Loyal' for a good price, since no one from the city would be wanting any. But even two days from the city, the smoke could still be seen, like an ugly smudge on the not so distant horizon.

Horizon... Fa had wondered about him and Rustling, she hoped that they had escaped the city in time, but she supposed that she would never know for certain. She had thought of many people in the past two days, Vision, the woman Dese had known in the Harbour Ring- what had come of her? and the boy and his father- the ones she and Fess had followed to the caves- had they escaped the city? For all this Fa had no answers. Yet even still, Fa found that she was at peace.

She sat with her hands in her lap, and her back against the ship wall, the sensation of sailing felt almost calming to her, and she marveled that it had only been a few days since they had landed in Tarva to begin with.

She had removed her clean bandages, her burns completely visible; from fingertip to mid forearm was red and raw. Yellow blisters had only stopped oozing the night before, the strange burns still seemed to heal faster than normal burns- but Fa was long past wondering about them.

"I dreamed again last night," she said at last.

Rave huffed and sat down heavily beside her, obviously preparing himself for the worst.

"I dreamed I was in a garden... a good one- one without cherry trees. But all the stars had fallen from the sky. Then you helped me put them back." She smiled faintly at the memory.

Rave frowned, "What do you think it means?" he asked softly.

Fa took a deep breath, "I think my heart stain is gone; I can feel it- or rather, the space it once took up."

"What was it like?" Rave asked, he looked a bit guilty for asking- but Fa didn't blame him for being curious.

"It was wonderful!" she breathed as she thought back to when the presence took full command of her, "but also horrible. To make room for it, I had to give up so much... It was like seeing beauty in the darkness, but also terror in the dawn. It was like... Eloi is the only thing in this world that will never change, and yet is the only thing that we will never understand."

Rave frowned, and Fa sighed- Rave always had a hard time understanding that kind of thing, so she changed the subject. "It's gone though, I think the presence would have burned me up if it had stayed much longer. I won't be having anymore of the 'dreams'- I think..." they were silent again for a moment, "And I think my hands will be all healed up by the time we get home."

"Home?" Rave asked, his tone suddenly much more serious, and he watched her face closely.

"You always said we'd go home at the end."

"Eamers gone though," he said, and for the first time Fa saw true despair in him- how strange that she should be the one to hang onto hope more than he!

"Eamer was just a place," she reminded him.

"A *good* place," he insisted.

"But not our *home*," she emphasised, hoping he would understand what she meant.

They were silent again and sat listening to the creak of the ship around them.

"We did it!" Rave breathed in wonder, "You crumbled Tarva."

Fa wondered for the first time what that would mean for the rest of the world. "I didn't do that," she shook her head slightly, "I was just the voice of the one who did."

"Still... we did it!" Rave insisted with a note of jubilation.

"Not yet little brother," she cautioned him, "We're still a long way from mother and father's arms."

Rave refused to be scolded and he grinned widely, "Do you think grandfather will be angry that I stole his dagger?"

Fa smiled ruefully, "You had better have an apology ready just in case- it would be twice as better if it was a neatly *written* apology."

Rave laughed, "We'll see!"

Fa smiled at the thought of teaching Rave to write on the long voyage home, and then she sighed as she looked at him beside her; the two of them together against all odds, just as they started... well not *quite* the same.

Fa hadn't told Rave the rest of her dream, it was because it was meant just for her. In it, the Dream Child had appeared one last time, and they had walked hand in hand through the garden, and the child had spoke to her... about Desert.

'His destiny was not the same as yours...'

A tear slipped unbidden down Fa's face- oh what she would give to relive her time with Desert... she didn't think she would change anything- just cherish it a little more. For it really *had* been a great adventure! And not just in Tarva with Dese, but before that, on 'The Prestige' and 'The Liberty'- horrid though it had been, and before that, in Garatin, when she had only an inkling of what her future would hold. It made her wonder if she really had any idea of what her future now held... what else did Nity have planned for her - the girl of fire and ash. Although Fa didn't know the answer, she was not afraid, not anymore, fear had no place in her now. For now, she knew that her fate, was in good hands.

The End

Epilogue

On the morning after the great fire of Tarva, a group of men, fishermen from a nearby village came into the harbour on a small fishing boat.

Wind blew ash across the water, and the air was still thick with smoke, it had rained in the night, and the fires in the Harbour Ring had died. But the flames still burned in parts of the Earls and Dukes Ring, only the Dragon Keep itself remained untouched by the scorched hunger of the flames. The irony of it was not lost on the fishermen; the castle remained- but it had no city left to rule over. Rumors of the king's 'unstable health' had spread, and some spoke of the army taking control of the country. A time of great unrest awaited Tarva, and the lands under its control, none could tell what would become of the empire.

The fishermen surveyed the city with sad eyes, the dangerous debris of the night before had almost all sunk, and there was no longer risk of sparks burning their own vessel.

Suddenly, one of the fishermen called out sharply and the group of them rushed to the side of their boat to help pull a young Tarven man from the water where he had been half clinging to a bit of wreckage.

The young man had a nasty wound in his shoulder and a cut on his forehead; he looked half dead- but he was awake and lay sprawled out on their deck, heaving in air, his dark eyes staring up at the blue sky.

"Your half a mile out- how did you get here?!" one of the fishermen asked in bewilderment. Anyone could see that the young man had no strength left in him- yet still he had stayed afloat!

"I swim like a fish," the young man breathed with a tired smile. The city had thrown him out and the sea had tried to swallow him up, but Eloi was not done with him yet. No, he had a story to tell; a story of a girl with fire hair who had stood before Triumphant the Great on the day that Tarva fell.

And he would tell that story to the world.

Rachel Lang lives in Orillia, Ontario. *Heart of Ashes* is her third book in the Namesake Chronicles, she also has written a short story series, Bland, that can be found on Wattpad. Aside from writing, Rachel enjoys art and finds great inspiration in nature. She is a little sister, a proud aunt, and college student.

The final installment of the Namesake Chronicles will be *Heart of Flesh*.

www.ingramcontent.com/pod-product-compliance
Lightning Source LLC
Chambersburg PA
CBHW022135170626
46807CB00005B/1942